The Two Roads

part one
of the
two roads
trilogy

Eliza White Buffalo
with Nicholas Black Elk

Outskirts Press, Inc.
Denver, Colorado

This story is based on my experiences as a shaman. However, the actual personal and family life of Rose and Lissy is fictional...Eliza White Buffalo

The Two Roads
part one of the two roads trilogy

v2.0

Outskirts Press, Inc.
http://www.outskirtspress.com

ISBN: 978-1-4327-5214-9

PRINTED IN THE UNITED STATES OF AMERICA

For Ben

Acknowledgements...

All of these wonderful souls, in their own special way, have contributed to the writing of this book. Many thanks to you all – for your individual gifts:

My husband and soulmate...You taught me what love is.

Our children...You guys were my hope and inspiration.

My dear sister, Lu...Lu, you believed in me, thank you.

Gusta...I am blessed to have you near.

David and Nancy...my wonderful, loving soul friends.

Dearest Brother Matthew...You are truly amazing. Thank you.

John...You're a star! Love your energy.

Anne ...You were Heaven sent. I'll never tire of saying thank you.

A true friend...Valerie, you helped me find my voice.

Peter...The White Brothers applaud you. Thank you.

Dearest Patsy...You were the light in the darkness. I'll never forget.

All you dear ones in spirit...Love you guys!

Teri, Dympna, Peter and Hilary...Thank you for your help and patience.

All my guides and spirit helpers ... I'm blessed to have you guys.

John and Ben...You're a huge part of the project – thank you for your help, past and present.

Special thanks to Valerie and Reggie for the front cover. Thanks to my editor Denise Ward for all your hard work. And to Stephen for all the research, support and technical help. Also thanks to Brooke Medicine Eagle for your guidance and support.

Lastly, how could I have ever done this without your unconditional love and guidance...May, A Mother's Love is you...Black Elk, my heart, I would do it all again for you.

Front cover – *The Dawn* – artwork by artist, Valerie Whitworth www.valeriewhitworth.co.uk

Photographer – Reggie Jameson

Related books:

John G. Neihardt...*Black Elk Speaks*

Brooke Medicine Eagle...*The Last Ghost Dance* and *Buffalo Woman Comes Singing*

www.medicineeagle.com

Eliza White Buffalo can be found at www.elizawhitebuffalo.com

Prologue…

I am Nicholas Black Elk. Some of you know of the great vision I was given when I was nine years old, upon the earth. For those of you who do not know, I shall speak what I feel is right to speak. In 1873 I was a young Lakota boy. The Lakota was a large tribe – part of the Great Sioux Nation. I belonged to a particular band of Lakota called Oglala. In those days, if a boy of nine years received a vision, it signified that that boy would do great things for the tribe and maybe would be chief one day. I was never meant to be a chief of peoples. Rather, the vision taught me that by walking two roads upon the earth, I would show my people the way out of the separation, where they depend on one man to be their leader, and into wholeness, where they would be their own chief. When I passed from the earthly life, they wrote 'chief' on my grave, but I never was an Indian chief. For a short while though, in my great vision, it seemed I was chief of all the universe. The Powers of the universe gave that vision to me. In that vision they each gave me Their power. Those Powers are yours too. For me, it was the Power of the West that I most abundantly portrayed on earth. For Eliza, it is the Power of the North. It was from the North that White Buffalo Calf Pipe Woman came bringing the wisdom of the pipe to our people.

Oh, how I wish that you all would view reality through the eyes of that wisdom! My people! My beautiful, brave, warrior people! In Lakota tradition, there is a saying – *Mitakuye Oyasin*! It means 'all are relatives'. When I was a young man upon the earth, I thought that my relatives were the Lakota Nation only, but when I came to be an old man, I realised that all people are my relatives. Now, that I see with eyes of wisdom and know with a heart of flame, I know that all peoples are within, and that by going within, each and every one of us can lead the nation into wholeness. It is this truth my people, my truth, which I call 'The Two Roads Truth', that is the teaching of this book. It is the way by which Eliza has brought herself into wholeness wherein dwell all her relatives.

Let me speak for a while of Eliza. All of us here in spirit stand in ovation for her homecoming. Her bravery, commitment, and devotion to all that is, have been the human attributes that have revealed the beauty of the heart within. My soul rejoices in the light of freedom, for she and I are one in spirit. And she is not the only soul on earth at present who is turning away from the forces of limitation and bravely making their way home. Many of you are walking that road now – the good red road. The fact that you are reading this book speaks of your willingness to succeed and the guidance within your own divine being that is *your* salvation – *your* wholeness. I love you all my dear brothers and sisters. My words in this book are my gift to you. For many years, Eliza has thought of writing this book. She has attempted many times to do so, but the time was never right. It was not until she had made the journey into wholeness, that together, she and I would write the words that, in hope, will help you on your journey. In this wholeness, Eliza and I as one, speak with purity of intention and with positive energy. She wrote the words on paper and I honour her for that. It was an awesome task for her to do so.

But this is not the first time I have put my words in a book. Many years ago, when I was a grandfather upon the earth, a beautiful and poetic soul was sent to me by the Powers of the Universe. He is Flaming Rainbow, though you may know him as John G Neihardt. He was sent to save the vision for all peoples. He wrote my words down in a book and named it *Black Elk Speaks*. It is a good and true book. To John, I will be eternally grateful. He and I seeded a dream together on earth, of bringing the great vision into the hearts and minds of all people. It is indeed a very beautiful dream and it belongs not only to John and me, but to the world. And so it is, that with that same intention of love and oneness, I speak again, through Eliza - through the Wisdom and Love of our wholeness.

Nicholas Black Elk

Part One

The Fearful Black Road

Chapter One

Rose

Belfast Ireland, July 1970

Rose was in the cupboard. She had been there all afternoon. No-one was looking for her.

In the kitchen Clare was fixing dinner. The heat was stifling and she had to wipe her face and neck with a cold wet cloth every few minutes in a necessary attempt to cool down. The radio had announced earlier that morning that today was going to be the hottest day in five years. In August 1965 temperatures had soared to thirty two degrees centigrade. This morning it was thirty and rising. Clare went to the back door with her cold comfort and exited into the garden unaware that her youngest daughter was just behind her in the cupboard. There were three girls in the house and two boys. The boys were only babies really – Kevin was eighteen months and Brian was three months. Clare stated proudly at every opportunity that Brian was the easiest baby by far, Rose being the most difficult. The two oldest girls were a delight to have and so helpful around the house: Caroline who was almost ten now never had to be asked to clear the table or tidy her bed and sweet little Angela was an angel at only eight years old. She loved to watch the boys when Clare was busy and was nearly as good as Clare at changing nappies. Rose was now five. From the moment she arrived in the world she had screamed.

Clare sat in the shade on the red painted bench. The kitchen window was directly above her and she could hear the spuds bubbling away as she surveyed the state of the grass which was brown and patchy with the summer sun. She frowned; irritated at the hose-pipe ban which had been declared by the local council four weeks ago and still hadn't been lifted. The garden was one of six in a row, identical except for the end one which had a hedge around it instead of the four foot high council estate fence. The back gardens faced another row of back gardens with nothing but a narrow path between them. To the front and to the sides of these rows of houses, stood more rows of houses. 'Chimney pots' was the common name for them, for if one viewed them from the sky that is what would be seen – row after row of chimney pots. This was where the McDevit family had lived since Clare and Sean got married in 1959. Clare's sister Colette had moved in with them four years after that when she had secured a job in the bakery that Sean worked in. Since she had been living in her family's home town of Cloughbeg at the time, a long distance away, lodging with Clare and Sean seemed the sensible thing to do. Cloughbeg was only a 'townland' really, on the edge of a small country village by the coast in County Mayo. Sean's family also came from Mayo but Clare and Sean had always wanted to live in the city so Belfast was where they had decided to start a family.

When Colette had moved in it was 1963. Caroline and Angela were little girls and crazy about Auntie Lett, as they called her. She was a huge help to her sister and spoiled the girls something rotten. At first Colette had gone home to Cloughbeg at the weekends but after meeting a local man from the estate, her home visits had become few and far between and she chose instead to spend her free time with him. It was a good estate to live in, at least most people would have said that until the two families from Donegal were set up very nicely in two of the four bedroom end-houses. It wasn't that they were undesirable families. Actually they were good Catholics who never missed Mass and whose children were impeccably turned out every day of the week even during the school holidays. No, the Donnelly and the O'Hara families were decent ordinary people. It was just that nasty rumours had begun to sully their presence in the area.

There had been talk! Some said that back in Donegal there had been trouble with the Donnellys and the O'Haras – the kind of trouble that warranted them being exiled as far away from Donegal as the thickset Irishmen could muster. A few dared to discuss rumours of anti-church goings on. But Mrs McDevit and Mrs Gormley, who were noted for their respectability, wouldn't entertain such unchristian gossiping and had spread it about that the two new households were decent God-fearing, law-abiding citizens who deserved to be welcomed into the area and treated like anyone else. They were, of course, especially by the kids in the estate. Caroline and Angela McDevit played with the Donnelly girls all the time and the O'Hara boys were always kicking a ball about with some or other of the local boys. And of course all of the kids were united in a favourite pastime - taking the piss out of creepy Rose McDevit.

Clare got up and hurried back into the house. She quickly checked on Brian who was sleeping peacefully in his pram placed in the space under the stairs, the coolest place in the house at this time of day. Back in the kitchen she lifted the lid of the bubbling saucepan and stuck a knife into one of the spuds to see if they were cooked. Having decided they were, she lifted them away from the gas, drained the water into the sink and left them on the drainer for a few moments. She went to the sitting room where Caroline and Angela were fanning themselves with home-made paper fans. They had made one for Kevin too and the toddler was having a busy time trying to copy his sisters' technique. His fat little fist couldn't hold on to his fan and he kept dropping it and picking it up again and dropping it again. After a while he became wiser and grasped more and more of the paper in his fist until what he held no more resembled a fan than the man on the moon. But it stayed in his grasp when he waved it and his little face which was red with the heat, was lit up with pleasure and pride at the achievement. Clare stood in the doorway beaming at the child's pleasure.

"Good girls," she said to her daughters. Her husband would be home soon and it was a huge help that Kevin was well supervised as she made the family dinner. "Dinner's almost ready. Bring Kevin and put him in his high chair will you, Caroline pet? And Angela where did Rose go to? Go and fetch her please. I don't know! Where does that child go to? It's beyond me!" Clare disappeared to the kitchen to dish up.

"Do you know where Rose is?" Angela asked her big sister.

"Where that child goes is beyond me!" was the reply. Caroline often mimicked her mother like this, but only when it was about Rose and she could get away with it.

"Is mummy going to be cross with Rose?" the smaller girl asked, eyes as wide as saucers. Angela's eyes were a definite talking point for any occasion. They were a soft blend of blue and green with huge curly lashes that went with her curly blonde bobbed hair style. The other children were plain in comparison. All of them had mousy brown hair except maybe the baby who was showing signs of the lovely blonde locks of his sister. They all had blue eyes, were all of slight build like their mum. Rose however, was becoming quite stocky which didn't surprise her parents in the least because she ate so much. Every mealtime Rose was the last to leave the table having devoured her meal and everyone else's leftovers. Her hair reached halfway down her back like Caroline's and although it was wavy of itself, Rose still often longed for Angela's curly wisps.

From her perch in the cupboard, Rose could hear every word her sisters were saying about her. She stiffened when Angela asked – *is Mummy going to be cross with Rose?* Had she done something wrong? Was she going to get the blame for something Kevin did? Did she forget to do something Mummy had told her to? She looked down at her hands. She couldn't see them in the dark to know if they were dirty or not. Her heart thumping, she opened the cupboard door slowly and tiptoed into the downstairs toilet. She washed her hands under the tap whilst checking her face and hair in the mirror. She looked okay! She flattened her hair with her wet hands just in case and brushed her teeth with her finger for fear that they might be 'as yellow as a duck's feet' as her mother said to her all too often. Then, with fear in her throat she went silently to the dining table and took her place. Caroline and Angela were there already and wee Kevin was chatting to himself in his high chair and playing with his plastic spoon. Rose kept her head down and studied her hands in her lap, waiting. When her mother sat a plate of food down on the table in front of her without as much as a *where have you been*? Rose began to relax as, still with her head down, she realised that Angela hadn't bothered looking for her and so Mummy hadn't been given a report. Mummy seemed focused on dinner so she wasn't cross – if she was cross she would be focused on her and anyway, if the dinner was on the table that meant that Daddy was nearly home and Mummy was hardly ever cross with her when Daddy was home. She brought her head up and lifted her knife and fork making sure she was holding them correctly. She was five and a half now and, like all the McDevits, knew how to have good table manners – how to sit up straight and not slouch, how to use a knife and fork properly and not put the knife in your mouth, and how to not make a noise with your mouth when you're eating. She wasn't very good at this last part. Hard as she tried not to, she would forget to close her mouth and then Mummy always heard it. "Quit that 'smackin'!" she'd snap at her. "Keep your mouth closed when you're eating!"

Rose dreaded a repeat of that one time ages ago. Daddy and Auntie Lett had been late for dinner and their plates were getting cold. Mummy had been in a foul mood and she, Rose, was concentrating really hard on being good so that Mummy wouldn't be cross with her. Everything was very quiet and it was safe until she forgot to keep her mouth closed and Mummy heard the 'smackin'.

"Quit that smackin'!" Mummy had snapped at her. Rose had jumped in her chair and dropped her fork which fell to the floor with a clang. She didn't dare try to retrieve it'cos that meant leaving the table before she'd finished her dinner and that was bad. She'd kept her eyes on Mummy, watching her mood shift from foul to furious. She held her breath and switched off, turning into herself for safety. She saw, as if in a dream, Mummy getting up out of her place and coming towards her. She was shouting "Get out of my sight, go on, out! I don't want to look at ya, get out now and stay out. Ya make me sick looking at ya!" The other girls had stared wide-eyed at their mother. They, like Rose, didn't know what had made their Mummy change into this wild thing, shouting at Rose and hitting her on the head with a tea towel. And she was crying, they could see the tears in her eyes and hear it in her voice. They racked their thoughts but couldn't remember Rose being bad that day. But then, Rose was often bad without anyone seeing what she'd done. They had all watched, mesmerized, as their out of control Mummy chased Rose out the door with the tea towel and then come back wiping tears from her cheeks and sitting down at her place again. "Eat!" she had snapped at them and they had all too readily obeyed.

Outside, Rose was standing in the centre of the garden trembling. Her short little legs rooted to the spot. She had seen this monster before when Mummy had been giving her a bath, and it had caught her off guard. The monster suddenly was there and was holding her down in the water. She didn't remember when or how it happened, or why, it just did. All Rose knew was that she had a picture in her head and it was a picture of the monster's face looking at her blackly whilst holding her under the water. Rose always remembered this when Mummy was cross but she had no real memory of it, just a picture of a monster. She was too scared of that monster to go back indoors and too scared to stay outside and get dirty and way too scared to even think about it. So she retreated inwards again inside herself where she could be still and safe. She never thought about how or why she did that, she just did instinctively. Without thinking she went to the coal bunker and climbed up onto the big block of concrete that served as a step for children to get up and sit on the top of the bunker. She opened the lid and swung a leg over the edge and then another until she was sitting in the bunker. Thankfully, it was empty. She sat down closing the lid as she did so and sat there in the dark. She had stayed in the bunker until Auntie Lett had opened the lid and lifted her out. "What are you doing in there Rosie? Come on, let's get you out, and my god! Look at ya child … you're filthy!" Auntie Lett never got cross. "Come on now, up to the bathroom and get cleaned up before Mummy sees ya."

Now as she sat hungrily eating her dinner, Rose was happy that it was Friday evening. Auntie Lett didn't go to work on Saturdays and Sundays and that meant Mummy wouldn't be on her own with the children. Sometimes, when Mummy decided that she was especially bad, Auntie Lett took her and her sisters out for the day. Last time they went to the zoo very far away and didn't come home until after bedtime. Auntie Lett's friend Alan took them in his car. Rose liked Alan. He liked her too. He never seemed to see that Rose was a bad girl or if he did, he never showed it. He had carried her around the zoo on his shoulders and bought her a great big red lollipop with a smiley face on it. Caroline and Angela got one too but they didn't get shoulder rides. Alan had fair hair and big, kind hazel coloured eyes that smiled with his whole face. Rose couldn't think of one other real person who smiled with their eyes like Alan. He loved the monkeys every bit as much as she did and he laughed when Auntie Lett was scared of the snakes. He made Auntie Lett smile and laugh all day and he had held her hand as he walked along with Rose on his shoulders. Rose was in her heaven as she made believe that Auntie Lett and Alan were her mummy and daddy, that Caroline and Angela were her cousins and her mummy was being very kind in taking them along on their family day out.

Just then there was the sound of a key in the front door. Rose was eating and lost in a reverie about Alan at the zoo. The sound had made her jump and she sat up straight, eagerly waiting to see if it was Auntie Lett or Daddy that would come through the door. It was Daddy. He had sweets with him the same as every Friday. Daddy took off his big blue overcoat and hung it over the newel at the end of the stairs, then he sat down in his place at the top of the table. The sweets were placed beside him and the children eyed them excitedly. They knew they wouldn't get any until Daddy had finished his meal and they were all gathered around him as he sat on the settee resting after a hard day's work at the bakery. He got up every morning at four thirty in time to start the daily bread and finished work at three in the afternoon. Then he usually popped in to the local pub for a 'wee one' before coming home. Dinner was at five pm on the dot and you could always hear the key in the door at that time, unless a 'wee one' turned into several wee ones and then – well, Rose knew all about that. It's not that Daddy was ever cross with her – well maybe sometimes he was but not like Mummy – not like her – not like the monster. And if he was cross it was usually with everyone and then you would just 'stay out of his way and give him peace' like Mummy said. No, several wee ones didn't normally make Daddy cross but it did make Mummy cross.

Rose often wondered if she wasn't so wee herself would Mummy like her more and not be cross at her so much. She was cross with the others too sometimes, especially when they really had done something bad like the time Caroline and Roisin Donnelly were caught eating an entire packet of biscuits smuggled from the Donnelly's pantry. But she was always cross at Rose it seemed. She said that it was because Rose was a bad girl, that she was born bad and that she'd always be bad. Rose didn't fully understand the whole being 'born bad' thing. She reckoned that it had something to do with Daddy and how she was his girl – special. Being born bad makes you special – that's what she reckoned. And being special was confusing in itself, just like being born bad. It had its good points like when Daddy was around Mummy didn't get cross 'cos Daddy said that Rose was his girl, but there was a bad side to being special too. You had to play Daddy's wee game which Rose didn't like but Daddy did. He said that she was chosen to play it instead of the others 'cos she was special – she was *it* – and when you were *it* you kept it a secret especially from Mummy and Auntie Lett because if they knew she was *it* they would give her to the gypsies who didn't like wee girls at all and might give her to the divil himself if they had a mind to. Rose was convinced that Daddy was right – Mummy had often threatened to give her to the gypsies. It seemed to Rose that being wee wasn't in the least bit a good thing. She reckoned that all wee things made Mummy sad and that's why she got cross and so she was hopeful that when she was big like Caroline Mummy would never be cross with her again, even if she was born bad.

Sean McDevitt ate his meal with his mouth open and 'smackin' noisily, Rose noted, chatting all the time to his children who all wanted to know had he brought lemon drops or barley sugar? Rose's favourite was clove rock but no-one else preferred that so clove rock was reserved for special occasions like Rose's birthday or Christmas or when Auntie Lett's Alan took them to the corner shop and let them each choose what they wanted. "So girls, what have you been up to today, eh? Helping your mother I hope," Sean asked them. He ruffled Kevin's hair who was placed beside him 'cos it was the only space big enough for the high chair.

"And how's my wee man, eh?"

"Da da!" said Kevin reaching out and grabbing his father by the beard with a potato- smeared hand. Sean laughed wiping the potato from his beard and swayed a little on his chair.

Oh no! thought Rose, *Oh Daddy, you've had too many wee ones.* She peeked a glance at her mother and quickly surmised that she was cross. Rose was an expert at guessing her mother's moods. She had to be, she had a lot to think about when Mummy was cross. She had to get out of sight for starters because Mummy didn't like to look at her when she was cross, and she had to concentrate really hard on being good which wasn't easy when you were born bad. She'd have to go to the cupboard again or hide under the bed. She didn't like that idea much since the last time she had done that she fell asleep and everyone was looking for her for ages before she climbed out all sleepy and cramped. They were cross that night – Mummy, Daddy and even Auntie Lett. Rose decided on the cupboard. She had made a comfy seat in there earlier that day out of a folded up blanket and she had another blanket to cover herself up with. Yup! The cupboard would do nicely. She watched closely as her father ate his meal, ready to start 'clearing away' before being told to. As soon as the last forkful was in his mouth she jumped up and lifted his empty plate and, holding on to it very carefully, brought it to the drainer and placed it there before turning to go back for another plate. A mild panic came over her when she saw Mummy carrying them all at once and coming towards her. She stiffened and held her breath, feeling her face flushing red and hot. Mummy sat the dishes down on the drainer and began to fill the sink with hot water. Rose very quietly went to the table and helped Caroline to bring over the beakers. Both girls moved quickly and quietly and when the table was clear Rose was relieved to hear Caroline ask Mummy for a cloth to wipe the table clean. She stood in the corner and watched her sister as she wiped, noticing how she did it without getting any crumbs on the floor. Then she held the high chair steady as Caroline lifted their little brother out and on to the floor. The child's face and hands were covered in dinner and Rose dashed up to the bathroom to get a flannel. However, by the time she returned Caroline had expertly wiped the child clean with the dish cloth and was chatting happily to him, saying what a big boy he was for eating up all his dinner. Daddy and Angela had disappeared into the sitting room with the sweets and Brian was still sleeping peacefully in his pram. She ventured over to the sink.

"Mummy," she said in a quiet little voice, "can I go and see if Auntie Lett's coming yet?" When Daddy had had several wee ones and Mummy was cross it was best if Auntie Lett was there. Auntie Lett was her safety net 'cos she and Mummy would be too busy discussing Daddy having several wee ones to notice what she was doing. She waited with bated breath for a reply. Clare turned and scowled down at her, wiping her hands viciously on a towel.

"Go!" she shouted, "get outta my sight." Rose scurried

out of the kitchen as quick as her little legs would go and ran to the back hall where she climbed onto her perch in the cupboard. She held her breath and listened for a few moments to make sure there wasn't anyone close by and then, pulling the blanket over her head she leaned back against the cupboard wall and cried. She didn't really know why she was crying. Was it because Mummy was cross? Well yes, because of that, but mostly because Daddy had had several wee ones. She cried for just a few moments – but only a few moments. She had learned a long time ago that crying got you into trouble and she was very careful not to lose control. The tears stopped and after a few more moments of vigilance, Rose relaxed. She knew she was okay now till at least supper-time. She felt different when she was away from everyone with a blanket over her head. It was like a little cave – her own special cave where she didn't have to be careful all the time. It was kind of safe – a safe cave like the one at Granny's beach in Cloughbeg.

That's where she had seen *her* for the first time. A lovely lady – old like Granny, with nice kind eyes like Auntie Lett's Alan. Rose smiled to herself now as she allowed the memory to form in her mind. It was last year on their summer holidays at Granny's house. Granny had taken the girls to the beach and Caroline and Angela had been allowed to go and play in the rock pools. She was busy making a sandcastle in front of the deckchair where Granny could watch her. It felt good to sit on the beach and dig her hands into the sand. The sea was making a nice noise as the waves came in and crashed on the shore. It was a kind of shooshing noise like when she held her hands over her ears. The seagulls were very noisy, screaming and jabbering away in seagull talk and she could hear her sisters giggling as they played together. It had seemed that everything was nice for a while; while she sat there lost in the noises of the beach everything was nice in her little world. She had giggled as she let the warm sand fall through her fingers and lifted her face up to the sky squinting at the brightness. A seagull flew overhead and glided off across the beach and she had let her gaze follow it until it flew out of sight behind the cliffs.

"Bye bye birdie," she had said softly. One glance at Granny had told her that her watcher was asleep. Without hesitation she jumped up and ran over to where she had seen the bird disappear. When she reached the cliff-face she saw her sisters playing happily and called to them about the birdie, but her voice went unheard. Just then she noticed an opening in the cliff face. She went closer to the opening and peered in, unsure of what to make of it. The nice feeling of the beach and the lure of the birdie were still very strong and she had entered the cave in wonderment. The inside wasn't as dark as it had seemed from the outside 'cos it had no roof. The floor was soft golden sand, some of it warm and some of it cold. There were little crunchy shell bits all around that hurt her bare feet as she stepped on them and she had to pick her steps very carefully. There was a lovely warm bit in the middle with a stream of sunlight beaming down on it from above. She had lain down there and squinted up to the sky with one hand shielding her eyes. And then out of the pale blue yonder, *she* was there – standing at her head and smiling broadly down at her. Rose hadn't moved. She seemed to know that if she did the lady would go away. She wasn't scary or strange in any way at all that might have frightened Rose; she was nice and warm and comforting and familiar, very familiar. She didn't speak and Rose didn't speak to her. The two had simply observed each other, both smiling, both happy, both sure that everything was perfectly okay. The lady had brown hair tied up in a bun and was wearing an apron with little flowers all over it. She smelled of baking buns and nice smells like that – flowers and sunshine. Rose had felt very good lying on the sand and smiling at that lovely lady, but it was over very quickly. She had taken her eyes off the lady for a second 'cos the sun was hurting them and making them water, and then she was gone. Disappeared, just like the seagull. Rose stood up and contemplated what had happened. She had known the lady was not a real lady – that she was a picture in her head like the monster only a nice picture. She had known that inside her was a tiny little place in her heart where good things were and that the lady came from there.

She shifted her position in the make-believe cave in the cupboard and realised that she had a big smile on her face as she thought about the lady. It wasn't the last time the picture came to her. A lot of times in bed the picture would come and the lady would be smiling at her again. Recently, the lady hadn't been the only one – lots of people came and stood around her bed smiling at her. She only ever smiled back if the lady was alone. She didn't like other people coming around her bed. It made her scared a little and reminded her of Daddy's wee game. Sometimes she would be scared a lot and cry out especially if the picture came too quick. Normally, like the first time in the cave, she got a nice funny feeling before she got the picture. Other times she would get another funny feeling which wasn't nice at all. It was like being in the sitting room watching the TV. Everything that was happening, for example at dinner time, or when people were talking or even when she was just looking around her, was as if it wasn't really happening, as if it was a TV show. It didn't seem real. Sometimes when she had that funny feeling she didn't just get pictures, she did things – very strange things. One time she had flown up out of her bed, out of the window and up over the houses. Another time she went outdoors and played on the swings and came indoors again only to realise that she hadn't gone anywhere at all – she was still curled up in the cupboard. And she hadn't been dreaming because… well she didn't know how she knew but she just hadn't. On the swings, lots of pictures came to her that moved and said things to her. They weren't so scary during the day, particularly when it was outdoors and there was loads of space around her. It was important that there should be loads of space around her. If there wasn't, she almost always got scared. She was scared of a lot of things. She was scared of the dark, of monsters, of Daddy's wee game, of pictures around her bed and of being bad.

She stopped thinking about that for a few moments to take stock of what was going on in the house. Straining her ears she tried to catch the conversation in the kitchen between Mummy and Auntie Lett who must have come in while she was thinking about the nice lady. She tried very hard but couldn't make out what was being said so she very bravely opened the cupboard and went to the door in the back hall that opened out to the kitchen. Pressing her ear against the door very quietly she held her breath and listened. Auntie Lett was speaking in a hushed voice. Rose knew that was because she didn't want Daddy to hear her. Rose knew a lot of things people didn't say out loud. She knew that Daddy and Auntie Lett played Daddy's wee game even though Auntie Lett wasn't *it*. She knew that Mummy knew this as well and wondered if Mummy knew that she played Daddy's wee game too. She reckoned she didn't 'cos she hadn't given her to the gypsies.

"Well what can ya do Clare? – nothin!" Auntie Lett was saying. "And even if ya did say somethin to 'im, what d'ya think he's gonna say eh? If ya ask me it's all best left alone."

"Aye well – that'ed suit you down to the ground wouldn't it?" answered Mummy sarcastically.

"And what's that supposed t'mean?"

"Work it out Colette! Anybody would think I'd have a bit a say in me own home but no – I just have ta go along with what yous think." Mummy was crying and Rose's little heart was beating nineteen to the dozen. She hated it when Mummy was sad. It nearly always ended with a Rose-hating session. She wasn't wrong – Mummy's next words confirmed it. "Where is she anyway? You'd think she'd want some sweets but oh no! – she has to have the whole house lookin' for her – attention seeking wee madam!"

Mummy had made Auntie Lett angry – "For God's sake Clare, wise up. It's not the child's fault she was born and it's not mine either before ya start. Look, let's not do this now eh? Come on now an' settle yourself. She's probably behind the sofa with her sweets ate by now. Anyway, never mind where she is, she'll come out when she's ready." Rose didn't wait to hear any more. If Mummy came looking for her then she'd best be behind the sofa like Auntie Lett said. She tiptoed to the opposite door in the hall which led into the sitting room. She paused as she put her hand on the knob. She had that funny feeling again – that funny TV show feeling. It was good in a little way 'cos it stopped her from crying and feeling angry or sad – it stopped her from feeling anything at all really. She gently opened the sitting room door a very small piece and sidled in. The sofa was right beside the door so it was easy to get down on her hands and knees and crawl behind it without being noticed. She lay down on her side and waited.

At seven thirty Rose was behind the sofa. She had been there all evening. No-one was looking for her.

Chapter Two

Lissy

She had been christened Melissa Mary Brigit Brenning, in the Church of Our Lady of Perpetual Succour, Lanesworth, Dorset, England in the year 1978. Everyone called her Lissy, Lissy Brenning. The Brennings were a religious family belonging to the Church of England but when Lissy's dad Russell married her mum he converted to the Catholic Church as was the expectation in those days. Brenda, her mum, was born and raised in Ireland in a place called Moor on the outskirts of Dublin. Her family, the Cassidys, were devout Catholics. Brenda Cassidy came to England to stay with her aunt and uncle after shaming her parents by getting pregnant by a local lad when she was only sixteen. As soon as he found out Brenda's condition, the young lad denied all responsibility and so Brenda was sent to a home for wayward girls where she was to give birth to the baby. Alas, the little boy died just as he was coming into the world and poor Brenda was expected to go to England to her aunt and uncle and forget the whole thing. She and Russell were married for five years and had lost three more children to still birth before they decided to adopt. And then Lissy came along. The Brennings had been waiting for a suitable child for well over a year when one day they had a visit from Father Peter Kearns. The priest had received a letter from his old parish in County Mayo in Ireland. In the letter a colleague requested that he find a good Catholic home for a baby girl born just two days prior. The child's mother apparently was not married and circumstances made it impossible for the child to be brought up within the birth family. Adoption out of the country was the only way forward for this child. The mother would be taken care of, there was no need to concern himself about that. His colleague was not prepared to answer any questions and he would be very grateful if his good friend Father Kearns would get back to him with a suitable placement arranged as soon as possible. The Brennings were overjoyed, at last they would be parents. Of course it was a sad business, the poor girl getting pregnant like that and not being fit to raise the child herself but oh, what joy! What a blessing! A little girl! A daughter! They could hardly believe the day had finally come. The arrangements were made with Father Peter and six weeks later he placed in Brenda's arms a most adorable little girl. Brenda Brenning had fallen in love with the child immediately and vowed she would never want for anything.

December 2007

Lissy was restless. Yet another night had she spent tossing and turning in a vain attempt to relax. Sleep eluded her. Never before had she known such restlessness. Each night she would collapse into bed physically exhausted only to battle with the constant thoughts and pictures rattling about in her head and vying for her attention. Each day she would go through the routine of rising, putting in a day's work at the shop and then coming home to paint. Lissy loved to paint. She lived to paint and although these days she was often so tired that she felt she couldn't lift a paintbrush, painting was her only escape. Now that proper sleep was a distant memory, painting had become not only an escape from the daily grind but provided a place where she could get as far away as was possible from the turmoil in her mind. Yes! Painting was her respite; her solace; it was who she was. She was the artist and when she put that brush to canvass it was as if she would melt away out of the restlessness and become one with the paint – she would become the very image she was creating. She sat up in bed and stretched her arms above her head, yawning deeply. Nodding at the realisation of the small truth, she smiled to herself and felt more alive than she had done in a long time. Springing up out of bed, she pulled open the bedroom door and skipped across the landing to the stairs. "Shit!" she muttered under her breath, "slippers." The cellar was always freezing cold first thing in the morning and the stone floor had no carpets. Mum had insisted on that for fear of paint spills on her well cared for furnishings. Mum cared for everything more than Lissy deemed natural. She cared for her of course and although Lissy knew that was because she loved her, it seemed that she cared too much for her in the same way she did for her home and Lissy would never understand that. She felt suffocated by her mother's all- consuming desire to please her, to make her happy and to keep her safe. But this morning, just for a few moments Mum would be unaware that Lissy was going somewhere where she couldn't follow. She went very quietly back to her room and retrieved her slippers, grabbed a cardigan from the bedpost and made her way tentatively to the stairs. Then, without a sound, she moved down the staircase. If Mum woke and started going on about *what would you like for breakfast dear*? or *what are doing down there in the cold dear*? she would ruin the special moment Lissy was about to relish. At the bottom of the stairs the early morning sun streamed into the hallway filling it with an aura of mysticism. Lissy felt encouraged. Giddy now in her heightened state she allowed the image to form in front of her eyes and as it became clear to her she almost ran down the cellar steps, threw open the door and danced over to the easel. She took off the beautiful blue scarf she used as a dust sheet and let her gaze fall upon it, the most wonderful image she had ever painted. Sitting on a red rug beneath the trunk of a huge oak tree was a lady. She held on her lap a little girl of about three years old and the little girl was gazing up into her mother's face with devotion and contentment. The lady looked down on the child smiling gently and Lissy believed no-one could fail to see the amazing love that she had for the child. As she fixed her gaze upon the woman's countenance, Lissy felt her heart swell with longing. She had never known the kind of love that this mother had for her child and even though she loved her Mum dearly and knew she loved her, it didn't feel like it was enough. She had known for years that she was adopted. Mum and Dad thought that she should know as soon as she could understand. It wasn't dropped on her like a bombshell nor did it ever feel like that. In fact, Lissy had almost welcomed the news. As a child she sensed that something wasn't adding up. She was nearly twelve when they told her and already beginning to feel like one of her mum's valuable pieces of china. She wasn't allowed to play with other kids in the park a few blocks away and she had to have playtime structured around Mum's watchful eye. The girls at school isolated her because she was always flounced up like a doll, Mummy's little princess. Even at home she was put on a pedestal and admired. Aunt Marion would say -

"Oh Brenda, you are lucky to find such a beautiful child and so gifted." When they went to visit Nan Brenning in the Lake District she would tell Mum every time in case she would forget –

"Brenda, God has been good to you. He has brought Lissy to you and you must cherish her as you would the child Jesus Himself."

She took her eyes from the beauty of the painting and lowered them to the floor. Her heart sank as she looked around the cellar. It resembled her life – everything all boxed in and suffocating, just the way she felt. She was twenty nine years old, still not married, still living with her parents, still Mummy's little princess, still wanting for nothing and still going slowly stagnant in her mother's obsessive control over her life. It wasn't much of a room. About twelve by eighteen feet, the walls were stone, painted white to help the room appear light as there were no windows. The floor had stone flags which were scrubbed clean regularly by her mum. Lissy wasn't even allowed to do that – clean the floor of her own studio. She sat down on one of the many beanbags she had scattered about. Beside her, stacked carefully against the wall was a line of paintings finished and ready for the local art group's exhibition next month. In the very centre of the room stood the easel, complete with the magnificent painting she had finished a few days before. It was done in oils. Usually Lissy liked to work with acrylic which was cheap plus it didn't take too long to dry. She hated the long periods of waiting for the paint to dry before she could proceed with a piece. Sometimes she would start tidying the studio. She knew she oughtn't to be so messy. Many a time she spent extra money on new tubes of paint only to find, weeks later, several half full tubes all dried up and useless since she had left the cap off them. She would have flung them aside at the end of an evening's work with full intention to recap them and then forgotten all about them as she drifted off into dreams on one of her beanbags. Looking around the many shelves and sideboards now, she was able to pick out several such neglected tubes from where she was sitting. The shelves were groaning with the weight of endless art magazines, sketch books and texts about the great artists. She had four such books on Leonardo Da Vinci who was her favourite inspiration. She loved *The Mona Lisa, The Last Supper* and *The Virgin On The Rocks*. They had such depth to them she thought. In fact, the latter was the inspiration for her latest piece which she entitled *A Mother's Love*. She had read a book lately giving several different theories on the meaning of Da Vinci's religious works and she was enthralled. "*A Mother's Love,*" she had said to her workmate Anne, "is about a love that is ideal, perfect, divine if you like. It's about the love that a mother has for her child: a love that can equal no other. A love that is nurturing and unrestrictive and well, holy I suppose."

"And do you think such a holy love exists?" Anne had asked her.

"Definitely! If it didn't, how come I feel it so much in my heart? How come I dream about it every night calling to me, waiting for me? I can't deny that she exists and I know she loves me 'cos I, well I just do." Anne had heard the story before ... Lissy's real mother couldn't look after her for some hugely significant reason, that Lissy was sure about, and when they were re-united Lissy's boring life would be transformed. The power of her mother's love would wipe away all traces of sadness from her life and she would be happier than she ever thought was possible.

"You're talking about your birth mother aren't you?" she had replied knowing that it was what Lissy wanted to hear.

Lissy drew her eyes back to the painting. Anne understood how she felt. She would love the painting no doubt and agree that it portrayed her real mother perfectly. She had been very careful not to make the image of the child too much like her at that age, as she didn't want to hurt her mum's feelings. After all, Mum did give her a loving home and loved her, as did Daddy, and she loved them too of course. No, she shouldn't trample on their feelings. They deserve respect and gratitude but they had to understand how important it was for her to find her real mother. She would always feel that a piece of the jigsaw was missing unless she could meet her and find out, from the horse's mouth as it were, why she hadn't been able to keep her. The woman in the painting was sitting under a tree on a red rug spread out on the grass. On her lap sat the adoring child and in front of them on the rug lay a little rag doll with bright yellow hair and a large black volume with a white cross embossed on the front. In the background was the faraway image of a forest and the sun setting over the tops of the trees. Lissy took a deep breath and drank in the scene. She imagined what it was like to sit there in the woman's loving arms and to feel complete, to know that when she went to bed that night her dreams would be deliciously filled with warm embraces and angels' kisses. She would have drifted off to sleep had it not been so chilly in the cellar and she pulled her cardigan around her and snuggled into a ball on the beanbag. Just then mum shouted down from the kitchen.

"Lissy dear, are you down there? Do come up to the kitchen dear and keep warm, I'm just putting the bacon on."

Lissy cupped her hands over her face and hung her head as she brought her thoughts back to the moment. Things had been difficult lately. She and her mum rarely saw eye to eye. They were simply too different and the latest arguments had left emotions running high for both women. Lissy felt it was very natural for her to be curious about her birth mother and her mum's reluctance to understand that was frustrating to say the least. As far as Lissy was concerned, Mum was much too stubborn. She hadn't even tried to understand last night when she and Lissy had gone at it again for the umpteenth time. Lissy felt a wave of regret sweep over her as she recalled the horrible things they had said to each other.

"Melissa!" Mum had insisted through clenched teeth, "I am your mother and that is that. For God's sake child, the bloody girl wasn't fit to be a mother. She gave you up for that reason. What makes you think she would relish you just walking into her life now, eh? Did it ever occur to you that she didn't want you then and she won't want you now?" Brenda felt awful as soon as the words were out but she was just so angry.

Lissy had leapt from the chair and stormed over to the

hall door. Poised there dramatically she retorted, "You may be my mother but let me tell you this – right now I wish you weren't. I wish someone else had adopted me and … you need to hear this…" she pointed a finger angrily at her mum "I am twenty nine years old. I am not a child and I can most certainly do whatever I want and I am going to go ahead with this with or without your consent."

Lissy sighed deeply as she slumped on the beanbag. She realised what a mess she had made of things. She still felt angry but she was angrier with herself at the moment for having been so hurtful. She never meant to be so but the woman was so exasperating and dammed stubborn. Why the hell did everything have to be about her and how bloody perfect she is? Getting up from the beanbag Lissy picked up the blue scarf from the floor. Before replacing it over the easel she looked into the face of motherhood perfected and felt an all too familiar stab of pain in her heart. "This is all your fault," she accused the woman, "why couldn't you have just tried?" With that she put *A Mother's Love* under wraps again. She took several deep breaths and did the exercise Anne's sister Linn had shown her. Linn had said -

"Lissy, all our problems are created in our minds. The mind is a powerful tool and as long as we understand that the heart is also powerful, more powerful for there is nothing more powerful than love, then we can use this knowledge to heal our lives."

She had shown Lissy how to visualise herself in a bubble

with her mother and how to let her mother float away from her in another bubble, taking with her all the difficulties between them, and as she floated away Lissy was to send her love. Linn had been using this technique with her own relationships and swore that it could transform Lissy's relationship with her mother and bring about harmony between the two of them. Having done the exercise Lissy felt a little calmer and tried to shift her attention to something else. It was going to be a busy day today and she would be meeting up with Linn and Anne which she was looking forward to. She enjoyed talking to Linn. She always felt so inspired listening to her talk about love and harmony and all that 'new age stuff' as Brenda called it.

She entered the kitchen with her usual morning smile for Mum and perched herself on a stool next to the breakfast bar. Mum was standing at the cooker with her back to her. "Morning dear," Mum said busying herself with cracking the eggs into the pan. She didn't look round. "Sweetheart, do go up and get some clothes on. You know how I feel about being dressed for breakfast. Oh! By the way, John will be dropping by later this morning so it might be nice if you wear that lovely white sweater I bought for you, that's a good dear."

"Oh Mum, John doesn't care what I'm wearing. I don't think John would even notice what he is wearing himself. Besides, he and I are just friends and that's the way we like it. I wish you would stop matchmaking Mum, I really do.

I'm perfectly fine as I am. Why is he coming over anyway?" Brenda wiped her hands on her apron and turned to face her daughter.

"Lissy, you know as well as I do that John has a fondness for you and before you start, just listen! I have asked him over to help Daddy carry the bed settee down to the cellar. You can't be sitting on those bag things, much too close to the floor. You'll catch a chill. I'll get Daddy to bring down the electric heater too and then you and John can enjoy a nice cup of tea while you talk about art or whatever you young ones talk about." Lissy waited a few moments before responding. Her mum's matchmaking could be annoying at the best of times but for goodness sake! This takes the biscuit! She couldn't be bothered arguing.

"Whatever! I dare say I could have helped him myself but as it is I'm not going to be here. I'm off to town to meet Anne and discuss the arrangements for the exhibition, and after that we thought we'd have our lunch in The Shepherd's Inn. Then there's that psychic fair on in the hotel at two. Might be fun to do that. Anne's sister swears by all that stuff. Anyway, I won't be back till at least teatime and I dare say John'll be gone by then so you can give him my apologies and tell him I'll catch him again." You just had to tell Mum what's what sometimes. Lissy was pleased at her assertiveness.

Her mum moaned - "Oh Lissy, can't you wait and take John with you then. I'm sure he'd love to have lunch with you. He'll be very disappointed I should think." She was trying her best for the poor child, not married and at twenty nine. *I don't know,* she thought to herself *what will become of her spending all hours God sends down there painting pictures (* which were she admitted very good) *instead of going out and meeting a nice young man and settling down and maybe then she'd forget all this nonsense about meeting her birth mother. I do my best and John is a lovely man indeed. Would be perfect if they got together.* She knew Lissy was talented and she was very proud of her. No other mother could be this proud of her daughter and art was a nice thing to be at. She even sold a few paintings to date and it gave her a little extra pocket money. It would do nicely until she found herself a husband and then she would settle down to real woman's work – caring for a husband and children and keeping a nice home. She herself hadn't been blessed with any children of her own and she never knew why they didn't adopt another child, perhaps a boy, but she did do the best with what God gave her and she did keep a lovely home. She prided herself on her achievements. No-one could say that Brenda Brenning was a failure, No! Not at all!

Lissy stood up. "I'm going to get dressed Mum. There's no point sitting here until he comes then he'll be seeing me in my p-jays. And that wouldn't do would it mother?" She was feeling quite daring now and decided to bring up the subject again. "Mum, I want to say to you, well, I'm sorry that we argued last night about you know what. But I'm very sure that it's a good thing for me to do. It'll satisfy my curiosity and well, John thinks I'll never be able to forget about it unless I meet her. It doesn't have to be a big thing anyway does it? I'll just see what she's like and let her see how well my mum and dad have brought me up. She might not even want to know me at all and then that will be that, what do you think?" She didn't really believe that but it was what Mum would want to hear and she had to be careful not to hurt her again.

Brenda turned and lifted the pan of eggs off the gas. She began getting plates and such ready whilst ignoring the lump in her throat. She had done everything to ensure that Lissy had all she could ever need and she just couldn't understand why the girl would throw it all back in her face like this. It isn't as if she had mistreated her or anything and Daddy doted on her. No-one had a father as devoted as Russell was to her. He did everything in his power for her. He worked all hours to make sure she had anything she wanted and he was never shy with his money. He never went to the pub or the bookies like some people she could mention. Instead he spent all his spare time with his family making sure they were happy. "Oh Lissy dear!" Brenda implored. She was tired this morning. She had lain awake until two pm this morning going over all this in her head and felt there was nothing more could be done. They had been through this more times than enough and nothing had changed. "Don't you think it's best to leave well alone? Why in Heaven's name do you need to bring up the past? The poor woman was unable to give you what we could and she most probably would be embarrassed to have it all dragged up again. I do wish you'd think about it properly dear, I really do."

But Lissy was determined. "I have thought about it properly Mum. I've thought about nothing else for weeks. I love you Mum, and Daddy, you know I do but it's just that I have to see what she looks like and find out for sure why she gave me up for adoption." Lissy felt insistent. She had thought about going about it without her parents' knowledge but she couldn't bring herself to be sneaky like that. Anyway Mum and Dad deserved better than that. "Besides, it won't do any harm to make enquiries will it? Maybe to begin with I could talk to Father Kearns. I'm sure it won't be too difficult to question him. And then if he knows anything I can cross that bridge when I come to it, eh?"

Brenda could feel her daughter's enthusiasm and knew she had lost the battle. She just prayed to God that she wouldn't get hurt. 'Cos that's what it could all end up with – Lissy getting disappointed and her picking up the pieces. And God forbid it that the woman should reject her completely. *She* knew she wouldn't want *her* secret broadcast for all and sundry to know. She was sure the woman would be no different. Against her better judgement she said -"Well I suppose so dear, if you're sure that's what you want."

"I am Mum," Lissy replied. There were a few minutes of awkward silence as Lissy watched her mother set out the breakfast with deliberation. Brenda never allowed her emotions to show, even when she was standing in her own kitchen with her own daughter, her face confessed nothing other than the careful application to the domestic task at hand. Lissy noted a flicker of irritation when Dad came into the kitchen with his newspaper under his arm.

"Morning dear," he said to Lissy, "has anyone seen my glasses? I had them last night but I can't see them anywhere now."

"Morning Daddy!" answered Lissy, glad for the distraction, "just gonna get dressed. Have you looked down the side of the chair?"

"Right dear," Dad reached for the kitchen door but Lissy was through it as quick as a flash. She dashed up the stairs two steps at a time and into her room throwing herself on the bed. Mum had finally given in. Today she would begin her quest to find her real mother.

"*Yes*!" she grinned as she hugged her pillow.

Chapter Three

The Indian

Co. Mayo, August 1977

Twelve – not an easy age for a girl like Rose – a girl with demons lurking in every shadow – fear in every thought – pain in every movement.

She was lying down amongst the trees, a layer of lime green moss under her back comforting her with its softness and its pure sweet fragrance. It was summer and the mid-day sun was filtering down through the high branches of the trees. All around her insects droned and birds chirped. The seagulls could be heard squealing as they flew high over the beach and swooping to grab a tasty morsel from the surf. The little cove would be deserted. No-one had access to it except Granny Doyle who lived in the cottage beside the wood where Rose lay. It was only a small wood, a little copse really. Granny Doyle's father had planted those trees. "Ah, well now, let me see," she would say with her eyes closed and her head tilted to one side as if she hadn't recollected the information a hundred times before, "it must have been nineteen sixteen or seventeen. I remember it was the year Daddy got this place from the Bradleys. I was only a wee thing, would'n have been more'an five or six I suppose, but I distinctly remember him putting them there trees into the ground. Wee tiny things they were, barely came up to my shoulders and would ya look at them now. My god! Where does the time go?" Rose didn't care if Granny Doyle's father planted the trees. What did it matter anyway, they were her trees, this was her wood. Her great grandfather didn't stick around long enough to see them grow anyhow. He went and got himself pneumonia and died when Granny was young. He had left her with just her mother and baby sister. Rose believed that that was why Granny was so hard, that and the fact that her husband had deserted her too. He went and died as well, leaving Granny with her own daughters to bring up when they were only just little. Rose felt she understood Granny. She admired her too, looked up to her – so strong and so holy. She was a strict woman, hell bent on being the perfect Catholic. She took her catechism very seriously indeed and made sure that the grandchildren were well taught by it. She didn't have her father to make her strong and Rose's mummy didn't have her father to make her strong and they never complained about that. So she, Rose, had no business not being strong since she had her father. The problem was, it seemed to Rose, was that her father wasn't strong himself – he was kinda weak – which was more of a reason why she ought to be stronger still. Fathers it seemed, were no good at all, only thinking about themselves.

She got up off the ground and winced as a sharp pain seared through the private area at the top of her legs. She doubled over holding her privates and let herself down again with her free arm. She couldn't sit. The pain in her bottom had eased a lot since a few days ago but just then it hit her like someone sticking a needle into her. She lay back onto the moss again and let the pain subside into the general ache she had been experiencing moments earlier. With her eyes closed she became aware that the area under her hand felt wet. When she brought her hand up to her face there was blood on it. She plunged her hand into her knickers and almost screamed out loud when she realised how much blood there was. The first thing she registered was that there was no-one close by to see. The second thing was that there was too much blood – she was used to little stains of blood recently and even little sores inside her that hurt like hell but went away very quickly when she bathed them in salted water a few times. But this much blood was scary – she didn't know how to deal with this much. The third thing that registered was fear. She held her breath and tried to think but nothing was coming. She couldn't think, she didn't know what to do next and she always knew what to do next – she always had it worked out beforehand – but now she didn't, she was trying, but nothing. A feeling came over her – the same feeling she had been getting since she was wee – the TV show feeling. She was in familiar territory now. She knew what to do. She reached out both arms and grabbed two handfuls of moss. Holding on she pushed her body tight to the ground and looked upwards through the branches. She was keeping herself on the ground – stopping herself from flying off the earth until the lady came. She was there within moments. Rose relaxed and allowed herself to drift away with the lady. Round and round she went and then up and up in the arms of the lady to her place.

The lady's place was nice. There wasn't any pain there and Rose never felt scared there. It was a small house which stood in a circle with other similar houses. In the middle of the circle was a green – an area of grass with a solitary tree in the centre. Rose had been going there quite a long time now. The first visit was around the time Daddy's wee game changed. Daddy had started to turn into a monster. His eyes would go dark and wild and he would get on top of her and it felt like she was being pushed down into hell. She wouldn't be able to breathe and then the lady would come with the TV show feeling and take her away. She always associated the pain between her legs with Daddy's new game but could never remember how it all fitted together. All she remembered was the time spent with the lady. And they were lovely times. She and the lady would bake cakes and buns and have tea out on the green under the tree. The tree was always laden with ripe red apples and after tea Rose would pick an apple and eat it lying back on the grass. Sometimes they would go visit people in the other houses. In one of the houses was an Indian man – a real honest-to-goodness Red Indian. He never spoke to her or to the lady. He would just sit there on the doorstep reading a little black book. From time to time he would glance up at Rose and smile and Rose would feel that he was telling her things straight into her mind and her heart. He didn't need to talk out loud – Rose understood. He was her friend, like the lady, and he and the lady and that place all came from inside her heart where good things were. Now, as she came there with the lady once again she saw the Indian sitting on the doorstep and a rush of joy filled her heart. She walked over to him and waited. As she felt his words come to her she watched his face shine as if a bright white light was behind his eyes. She felt his love for her deep within her and she loved him too. It felt to her that he was a part of her and she knew – a very deep, wise and ancient part of her.

Rose opened her eyes. She was back on the ground and the ache in her private area was still there. She lay for a while staring at the sky through the branches aware still of the love she was feeling. She knew it would fade, like the lady's place. It always did, and she was always trying to hold on to the memory between visits but to no avail. Her thoughts turned to the situation at hand and what to do now? *Ask Angela*, she said to herself. The idea came to her as if she already knew that she should do just that. *Angela will know what to do and she won't tell.* Thinking quickly, she pulled a tissue from her trouser pocket, folded it up and placed it inside her knickers. Then, very sheepishly, she left the trees and made her way back to the cottage. She found Angela in the front yard with Brian who was carrying a plastic bucket and spade set in his hands. Rolled up and tucked under the other arm was his big red beach towel. As Rose neared them she noticed that Angela didn't look too happy. *Must have to take them down to the cove,* thought Rose.

Angela pounced on her as soon as she saw her coming. "There you are" she said pretending she had been looking for her. "Mummy wants you to take the boys down to the cove."

"Oh aye, me or you?" asked Rose, irritated at her sister's trickery.

"You can go. Me and Caroline are going into the village with Mummy. We need to get some things for going back to school. Kevin's just fetching his sandals. You're not to stay too long and don't let the boys go out too far and no matter how many times they beg – no bringing back anything from the rock pools."

"I'm not stupid, I know right well it's you was told to take them. Besides, you don't need any more stuff for school, you just want to go off gallivanting to Cloughbeg having a good time while I'm stuck here with the boys," insisted Rose angrily. Everyone dumped on her – it wasn't fair. Angela wasn't listening. She had offloaded her chore and made sure

Rose knew the ins and outs. Now she was already planning where to go in the village. Rushing off to tell Caroline she was coming too she shouted back to Rose –

"Granny will be in the hen-shed. Any complaints take them up with her. See ya!"

Rose was livid. "Wait there!" she snapped at Brian, "I'll be back in a minute." She stormed off back in the direction she'd come and didn't stop until she was in amongst the trees again. Her mind raced with thoughts about what to do now and the implications of whatever she did. She needed Angela to tell her what to do with this much blood. She couldn't ask Mummy or Caroline and what would Kevin and Brian know? Dare she risk telling Granny about it? Granny didn't know she was *it*, and God! If she found out she'd be raging. It's a very wicked thing to be *it* – to be different. The worst thing was that she was just that – different – weird. A witch they called her sometimes. The time she told Maria Donnelly about the Indian she was mortified when Maria laughed and told everybody that creepy Rose McDevit was officially a lunatic and belonged in a mad-house. To make matters worse she confided in Angela that she thought everyone had an Indian and Angela said she was what was commonly known as a 'psycho' and she would end up dribbling from the mouth with a straitjacket on her. Psychos didn't belong in civilized society and normal people needed to be protected from them. Another time Rose had spoken to Auntie Lett about her differences. Well, not entirely! She spoke to her about one of her picture people that she often saw around her. Rose realised now that these people were privy to her and her only but she had to take the risk of mentioning this particular picture person to Auntie Lett. It was a boy, the same age as her and each time he had come he had changed. Rose could see that the boy always happened to be exactly the same age as her. Now the boy kept making her see a picture of Auntie Lett. Rose thought he wanted her to tell Auntie Lett that he was there, so she did. But Auntie Lett was awful! At first she just sniggered a little, but then she got cross and said sarcastically that there was no such thing as ghosts. Well, Rose never knew the boy was a ghost but then she decided that was exactly what he was. She didn't speak to anyone now about being different in any way. The more she could keep it secret the safer she was, especially now that Mummy seemed to be going mad as well. That was the only explanation Rose could come up with to explain her mother's behaviour of late. Around about the time Daddy's new game started Mummy started going mad. Occasionally, usually at the weekends, Mummy and Daddy, Mr and Mrs Donnelly and Mr and Mrs O'Hara would all gather in the kitchen and have some drinks. They would all sit around the dining table and talk about stuff. The children would be in bed sleeping but sometimes Rose would listen to them from the top of the stairs. She never understood what they were discussing. It was all very funny talk like it wasn't anything real – just made-up stuff. One night she overheard Mummy mention the word ghost and Rose strained her ears to hear what came next. She was sure they must have been talking about her but she couldn't make head nor tail of what they said. The adults would talk and drink whiskey and beer and smoke cigarettes which gave off a sickening, sweet-smelling smoke that reached Rose's nostrils on the stairs and made her feel quite dizzy. The adults would talk on and on and their voices became like a low murmur as it got late. Rose would give up trying to listen and go back to bed.

When she thought about these times she was confused and anxious. *Why did I not stay in bed all night? Why did I get up and go to their room?* She seemed to have a faint idea of Daddy waking her but it was very foggy. She could not remember, no matter how much she thought about it, how she would come to be in her parents' room – in her parents' bed.

When she was wee she had thought that Mummy had turned into a monster or that a monster had come and made Mummy disappear, but now it seemed to her that Mummy had gone mad. Rose sat down on a soft patch of moss. Ignoring the pain shooting up her bottom she hugged her knees and buried her face in her hands weeping. She didn't want to think about Mummy going mad. It was too frightening, but the memory of it came anyway. Mummy had shouted at her. She had accused her of being evil and of ruining everything. From the things she said Rose believed that she thought she was talking to Auntie Lett, especially when she talked about Rose as if she hadn't been sitting right in front of her. One of the things she said was "I should've kept the boy" - just like that. Rose hadn't had a clue what she meant by that.

She cried for a long time. She could hear the boys calling for her but she didn't care that they were or that she was being bad. She wanted the lady to come and make her feel better. She wanted to go to her place and see the Indian, but the lady didn't come. She wanted Mummy to come and be nice to her but that wasn't going to happen. She cried and cried and when she was tired of crying she lay down on the moss and sobbed some more. She felt so tired and she closed her eyes. She wanted to feel the trees around her and the heat of the sun on her body. She wanted to smell the moss and listen to the birds. She did not want to hear the boys calling for her and she most certainly did not want to hear Mummy's painful words in her head. The niceness of the wood enveloped her and offered her comfort which she hungrily accepted. Inside her shut eyes she began to see beautiful colours – vivid and swirling – blues and purples and pinks. It felt good! She didn't question where the colours came from but allowed them to be, enjoying the lovely warm safe feeling they gave her. And then, in a split moment the Indian's face flashed amidst the colour. She gasped in surprise opening her eyes and the Indian disappeared. Not wanting to miss seeing him again, she closed her eyes and relaxed. The colours were still there, growing in intensity. After a few moments the Indian's face came again and this time Rose tried desperately not to react. The face became clearer and soon there he was, smiling at her as he always did and pouring silent words into her mind and heart and filling her with the same joyous feeling she had felt before upon seeing him in the place the lady took her to. All too soon, he was gone and Rose was aware that the warm feeling she was experiencing now came from the heat of the sun and not his bright light. The ache in her private area had gone and although her abdomen continued to pain, it was so faint Rose hardly noticed it was there. She lay for a few moments still and quiet, relishing this new-found comfort. She could hear Brian's voice calling as if from a distance and then she heard Granny's voice demanding that she come at once. Reluctantly she turned her attention to the situation at present. She knew what to do next – she was going to tell Granny about the blood. It wasn't connected to Daddy's new game at all – there was something else – she felt it was connected to what Caroline and Angela called their period. Angela had got blood on her bed once and when Rose had started crying about it, Caroline had tutted at her and told her not to be a drama queen 'cos it was only her period. *Yep, it must be that*, she decided.

She stood up and dusted herself down as she was covered in pine needles. Rubbing her face with the end of her sleeve she hurried out of the trees and ran towards the cottage. Granny was back in the hen-shed. The hen-shed was huge. It was made entirely of tin painted red. The door remained open all day long and was only shut when the hens were put in for the night which was unfortunate to say the least since the shed also served as the toilet. The toilet was just a bucket really. There was a wooden box built around it with a hole in the lid. It was bigger than the toilet at home and Rose had to leap up onto it and shuffle backwards on her bum until she was over the hole. It's a wonder she never got a splinter in her bum. She would sit there watching through the cracks in the tin wall for anyone coming. If there was, the rule was to shout 'there's someone on the toilet!' as loud as you could. It wasn't a foolproof plan but it worked most of the time. When the bucket needed emptying Daddy, or Granny she supposed when the McDevits weren't there, would dig a hole in the midden and empty the contents into it. The midden, which was a heap about two metres square, was a safe distance away from the cottage but on a hot day like today was very noticeable to the nose indeed. Everything went in there from the toilet contents to the kitchen waste. Of course it attracted mice and rats. That's why everything had to be buried and why Granny always kept one or two cats. The cottage itself was very small. Only two rooms, three really if you counted a narrow strip along one gable that was called the pantry but only served as a dumping ground for old magazines and newspapers and anything else that needed storing 'out of sight out of mind' as Granny often described it. The kitchen was the main room. It had the range cooker surrounded by a huge chimney brace which was once whitewashed like the cottage but was now yellow with all the smoke from the range. There was a sofa and two chairs around the range, and at the other end of the room were the big kitchen table and a cupboard on top of which were Granny's precious ornaments and a big radio. Beside the cupboard was the pantry door which was always shut and God help anyone who left it open. The bedroom door was beside the chimney. It was a big room, again. It contained three big double-beds with massive mahogany headboards that almost reached the ceiling. There were two large mahogany wardrobes and several rugs on the stone floor. Underneath each bed was an enamel potty or *po* as it was commonly called for use at night when the trip outside to the toilet was undesirable. The entire family slept in this room at times, all crushed together in the big beds. There was only one little window and one in the kitchen. On a clear summer night the moonlight would stream into the bedroom. Rose would watch it mesmerized and play a game with the ghostly people she saw coming in through the moonlight. She would count in her head, guessing how long it would be before each disappeared.

The back of the shed was devoted to the hens. It didn't smell too great either and had to be cleaned out frequently which was what Granny was doing in there. Rose entered and stood inside the door waiting for Granny to speak. "Ah! There ya are Rose. Where did ya go off to? Your mother can't leave until she sees ya. Needs to measure ya for the cardigan she's getting knitted. Go and see 'er in the house and then come back here afore ya go to the cove. Go on then, hurry up." Granny didn't seem in the least bit annoyed and Rose's hopes picked up.

"Granny," she said quietly having gone right over to her until they were nearly touching, "Granny, I need to tell ya somethin'. I'm sore here so I am," she said, indicating her abdomen, "and there's blood in me knickers."

"Pants child! Don't say knickers, it's not nice. Okay, never mind about it. Your mummy will get ya somethin' for it from the village. Now on ya go, time's marchin'." Feeling somewhat dampened by Granny's flippant reaction to her crisis, Rose went down to the cottage to find her mother. She was in the kitchen, bag in hand ready to go to the village.

Rose obediently went over to her and said "Mummy, Granny said you'll get me somethin' from the village. I think I got the period Mummy."

"Oh! Right!" answered her mother, a little surprised it seemed. "Okay, em… let me think now. Right! Where's Angela? Is she in the car? Go and tell Angela I want her will ya?"

Angela *was* in the car and wasn't happy about being told to get out again. She knew where this was going. *Creepy Rose has wrangled out of minding the boys*, she thought. When she entered the kitchen with Rose behind her she started to complain straight away. "Mummy, why do I always have to mind the boys? It's not fair, Rose never does," she moaned.

Rose thought that was completely untrue – she had done more than her fair share of minding them lately. Caroline on the other hand never had to do anything. She was Mummy's wee pet. Besides, Rose didn't mind it as much as Angela seemed to. The boys could be fun sometimes and it got you out of doing housework.

"It's nothing to do with that Angela. Stop being so bloody difficult will ya?" replied Mummy. "I want ya to go and see if you've got anything for Rose. She's got her time. It's just for now – I'll get her somethin' from the village."

"Oh, aye I have! Hang on," muttered Angela and went off to the bedroom sneering at her younger sister. She came back with the required item and handed it to Rose without so much as a 'there you are'.

"Rose, come here till I measure ya," Mummy said to Rose taking a tape out of the top drawer of a cupboard. "There's a great knitter in the village – a friend of Lett's. She's gonna make ya a cardigan for the big school."

"Is she gonna make one for Caroline and Angela as well?" asked Rose holding her arms out from her sides.

"No, their cardigans are fine. They'll do them another year but you need one for sure. Well then, Rose, the big school now and you startin' your time an' all eh?"

Rose didn't know what her mother meant by her *time*. It must mean the same as her period. She felt a little proud just then that she was starting her time and going to the big school as well. Especially if it got her this much attention from Mummy and her talking nice to her like she did to Caroline and all. Rose was almost twelve – it was her birthday next week. They'd be back at home then which was a bit of a bummer – Rose much preferred being here at Granny's. Anyway, she'd be going to the secondary school after the hols and because she would be twelve, she'd be one of the oldest in the class. She was a wee bit scared of going to the big school which was three times the size of her primary school and catered for twice as many pupils. However, Angela had been scared when she started three years ago and it hadn't been long before she was proclaiming it to be the best place in the world. Rose didn't like school that much, in fact sometimes she detested it. Rose didn't like anywhere that had too many people all in the one place. She liked being alone so she could watch her picture people and go on her little mind adventures to visit the people that she thought were wonderful and who thought she was wonderful too.

"You're a woman now," Mummy added.

Wow! This startin' your time business is great if it makes Mummy like me now, thought Rose to herself with a smile. She was so pleased she could have tackled any school, any name-calling, any amount of blood. Mummy was being nice to her and that was all that mattered, and it got better…

"Now, I don't want you going down to the cove today Rose. You're to stay here and rest. Angela can take the boys for me and I want you to fill the hot water bottle and hold it to your back, okay? It'll help with the pain. Oh, and you'd better take those pants off and put on some clean ones."

Rose trotted off to the bedroom to do the necessaries. She was elated. Having your time was fantastic – the best thing ever. She didn't know what to do with the bloody knickers though so she stuffed them in her pocket. She didn't want anyone seeing them for fear they'd know by looking at the blood that her time wasn't the only issue. When she returned to the kitchen Mummy had gone outside. She lifted the lid off the range quickly and dropped the knickers into the fire. Then she went to the window and looked out for Mummy. She was talking to Angela who was by now back in the car impatiently waiting to go to the village. Rose watched as Angela got out and stormed back towards the cottage door. Getting off-side, Rose nipped into the pantry. She listened as Angela banged doors and complained loudly to herself about it not being fair. She heard the car starting up and driving away down the lane to the main road. The two boys were laughing and jumping around in the front yard excited about finally getting to the cove and then she heard Angela bang the door on her way out. She shouted at the boys - "Shut up you two and don't annoy me or you'll go nowhere."

Rose waited until she could no longer hear their voices as they left the yard before she re-entered the kitchen and filled her hot water bottle with piping hot water from the kettle on the range. She fetched her book from the suitcase stashed under the sofa. She was reading Enid Blyton's *Famous Five*. Settling down on the sofa she placed the hot water bottle at her back and began to read. The *Famous Five* books were her favourite and she had read them all a couple of times. This one was number three – *Five Run Away Together*. One of the characters was a girl called Georgina who wanted to be a boy and wouldn't answer to anything other than George. Rose could identify with George wanting to be different than she was and sometimes she pretended that she was George going on amazing adventures. The hot water bottle was doing its stuff – the ache in her abdomen was easing greatly. "My mummy loves me," she said to herself with tears in her eyes.

Rose opened her eyes. It was morning. Today she was twelve years old. It had been a whole week since she had started her time and she was all better now, although she was shocked when Caroline told her that it would happen every month until she was an old woman like Granny. Mummy had been okay with her. After that initial exchange between them when she'd been so nice, things didn't go back to being normal but she wasn't particularly nice to her either which was devastating for Rose. She had got her hopes up and now that they were home again it looked like nothing really had changed much. Brian came running into the bedroom delighted because there were several birthday cards on the mat by the front door. Brian always woke up way before anyone else in the house. He used to wake her up about six in the morning and Rose would get up and watch cartoons on the telly with him, but since he was seven now he thought he was a 'big boy' and so he got up and watched his cartoons all by himself. Rose knew that the boys liked her especially Brian. Sometimes, when she studied him, she thought she felt a connection between them as if he was able to see things as well. She never questioned him though 'cos she couldn't risk him saying anything to the others. She was in enough trouble just being her, being born bad. "Rosie! Rosie!" the delighted boy was saying with glee, "You've got four cards. Can I bring them up to ya? Please, can I?" Rose giggled at her brother's excitement and began to feel a flow of excitement herself. It was her birthday and later on they were gonna have a tea party with a real birthday cake and candles an' all.

"Go on then Brian. Bring 'em up." Caroline and Angela were awake now too and although Caroline wasn't interested Rose knew that Angela was just putting on an act that she didn't get excited about kid's things. She wouldn't flaunt her cards though. She knew what it felt like when Angela had birthday cards, and she had got nine of them. Rose was happy with four and she wouldn't hold out much hope for any more. They'll be from Granny and one from Uncle Tommy and Auntie Theresa. There'll be one from Auntie Lett and Alan and one from Auntie Anne and Uncle Gerry. Mummy and Daddy never gave any of their children birthday cards. Mummy said that a present was all they needed and that cards are only from people outside the house and besides, they're a serious waste of money. Auntie Lett always sent birthday cards to them so Rose was a little confused about that, but she would never question that what Mummy said was right. Brian already had the cards. They were stuffed up his pyjama top. Rose laughed. It was all part of the silliness that birthdays allowed – like Christmas when Santa Claus came. Personally Rose never believed in Santa but the boys did and it was fun sharing their excitement. Brian handed over the cards – four. Rose was right about who they were from. What was really exciting though was that in each card was a crisp clean one pound note.

"Wow! Four pounds!" exclaimed Rose. "I'm gonna save it for my first school trip. You went to the zoo on your first year didn't ya Angela?" she asked her sister.

"Ya don't need four pounds just to go to the zoo," Angela replied, joining in with the excitement. "One pound is more than enough for a school trip. If I was you I'd buy a tape recorder. It's the in thing to have nowadays and ya can record your own voice an' all as well as play songs on a cassette."

"Aye, that's a good idea," said Rose, "maybe I'll buy one of those, or I could keep it for the zoo and still have money to buy presents at Christmas."

Angela was disgusted. She wanted Rose to get a tape recorder. She was the only one in her class that didn't have one, so if Rose got one she could pretend it was hers. She nearly always ended up getting Rose's things anyway. "Well if you want to ignore good advice and be the odd one out in your class so be it. Don't come crying to me when you're sorry ya didn't get a tape recorder when ya had the chance."

Rose thought about it, but she wasn't sure that's what she wanted to spend her birthday money on. She'd be starting school on Monday coming so it was no big deal to wait and see what she wanted then. She leapt out of bed ordering Brian to get out of the room till she got on her clothes. It was another hot sunny day and it was a Saturday *and* it was her birthday. What could be better? When her mother and father came down the stairs at seven thirty, Rose showed them her cards and the four pound notes. Her mother didn't seem all that interested which was nothing new for Rose and which she passed off very easily, but her father said -

"Ah! Sure that's great Rosie, what'll ya buy with your money?"

"Dunno yet Daddy," was the response, "I might buy a tape recorder 'cos everybody's got one these days."

"Everybody except Angela, eh?" asked Daddy winking at her. Rose knew what he meant. She wasn't slow in the uptake, as Daddy often said. "There's no flies on you, eh Rosie?" he would add, much to his wife's disdain.

She received a brown paper package from her parents. Inside the package were a bright green skirt and a green blouse with little rosebuds all over it and a big wide collar with a rose coloured trim. They were the most beautiful clothes she had ever seen, she thought, and they were hers from the start – not hand-me-downs like she was used to.

"And when Auntie Lett gets up she's gonna take ya into the town to get new shoes to match. What d'ya think o' that, eh?" Daddy said with a broad grin. He really loved his wee Rosie and was delighted to see her get so much attention. *God knows,* he often thought to himself, *poor wee lass has no life with the way Clare treats her.* Sean was well aware that his wife resented the child but at the end of the day it was her decision and he never believed that there was any real reason why things should change. If Lett and Alan get married it would take a load off no doubt and maybe things would be better for wee Rosie then. Still, he loved her more than the others – she was his wee girl and that counted for something. *She'll be grand*, he often said to himself, *if she wasn't so strange.*

"Yeah!" Rosie said in the little baby voice that always worked with Daddy. She was jumping up and down with glee when Mummy piped up with –

"Don't' be getting too excited. You're all getting new shoes for school. Just so happens that I don't have time today so Lett's taking ya in." Clare's remark had the desired effect on Rose. Her little heart sank at the disappointment. She thought she was getting to the town with Auntie Lett on her own and getting new shoes as a special birthday present.

Ah well, she thought, *at least I'm getting new shoes to go with this lovely outfit.* And she suspected that Alan would take her to the shop and let her choose whatever sweets she liked. Unfortunately, it turned out that Alan was not going to be there and he would not be at her tea party either. He had to go away on business according to Auntie Lett who seemed to be every bit as disappointed as Rose was. Still, they had a nice time in the town. Auntie Lett got them all new shoes and Rose got a 'Bay City Rollers' T-shirt from the market stalls that lined up along the main street.

"Your ma'll kill me for spoiling ya," Auntie Lett had told her when she was sizing the shirt up for her, "but sure it's your birthday. If I can't spoil ya on your birthday it'd be a sad day indeed." After the T-shirt excitement they all had chips in the café and washed them down with coca cola which was a rare treat indeed. Rose was having a great birthday.

At three o'clock the party tea was sitting on the table but there was no sign of Auntie Lett and the children. Caroline, who had stayed at home 'cos she wanted to pick her own shoes from the catalogue was playing her record player very loudly and the words of *Bye Bye Baby* were starting to grate on Clare's nerves.

"For crying out loud!" she screamed up the stairs, "turn that racket off or I'll come up there an' turn it off for ya." Caroline lifted the needle off the record and turned off the player, muttering under her breath. She went downstairs where the first thing she saw was the tea party all laid out and waiting for the children.

"Nobody back yet?" She asked the obvious question and regretted it almost immediately when her mother went off on one of her rants.

"What does it look like?" she ranted. "You'd think she'd have the savvy to have them back by now. I said be here for at least two forty-five and it's now gone three. I've my own thing on tonight and there's gettin' ready to be done."

"I'm sure they'll be back soon Mum," said Caroline cautiously, "would ya like me to go and see if I can meet them and hurry them up?"

"Aye, you go love," replied Clare softening a little, "an' when you're passin' the pub will ya nip in an' tell that father of yours to come home. I don't want him drunk wi' guests comin'."

"Aye, no problem Mum. I'll go right now." Caroline nipped out the front door before her mother thought of anything else for her to do. It was always a delicate time when Mum was irritated. Mind you, it was worse for Rose but then Caroline always maintained that the creepy wee bitch deserved it. She had always hated Rose. She didn't really know why exactly but it seemed to her that Rose was the reason for a lot of disharmony in this house and she resented her being there probably more than Mum. If she had her way Rose would be long gone. She had witnessed her mother one time trying to drown Rose in the bath. At least that's what it had looked like and if she hadn't come into the bathroom God only knows what would have happened. Caroline thought about that often – the time she saw Mum holding Rose under the water. There was another time when Rose was only a toddler – she would have been about seven or so. Mum was coming down the stairs holding Rose and then suddenly Rose went tumbling down on her own. Mum said she wriggled out of her arms before she could stop her but Caroline was pretty sure that Mum had simply let go of her. Caroline never spoke about these things to anyone, not even Daddy, but at times it made her wonder if her mother was crazy or something. Anyway, what did she care about Rose? For all she was concerned it was a pity Mum had stopped her from throttling Rose one time there last year. She really hated the dirty wee bitch – creepy wee witch was what she believed.

She met her father on his way home and she was relieved not to have to go into the pub. It wasn't a nice place for a young woman like her to be and it was important to have a good reputation. Better still, as soon as she saw him she spotted Auntie Lett and the children coming walking behind him. She waited for them to catch her up and said, "Hi Daddy, Mum's waiting for ya all to come home. She's got the tea party waitin'."

"Aye well that's grand then isn't it?" said Sean drunkenly.

"Christ sake Sean. Could ya not stay sober just for once an' it the child's party an' all?" snapped Auntie Lett as she came up behind him. Sean smirked at her and walked on without answering. He seemed a little crestfallen, Caroline thought. She nudged Rose as she passed her and whispered -

"Mum's raging you're late. You're gonna get it ya wee creep."

By four o'clock the tea party was done. Rose had blown out her candles – there were only four of them – and everyone sang Happy Birthday except Caroline who hadn't returned to the house at all. Rose wished that her mother wouldn't lose it today of all days. She did seem too busy getting ready for her own party to be cross at Rose or Auntie Lett for staying too long in the town. She didn't even say anything to Daddy who was obviously drunk. Rose remembered that when she was wee she used to call that 'too many wee ones' and how could she forget the implications of that? She knew only too well what happened when Daddy was drunk and that was not something she wanted to even think about. Anyway, the birthday was ruined and Rose never felt as angry as she was now. When the kitchen was cleaned Rose lifted her cards off the wireless where she had displayed them for the party and went outside to the back garden. The shed door wasn't locked and with much despondence, she stepped inside and shut the door behind her. She sat down on an old rolled up mat and folded her arms. The angry feeling had left her and all she felt now was hopelessness. She leaned back against the wall prepared for a long stint in the shed. What else was there to do? Nobody wanted her – nobody liked her – she might as well just die here in the shed. She hadn't seen the Indian since last week in the wood and the lady hadn't been around either. It was probably best for her that she forget about that nonsense anyway since it just made people think she was a witch.

"It's all my imagination," she sighed and gave in to the

feeling of hopelessness – a hopelessness that had become the very core of her being. She sat like that in the shed for an hour before the Indian came. He hadn't forgotten her and when he came she was once again filled with joy. He looked at her and smiled and she smiled back soaking up all the delicious energy he created. They remained like that for what seemed to Rose to be only a short time but when he was gone and she looked at her watch, a half hour had passed. It was enough for Rose. She perked up and dared to hope again. By the time she went to bed that night she was eager to get by as long as the Indian was her friend. Little did she know that she was about to be shoved violently into a world such as she'd never encountered before, even in her worst nightmares.

Twelve – it was to be a terrifying age for Rose – a girl whose every night was to be filled with terror – whose every day was to be filled with fear of death – and who had no-one to save her, only 'dead' people.

Chapter Four

Grow up Lissy

Dorset, England December 2007

Lissy put down the receiver. She was bitterly disappointed. Anne had cancelled their meeting that morning, and their lunch date. Anne was always doing stuff like that. It seemed to Lissy that she couldn't rely on her to see anything through. She would be full of enthusiasm for their plans from the start especially when it was her idea but she very often fell through at the last moment. Lissy wasn't even confident that she'd help her with hanging her paintings like she promised. Many a time she felt like cancelling their friendship altogether, if that's what you could call it – sometimes she wondered. And now, today of all days, when she had the most exciting news to tell, she'd gone and let her down again. She was so disappointed – and dammed angry too! "What was it you wanted to tell me anyway?" Anne had asked at the end of their conversation on the phone.

"It doesn't matter, it'll keep," was Lissy's curt reply.

"Fair enough then. I'll see you tomorrow, bye!"

"Hang on. Are you not going to the psychic fair this afternoon?" Lissy needed her to go to that. She wanted to see Linn.

"Oh yes! I totally forgot that. Em... yes, yes, why not. Oh yes, that's right – Linn was to go as well, wasn't she? Fine, fine, no problem. I'll phone her now – see what she's doing. You and Linn could go on anyway couldn't you? I might stay in and shake this cold. That'll be alright won't it? Tell you what, I'll give you Linn's number and you can chat to her yourself. I'll text you it, okay? Gotta go babes, see'ya later."

Yea, fuck you an' all, Lissy had thought to herself. She told herself that on Monday she'd let her know on no uncertain terms exactly how pissed off she was with her, but she knew she wouldn't. She and Anne worked alongside each other in the local tourist information centre. Both women loved their work but it wouldn't be so great if there were bad feelings between them. Moments later while she was still standing in the hallway the doorbell rang, startling her. She opened the door with one palm stretched across her chest. It was John. "Hi John," she said with a smile. She liked John. He was one of those people who never argued with you. Plus, he hung onto her every word. "You made me jump, come in."

"Hello Lissy, how are you?" he asked, stepping in

through the door and shutting it behind him. "Whoops!" he said quietly to her, "forgot to wipe my feet, didn't I?" He took off his trainers and placed them on the mat by the door. John was well aware of Mrs Brenning's rules about good housekeeping. It had become a bit of a joke between him and Lissy who saw it as her attempt at rebellion. Sad really - she knew! but she never had the guts to stand on her own two feet. She was still living at home for Christ's sake. She shook her head and tutted in feigned disapproval.

"I don't know John Brunt, what shall I do with you?" she said.

"Do what you should've done a long time ago," John was grinning from ear to ear, playing along with her little game.

"And what might that be then dear neighbour?"

"Lock me up in your cellar and keep me as your sex slave." He laughed, ducking down to evade Lissy's right hook.

"Cheeky git," she gasped. They stood giggling for a while and then came a very uncomfortable moment for Lissy when they locked each other's gaze. She was the first to turn away. She knew her mother was correct when she said that John had a fondness for her. *Bloody hell! More than a fondness – poor bloke's fallen for me,* she told herself now as he tried to pass over the awkwardness with another joke.

"Maybe Brenda could use me around the house a bit more. What d'ya think eh? Would her pinny look nice on me?" Lissy didn't answer him. She giggled nervously. She wasn't sure she wanted to get involved again. God! She wasn't falling for him too, was she? She was just about recovered from yet another disastrous relationship. Liam had been everything she wanted – charming, good-looking and very rich. Only problem was, he knew it and so did all the gold-digging, boyfriend-stealing tramps for miles around. It was as if they could sniff him out and snuff her out at the same time. Anyway, it was good riddance to bad rubbish. He was always trying to make her into something she was not. Pooh to him was her reaction when he dumped her. Lissy liked to be in control of a relationship and no self-absorbed shopwindow dummy was gonna mould her into the perfect girlfriend. The reality was that Lissy Brenning was a spoiled child. Even at twenty nine years old she was incapable of seeing anyone's point of view except her own. She still lived with her parents not because her mother had too much control over her but because deep down she knew that moving out meant taking responsibility for her own life and that was something she was scared shitless of. But she would never admit that to herself – instead, she manipulated people into giving her what she wanted. Boyfriends came and went leaving Lissy wondering what had gone wrong, convinced that all men were selfish bastards.

"Ah, the very man!" came Dad's cheery voice from the kitchen door. "Come to give me a hand, lad? Appreciate it lad, ta very much." John gave a friendly nod to Russell Brenning and went to the kitchen. Lissy watched him go from behind, sizing him up as he walked away from her. He wasn't what you would call good-looking. His face was pleasant enough but he was short. Lissy usually went for tall men - very protective. His sand-coloured hair curled around his ears and the nape of his neck. Lissy thought that was cute and found herself blushing as she looked at him now, the hair just touching the collar of the pale blue shirt he wore open at the neck. Although he was short, his body was fit in a sinewy kind of way. She knew he played rugby and supposed that was how he'd come to have such a tight bod. He was a journalist by trade – not something that resulted in physical strength. Lissy thought about the moment they had just had and smiled at the memory of those blue eyes looking at her from under those long curly lashes. She felt a sudden flutter in her stomach and shook herself out of the trance she was in. No way was she going to fall for John – it was what her mother wanted, not her. She watched as he went into the kitchen and she heard him saying hello to her mother. She was just going to fetch her mobile from the bedroom when the phone rang again. She came back down and answered it. It was Linn.

"Hello, is that Lissy?"

"Yes. Oh hi, Linn. I suppose Anne rang you did she?"

"She did, yes. Listen Lissy pet, I can't chat now. I was wondering if you wanted to meet up at the hotel. Mark and I are having lunch there so if you want to meet us at two, say, or you can join us if you like, for lunch I mean. What d'ya say?"

Lissy was delighted. She'd love to have lunch with them. Mark was Linn's husband. She wondered if John would come along. "That would be nice Linn but would you mind if I brought a bloke along?"

"Not at all, the more the merrier. Didn't know you were seeing someone again. Who is it?"

"Oh no-one really, we're just good friends. He's my neighbour actually – John. I kind of promised he could tag along to the psychic fair you see," lied Lissy.

"No probs pet. See you both at twelve in the foyer. Gotta dash, talk later, okay? Byeee!"

"Bye!" said Lissy brightly. She went to the kitchen door and opened it a little bit, peeping in. John and Russell were struggling with the bed settee. She moved out of the way and held the door open against the wall, pinning herself up against the wall too. As the two men struggled to get the settee through the door she flashed a smile at John just to ensure he would go with her to the hotel. Once the settee was through she skipped over to the cellar door and held that open for the men. It wasn't long before the settee was in its new home in her studio and Russell was slumped onto it taking a breather.

"John, Come on, I'll show you where the heater is. That has to come down as well," said Lissy leading John up the steps again. "Daddy darling, stay there and I'll bring you down a cup of tea."

"Thank you dear, but I'll come up for it," replied her father. Once in the hall she told John of her plans for lunch and the psychic fair. She didn't have to ask him twice – he'd love to spend the day with her and her friends.

"Are you sure now I'm not taking you away from anything important?" Lissy added knowing fair well that he'd drop anything to be with her.

"Hell no! When it comes to a toss-up between you and a bunch of papers, I'd choose you every time. Just gotta nip home first to get changed and I'll pick you up before twelve."

"Mum'll have tea ready. You have time to stay for a cup before you go. You know Mum. She'll be annoyed if you don't." Lissy grabbed his arm and ushered him into the kitchen where Brenda had indeed prepared elevenses.

"Oh thank you Mum," she said kissing her on the cheek, "you're an angel."

"Well you've picked up from this morning dear. Doing anything nice today?" asked Brenda, relieved that her daughter had stopped going on about that woman.

"Mum!" Lissy said, "I told you. I'm having lunch with Linn and Mark and I'm going to the psychic fair at the hotel. Don't you remember?"

"Of course dear, did you not say you were meeting Anne though?"

"Nooo," said Lissy, feigning amusement, "What are you like? Anyway, John's coming too, so he can't stay long Mum. Have you got any of those cherry scones he likes?"

"Don't be going to any trouble for me Mrs Brenning. This is just lovely as it is," chipped in John as he pulled a stool out for himself.

Brenda was delighted. "No trouble dear, you help yourself. I'm afraid I haven't any cherry scones made. I must do a bake this afternoon. Russell's very grateful for your help dear – it's very kind of you and I'm sure Lissy appreciates it too."

"Gosh, yes, thanks a bunch John," Lissy added.

"Anytime!" John smiled at her. "Gosh, yes, what about that heater?" Both Lissy and Brenda noticed the way he had repeated her phrase. Russell came in before she could speak and answered for her.

"Ta very much lad," he said to John, and to Lissy he said, "Just looked at that heater you wanted dear. I don't think it's too safe to be honest. Best get a new one really."

"That's fine Daddy. It doesn't matter anyway. I can do without. No big deal." It wasn't Lissy who wanted the heater down there anyway. Russell went to the sink and washed his hands.

"Not in there," Brenda shrilled, "how many times do you have to be told. There's a perfectly good bathroom to do that in and nooo, don't wipe your hands on that towel – that's for drying the dishes." Lissy looked at John and shook her head.

"Er, I'll be off then folks. Thanks for the tea," John said having jolted off his stool.

"But you haven't finished your crumpet dear," Brenda said sweetly.

"Thanks Mrs Brenning, but I'd best be off or I'll be

pushed for time. See ya soon Lissy, I'll let myself out." And he hurried out the door.

"What a nice lad!" exclaimed Brenda when he'd gone, "I'm glad you're spending time with him Lissy dear. Just what you need."

"Mum! You said that about Liam," answered Lissy, exasperated.

John's car pulled into the drive at precisely eleven forty five. He had gone home, showered, shaved and dressed in his smartest shirt, all in record time – thirty minutes. His house was only fifty metres away from Lissy's. He lived on his own now. He had bought the house with an old girl-friend, Carla, ten years ago. He was only twenty five then and was pretty sure he didn't want to be tied down with kids so young but Carla had different ideas. She was Italian and had wanted to settle down and raise a large family like most of the women in her family. Anyhow, to cut a long story short, in May of 1998 she had got pregnant but had mis-carried three months into the pregnancy, and although he couldn't say he wasn't relieved, he shared in Carla's pain as well as feeling a sense of loss himself. The whole thing had put a strain on the relationship and they broke up just two months later. The last he heard, she was living in London with a husband and three kids.

He waited for a few moments and then beeped the horn.

Lissy was keeping him waiting. "Typical Lissy," he laughed to himself. It was exactly like her to do this. She was trying to keep him on his toes – she wanted him to run after her. He'd known her type before – spoiled little rich girl who would want him to bow down to her at a moment's notice. You only had to take a look at the mother to see how she'd turn out. Like mother – like daughter, he always said. Mind you, Lissy was no child - she was nearly thirty, although she did act like a child. Still, he hadn't been able to keep his eyes off her since that first day, the 10th of July 1906. He knew the very day 'cos it was his birthday. She had been running down to the post box at the end of the street and he'd come round the corner and walked straight into her. He had seen her about before but never really noticed how pretty she was til then. Her cheeks had been flushed and her skin glistening with little beads of sweat. Her long thick auburn hair clung to her face and she had been picking it off all the time they were talking to each other. John hadn't been able to stop himself from staring at her, especially at her huge blue eyes. Now, as he watched her skip down the steps from her front door, he reminded himself of her loveliness. She could be difficult yes, but John knew that was just a mask that she wore to protect herself from the world. She needed someone who could teach her how to grow up, someone who would love her despite her tantrums and who would show her what the world was really about. Carla had been wonderful at a time when he needed someone to have fun with but now he was ready to settle down and Lissy fitted the bill very nicely. He had loved her since he met her that hot sunny Saturday last year and he knew he had been waiting his entire life for her. *Easy does it though, John old chap*, he said to himself as he reached across and opened the passenger door for her. She plopped herself into the seat and shot him a wide smile that melted his heart. She was gorgeous. Her hair was straightened and came down past her shoulders, lying on her red shawl that highlighted the natural auburn in her hair. She had make-up on her face with vibrant red lipstick which looked very sexy but could never compete with her natural beauty. He turned away quickly. He didn't want her to see his desire. He had to wait for her to come to him.

"Never been to that hotel for a meal before," he told her, "Is the food good?" He put the car into gear and set off out of the drive and along the main road towards the little town of Lanesworth. She didn't answer him. She was miles away. "Lissy? Hello, are you with me?"

"What? Oh, I am sorry. What did you say?" Lissy said, genuinely apologetic.

"I was asking what the food was like in this place. You were out of it there – something on your mind?" John was hoping she wasn't regretting asking him along.

"Dunno, never dined there before."

"And the second question?" He said stopping at the traffic lights. He turned to face her. "I asked if you had something on your mind."

"Yes, yes I have actually."

"And...?" God, it was like pulling teeth.

"And we talked about it before. Do you remember how I told you that I was adopted and that I'd love to meet my birth mother?"

"I remember," said John, "I said it was a good idea."

"What you said was I'd never be able to forget about it until I meet her."

"And?"

"And I've decided to look for her, that's all. That's what was on my mind just then when you said I was out of it." She sounded so vulnerable just then and John noticed a hint of sadness in her voice that he hadn't seen before. He wanted to take her in his arms then and there and make all her wishes come true. He was quiet as he drove off again and neither of them spoke until they reached the hotel car-park several minutes later. When he had turned the engine off he turned towards her and took her hand in both of his.

"Lissy, are you sure that's what you want?" he asked her in a fatherly kind of voice.

"I'm sure John but, well I am scared a little. What if she doesn't want to know?"

"That's something that we'll deal with *if* it happens," he stressed the *if*.

"We?" asked Lissy, almost in tears. She hadn't realised until now how frightened she was of rejection. She had built the woman up in her mind to be the perfect mother but what if she wasn't her idea of the perfect daughter?

"We," echoed John, "you don't think I'd let you go

through something like that on your own do you?" Lissy just smiled and shook her head. "Well then, we it is and we'll start as soon as you say, okay?"

"Okay!"

"Good! Now let's eat, I'm starving."

The conference room was crowded. People must have come from miles away for the fair. The stalls were lined up along each wall and there was also a row of displays down the centre of the large room. Lissy and Linn stood at the back surveying the scene, not sure where to begin. The men had cried off to the bar after lunch, not that interested in pushing their way through hordes of people scrambling for first place at Madame Lee's fortune-telling tent. "It won't be like that," Linn had said trying to persuade John to join them. John had watched Lissy – looking for any sign that she wanted him to go in with her but she seemed unconcerned. All through lunch she had ignored him and had eyes only for Linn who must have been a good bit older than Lissy – at least fifty. It was evident to John that Lissy hung on her every word. She'd been talking on and on for the entire time they were sitting there about Christianity and Buddhism and how she believed that the correlations between the two faiths were much more than the differences and how all religion is a creation of humanity and not God, whatever 'God' is. Personally, she believed that 'God' is only a concept that people used to define what really is.

"And what really is," added Mark, supporting his wife's philosophy, "is that this 'God' as people call it is the source of, and permeates, an invisible energy – an energy that all of life is essentially made up of."

"Exactly," said Linn passionately, "we call it God, although it is something that can never be defined. It's a mystery – life's a mystery and it will always be. That is what is real." She sat back in her chair beaming at Lissy, obviously satisfied with her account. John had to admit that what Linn had been talking about was interesting but he noticed that Lissy was agreeing with her whole-heartedly, going as far as to say –

"Well that's what I've always believed myself. As it is I don't even believe in the Catholic church any more." He knew that Lissy's parents went to church every Sunday and that she no longer went with them, but up until now he'd never heard her talk like this. She was easily led, he understood – for fuck's sake she had believed every cock and bull story that Liam fella had fed her, to say nothing of Colin who came before him and told her he was working for the government and that he had to go off every now and then on top secret missions. It was all bullshit of course. The bastard was married and was a used car dealer looking for a bit of posh on the side. John had had his suspicions from the start and made it his business to find out exactly who Colin Marshall was.

"Poor Lissy," he had said to his mate Marcus in the pub earlier that week, "she's such an easy target for bullshitters."

"She can look after herself though," Marcus had added with a wink, "I've experienced her temper first hand remember." Marcus had been going out with Lissy for about six months when John met her and the two men had struck up a friendship. Marcus wasn't a bad bloke according to John and he was about the same age as him so they got on pretty well.

"I know she can be a spoiled bitch and she can seem hard-hearted at times but that's just an act. She doesn't know any other way to be, does she? She just needs to grow up a bit that's all."

"Grow up a lot, mate," Marcus snorted. "That mother of hers – did you ever see anything like it? She treats her like she's a child. Why the fuck she puts up with it I'll never know. Anyway, I couldn't take much more of it. Nothing I did was good enough, it was as if she expected me to do everything for her, just like her mother. Did you know she's adopted?"

"She told me that not so long ago. She looks up to me a bit. I suppose she sees me as an older brother or something. I wish she wouldn't. I like her, mate, I really do. I wouldn't mind taking her in hand."

Marcus snorted again and said, "Sooner you than me, mate – a bit too much baggage for me."

John had been slightly annoyed at Marcus for his attitude towards Lissy but he knew he didn't really mean to be horrible. In fact, he treated her with the utmost respect any time they met her out and he had been very gentle they way he went about breaking up with her. Marcus was alright! Observing her now from across the table John wanted to protect her from herself. He could see that what was really going on with her was that she was projecting her feelings for her birth mother onto Linn and that she was simply pleasing her by believing her every word. If he was going to help her find this birth mother he would need her to be her own person – to grow up and stand on her own two feet. He changed the subject, chatting animatedly about rugby and Mark took the bait hook, line and sinker. He and John had then slipped off to the bar and left Linn and Lissy to enjoy themselves.

The two women had been standing at the back of the room for several minutes when Linn pointed out a man she knew, standing behind his stall, and waved over to him as he spotted her. Pulling Lissy by the hand she manoeuvred their way through the crowd towards him. "Hi Bobby, doing okay?" she asked him and stretched across the stall to give him a hug.

"Hello my love, how are you? Who's your companion?"

"This is Lissy, a good friend of mine," answered Linn smiling at Lissy warmly. Lissy felt her heart swell with encouragement and shook Bobby's outstretched hand, saying hello.

"Well hello Lissy, it's a great pleasure to meet you. I feel

I know you already. I recognise your spirit."

Lissy must have looked surprised at his words because Linn offered an explanation very quickly. "What he means is that he feels you may have known each other in a past life."

"Reincarnation?" Lissy was intrigued. This was a subject she had always believed in. However, the church was dead against the idea and forbade it to be entertained.

Linn didn't answer her question directly. Gesturing towards the information on Bobby's stall she said – "Bobby is a past-life regression therapist. He is able to help people remember previous incarnations, which aids them in understanding themselves better. For example, a woman may have a recurring illness of unknown origin. If she goes back to a particular lifetime she may discover the reason for the illness and in doing so is better informed as to how to heal herself."

Lissy was a little taken aback. "Oh, right! But that's all in the mind is it – kinda hypnotism?"

Linn screwed up her nose and addressed Bobby. "Lissy is only beginning her journey. She's angry at her adoptive mother for smothering her all her life and at her birth mother for giving her up."

"Linn!" Lissy started, shocked at the frivolous way Linn had given out her personal feelings to a stranger. "I don't believe you just said that, is nothing sacred?"

"Don't be alarmed Lissy," Bobby said, gently coming around the stall and putting his arm around Lissy's shoulder. "Linn doesn't mean any harm. She simply is aware that

I may be able to help you with your anger." Linn stood there and smiled at Lissy and Bobby while Bobby added – "You do know darling that you were meant to be here today. You were meant to meet me and I am meant to help you. It's all written in divine order. I knew as soon as I laid eyes on you that I'd be helping you."

"That's as maybe but you can't help me find my birth mother though," stated Lissy more relaxed.

"Maybe not, but you never know what you can do unless you take the first step." Bobby stood back from Lissy and took her hand in his. He reached for one of pamphlets of the stall and placed it in her hand. "Take this with you and give me a ring when you're ready to talk, or don't, if that's what you want. You can always contact me through Linn and Mark anyway."

Lissy took the pamphlet and thanked him politely, stating that she would like to see around the place and maybe she'll come back to him later. With that she moved away not caring if Linn was following or not. She was.

"You know Lissy, I think you really would benefit from seeing Bobby. You don't have to have past-life therapy, you could just talk to him. He knows a lot of stuff. I really do think he can help you more than I can," Linn offered, seeing that Lissy was curious despite being uncomfortable with the idea.

"Gosh, it's certainly interesting, I'll give him that, but what could he possibly do that will help me?"

"Mark met Bobby two years ago through a friend who

had seen him for therapy. He started asking questions just like you are now. His friend set up a meeting with Bobby and Mark went along to see him. He found what he had to say very interesting and he arranged to meet him again. Bobby had a meditation group going at that time and although we didn't know anything about meditation, we agreed to go along and try it for ourselves. We haven't looked back since. You know all that stuff I've been telling you about? Well we learned all that from him. Well, learned is not the right word but it was he who helped us to see it for ourselves."

Lissy had been listening with increased curiosity. She had to admit to herself that the idea that she knew this man in another life was fascinating. If nothing else, she wouldn't mind following up on that. Plus, Linn had been talking about meditation for ages now and she was keen to learn how to do it. She decided she would give Bobby a try.

"I might try that past-life stuff you know," she told Linn. "I would like to have a chat with him anyway."

"I believe you'll be glad if you do," replied Linn, taking a hold of Lissy's left arm. "Now let's see what else is exciting here. How about a tarot card reading? That's always good fun."

"Why not?" Lissy answered lightly, beginning to enjoy herself. "Won't do any harm I suppose."

"No, of course not. Besides it's not the cards that do the work. It's the psychic who gets it all isn't it? She just uses the cards as tools or props or whatever."

They set off towards the stall at the top of the room that had a huge sign hanging over it which read – ASK A QUESTION AND LET THE CARDS GIVE YOU AN ANSWER – and in smaller print underneath – 'pick 3 cards for a pound'. There was a long queue at it but they decided to wait since it seemed to be moving fairly quickly.

"She's either on the ball or making it up," Lissy joked quietly in Linn's right ear.

"No she's on the cards actually, crystal ball's on the other side of the room," was the witty reply.

"Ha ha," laughed Lissy. She was glad she'd come today, and what a day it had been! What with the big decision after last night's fight with Mum and then meeting Bobby. Then of course, there was John. She smiled to herself as she thought about him waiting for her in the bar. He was going to support her in her quest and you never know, maybe she'd be safe enough falling for him. After all, she had known him now for well over a year and she liked him a lot. He's a good man. She was one from the top of the queue when she realised she hadn't thought about what her question was going to be. There were lots of questions in her mind but only one seemed the obvious one to pose – 'Will I find my birth mother and will she accept me?' That was two questions actually but maybe if she phrased it like that it would count as one.

"Hello my dear, do you have your question? No, don't say it out aloud. Keep it in your head and choose three cards please," the fortune teller said.

Lissy asked the question again to herself. She noticed her heart was fluttering and she laughed at how silly she was being. She selected three cards very carefully and gave them to the fortune teller who gave a little smile as she placed them down face up on the table. "The first thing I'm going to say to you dear is that the happiness you seek is within you. No need to go searching. I see a lady here – a lot of power – a good woman. My dear, may I ask if you are actively seeking this particular lady?"

Lissy couldn't believe what she was hearing. How could she possibly know she was looking for her. "Em, yes I am actually. Will I find her?"

"No my dear, I'm afraid not. At least that's what the cards say."

"Oh," said Lissy, her heart sank.

"But she will find you."

Chapter Five

The heart of a child

Belfast 1978.

Someone once said – 'whatever you write on the heart of a child, no water can wash it away.'

Was Rose McDevit's heart gone forever? Was it so damaged, so filthy that no-one would ever want her? Was her soul so black that only hell would accept her? Rose believed the answer was yes, although she had gone to sleep on the night of her twelfth birthday with new-found hope taking seed in her heart. Her dreams had been of far-away places and loving friends. Downstairs a 'meeting' had been well under way. The adults had talked about things that children ought never to be aware of, but for Rose there was another rule – *what the child knows no-one should be aware of.*

She was now thirteen years old and was beginning her second year at Hexton Comprehensive School. She and Anna Welsh were helping to clean up the science lab after the class's last chemistry lesson. They had just washed out all the test-tubes and Petri dishes when Rose came over all hot and dizzy. It hadn't been the first time this had happened. For quite a few months now she had found herself having to sit down every so often. She was eating just as much if not sometimes more than she had always done but lately she didn't seem to have much energy at all. She had been sick way back – very sick indeed. Every day when she'd come home from school she had vomited in the toilet. At first her mother let her stay home from school but when she didn't get any better her mother became angry and said things like 'go on to school with ya. Ya'll be grand' and 'there's nothing wrong with ya. It's just your imagination'. That was something she said a lot. Rose didn't know how her imagination could make her actually vomit, but then her imagination was supposedly responsible for a lot of unpleasant things in her life. Sometimes she asked Anna to help her out with a few little experiments. For example, she had devised a game where she and Anna would talk about certain situations at school like who was in the playground for instance – what did they play? - did anything unusual or interesting occur? She would suggest certain scenarios to her friend who would then respond with a yes or no according to whether or not Rose's imagination was playing tricks on her. On the whole she got a yes answer which left her wondering if her imagination only played tricks with unpleasant stuff. It had been only a few days since she had shown Anna a big red swelling she had on her inner calf.

"I know what that is," said Anna proudly, "It's a boil. You get it when you're run-down. You know, when you're not getting enough vitamins and stuff. I had one when I was about ten. Ma took me to the doctor and got me a tonic."

"What's a tonic?" Rose asked, "In case I have to ask Mummy for one."

"You know, a tonic – it's like medicine to build you up and make you more healthy. I think it's called iron."

"Oh, but I don't want to go to the doctor. Mummy doesn't like it. D'ya think there's iron in the shops?" Rose knew Mummy didn't take her to the doctor in case he would see her sores down below and find out that she was born bad or that she was *it*. Mummy was ashamed of that and she wasn't gonna let anyone know about it.

"Dunno, but I can find out for ya. But you know the worst thing? I had to get it sliced open with a kinda knife thing. All this puss came out and everything. It was disgusting. If I was you I'd keep me mouth shut. Just eat your vegetables more if ya can and maybe it'll go away."

Rose thought for a few moments before answering. She wasn't sure if she should say this or not. She was wondering if Anna had been sick the same as her... with the same sickness that is – the kind that you shouldn't tell about. She decided not to – Anna might think she was stupid and wicked like Mummy had said she was.

"I might sneak some more of those wee vitamin tablets we get in the morning before school. You know the wee orange ones?"

"Aye, we get them as well," Anna announced, satisfied with the plan of action.

That had been only two days ago and Rose had already consumed several of the little orange tablets. She would have liked to have more but she was afraid of her mother discovering that they were going missing. It wasn't worth it. Plus, she felt so guilty that she just could not bear the feeling any longer and had already decided this morning that she would not sneak any more extras. As she sat on the science lab floor now she wondered if she had taken too many and made herself ill again. Her forehead was hot and clammy and she could feel the sweat trickle down the back of her neck. The light-headedness had taken over her and she could feel herself losing consciousness. It wasn't at all like the TV show feeling during which she could still hear and see. This was more like when she got gas at the dentist's to make her fall asleep very quickly. She blacked out. When she came to, Master Collins and Miss McArten were there. Miss McArten was wiping her forehead with a wet cloth and had been saying to Anna to run and get the school nurse. Master Collins had been filling a glass with water from the classroom sink and then it happened. She had started to gain consciousness again and someone was kneeling over her. Maybe she thought it was Mummy gone mad or maybe she thought she was in bed and Daddy wanted to play his game. When she thought about it afterwards she didn't know what happened only that she was terrified. She knew that she had acted out of some kind of instinct. She had been trying to push people away from her – stop them from hurting her. She had been looking around for the lady and the Indian but they weren't there – why weren't they there? She needed them. She needed them to come and take her away like they had been doing all along. Why desert her now?

Later, in the sick bay with the nurse forcing water down her throat, she knew she had acted out of pure instinct. She had come to and there was someone kneeling over her. There were others there as well because she heard voices although she didn't understand them. It seemed to remind her of something at home. When Mummy and Daddy had their meetings the O'Haras and the Donnellys were there and Mr Donnelly always scared the hell out of her. He was creepy, like when Daddy played his game – the same creepiness. Rose always felt very uncomfortable around him even when it wasn't a meeting night. One time she had stayed overnight at the Donnelly house when Mummy and Daddy were gone somewhere. She had a picture of Mr Donnelly standing at the bedroom door and she was pretty sure that something bad happened between them that night, she just couldn't remember it. She reckoned the lady and the Indian must have taken her away but she couldn't remember that either. Now Rose was pretty convinced that when she had come to she thought she was at the meeting and something terrible was about to happen. She had panicked and fought because it seemed that the lady and the Indian were gonna leave her there. But, instead, it was just the teachers and poor Anna, and she had scared the hell outta them, screaming and fighting and shouting, "No no! Leave me alone! Get away, Mummy!" The teachers had tried to quiz her when she'd calmed down but by that time she had withdrawn into herself and the TV show feeling was very strong. She wasn't gonna say anything at all 'cos she couldn't think about what to say – she couldn't even listen to the teachers.

"Feeling better Rose pet?" asked the school nurse. Rose looked at the woman's face and remained silent. She still felt a little queasy and she sipped from the glass of water the nurse had placed in her cupped hands. She was sitting on the sick bay bed with a couple of pillows propping her up and her legs stretched out in front of her. The nurse had her back to her, busy with something at her desk and she spoke again, "Tell me pet, have you fainted like that before today? Maybe at home eh?" Rose still didn't answer. She was frightened. She didn't want the nurse to see that there was something wrong with her. She didn't want her to see the boil which she had suddenly realised was burst and was oozing puss and blood. It must have happened in the struggle with her imaginary attackers. The nurse turned around and began to wash the boil with very hot water. Rose watched as if in a dream. "And how long have you had this then?" the nurse went on. She wasn't going to be beaten by the child's reluctance to speak. She had examined the poor wee lass thoroughly and she was taken aback to say the least at what she found. The child's abdomen was greatly extended and by the look of it, it seemed that the poor little thing was pregnant. *God knows how the poor wee lass got into that state*, *she had thought to herself, mind you, there's no way I'm getting involved with that. God only knows the mess I'd be getting into*. She wondered later on that night if perhaps she should have tested the girl's urine but decided that it was best to leave well alone that which doesn't concern you. "Bit of a nasty one that," she said to Rose indicating the now bandaged boil. The child just looked at her with those big frightened eyes and her heart broke for her. *God only knows what happened to 'er, a bad'un I suppose – must 'ave caught 'er on 'er own,* she thought. She decided to take the problem out of her own hands and told the child she'd be back presently. Off she went to the headmaster's office.

The man couldn't believe that a thirteen year old girl in his school could be pregnant and agreed to question the child for the sole purpose of dispelling any such crazy thoughts from the nurse's mind. The child was crying when he entered the sick bay in front of the nurse. He recognised this girl. It was Rose McDevit. The primary school master had warned him that there might be trouble with this one. Apparently she had been 'picked on' a bit and had a tendency to dream in class. This headmaster was not going to put up with any nonsense in his school and he had sought her and a few others out for his watch list at the beginning of term.

"Well Rose, what's all the tears about then," he said in a very headmasterly voice. The child didn't answer. She looked frightened out of her wits. He softened a little and sat down on the edge of the bed. "Now Rose dear, no-one can help you if you don't tell us what's wrong. Why are you crying, is everything okay at home?"

"Yis," the child sniffled.

"And have you fainted like this before today?" he went on.

"No."

"Rose, would it be okay if I have a look at your tummy? Can you lie down for me?"

The child wouldn't budge. She wrapped her arms around her abdomen and shook her head. She wouldn't look at him. The headmaster sat quietly for a moment thinking and then got up and ushered the nurse out of the door. "The girl's fine Anita," he told her. "I think there's nothing to be done except inform her parents of the incident and get someone to pick her up. No need to go into anything else eh? Let them sort it out if there's anything to sort out. I'll be in my office if anyone wants to see me." And with that he left it in the hands of the nurse. *All this girl stuff's not my department anyway* he told himself and went satisfied back to his office.

It was the first week in November and Rose had been off school for almost two whole months. She couldn't remember the last time she had been this bad. Mummy was cross all the time and even Daddy and Auntie Lett were irritable at best. Rose stayed out of their way mostly, appearing only at mealtimes and bedtime. Her sisters had started asking questions as to why Rose was off school. Not only that but she had begun to act even weirder than usual. She hardly went outside anymore and spent more time than before reading, often in the back hall cupboard or behind the sofa. Even Mummy had started acting strange. She had to know all the time where Rose was when they knew full well that she never gave a toss before where she was or what she was doing. On bath nights she locked Rose in the bathroom till she was done and often spent the time in there with her. Very strange behaviour indeed! As well as that, Auntie Lett was in tears most of the time. Mummy just shouted at her the way she shouted at Rose and made poor Lett worse. No-one knew what was wrong with her and no-one seemed to give a monkey's toss if she cried all day and night except Alan who got shouted down by Mummy when he expressed his concern.

Caroline and Angela and even the boys were greatly upset that evening. Alan had arrived just after the boys went to bed and the three girls were shooed out of the room.

Rose was quick to disappear but Caroline and Angela hung about in the kitchen trying to find out what was going on. Mummy had been too smart for them though and had caught them listening at the door. They were marched up to bed early with a right roasting and sat there discussing what was happening whilst all the time tempers flared downstairs. That had been ages ago now but it was just before Daddy announced that they were going to move house. He had been sussing out a great job in a large town near Granny Doyle's village, Cloughbeg and they were all going to live there as soon as they find a house.

"Mummy said that we've all got to go to Mayo 'cos you went an' shamed us all an' we can't stay here any longer" Caroline hissed at Rose one day. "Hope you're happy with yourself ya wee witch. Now ya have us all havin' to hide 'cos of your creepiness." Caroline was bitter. She did not want to go anywhere least of all so far away. She was going to be eighteen soon and she had a good mind to tell Mummy she was staying. They wouldn't be able to do a thing about it 'cos she'd be an adult then. Unfortunately, they were still in the old fashioned way of thinking that you were an adult when you reach twenty one and not until then.

Rose was not even gonna try and defend herself, the wee witch just sat there looking like she'd been on the weed. *Wouldn' be surprised if she was. I know Mummy has a stash somewhere. I bet the miserable wee witch has found it, always snooping around the way she does*, Caroline thought to herself, eyes half closed in suspicion. "Hey weirdo!" She pushed on Rose's forehead. "Have ya bin on the weed eh?" Rose didn't reply but silently turned her back on Caroline. "Aye well, see if ya have, ya can get me some an' all." There was no response. Caroline was becoming very uneasy. What the hell was wrong with the creepy wee bitch? Why was she behaving like this, like she was some kind of hospital case? She didn't care much for her that was true but she wouldn't like to see her go completely doolally. Fuck it anyway, it was no loss to her. Except it was if she was forced to go and live over a hundred miles away. "Why the fuck didn't they give ya to the gypsies when ya was born?" she sneered slamming the door as she left the room.

When Caroline had gone Rose sat still as she was for about five minutes staring at the door and pondering what her sister had said. *Why did they not give me to the gypsies when I was born? Why did they keep me here to torture me and make me sick? What if I run away and just lie in a ditch somewhere and die?* All these questions flew around in her head like poison, stabbing at her, accusing her and reminding her of the evil that was inside her - the evil that was now desperately trying to get out and take her to hell. It was making her tummy grow and stretch and any day now it was gonna make it burst wide open. Then everyone would see. Everyone would know that she was evil, that she was born bad. In a way she felt that at least it would be over and she would be dead. She was hoping that the lady and the Indian would come when she was dead and take her to be with them but she believed it was more likely that they wouldn't want to know once they saw the evil inside her. There was nothing she could do but wait for the inevitable.

"Mummy," she had stated miserably when she was getting fitted for a bigger skirt – one of Caroline's that went halfway down her shins - "Mummy, I've bin thinkin', what if I go an' see Father Corrigan? He might say some prayers for me and make me better?

"For God's sake child. Father Corrigan has got better things to do than worry about the likes of you. You'll be grand when it's all over. Just keep your tummy in an' no-one will see. It won't be long now."

"But what if it takes me to hell when it gets out? Mummy, I don't want to go to hell," Rose pleaded.

"If ya don't shut up and quit your whingeing I'll send ya to hell meself. Keep your mouth shut and your tummy in an as long as no-one sees then you'll be grand."

Up until now Rose had kept her mouth shut and her tummy in as best as she could, but the girls had already started to call her fatty. Granny Doyle had called her worse. Once she knew that Rose was dying she had to have Auntie Lett bring her to Cloughbeg in her car. Rose thought it might be a good thing to stay there until she died since she could be with her trees and the cove. Those things always helped to make her feel a little better. But she wasn't to stay at Cloughbeg at all. Granny just wanted to see her tummy and check the situation out for herself. She went crazy when she saw how sick she was. She yelled and yelled at Rose and poor Auntie Lett who was crying more than usual.

"Ma please," Auntie Lett had begged, "She's only a wee wee'n. You're scaring her. She doesn't understand what's happening to her, how could she? She's only thirteen for Christ's sake."

"Don't you dare bring the Lord into this Collette. The Lord has nothing to do with this evil," Granny had yelled, her face like thunder. "Like mother like daughter. I should 'ave known she'd go bad. It's in 'er. Well I wash my hands of the pair of ya, I really do. You can go to hell for all I care."

Granny didn't wash her hands of Rose and Auntie Lett that day, instead she let them stay for the whole weekend and on Sunday she took Rose to see the parish priest. Auntie Lett disagreed with her plans and insisted that Clare and Sean wouldn't like it but Granny was adamant. According to her there was only one person who could amend this mess and that was God.

"Rose, this is the parish priest, Father Murphy. He's gonna talk to ya an' see if he can make this horrible mess a bit better. I'm gonna leave ya here for a while an' then I'll come back, okay? Be good now an' do what Father Murphy tells ya to." With that Granny left the room in the priest's house where she had taken Rose just ten minutes earlier.

Father Murphy looked down at Rose and said – "Now then young lady, what are we going to do with ya eh? Your Granny says you're in a spot of bother, what?"

Rose studied his face carefully trying to surmise if she could be frank with him. It was an old face deeply ingrained with laughter lines around the eyes and mouth. His hair was grey and only came around the back and sides of his head the top of which was completely bald. His skin and teeth shone so clean that Rose thought he must scrub them five times a day. She liked him instantly and at the back of her mind she could see the lady smiling and nodding, encouraging her to go ahead. Rose smiled. She was smiling at the lady but the priest of course thought she was smiling at him.

That'll do, Rose thought secretly, *He's okay if the lady says he is.* "I'm sick Father, very sick. I think I'm dying," she bravely stated.

"Dying!" the priest exclaimed, "well, let's see about that, what? Tell me how ya got to be in this state my dear?"

"If I tell ya, you've gotta promise you'll never breath a word of it," Rose went on. The priest nodded, prepared for a story about some lad or other but what he heard made him angrier than he'd been in a long time and he had heard some hair-raising tales in the confessional, he had. "It all started at the meetings see," Rose went on, "The Donnellys and the O'Haras come to a meeting with Mummy and Daddy every other Saturday night. Well, at first they didn't involve me. I mean at first it was just Daddy but then Mr Donnelly started. At least I think he did."

"What on earth are ya talking about child, started what? At first it was just Daddy what? What did your father do?"

Sean Murphy did not like where this conversation was going at all. Rose took a gulp and crossed her arms around her body. She hung her head and began to sob. "Sweetheart," the priest said softly, unfolding Rose's arms and taking her hands in his, "What did your father do?"

"He... he... t'turned into a m' monster..." she stammered, "an' he hurt me th'there." She nodded down to her groin.

The priest sat back in his chair and crossed his legs. "Ah so!" he said so quietly that Rose had to strain to hear him, "and these meetings, what happens then?"

"I have to come downstairs and be part of the play." Rose's heart was thumping very loud in her chest and her mouth was dry – she found it hard to get her words out. She looked over at a jug of water and some tumblers sitting on a sideboard.

"Would ya like some water Rose?" the priest asked studying her closely. She nodded yes and waited for him to pour her a glass. When he had done so she reached out her hand to take it and then sat up straight sipping the tepid water, glad for a break from the conversation. He sat watching her in silence, an idea forming in his mind. He rose from his chair and said, "Rose, will you excuse me for just a moment. You finish your water and I shan't be long. Would ya like some tea, sweetheart, and a biscuit perhaps?" The child looked up at him with such fear, his stomach lurched and he gasped in fear himself.

"Yes please," she said in a timid voice.

My God, Father Murphy thought to himself as he dialled the number, *please let me be wrong.*

"Hello father, what can I do for ya?" came a voice on the other end.

"Good afternoon Mary. Get me the number of a certain Father F. Corrigan please, Hexton, Belfast."

"Is that Belfast in the north, Father?" Mary inquired.

"Yes yes hurry up please, it's important."

"Sorry Father, I'll ring back when I've got it"

"Ah so!" The priest put down the receiver and waited. He remembered the tea and went to the kitchen where his housemaid was busy peeling vegetables. "Roisin, I wonder would ya mind making myself and my visitor a cup of tea please? Plenty of sugar and some biscuits, if ya don't mind."

"Not at all Father. Be my pleasure," the young girl said. The phone rang in the study and Father Murphy half ran to answer it.

"Hello, Mary? Oh good, tis you. Read it out to me there, aha I'm getting it, aha, 5808. Ah now! That's grand. Thank you Mary, thank you." He replaced the receiver and lifted it again to dial. He listened to the ringing tone for a long time before someone answered.

"Hello, Hexton Parochial House!"

"Oh Hello there, is that Father Corrigan? This is Father Sean Murphy from Cloughbeg in County Mayo. How are ya there?"

"Hello Father, I'm fine yes, and how are you? How can

I help you?" replied Father Corrigan.

"I have a young girl here with me Father. She's one of yours. Her grandmother lives here in Cloughbeg and has brought her in to see me. Her name is Rose M'Devit. I believe her parents are Sean and Clare McDevit."

"Yes Father, I know the McDevits. What seems to be the problem?"

"Well, for a start I'm afraid the child is pregnant, at least seven months I'm told." Father Murphy found himself blushing at the mention of it.

"What? Good Lord in Heaven!" the other priest exclaimed, "I'll have to see Sean. Find out what's to be done with her."

"That's just it Father. It's what's been done with her that I'm afraid of," Father Murphy insisted.

"What do you mean? She's pregnant isn't she? That can only mean one thing."

"She's pregnant alright. But it's who got her pregnant. God help us Father but I think there may be evil in our midst."

"I'm sorry Father … em …Murphy is it? But you're not making much sense. Evil you say? What evil?"

"Meetings, rituals, you know! Well, have ya heard anything?"

"Oh Good Lord in Heaven, I *have* heard rumours. The schools have all been warned. Did you not hear? Ah well, I suppose with you being in the south and all. They were talking about black magic worshippers you know. Personally I don't believe it, not here in Hexton. We're a very religious community you know. None of that nonsense here. As if I would allow any such thing. No, ya can rest assured Father, there's no need to think like that. I'll have a word with the child's parents and sort it out. They're from your neck of the woods themselves you know."

Father Murphy wasn't at all assured that it was okay. There had been similar goings on in Donegal not so many years ago and it certainly wasn't rumours then. There had even been talk in a parish as close as forty kilometres away. No, he wasn't at all happy. Scared was what he was: scared that the little girl sitting in his front room had been mixed up in some kind of evil satanic ritual.

Bunch of rotten paedophiles is what they are, he thought to himself angrily. "I know Clare from when she was little," he said to Father Corrigan. "I married them so I did. I never thought …" he paused "… well it doesn't matter now does it? Perhaps Father, you'll call me back when you've spoken to them, what?" The two priests exchanged pleasantries for a while but Father Murphy was keen to get back to the child so he made his excuses and hung up.

Rose had been waiting a long time in the room. After a while when it seemed the priest wasn't coming back she began to look around her. The room looked just like anyone else's front room with a three-piece suite and a telly. There was a sideboard along one wall with the water jug and all and a huge big crucifix made out of wood. The statue of

Jesus on it looked really creepy with blood coming down the face. Rose looked away ashamed of herself for being evil and prayed that he wouldn't punish her for it. The door opened and a girl not much older than Caroline came in carrying a tray of tea and biscuits. Roisin put the tray down on the sideboard and shot a glance at Rose. She was startled at how young the visitor was. Young girls in trouble were a familiar sight in the front room but not as young as this. *Jesus, Mary and Joseph, that's an early starter,* she gasped to herself. She paused at the door and surveyed Rose with a scrutinizing eye. It was hard to tell by this one if she was in trouble or not – she was a right plump one though so you could never tell. "So what's to be done with ya then? Ya for the nuns?" she asked Rose with an unmistakable air of amusement. Just then the priest arrived back.

"That's enough Roisin" he scolded the girl, "and may I remind ya that what goes on in this house is no-one else's business and that includes whoever may or may not work here. Am I making myself clear?"

"Aye Father, sorry Father," Roisin said, her head hung low. Father Murphy was not at all happy. He had taken Roisin on just after she'd left school. Her father had pleaded her case since she was a bit too wild for his liking and needed a close eye kept on her. At that moment Father Murphy found it difficult to tolerate the behaviour of the young floozy when here was this poor child in his care with whom he had no idea what he was going to do – this innocent wee thing struck down by God only knows what kind of devilry – tainted for evermore through no fault of her own.

"Go on then, out with ya," he snapped at Roisin impatiently. He held the door as Roisin left and then turned his attention towards the child who had kept her head down throughout the exchange between him and the housemaid. "So now, young Rosie, what about that tea and biscuits, what?" He busied himself pouring tea and adding the sugar. He placed a couple of chocolate digestives on a plate for Rose. He did all this deliberately slowly playing for time while he thought about how exactly he was going to get to the bottom of this. After today, he had no idea how to deal with it. *My God! How am I gonna tell the bishop?* he thought suddenly. He put Rose's tea and biscuits on a little table beside her and sat down in his armchair with his own tea. He sipped the hot liquid slowly not noticing how it tasted. Keeping his eyes fixed on the floor between himself and the child, he prayed for the grace to discern the right course of action. "Rosie sweetheart," he said at last when his tea had turned cold in the cup, "I want ya to tell me about these meetings that ya say your parents have. Now, I know you're worried about it but let me assure ya that what ya say to me is in the strictest confidence okay? That means no-one will know what ya say to me unless you want them to. Do ya understand?" She nodded. "Now, as a rule I have to write down an account of all visits in my big red book here," he added, getting up and taking a huge red leather backed journal from a drawer. "What d'ya say, is that okay? It's just for me so that I can remember." She thought for a moment and nodded again. "Ah, sure we've got off to a grand start now, have we not?" She nodded again! "Indeed, indeed! And ya say the meetings were every two weeks is that right?" He waited for her to nod again and then continued – "And so, who did ya say was at these meetings?"

"Mr and Mrs Donnelly and Mr and Mrs O'Hara."

"Are ya sure now that the meetings were at your parents' home? You don't think they might have been somewhere else?"

"I don't remember anywhere else."

"But ya remember them being at your home?"

"Aye."

"Rosie, do ya know what the meetings are about? What do people talk about?"

"Dunno, weird stuff – and sort of praying."

"What do ya mean – sort of praying? Praying to God is it?"

"Aye, like Mass only in a kinda play Mass."

"Ah so, well you're doing good Rosie." The child was relaxing more and he wished he could say the same about himself. "Now, can ya tell me anything else about it? What do the people do?"

She reacted to this last question by recoiling into the chair. "Well…I…I…d'dunno," she stammered and put her hands over her mouth. She looked at the priest tears streaming down her face.

He had to look away from her. He couldn't face the

obvious pain and terror in the child's eyes. *Holy Mother of God, pray for us who have recourse to Thee*, he prayed silently, his heart aching with compassion for the child and rage for the enemy. Composing himself he reached for a box of tissues and handed them to Rosie. "There now, sure you're grand. You're doing very well." He waited for her to dry her tears and take a sip of cold tea. "Is it alright to go on now? Aye? Ah, sure you're a great girl altogether. Let's see now, I wonder is there anything else ya remember?" Rosie said nothing but seemed more composed. "Rosie, did someone hurt ya?"

"Aye, but the lady took me away in case he would kill me?"

"Kill ya Rosie? Are ya sure? Who is the lady that took ya away? Is that your mother?"

"No, she can't see the lady, no-one can 'cept me. She always takes me away and we go to see the Indian. He's great and he always makes me better." The child sat up straight, her eyes flashing as she talked about her lady and an Indian. Sean Murphy almost lost heart again. It was worse than he thought. The child was obviously deluded.

"Rosie, tell me what else ya saw – before the lady took ya away that is." The child was keen now to disclose what she could and he listened intently as a horrifying picture began to form in his mind.

"Everybody wears costumes like priests do in Mass an' they have a cross too but it's a funny kinda cross – I never seen it afore. An' everybody has a false face too but Mr Donnelly has a different face than the others. I don't have a face 'cos I'm the main thing in the play."

He interrupted her to ask, "And what's the play about Rosie?"

"Dunno, it's something about Jesus I think. They make me into Jesus. I'm bad an' then when they make me like the cross I'm good. That's the same as Jesus isn't it? Everybody said He was bad and deserved to be punished an' then when He was they were sorry and said He was good. An' anyway, He went up to Heaven when He died, didn't He. That's like me kinda – I kinda go to Heaven 'cos that's where the lady and the Indian are."

Good God! thought Father Sean Murphy, *the devil is inside her, the bastards! Dear God, deliver me from this evil. Show me the way Dear Lord to save this poor soul from eternal damnation*. He covered his face with his hands and took several deep breaths. The child began to go on and he got up off his chair eager to get as far away from her as possible. "Back in a moment Rosie," he said reaching for the door. He closed the door behind him gasping for breath. He felt sick. This was not a situation he was prepared for. In forty five years of priesthood he had never encountered such a crisis. He went to his study and paced the floor trying to decide the best course of action. He would have to inform the bishop, no doubt and maybe he should inform Father Corrigan. No, that wouldn't do. Best kept contained for now. Bishop Cleary will know what to do and that will take the onus off him. But something would have to be done now about the child and the grandmother will be back soon. Probably best not to mention it to her – such a God-fearing Catholic – too old to receive such a shock – likely to kill her, bless her! "Okay, I know what to do," he decided, "first thing is to give the child a blessing – might not be too late. She certainly shouldn't be receiving the Blessed Sacrament though – not till the baby's born anyways." He took some holy water out of a cupboard, left the study and returned to the front room. "Now Rosie dear, you've done very well indeed and your grandmother will be back soon. But before she is dear we have a little matter to attend to. If ya would be so good to come over here now and kneel down. I'm going to hear your confession, okay?"

Rose hated confession but she had no choice, the priest said she had to. She knelt down where he had indicated and began her confession – "Bless me Father for I have sinned. It is two months since my last confession. These are my sins..."

When the confession was heard Father Murphy stood up and anointed Rose's crown with holy water. Making the sign of the cross with holy water on her forehead, eyes, ears, lips, palms and feet he repeated – "*In the name of the Father and of the Son and of the Holy Spirit.*" Then with his hand on Rose's head he made a demand which was to seal her fate for a lifetime – to Rose it was plain to see that the priest in his wisdom was telling the devil himself to come out of her. She just hoped against all hope that when he did he wouldn't take her with him. Having done what needed to be done, Father Murphy left the child in the hands of God and went to the bathroom to wash his hands and face – the stench of evil was clinging to him.

Mrs Doyle arrived back several minutes later and was welcomed sombrely by Father Murphy himself. As soon as she entered the house she was aware that something significant had transpired. She assumed that Father Murphy had given the child a good talking to and was satisfied that his sombre demeanour was due to his disgust of her predicament. Father Murphy was content to let her remain in her ignorance. "So what's to be done Father?" she asked. She trusted the priest completely.

"Ah well, Mrs Doyle, I've spoken to her own priest in Belfast. He'll have a quiet word with Mr and Mrs M'Devit and we'll see where we go from there, what?"

"I don't want this getting out mind. You know what I mean?" said Mrs Doyle.

"Don't worry about that Mrs Doyle. It'll all be as discrete as possible. In fact, I have a colleague in England. You remember Father Kearns don't you? He served his time here as curate. Aye? Well, I'm sure he can move the baby on once it's born but that leaves us with the problem of taking care of that side of things."

"Oh there's no problem there Father – there'll be ample discretion at my place. No need to involve the nuns. I've delivered many a child myself. No, she'll come to me as soon as' an' that'll be that," insisted Mrs Doyle. "Does she know what she's done wrong?" she added.

"Ah well, I think there's no need to fret about that now," said the priest evading the truth. After Mrs Doyle and Rose had left Father Murphy went to his study to face the difficult task of informing Bishop Cleary of the situation. He spoke to the bishop for an hour and then reached for a bottle of whiskey. Having pored himself a generous measure he opened his red leather backed journal and began to write. He had already written an account of Rose's predicament and the proposed course of action. However, after speaking to Bishop Cleary, he felt that for his own peace of mind, he should do something he had never done before and add his suspicions to the entry.

The bishop had reacted to the information very differently to how Father Murphy thought he would have –"Father, we need to be very careful that we don't make trouble where there isn't any," he had said to the surprised priest, "there's already a story passing throughout the north and we know what that can do, don't we? Rumours like that have a tendency to get out of hand and before ya know it we'd have a full scale panic on our hands. We can't have parents everywhere afraid to send their children to school because of one priest's vivid imagination. How do ya know the girl isn't in need of psychiatric help? It certainly sounds like it to me."

"But I thought the same thing at first. And that most likely is true but I believe that this kind of thing can send a child out of her mind," replied Father Murphy trying to get his concerns across. *How dare he suggest that I'm imagining this?* he thought angrily.

"And what kind of thing is that?" demanded the bishop refusing to accept the obvious. Father Murphy couldn't believe the other man's attitude towards something so serious. Did the bishop actually think that if he told himself it wasn't happening it would go away? Maybe he was mistaken. Maybe his imagination was running away with him. After all, he was going on the testimony of a thirteen year old child who was quite evidently not in her right mind. However, there had been rumours since the incidents in Donegal and if they were actually true then God forgive him if he should be instrumental in covering up such a threat to all God-fearing Christians.

"Please don't make me say it Your Grace," he had replied anxiously, "ya know what goes on in these pagan ritual things. Total renunciation is crucial."

"Father Murphy, I understand your fear, I really do but I believe you are being totally irrational. Now I suggest you forget all about it. See that the unfortunate child receives absolution and deal with the situation. That's all ya need concern yourself with. Leave anything else that may or may not be up to me. I assure ya though that there most certainly is no cause to worry."

With that the bishop cut off the conversation and Father Murphy was left with the receiver to his ear listening to no-one. "Might as well have been talking to no-one," he had complained out loud. He was aware that Bishop Cleary was one of the favourites for Archbishop and acknowledged guiltily to himself that it was more of an issue in the attitude of the bishop than he would care to admit. He suddenly felt very tired. It had been a disturbing day and he needed to rest. Having put down his thoughts in the journal below the entry headed '*Sunday 20th October 1978, Rose C McDevit*', he put away the bottle of whisky which was now half empty and climbed the stairs to his bedroom. He lay down on top of the bed and stared at the picture of The Sacred Heart on the wall opposite. "But deliver us from evil," he muttered making the sign of the cross.

Rose had gone home with Auntie Lett that evening after she had sat in Father Murphy's front room. She had a very interesting conversation with Auntie Lett on the way up to Belfast in the car. Auntie Lett had been curious as to what the priest and Granny Doyle had arranged for when the time came. Rose wasn't sure what she meant by 'the time'. Did she mean her period? She didn't think so. Why would that involve Granny and Father Murphy? Besides, the priest didn't ask any questions at all about her time. "What d'ya mean – when the time comes?" she asked her aunt.

Auntie Lett bit her lip and thought for a while about how she was going to help Rose to understand what was happening to her. Granny Doyle and Clare both thought that the best thing for Rose was that she would never know that she was going to give birth to a baby. The child believed she was sick and that she would get better and that was best left as it was. As far as Lett was concerned it was a ludicrous plan but she had given up all rights as far as Rose was concerned and she had no choice but to heed by her mother's and sister's wishes. She had a feeling though that Rose did not think that way exactly. The child had said some very strange things about *dying when it comes out*. Lett realised that Rose must know to some degree that something was growing inside her and she thought that she owed it to her to give her some inkling of what that was. She couldn't bear the thought that Rose believed she was going to die. "Rose, ya do understand don't ya that you're gonna be alright? This isn't gonna last forever ya know" she told her.

Rose wanted to know – "D'ya mean when *the time comes* is when it's gonna get out?"

"Aye that's right. And when it comes out ya'll be okay. Listen to me now Rosie – you *will* be okay."

"But when it comes out, will it take me to hell?" cried Rose. She began to sob and shake. Lett couldn't believe what she was hearing. She pulled the car over to the side of the road and took Rose by the shoulders.

"Now you listen to me child," she said sternly, "No-one is gonna die, never mind go to hell. Where on earth did ya get that idea from anyway?"

Rose didn't answer. Auntie Lett was scaring her. She wasn't normally so cross but when she was she was a match for Mummy an' no mistake. She stopped crying immediately for fear that Lett would get even more cross. It had the desired effect. Lett sat back in her seat and drove off again. Rose thought that Lett must have remembered that she was born bad too and that it made sense to her that hell was the only place they belonged. After all, that's where they came from wasn't it? She recollected a time in primary school when she was only about six or seven when the headmaster had asked the entire school during assembly – "If I asked you all, who is the one person you love above all others, who would you say?" She had thought, Mummy of course – the answer was Mummy. The headmaster had continued – "I am sure that each of you will have answered God." Rose was surprised and felt very bad indeed that she didn't put God first. She was convinced the right answer had to be Mummy who held control over everything in Rose's life. "Well," the headmaster went on, "it is a very good thing to love God first and that is what the Bible teaches us, but it is also important to love your mother. You see, God gave life to you through the Holy Spirit but your mother gave life to you through her body."

Rose had been very confused that day and had become quite upset during break-time. When asked by a teacher what was the matter with her she had replied in tears, "But God didn't make me, the devil made me and now I'm even badder 'cos I didn't know the right answer." But she was thirteen now and that was big and she knew that even if you were born of the devil you should love God and keep His Commandments and do what the priest and your parents tell you. In that way you get to go to Heaven when you die, like the lady and the Indian. Sadly, she believed it was too late for her. The devil had got into her belly at the meetings and he was coming out soon. But from the way Auntie Lett was talking it seemed that the priest had managed to make the devil leave her alone. There was a good chance she was going to be okay.

"Let me tell ya a wee story from when I was not much older than you," began Auntie Lett. Rose sat up to attention and waited eagerly for her to go on. "I used to have a wee doll. Now, it wasn't like a normal doll – this doll was inside my tummy. It got bigger and bigger inside me until it was so big it had to come out."

"Did you get to play with it when it came out? Like it was a real baby?" Rose was intrigued.

Lett was taken by surprise. She hadn't realised that the child knew where real babies came from. But then, she had seen her Auntie Theresa pregnant before. Caroline and Angela would have told her all about it. She wondered just how much the child knew about sex and if she linked that to what had happened to her. She decided not, the child was obviously unaware of the reality of her situation.

"No I didn't, an' I was very sad about that, but as time went on I got used to it an' then the wee doll didn't even seem real anymore," answered Lett. *God! What am I saying?* she thought to herself. She looked at Rose who seemed engrossed in the story. "What I'm saying is that what's inside you is like my wee doll. An' when it's gone ya'll forget about it just like I did."

"Hope so," said Rose in a small voice, "but it's not a doll."

28th November

Rose was in the cupboard. She had thought a lot about Auntie Lett's doll in the last few weeks. Auntie Lett never mentioned it again and Rose knew better than to ask her mother about it. She felt sorry for Auntie Lett, not only because of the doll which she strongly suspected had been a real baby, but because she had been born bad too. It was pretty obvious actually, since Mummy and Granny Doyle said similar things to her as they did to Rose. And Rose was aware that Auntie Lett played Daddy's game which was part of being born bad. In a way Rose wished that what was inside her was only a doll as Auntie Lett so obviously wanted her to believe but the reality was clear – the devil was inside her and very soon he would come out and God only knows what will happen then. She had prayed since that day with Father Murphy that the devil would leave her alone as the priest had demanded but she wasn't so sure. She spent her days indoors, reading mostly – pretending she was George from the *Famous Five*. When she wasn't reading she would hide in the cupboard or in her bed with a blanket covering her. She would go off in her mind to meet with the lady and the Indian. Hours passed by in this way which felt to Rose like minutes. The strangest thing to her was that when she went there she was not the Rose that was thirteen years old and had the devil growing in her tummy. Instead she was a very big Rose who was wise and knowledgeable and oh! so good, so strong and so loving and loved. She would stand with the Indian and the lady holding hands in a circle and an invisible energy would pour from them through the circle and into her. In this energy were strength, hope, love and wisdom. It was as if she was being renewed – as if she had gone back to a time way before she was born. It was a time when she was good and she knew who she was and what she wanted to be.

The cupboard door opened suddenly and Rose was startled back to her physical reality. Brian stood there not in the least bit surprised at finding her in the cupboard perched on a box of toys and covered in a blanket. "Mummy wants ya," said Brian softly. Rose didn't reply. She remained very still. He wondered what she had been doing. It had never occurred to him before that Rose would actually be doing something while she spent hours in cupboards but now as he saw her there completely still with a blanket over her the thought came to him that she was privy to something, some kind of game maybe, that none of the rest of them even knew about. "Rose? What are ya doing Rose?" he asked in his soft voice. Rose threw off the blanket and looked into his eyes. There was an eeriness to her face that caused him to step back considerably. He didn't take his eyes off her. It seemed that her eyes conveyed a seriousness – a momentous awareness of him; and he felt stripped of all he knew to be real. As he continued to lock into her face he became aware that she was seeing him as no-one had ever seen him before and he knew that nothing was hidden from her. Then he felt himself relaxing into the experience as she began to exude a brightness – a light that enveloped her and grew bigger and bigger until it touched him. In her eyes he no longer saw severity but a gentleness that warmed his heart and brought a feeling of joy to him. He stood in her great light for a few moments until it began to dissipate. She moved and said nothing to him as he quickly shook himself out of the trance, and then silently she left the room and went in search of her mother. Brian went and sat down on the bed. He didn't know how to react to what had just happened – or had it just happened? - he wasn't sure now. Perhaps she had put a spell on him. Caroline had told him that she was really a witch. He hadn't believed her then but maybe he did now. Many a time he had seen things around her that came and went in an instant, like the time when he was wakened out of his sleep. Rose had been screaming and shouting for Mummy. She had been having one of her bad dreams. He and Kevin had run into the girls' room after Mummy to find Rose sitting up in bed screaming and trying to get something off her head. Mummy had a hard time convincing Rose that nothing was attacking her but *he* could see something hovering around her head. It was like a black cloud right around her head and Rose was swiping at it and screaming. All the time it was getting darker and darker. Rose had scared the hell out of him that night. Mummy had shouted to Kevin to run and get a glass of water from the bathroom. After he had returned and handed it to her, Mummy had thrown the entire contents over Rose. Brian had remained rooted to the spot speechless, but Kevin had started to cry. Even Angela and Caroline had begun to whimper and cry, "Mummy, what's wrong? What's wrong with Rose?" Brian thought about that now as he sat on the bed and concluded that Rose had to be some kind of witch, although it seemed to him that she was a good witch and not the kind to turn people into frogs. He didn't like to think of her as anything other than good 'cos he knew that he wasn't too different from her. In fact, the very thing which just happened proved to him that what she was wasn't bad and that she had an understanding of these things that he himself was very curious about.

Downstairs, Rose found her mother in the kitchen doing the weekly wash. Rose felt sleepy and timid since her latest encounter with her friends and she went quietly over to her mother and touched her arm to let her know she was behind her. "Brian said you want to see me Mummy," she told her in a calm voice.

Clare closed the lid of the laundry machine and dried her hands with a towel that was slung over her shoulder. She looked at Rose intently, her gaze falling to the child's abdomen. A look of concern came over her face and Rose felt a pang of guilt. She lowered her head. "Granny's expecting us tomorrow," Clare stated with a tone of regret, "probably best if ya pack a few things. The brown case is under the stairs. If ya go and fetch that now and then come back to me." She walked over to the kitchen table and picked up a bathroom bag which she had filled earlier. "Now, I've put everything else ya'll need in here and, and stop looking at me like that would ya? Anyone would think it was the end of the world." Rose's eyes were filled with fear and she stared into space, not seeing her mother, not noticing the tears falling down her face. Clare was worried. She had seen the child in a trance before – for God's sake, sure she was always away with the fairies, but this time she was worried. The child had slipped into a world of her own. She had been behaving very oddly of late and both she and Lett had noticed it but now it seemed that maybe they should have done something about it. For the life of her though, she had no idea what that could have been. *Well, too late for that now – most likely she'll come round,* she thought. She took Rose by the arm and led her into the sitting room where she guided her down onto the sofa.

Caroline was busy studying at the coffee table and she put down her pencil and stared when she saw the caring way her mother had dealt with Rose. "What's wrong with her?" she asked her mother.

"Never mind, just watch her for me a minute will ya? Talk to her a bit and see if ya can snap her outta it." Clare went back into the kitchen and made a cup of strong tea with two spoonfuls of sugar. She carried it back to Rose who took the cup obediently and began to sip. She didn't speak a word. "Did she say anythin'?" Clare asked her other daughter.

"Not a word. D'ya think she's okay?" replied Caroline, surprised at how concerned she was about her little sister.

"Oh aye, I'm sure she's okay. Rose? Rose speak to me. Come on now, stop this nonsense at once." Clare spoke very sternly trying to snap the child out of the trance.

"Rose!" she repeated more urgently, slapping her cheek a little, "Come on, snap outta it."

Rose looked at her mother and began to cry – really cry. "Mummy I'm scared, help me please Mummy, help me" she wailed.

Clare really did get angry now. She couldn't have the child talking like this, especially in front of Caroline who, as far as Clare knew, had no idea that Rose was pregnant. She took the cup of hot tea out of Rose's hand and slapped her hard across the cheek. She stopped panicking. "Now you listen to me girl," Claire said again very sternly, "there's nothing wrong with ya. It's all in your imagination. Now, I don't want you going down and scaring the hell outta Granny, d'ya hear?" Rose was sobbing and Clare lifted the cup of tea again and urged her to drink. As she became calmer Clare cooled down and began to feel less panicky herself. *Thank God for that*, she thought to herself. She left Rose with orders for her to go to bed and rest for an hour after she finished the tea and then she went to the space under the stairs where she retrieved the brown case.

She grabbed the bathroom bag from the table and went upstairs where she proceeded to fill the case with whatever she felt Rose was going to need for the next few weeks at Cloughbeg.

They arrived just before teatime. Granny had heard the car driving up the lane to the house and she was standing on the doorstep waiting for them, arms folded across her chest. She was sick with worry about the child ever since she had sent her and Lett back to Belfast. Many a time she had wondered if maybe she should have kept Rose with her but Clare had been insistent. Well, it wasn't long to go now and all seemed to be fine so far. The next few weeks would be easier now that the child was away from seeing eyes. She had everything she thought she would need to deal with the birth and Father Murphy had been so good in arranging the handover in England. One of Clare and Sean's friends, a Mr Michael Donnelly, and his good wife, had offered to take the child with them when they went to England next month. Apparently the Donnelly family were in the process of moving to England permanently and wasn't that lucky that they were able to offer such kind help. Granny wasn't too happy about the Donnellys knowing about the situation but she had to agree that it was the only way they had of getting the child moved on. Besides, she knew Clare spoke very highly of the Donnellys and that was enough for her. The car pulled up and Sean and Clare got out. Granny could see Rose sitting in the back and when she didn't get out she went to open the door for her. "She's asleep Ma," Clare told her, "Sean, leave the case till later. Let her sleep for now," she said to her husband. Clare seemed very stressed and Granny led her inside with a comforting hand on her back.

"Sit down Clare and I'll get the tay on," Granny said busying herself at the range.

"Oh Ma," moaned Clare, "I'm at me wits end, so I am. It was an awful drive down ya know. He never stopped complaining the whole time an' she hardly uttered a word. She's got worse ya know. Yesterday she scared the hell outta me and poor Caroline. She was in a bad way – kinda shocked I think. She's scared anyway that's for sure. I swear, if I got the pig that did it I'd kill him with me own hands."

"And you're sure there's no way of finding who did it?" asked Granny. She must have asked that question a dozen times and each time she wasn't sure that her daughter had been completely honest with her.

"No, none at all," replied Clare. "Christ sake Mum, we've bin over this. The only thing I can think of is that she must have bin attacked outside amongst the bushes or somethin'. Ya know what Rose is like. It coulda' happened and she'd not say anythin' at all about it. Just go into that wee world of hers and say nothin'. Besides, it's done and that's that… Can't turn the clock back now as much as we'd like to."

"Aye well, that's the truth now. Can't turn the clock back," nodded Granny. She had the tea in the pot just as

Sean came in settling himself in one of the big armchairs. "Is the child still sleepin'?" Granny asked him.

"Aye, that she is," drolled Sean, "sparked out halfway down. Aye, I'll have a mug of that tay there Granny and some of that scone-bread there." Granny cut some bread and smothered it in a generous layer of home-made butter. The O'Hagans at the farm up the road made their own and Granny always received a generous packet or two in exchange for a dozen eggs or so. She put the bread on a plate and placed it down beside Clare on the small sofa. As everyone took their tea the subject of Rose was put aside and small talk filled the conversation. About ten minutes later the latch rattled on the door and everyone looked over to see Rose coming in sleepily.

Oh Good God in Heaven! exclaimed Granny to herself, *she's gotten a lot bigger than the last I saw of her.*

The child came into the room and stood sheepishly before them and cried – "Mummy, I think I wet myself. I couldn't help it. I just got outta the car and it kinda just gushed out. I couldn't stop it."

"Oh Christ, Sean," Clare shouted, "she's started. Mum what'll we do? Get her down here, have ya got an old blanket? Shit! It's too soon is it not? It can't be time yet."

"She's just a child Clare for goodness sake, probably for the best. If it got much bigger she'd not cope with it." Granny was annoyed at the sudden turn of affairs. Nevertheless, she went into full speed and had everyone calm and ready in no time at all. Everyone that was except Rose who once she realised that *the time* had come had withdrawn completely into one of her trances. The adults watched her closely and were at a loss as to know where she was or if indeed she was okay. She hardly winced at all and Clare and Granny were convinced she must have started contractions by now. An hour passed and Rose never showed any sign of being in pain. Sean had been sent into the village to telephone Lett and tell her what was happening. She was to leave the children in the care of Mrs O'Hara and get down here at once.

At ten thirty Lett arrived in the front yard. Sean's car was sitting right outside the door and she pulled up alongside it. She went into the cottage half expecting to see the baby there and Rose tucked up in bed but that's not what she saw. She saw no-one in the cottage at all. She went outside to her car and retrieved a torch from the boot. It was a very cold night and she shivered, half from the cold night air and half from fear. She opened the car door on the passenger side and snatched her coat from the seat there. Putting it on she made her way carefully around to the back of the cottage and up to the hen-shed. As soon as she neared it she heard the child scream. As long as she lived she would never forget that first sound – that first indication that poor little Rose was enduring the worst pain she would most likely ever experience in her life. Lett said a silent prayer as she stood outside the shed door – "Dear God," she prayed, "give us all the strength to do what needs to be done. Send down your angels to watch over this child and her baby and see that no harm comes to either of them. Promise me this one favour Oh Lord and I promise I will stand by that child for as long as I live." She entered the shed to an unforgettable scene. The child was lying on a blanket on the ground and Clare and Sean were crowding around her obscuring from her vision what Granny was doing at the back of the shed. Lett turned her head towards her mother and saw her wrapping the newborn infant in a sheet. The baby was crying and Lett felt a wave of relief sweep over her at the realization that the baby had survived. She turned her attention towards Rose and knelt down beside Clare. Looking at Rose's terrified face she instinctively took the cloth that Clare had been clutching and dipped it into a basin of water there on the ground. Then she gently wiped the child's forehead with the wet cloth saying all the time – "There, there now Rosie, you're gonna be alright now." The child was whimpering, exhausted from screaming so much. She tried to talk but no-one could understand her. "Shh now, just relax. It's alright, you're gonna be alright." Lett found herself crying bitterly and made no attempt to wipe the tears from her face. Clare had been crying too it seemed and was glad that Lett was finally there to take over for a while. She shot her younger sister a hateful glare as she rose from the ground and Lett felt powerless to defend herself. *If I'd never been born none of this would have happened*, she told herself.

It had never occurred to either woman to blame any of it on the man kneeling in front of them. Sean McDevit hadn't spoken a word to any of the three women since the crisis began. He kept his mouth shut and followed orders as they were given. He had never seen a baby born before and the fact that it was his wee Rosie lying there and her not much more than a baby herself was unbearable to him. He watched as Lett mopped the child's brow and marvelled at how gently and lovingly she spoke to her. He had never known Lett nor Clare to be so soft. They were normally rigid and bitter like their mother. *Not my Rosie*, he thought to himself, *she's not like them. She's special – aye, there's somethin' very special about my Rosie.* He stood up as Granny came over to gather the extra bits – whatever they were called – how would he know? She wrapped them into the end of the blanket that Rose was lying on and ordered Lett and Clare to pick Rose up and bring her back to the cottage. Once Rose and the two women were out the door she gathered up the blanket and followed them, ignoring Sean who was left wondering what on earth he was to do then. He followed then and attempted to help the women who seemed to be struggling to get Rose back to the cottage in the dark. After realising he was getting in the way he stopped them and picked Rose up into his arms and proceeded on down towards the cottage with Clare going in front with the lantern and Lett shining a torch from behind. In through the cottage door the little procession went. It was the eleventh hour and the big clock was striking loud and shrill magnifying the deathly silence that had fallen over everyone. Sean went to lay his daughter down on the sofa but was stopped by Granny who with one hand firmly gripping his arm ushered him in through the pantry door. They were followed by Lett and Clare who went to work immediately. Clare grabbed a plastic basin and went to the kitchen were she filled the basin with hot water from the kettle on the range. She carried it carefully back into the pantry and placed it on the stone floor. Lett had been stripping Rose of her clothes and was ready to hold her standing up in the basin whilst Clare sponged her down with hot water. Sean was chased into the kitchen to make tea and to get the fire in the range stoked up to give out plenty of heat. Granny Doyle had quickly disappeared back to the hen-shed to fetch the infant who was wrapped up safely in a large sheet and lying in a basket. She hurried back to the cottage and waited for Clare and Lett to finish washing Rose and bring her into the kitchen. When she saw the pantry door open she turned her back to them until Rose was on the sofa and then she deftly moved into the pantry with the infant in her arms. It was crucial that Rose didn't see the infant. On no account was she ever to know that she had just given birth to a baby. The little infant girl cried piercingly, little arms and legs flailing as Granny placed her in a basin of clean warm water which Clare had had the presence of mind to provide. Granny had delivered babies before and she knew exactly what she was doing. She thanked God though that there had been no complications, especially since it appeared that the little mite had come early.

All this happened with the least amount of talking

possible. Rose was so weak that she didn't want to talk. She was lying on the sofa which was just big enough to take her full length. Lett had dressed her in her nightie and dressing gown and had tucked a blanket around her. She turned and stared into the grate of the range at the bright orange glow of the fire. She was aware that she was still alive. The devil hadn't taken her to hell. Father Murphy's orders had been obeyed and God had been on her side. Before the devil went, though, she had caught sight of him. Mummy and Daddy had been holding her down telling her not to look. The devil had come out already and she had felt it violently and painfully. She had been terrified and held on to her parents' arms for safety. Mummy had held a cloth to her mouth from time to time and she did it again at that moment. The cloth had a weird smell to it like the smell you get at the dentist and then she had felt something cold running down her throat. Voices had become muffled and people blurred as she began to drift out of the consuming pain. When she became aware again she shot up very quickly and what she saw then was to haunt her dreams for decades to come. Between her legs, lying on the blanket, had been a snake-like creature. It was covered in slime and had a huge bulbous head that looked like a lump of raw meat. Rose had screeched in fear convinced that it was the devil and it would take her there and then. Clare had been shaking her and soaking her head and face in water when suddenly Auntie Lett was there too. She had appeared beside her and talked to her gently telling her she was gonna be alright. "Is it gone, is it gone?" Rose had kept asking her between gulps of fearful tears.

Rose went through the entire nightmare in her mind as she lay staring into the fire. Flashes of pain and terror gripped her from time to time and each time she began to panic and cry for help. She was aware of Auntie Lett and Daddy near her – one at her head and one at her feet but they were no comfort. As each minute passed she slipped deeper and deeper into a trance full of fear that she would die. Just as she thought she was about to be taken, she felt a loving touch on her head and on her hand. She focused on the warm comfort the touch brought to her and she saw *him* there kneeling by her side and smiling at her. The Indian had one hand on her head and the other on her hand and as he stroked her gently he said – "*Be at peace child, you're going to be alright.*" A peacefulness came over her and she slept. She dreamed peaceful dreams floating amidst beautiful colours and all around her she heard wonderful comforting music. It was the music of the angels.

She slept until she was awoken by a sharp rapping at the door. She was still on the sofa and the fire was glowing dim in the grate. Her father was sitting on the armchair beside the range and he shot up quickly and went to the door. Rose attempted to look over the back of the sofa to see who was coming in but her mother had dashed out of the bedroom and ordered her to keep her head down. The door was opened and Rose heard the voices of two other adults now in the kitchen. Granny had sat down beside her and was telling her to close her eyes and go back to sleep. But Rose couldn't sleep – not now that she distinctly heard a little baby crying – not now that she recognized the voices as Mr and Mrs Donnelly. And how was she ever to sleep again when the whole terrible night's events came screaming back to her, overwhelming her with fear and confusion?

But Rose did sleep that night. She did the only thing she could. She thrust all awareness of the night's events deep down inside her where she would never have to know it again. With it went a childhood full of years of emotional, physical and sexual trauma. Rose shut down that night. She died… and all that remained was a shadow of the exceptional little girl who was Rose McDevit.

It has been said that at times simply making the choice to live is in itself an act of bravery.

Chapter Six

Beginning the search

January 2008

The Church of Our Lady of Perpetual Succour stood at the top of the hill surrounded by huge trees – mostly cypress which almost obscured the little graveyard from the road. On the opposite side of the church was a group of yews. They spread their branches wide across the entire left hand side of the perimeter grounds that were blanketed with a layer of snowdrops nodding and dancing in the cold winter wind. As the car climbed the steep driveway it passed a huge English Oak which stood in the middle of the front lawn that swept down to the main road. Lissy took a deep breath and composed herself. She had been here many times in her life. This was the church she was christened in and every Sunday for years she had come here for Mass. The parochial house was right around the back of the church amidst a little copse of conifers. The driveway went all the way around and came to a dead end at the gateway to the priest's little cottage. "We should park here," Lissy told John, indicating a spot to the left just in front of a large yew. She cleared her throat and reached for a bottle of water.

"Nervous?" asked John.

"My throat's dry," she offered. She took a sip and replaced the cap, her hand shaking a little. "Yes," she relented, "just a bit."

"Well, we're here," said John lightly as he surveyed the church. "Nice place." John wasn't Catholic. He wasn't anything really since his parents weren't at all religious but he had been in a few churches over the years – friends' weddings, that sort of thing. This one was in a very picturesque setting – very oldie worldie what with the yew trees and that. The building itself was natural sandstone and had a bell-tower that reached about forty feet high. The front entrance was a huge oak door that opened inwards from the middle. Today it was opened at one side only. "Shall we go in?" he asked Lissy who was sitting quietly looking down at her hands, in which she clutched the bottle of water. John saw that she was busy peeling off every little bit of paper from the plastic bottle. "Are you okay?" he asked her frowning.

"Oh! Yes, I'm okay. I just need a moment I think. Yes, I'll … erm … I think I'll just sit for a while and then go in."

"What time's he expecting you?"

"Four." Lissy took another deep breath and looked at John. He was so kind. Ever since she first decided to look for her birth mother he had been so supportive. If it had been left to her alone she would have put off doing this until she thought she would be less scared. But he on the other hand was a doer. He was strong and decisive and had actually dialled the priest's telephone number himself and thrust the receiver into her hand. Even now she could see how bewildered he was at her reluctance to press on.

"So why are we sitting here? It's gone four already."

Lissy glanced at her watch. It was two minutes past four. "Only just," she said. "Haven't been here in years. Do you think he'll remember me?" She turned her head to look across at the church. Nothing had changed much except maybe her. For eighteen years she had come here never questioning why – it was what was expected of her she supposed. It was no different from the way she allowed her mum to run her life for her. It was just the way things were done but not any more. She had left the church behind her over ten years ago and now it was way past time that she broke away from her mother's control. She breathed deeply again. This time because she felt a surge of nervous excitement at the changes she was about to embark upon. She swung round to face John again with a smile on her lips. "He should do. I mean I can't have changed that much, can I?"

John smiled back at her. She was so lovely. The sun was low in the sky and its amber glow fell on her hair and face accentuating her beauty. Her eyes smiled brightly as she spoke and John thought that the pastoral beauty of the churchyard could not compare with the godliness emanating from behind her smiling face. He reached out and pushed a curl back from her eye with his fingers and said softly –

"How could anyone forget you?"

Her expression said it all. A sadness clouded the bright smile and the light went from her eyes. She hung her head and he had to fight with himself not to take her in his arms. "Lissy, I …" he began.

"No, please don't. It's just, I don't… I'm not… sorry." She sighed deeply and shook her head. "Let's just go, shall we?"

When she looked up at him her eyes glistened with unshed tears. As he studied her face again, John felt angry. He opened the car door and stepped out into the driveway. Taking a deep breath of cold air he knew that he was angry at everything at that moment … Angry that she should be in pain at all … Angry at whatever stupid circumstances that lay down her life. But most of all, what he felt was anger that there was nothing he could do to stop her feeling like that. He walked around to where she was now standing and took her arm to prevent her from walking off.

"You know, Lissy, that I would do anything to make you happy?" She looked away. "And if I could I'd change history. You know that don't you?"

"John," she said brushing his hand off her arm, "I know you would but the reality is you can't – no one can, and well… don't get me wrong… I appreciate your help, I really do, but I can't love you. You have to know that. It's not that I don't want to – it's that I just can't. I can't love anyone John, it's not you – it's me. I just can't while I'm looking for her." With that she walked away leaving him standing staring after her. There was nothing else to say. He was aware of that.

You will love me, he said silently to her, *you'll see.* She wouldn't be able to stop herself. He'd be beside her every step of the way until she found what she needed and when she did, he'd be there loving her no matter what. He wouldn't let her down. He set off after her around the side of the church and caught her up. He might be feeling a little crushed by her words now but he could wait. "Right then," he grinned, throwing an arm around her shoulder, "*mates* it is." She grinned back. "So this is the guy that organized your adoption. Is that right? *Mate*!" he asked.

"Yes, Father Peter Kearns. He's quite old now I imagine. Crikey! He was old when I remember him and that's at least ten years ago," she said, her sombre mood lifted. She opened the little gate and passed through onto the garden path. John followed her. The garden was kept nice and trim. Along the little pathway were borders of box hedging about two feet high. They led right up to the door over which hung a rambling rose the colour of which Lissy couldn't tell since the buds weren't even out yet. She reached out to knock and was saved the trouble as the door was opened from within. There stood Father Peter Kearns.

He was bent over now – his tiny frame almost skeletal he was so thin. His eyes peered out from behind thick black spectacles. They were sunk into his face with age and were very bloodshot.

"Hello, you're Miss Brenning I assume?" he asked in a very quiet soft voice. Not the same voice Lissy remembered booming down from the pulpit many years ago. But it was him all the same. Lissy was a little surprised at the feebleness of Father Kearns. Truth be told, she had always been a little afraid of him but how could she be afraid of the frail old man standing in front of her. She smiled, offering her hand to him.

"Yes, I'm Lissy. I'm very pleased to see you again Father," she said shaking his hand, "and this is a very good friend of mine, John. If that's okay Father?"

"Yes, yes that's fine. Come on in then and make yourselves comfortable." He moved aside to allow Lissy and John room to enter the cottage. Inside the hallway was tiny. It smelled of fustiness and old man. Lissy took stock of the décor. It was very much eighties style and the walls were festooned with photographs of what she supposed was the old man's family. She and John followed him on in, having to squeeze their way past several chairs placed there, most likely for waiting parishioners. He led them into a front room which was decorated similarly to the hall but without the festoon of pictures. Above a red brick fireplace that surrounded an electric fire, was a huge Sacred Heart picture with a little cross lit up red in front of it. The electric fire was on and both Lissy and John were thankful for the heat it gave out. "Sit down my dears," the priest said nodding towards the large leather sofa against the wall behind them. They sat down sinking into the soft cushions with a squeaking noise.

God I hate these sofas, said Lissy to herself. She didn't dare look at John for fear that she would start giggling. The priest sat down opposite her and rested his clasped hands on his lap. He looked at her from over his glasses and said after several moments – "Melissa is it?"

Lissy nodded. "Please call me Lissy."

"Melissa," he went on, "I had a call this afternoon from your mother. She's very concerned about you my dear."

Lissy shook her head and glanced at John in disbelief. He put his hand up gesturing her to wait a moment and then said to the old man –

"Lissy's mother doesn't agree with what Lissy's … what we're trying to do. I think she's afraid of Lissy getting hurt. But Father, with all due respect to Mrs Brenning, and to yourself of course," he added, "this is something that Lissy feels she has to do and to be honest I agree with her."

He put his hand down on the sofa just between his leg and Lissy's and she took his hand in hers giving it a squeeze as if to say – thanks for that. She was indeed very grateful for his assertive response. She would have lost it and blown the whole thing probably. How dare her mother do that? What was she trying to achieve anyway? Putting a spanner in the works before she even got started most likely. She would have to tell her to back off and let her do this her way.

The priest seemed unimpressed by John's interruption. He had listened to him with half of his attention, devoting the rest to studying Lissy's reaction. Brenda Brenning had said that she was highly strung and it would need a firm attitude to make her see sense. He was aware of Brenda's concerns for her daughter but at the same time he was more than aware that his main duty lay with Melissa's concerns. After all this was about her. He felt that if Melissa asked for whatever personal information he knew about her then it was his moral obligation to give it to her. On the other hand, watching her then as the young man was speaking, he came to the conclusion that she may well be highly strung as her mother had said. She certainly seemed angry at her mother's interference. To be honest, he had also been a little exasperated at Brenda's phone call. It was the kind of thing he would have expected from the mother of a minor. In his experience it was best to deal solely with the person concerned, other people sticking their oar in only became a nuisance.

"I see, I see," he said, more to Lissy than to John, "I'm just wondering how you came to that conclusion." He scribbled something down in a notebook.

Lissy stared at the notebook and said exactly what she wanted him to write in it – "Look Father, don't misunderstand me. I love my parents and I will always be grateful to them for giving me a good life but it's a feeling I have. I feel that there's always something missing… That I can't be happy until I know where I came from – who I am. Mum thinks it means she's failed me in some way, I know she thinks that. But that's just not true. If anything she does too much for me and you know, I can't help but wonder if I met my biological mother and got a sense of the start I had in life then I could appreciate my mum even more."

"What do you mean – a sense of the start you had?" asked Father Kearns.

"I don't know, it's just that it's a blank in my life and if I could fill it in then I would have a better sense of who I am and what I'm about. Maybe that doesn't make sense to you but it does to me."

"And what if you don't like what you find?" Father Kearns suggested. He was concerned about this young woman. He had dealt with this kind of enquiry before and although the person involved had pretty much the same reasons for it as Melissa, that had been straightforward compared to this case. He had looked into the matter after she had first contacted him and there was a lot of secrecy around it. Melissa's answer gave him all he needed to make a decision on how much he was prepared to get involved.

She had stood up and walked to the window where she appeared to be thinking seriously about the answer to his question. She took her time and eventually turned to him and said – "It isn't a question of whether or not I like what start I had in life… Or indeed, if I like the woman who gave birth to me or not. She may not even like me or worse still, she may not want to entertain me at all. The thing is, I have to know. It's the knowing that makes all the difference. As long as I know who she is and something about her, about who my father is even and where I was born – that kind of thing." She paused for a while and sat down again beside John absentmindedly putting her hand on his leg. "And anyway, if it all goes pear-shaped I have my parents. Of course I love them and would never want to replace them. Even if she and I bond as mother and daughter she'll never replace what they are to me or indeed what she never gave me."

Father Kearns was astounded. It was clear to him that Melissa was as unrealistic as her mother had suggested. How could he even contemplate telling her the truth? That her biological mother was just a child when she gave birth to her and that the information he had gave her mental state to be psychotic at best. He would have to tread carefully with this case. Melissa's well-being had to come first. He turned to John.

"Can I ask who you are?" he asked him.

"No problem," replied John sitting up straighter in the sofa, "I'm John Brunt. I'm Lissy's neighbour and friend."

The priest wrote the name in his notebook. "And may I ask what your interest is in this business?"

John was somewhat offended. How dare this practical stranger suggest that he have any other interest in it other than to care for Lissy? "What do you mean? I'm Lissy's friend. Isn't that enough?"

Lissy could feel that John was angry at the priest and she didn't want him to get worked up. She would have to intervene to smooth things out –"Erm… what he means Father is that he cares about me and wants to help me, that's all. He sees what I'm like when I'm upset about this and he gets annoyed sometimes that there's nothing he can do. If I didn't have him I swear I'd just get depressed over it. He helps me to take action you see, he's wonderful, he really is. Didn't Mum tell you how much she admires him? Gosh, she must have. She absolutely adores him, doesn't she John?"

John nodded in surprise. Crikey! He never expected her to say all that about him. So what if this old priest thinks the worst of him. After what she just said the old boy could think whatever the hell he liked. It didn't matter a toss. It was a good thing he was feeling generous because the old boy didn't even as much as flinch at his response and had listened to Lissy sing his praises without as much as an acknowledgement. Lissy thought that he was probably pissed because John was obviously not a Catholic, and made a mental note to tell John once they were out of there.

"Yes, well Melissa my dear," Father Kearns said in a very patronizing way, looking over the top of his glasses at her, "your mother is a very respectable woman no doubt. Your dad, Russell is it? Yes, well they're here every Sunday. They often say hello after mass. I haven't seen you with them for a while though."

For fuck's sake, John thought.

"No I suppose you wouldn't have really. I'm mostly away at the weekends so I go wherever I can you see," lied Lissy.

John was always amazed at the ease with which Lissy lied but he had to hand it to her – it got the old boy off her back.

"I see," said the priest. "Good for you, business is it? Anywhere nice?"

"Oh, mostly social stuff you know. I go up to London a lot to see some mates up there. Anyway Father, do you think you can help me? I suppose I need to contact the adoption agency first. Mum says she wasn't given any information whatsoever."

"Just a minute now, let's not get ahead of ourselves," the priest answered getting into the patronizing mode with full swing.

Lissy could feel her blood boiling at his attitude and she knew John would be the same but she said nothing. Experience with priests in the past had taught her that they assumed they had total authority over their parishioners and that if she rocked the boat he might just refuse to co-operate. She waited for him to go on.

"Now then my dear, I have looked into the matter. I did get some information about you when you were brought to my attention. I received a letter in 1978 I believe. It was from a parish priest in Ireland, an old parish of mine."

"Yeah, Mum did say she knows I came from Ireland Did he say who my mother was?" interrupted Lissy eagerly.

"Have you got the letter there?"

"No, I haven't but I do have a report about the matter. There's no agency details in it but it says about the letter, although not the full contents as they were." It was the priest's turn to lie now but Lissy was completely unaware of that. John, however, was not so sure that the priest was completely forthcoming.

"What does the report say then?" asked Lissy, feeling disappointment coming on.

"Well, it says that this old colleague of mine needed to find a place for a baby girl that I assume was born in his parish. It doesn't say where you were born only that your maternal grandmother wished for him to make the arrangements for your adoption."

"Does it not say who my mother was? What was my maternal grandmother's name?" asked Lissy, very worried now that she was not going to get any decent information at all.

"It doesn't give any names I'm afraid my dear, only that you were born in November 1978. By the time you came here the adoption had already been finalized. Don't your parents know anything at all about it?" The priest was being very sketchy indeed.

John piped up. He had to say something. "They must have had to sign the adoption papers would they not?"

"Of course," replied the priest.

"Then," John went on triumphantly, "as the parish priest who organized this side of things, you would have had to witness that signing. Don't you have a report on that?"

The priest took off his glasses and began wiping the lens. *Trying to think up what lie will get him out of that one,* thought John suspiciously. Putting the glasses back on the priest stood up and pulled a piece of paper out of his back pocket.

"Let me see now," he began, "I made a few notes here from the report. Anything useful you know." He was obviously evading the question. "Ah, yes, I can give you the name of the priest who organized the adoption. He's dead now I know for I attended his funeral a long time ago but you can start at the parish. His name was Father Sean Murphy – a good man, yes."

"And you're sure it doesn't give a report on the signing of the adoption papers? John asked. "Surely you remember witnessing that don't you?" he insisted. There was no way he was going to be browbeaten by this old fart. If Lissy couldn't stand up for herself then he was damn sure he was gonna.

"Well if I did I don't remember it and there's nothing about it in the report. Sorry I can't be of more help but that's it I'm afraid." Father Peter Kearns was getting fed up with the young man sticking his oar in. That is exactly why these things are best left alone. If he were to tell all to this couple, the man would rush them headlong like a bull into disaster. Then where would the poor girl be to say nothing of his promise to Brenda Brenning that he'd treat her daughter with the utmost discretion. He remained standing and said with authority: "Now if you'll excuse me, I'm rather busy this evening." And with that he opened the door to the hallway and waited for them to leave.

John and Lissy got up and adjusted their warm winter coats. They were about to leave disheartened when John remembered – "Oh yes, what did you say the name of the parish in Ireland was?"

Lissy brightened up a bit and added – "And the priest was Father Sean Murphy is that right?"

"Yes that's right," said Father Kearns irritated at John's constant interference, "wait a moment now." He went down the hall to what appeared to be the kitchen and came back with a piece of paper and handed it to Lissy. On it was written – 'Father Sean Murphy PP, 1966 – 1992, Cloughbeg Parish, Cloughbeg, Co.Mayo, Ireland.'

Lissy thanked the old priest for the information and allowed herself to be ushered quickly out of the front door. She and John said goodbye politely at the gate and began walking back to the car, she disappointed and he angry.

"If that old fart was telling the truth about how much he knows then I'm a bishop's auntie," insisted John when they were out of earshot. Lissy giggled but John wasn't at all amused. "*Melissa my dear*," he mimicked the old priest, "*let's not get ahead of ourselves now.* I'm telling you Lissy I could have reached for him going on like that. Don't you think he could have told you more?"

"I don't know. I suppose if that's all it said in the report then what can he do? Besides, we have a lead if nothing else, don't we?"

"Crikey, you are so naïve at times, it's hard to believe," John said shaking his head in disbelief. "It was bloody obvious that he was lying through his teeth. I bet you that letter is there and I'd go as far as to say that it gives a hell of a lot more information than he wanted to give. There's obviously something he doesn't want you to know."

"But why would he not want me to know? I mean it's nothing to him is it?"

"None of his business no, but he may be hiding something." John was beginning to wonder if there was something fishy about the way all this business was carried out. Maybe Father Kearns knew something that could mean potential trouble for him if it got out... best not to worry Lissy at this stage. After all, they had a lead and he had no problem with going to Ireland to follow it up - no problem at all.

"Hiding what?" Lissy asked confused. "No John, I think you've gotten carried away. He wasn't very pleasant, no. In fact I suppose he was downright rude but I don't think he was blatantly lying to us." Lissy had grown up trusting priests and it never occurred to her that Father Kearns could be dishonest, even if he tried. She smiled reassuringly at John and felt a rush of fondness for him as he walked beside her, clearly wanting to protect her.

"I suppose you're disappointed that you didn't get a name or an adoption agency?" John said, letting go off the frustration he felt with Father Kearns.

"Yeah, I am but I realised something in there that means a hell of a lot when it comes to moving on with this thing," she replied smiling and linking her arm through his. He stopped and looked at her, his eyebrows raised questioningly.

"And what's that?"

"I realise that I'm very lucky to have you fighting my case for me. You were fantastic in there, you really were. I would have left with nothing. Thanks to you we have a lead."

"And is that all I am to you? Someone to help you fight your case?" he pushed.

"No, of course not. But you know I can't go there." She wished he wouldn't keep harping on about the two of them being a couple. She was falling for him, she knew that but she had to be strong. Nothing was going to stand in the way of her finding her birth mother. She thought of her painting, *A Mother's Love*, and remembered that tomorrow was the exhibition.

"Tomorrow is the exhibition," she said, thankfully changing the subject.

John had just parked his bum on the seat and didn't get a chance to add anything to the previous discussion. He relented, knowing full well that it was for the best. It's just that hearing her speaking so fondly of him had gotten his hopes up. "You said," he replied dejectedly. He couldn't offer any more than that.

Lissy knew how he was feeling and she kept going brightly telling him all about the organization that went into it and how Anne had helped her hang her paintings and all.

"You will come won't you?" she asked tentatively, eyeing him closely to ascertain his mood. "Oh come on. How am I meant to enjoy my big moment without you by my side?" she cried, hitting him playfully on the arm. It worked – he brightened up and gave her a wink. The butterflies started in her tummy and she tried to ignore the tell-tale sign. *Don't Lissy, don't you dare fall in love with him,* she told herself.

Lissy and Anne stood back and admired the professional way they had displayed their paintings. They each had ten pieces in the exhibition and there were eleven of them in the group so in total there were one hundred and ten pieces on display. They had been very fortunate to secure a proper exhibition hall at the local craft centre and the paintings all looked superb hanging there professionally framed with the title of each displayed below. They were hung on two thirty foot long plain white walls which, along with two massive windows one on either end, were the only features in the room. *A Mother's Love* was hanging second from the end of the left hand side. It was one of the largest paintings in the exhibition and was one of the most expensive. Lissy wasn't sure that she wanted to sell it at all and had stuck a 'sold' sticker on it for the time being. Down the middle of the two displays were placed three narrow tables groaning with the weight of platters of buffet food and bottles of wine and glasses. Everything was ready and it was almost seven thirty pm. The guests would be arriving shortly for the grand opening.

"Where are the lists of prices?" asked Anne flustered. Lissy was calm. She had gone into her performance role and was brimming with confidence. It comes from years of being made to feel important, she always said. Plus, she had learned it from her mother – *even if you feel like crap inside, look accomplished on the outside*. They weren't her mother's own choice of words but they said it well for Lissy. She was employing them right at this moment because Anne was getting on her nerves flapping about like that. She would have to avoid her company as much as possible tonight if she was going to pull this off.

"Fuck's sake Anne" she snapped, "would you calm down. They're over by the door. People will pick them up as they come in. Thank God some of us are thinking straight or it'll be chaos." Lissy snapped at her colleague often in this way – the woman just couldn't stop flustering for a second. She was the same at work where she just couldn't take constructive criticism. Last week she had the nerve to accuse Lissy of being exactly like her mother, thinking she was perfect all the time. God knew how her poor birth mother would live up to her expectations if she ever had the misfortune to be found, she had added. Lissy had been furious. How dare she say such a horrible thing when she knew how much this meant to her? It was typical of Anne to be nasty when she was caught lazing about at work. Lissy was only trying to buck her up a bit although she never knew why she bothered. Anne was the frivolous type who gave up on things before she gave them a proper go. She, on the other hand, prided herself in her ability to do things properly and with enthusiasm. She got that from her mother too, and if we were talking about her birth mother then what she learned from her was that if you want something in life then you go for it and take whatever help is offered because there are too many people all too ready to dump on you if you let your guard down.

Anne went off towards the double doors to check that Lissy had been right about the lists. She was. There they were on a chair. She opened the doors with a little too much force and banged them against the walls. "Bitch" she hissed under her breath. Lissy had been a real cat lately since this thing with her birth mother. Anne wished she'd hurry up and find her already so that she would give her ear a rest. All she ever talked about at work was 'my mother' this and 'my mother' that and if she wasn't boring her with that it was 'John' this and 'John' that. Anne had met John a few times before and she had to admit he was something to write home about but for God's sake, the way Lissy went on you'd think he was the bee's knees himself. It wasn't even as if she was shagging him. As far as she could tell Lissy was just stringing the poor bloke along after her with this adoption thing. Anyway, what the fuck was it to her? She only put up with her because of work. Funnily enough though, Linn seemed to like her and Linn was always a good judge of character. Ah well, she could be nice enough at times, when she wasn't being a bitch that is.

"Right on cue," said Anne in surprise as Linn and Mark walked through the door.

"What's that?" asked Linn puzzled.

"I was just thinking about you," replied Anne, "thanks for coming, both of you."

"That's okay sis, bit of support and all that. Hey! There's Lissy. Lissy, Lissy, hi!"

Lissy came walking towards them grinning from ear to ear and gave Linn a big hug. Anne had stormed off and left them to it.

"So how are you?" asked Linn lovingly. Mark stood beside her smiling at Lissy too. From the far side of the room Anne could see that her sister and brother-in-law were delighted to see Lissy. She busied herself with pouring a glass of wine for her guests. Lissy was in full performance mode and was chatting animatedly to Linn and Mark. She was just bragging about *A Mother's Love* when Anne returned with the drinks. "Ta sis," Linn said to her taking both glasses and handing one to Mark. "So, which of these paintings are yours then?"

Anne was delighted to drag them away from Lissy to look at her work. She was particularly proud of a watercolour she had done and enjoyed the oohs and ahhs that Linn so tactfully offered. The truth was that Lissy had a raw talent for art that Anne knew she could only aspire to. Lissy's paintings would be the main attraction of the weekend. And if she was being perfectly honest with herself, she was a little jealous of Lissy. At work she always achieved so much and the boss was well pleased with her and in her personal life she had men running after her all the time. She was very attractive and Anne was plain in comparison. Anne had shacked up with a few old boyfriends in the past and now she was very much on her own in a draughty flat. Lissy on the other hand never fell into that trap. Oh, Anne knew that she moaned away about living at home with her parents but she would have given anything to have that luxury. The fact was, she had never got on with her mum and dad. From an early age she had constantly argued with them and things never changed. Linn was different, she was agreeable to everybody and Mark was the perfect match for her – easy-going and happy all the time. Linn had been their parent's favourite but Anne could never dislike her for it. She loved her to bits and aspired to be like her. She had been practicing being as pleasant as her on Lissy for quite some time now even though she wanted to throttle her.

Linn and Mark moved quickly on looking at the other pieces of work and shouting out to Lissy to direct them to *A Mother's Love*. When they came to it they openly expressed their approval and Anne could see that Lissy was lapping it up. She strutted down the room with an air of royalty and began to go on about how she had attempted to portray a mysticism in the love between the mother and the child. Anne didn't know what to do now that she was left standing in front of her own paintings. Several people had come in and a small group were heading her way so she asked them if they would like a glass of wine which they accepted. She spent the rest of the evening topping up glasses and serving food whilst Lissy swanned about socialising with everyone. John arrived in shortly after eight and was very quickly by Lissy's side. It was plain to be seen that he adored her, he couldn't keep his eyes off her all evening and he was her biggest fan when it came to her paintings. Several people asked about *A Mother's Love* and were disappointed to discover that it was sold. It turned out at the end of that first evening that it really had been sold. Lissy had been shocked at first when she found out but she was even more shocked and greatly pleased when the new owner presented her with it later. John had purchased the painting in the understanding that it now belonged to Lissy and him. It was to be a symbol of their common quest and their future together. Lissy had been so overcome with pleasure at the romantic gesture that she forgave him the cheeky assumption.

The evening was a huge success. Many of the group sold some pieces. Anne, to her immense pleasure, sold four paintings including the watercolour she was so proud of which had been quite popular as it turned out. Lissy had sold three including *A Mother's Love*. She had been thanking everyone for coming at the end of the evening when she spotted a man coming in late. He seemed familiar to her although she couldn't quite place him. Several minutes later she saw him talking to Mark and remembered him then. It was Bobby from the psychic fair four weeks ago. What with Christmas and the exhibition and that, to say nothing of arranging to see Father Kearns, she had totally forgotten all about him and his claim that he was meant to help her. She hadn't thought much about it to be honest but she might like to try this past life therapy thing. John was bound to go with her if she asked and they'd have a laugh if nothing else. She pointed him out to John and quickly explained who he was.

"Do you remember me telling you about what he said to me?" she asked him, "about Linn saying we probably knew each other in a past life?"

"I remember you were more excited about him telling you that your mum would find you," answered John, amused at her enthusiasm.

"No no, that wasn't him said that. That was a fortune teller, remember? He said he knew my spirit. Did you ever hear anything so curious?"

"Weird if you ask me," John said, in a whisper now because Bobby was heading straight for them.

"Lissy hi," Bobby said before he reached them, "I am so pleased to see you again. Hope you don't mind. Linn invited me along. I'm not gate-crashing I assure you."

Lissy was completely at ease with him and eagerly introduced him to John.

"Nice to meet you" John said shaking the man's hand with a firm grip.

"Nice to meet you, John. Lucky man, eh? Lissy's a lovely girl."

"No, we're not… you know. We're just friends," giggled

Lissy girlishly.

Blimey, is she flirting with him? John thought. "For now anyway," he told Bobby. *Just so you know,* he said in his mind. Lissy thumped his arm in her usual manner and he took the liberty of pinning her arms to her body in a bear hug from behind. He grinned at Bobby letting him know that as far as he was concerned Lissy was taken so no trying to muscle in. Bobby smiled at John's antics. He saw right through them but his interest in Lissy was not romantic in the least. Her insecure boyfriend need not worry about that. He was interested only in getting to know her and fulfilling his part in her spirit's path through this lifetime. He addressed Lissy with an intense look.

"I'm glad for this opportunity to see you again. I wonder if you would mind having lunch with me soon. You too John, please. I believe you are aware of Lissy's quest to find her biological mother?" John could only nod. He was surprised at the directness of the man.

"We'd love to, won't we John?" Lissy said politely. "We could talk about this past life stuff and that."

"Well that would be great. And if you don't mind I'll bring my wife along, okay?" Bobby replied with a grin. He glanced at John's face and took note of the sudden change of interest in their proposed meeting. *That'll relax him,* he thought to himself.

"Right mate," John blurted out, "we'll be in touch."

Lissy wasn't thick. She knew that John had gotten jealous at Bobby's interest in her but she was aware from the start that it wasn't anything sexual. He was simply a lovely guy and for some strange reason they were about to find out, he was willing to help her in whatever way he could. That was good enough for her even if John didn't think so. She kissed Bobby on the cheek as she said goodbye and grabbed a shocked John by the arm ushering him away from Bobby and towards the door. She stood there for ten minutes saying goodbye to the leaving guests, a subdued John by her side.

In the time it had taken to clear the room and part company with the art group members John had done a lot of thinking. Maybe he shouldn't be so confident that Lissy would come around to him. Maybe she needed someone to tell her the way it is. That Bobby character had obviously come there solely to get Lissy to have lunch with him and hear what he had to say and look at the way she responded. But then she must have known he was married. Nevertheless, if he was to take a more positive lead not just in the whole mother quest but in their relationship, then she might just find herself going with it. She did love him. He was sure about that even if she wouldn't admit it.

Later on that night when they had had a nightcap and had discussed the evening's success, he didn't feel so confident. He wanted to tell her about ideas he had about the two of them just having fun together but found instead that he was talking about his plans for Ireland and how he could be of help.

"It would be a good idea to do some research first though, wouldn't it?" Lissy suggested.

"Gosh yes, of course we'd do some research. That's what I'm talking about silly, with my contacts there's a great deal of avenues I could go down." Lissy hadn't realised that John being a journalist would come in useful. When she thought about it now, she got quite excited. She treated him to a friendly squeeze and turned away quickly because she felt the urge to kiss him. John had sensed her feelings of the moment and was inwardly pleased. She loved him, she was about to kiss him. It was a plain as the nose on your face and it was enough for him – for the time being.

Chapter Seven

The fog

Sometimes girls go through their teenage years with rose-tinted glasses; more often they rebel. Rose would have liked to rebel but she was scared to; she was unaware of a thick fog around her that prevented her from seeing where she was going; all she could do was to move bravely forward without ever turning to see what was behind her.

January 1983

Rose was standing in the line for school dinners. Her classmate and only friend Marie was behind her. Marie was a lonely bean-pole of a teenager with long greasy ginger hair and a face covered with acne. Her grey school uniform hung on her like clip-on paper clothes on a cut-out paper doll, and her knee socks flopped around her skinny ankles. She had tried holding them up with elastic bands at the beginning of term but that had made her legs itch and she had gotten terrible stick for scratching all the time. *Marie's fleas – Marie's fleas* was the constant taunt from other girls. Rose had felt sorry for her then but in a way she was thankful that she wasn't the target for the girls' amusement. In fact, ever since they came to live in Drumgar in County Mayo, she didn't have a problem with teasing at school, not like it was in Belfast anyhow. Even at home her two older sisters had begun to focus their attention on other things, mainly boys and dances. At first, Rose had been dreadfully unhappy at school. She was only thirteen then and had gotten off to a bad start in Drumgar Convent School for Girls. Angela had still been school age at that time and had left just six months after moving house but she had several girls in her year well educated on Rose's strangeness. Thankfully it hadn't stuck and now that Rose was seventeen and in her sixth year at school those first few months were just a bad memory. She kept herself to herself though and had gotten a reputation for being a bit mousey.

Earlier this morning, she had written a letter saying that she had decided to leave school and get a job. She had handed it in to the secretary who had said she was crazy not to finish the rest of term. There was only four and a half months to go after all. Rose didn't care. She wanted out of this dump so she could begin earning some money. Maybe then she would be a bit more enthusiastic about her life. There had to be more to it than this. She couldn't say she was unhappy or anything 'cos what had she got to be unhappy about? But she spent most of her days going through the motions as it were. Everything seemed uneventful, boring, lifeless – a chore even. Aye, that's it – just putting in the days and weeks was a chore – a chore she would prefer not to have to do.

"Rose! Rose McDevit!" went the high-pitched voice somewhere along the corridor. Marie stuck her head out of the line and saw the headmistress marching up the line looking for Rose. She put a hand on Rose's shoulder and said discretely in her ear –

"Old Catweasel's shouting for you." Rose's chest tightened and her heart raced. No doubt Catweasel had read her resignation letter. She looked down the corridor and stepped out of the line in full view of Catweasel. She shot a quick glance at Marie who gave her the thumbs up and mouthed *good luck*! Catweasel strode towards her with a grim look on her hairy face. Her proper name was Mother Anne Kelly, the headmistress of the school. Most of the teachers were nuns and this one was the nastiest, most bitter one of them all. Her face, in particular her chin, was covered in fine white hairs which got her the nickname Catweasel after a long white bearded unpleasant character on TV. Rose had been on the receiving end of her nastiness several times to date.

Ever since their first encounter Mother Kelly seemed to have developed a grudge against her. The family had been in Drumgar for two months but it was only Rose's first week at her new school. She had been in the dinner hall and had just finished eating her dessert when she felt the most god awful pain in her abdomen. She tried to ignore it at first but by the time she had made her way back to class she was doubled over in agony. She didn't know anyone to ask for help but as it turned out she didn't need to because a stream of hot red blood began to run down her legs. Someone had screamed at the sight of it and scared Rose half to death. She was taken to the nurse and then to Mother Kelly who had called Mrs McDevit on the telephone. By the time poor Rose was sitting in the head's office opposite Mother Kelly and her mother she was in a daze, totally withdrawn. The nun had seemed furious at her for some reason and had been a real bitch, telling her to go home and sort herself out before she came back to school. That experience had scared the hell out of Rose, and her mother, who didn't offer any sympathy whatsoever, had dragged her home and sent her to bed with a painkiller. She had said at the time that it was a heavy period but as time went on and her periods didn't come until she was sixteen, Rose had begun to think that something was terribly wrong with her. What she didn't know, of course, was that it was connected to the event just weeks ago when the devil had come out of her. But then, she had shut that out of her conscious memory forever.

"Rose McDevit, follow me" Catweasel said with a sharp tone. She turned and walked back up the corridor, Rose reluctantly walking a few steps behind. As she walked several girls sneered at her; several smiled reassuringly and several looked the other way avoiding eye contact with the condemned girl. Rose knew they were all simply relieved that the unusual and ominous presence of Catweasel at the dinner line had nothing to do with them. With her heart thumping against her ribcage and a loud shooshing in her ears, Rose was not even completely aware that the condemned was herself. She reacted this way to any unpleasant situation in her life. It was normal for her, so normal that she never questioned it. In fact, she wasn't aware that other people were any different. She drifted in this semi-conscious state down the corridor and through the reception hall after the dreaded Catweasel. Into her office Catweasel went and Rose came to a halt outside the door.

"Come in here Rose, did I say to wait outside?" the nun snapped. Rose stepped into the office, her insides churning. She thought she was going to throw up. Holding her breath she sat down opposite Catweasel who stood behind the desk. She waited for the inevitable lecture on the importance of finishing one's exams. Catweasel surprised her. "So you're leaving us then Rose? May I ask when?"

"Today, I suppose." Rose hadn't expected that question. The nun's face was white with fury and Rose thought that the woman had never looked so ugly and terrifying.

"Yes well, don't think you'll be doing any GCEs this June. Qualifications are only for those who deserve them, not for quitters," Catweasel began. "And don't think I'll be giving you a reference to get a job. If I can't say anything good about someone then I won't say anything at all."

She waited for Rose to reply, half expecting her to defend her decision but she was disappointed. The girl just sat there staring into space and saying nothing. The nun leant forward, hands on the desk in front of her and shoulders rising up and down with her fuming breath. "Rose, I have to say – ever since you came here you've displayed the most atrocious attitude. You get a notion into your head and no-one can convince you otherwise. You put a half-hearted effort into your studies and if that's the way you're going to go into the world of work then you're doomed to fail."

Rose still didn't utter a word but stared straight ahead avoiding the nun's eyes. Catweasel slapped one hand loudly down on the desk and raised her voice almost to a squeal causing Rose to jump in fright. "Are you listening to me girl? If you think anyone's gonna want you to work for them you're wrong! You don't even have the decency to speak when you're spoken to!" She lifted Rose's resignation letter off the desk and threw it back down again. "This... this rubbish says it all doesn't it? Your mother knew it when you started here, crying and whingeing, expecting to be treated with sympathy. Oh no, not from me girl. You're on your own from now on."

Rose felt confused at the nun's words. Had she been aware of how unhappy she had been when she first came here? It just went to prove that she was a nobody like her mum made her feel. Now, this important nun was saying that she wasn't worth anything, as well. What was new? It did make her feel sad though.

"Well, have you anything to say for yourself?" Catweasel hissed. Rose didn't know what the nun would want to hear and she didn't know what she could say that would change things. Truth was she hadn't really thought this thing through. She just thought it might be exciting to get a job and she tended to grab on to any bit of excitement at all. Too late now, though, the ball was rolling. Anyhow she couldn't face Catweasel any more after what she just said to her.

"No, just that I hope I'll get a job and I'll try my hardest" she said in a sad little voice, tears stinging her eyes. They were lost on Mother Kelly as it was. The nun didn't stand for nonsense like that. In her opinion she was well rid of her. She remembered when the McDevit family came to Drumgar the whole way from Belfast in the north. The eldest girl came and went in a flash and there was not one bit of trouble out of her. This one apparently had been the reason the poor family had made such a big move in the first place. She couldn't be sure about that obviously but it had been true that the girl had gotten herself into trouble. She had missed a full term of school and came waltzing in here haemorrhaging all over the place and sneaking around completely non-penitent. Mother Kelly took one last look at the girl and shook her head.

"Sign this," she demanded, handing Rose a sheet of paper, "and then you're to clear your locker and go. Don't bother waiting to home time."

"I haven't been to dinner yet," Rose replied shyly.

"Go on," she shouted, "then get out of my sight."

That had been Rose's last day of school. She wasn't sorry although she really did not know how she felt only that she dreaded what her mother was going to say about it.

July 1984

The seaside town of Drumgar was situated just inland from the Mayo coastline. It was a large town with two magnificent stone bridges stretching across the River Bane. The Bane ran through the town and onwards to Cloughbeg where it joined the Atlantic Ocean at the estuary situated just outside the quaint little seaside village. Further along the rugged coastline were several little coves just like the one at the bottom of the hills where the little cottage belonging to Rose's grandmother stood. It was the middle of the tourist season and the main thoroughfare in Drumgar was heaving with visitors browsing the stores for souvenirs, and townsfolk trying to do their weekly messages as quickly as possible so that they could get out of the hot summer sun. The street was lined with brightly painted wooden benches on which people sat eating ice-creams and drinking ice-cold soft drinks. O'Hanlon's Ice-Cream Emporium was situated in the middle of the street and this afternoon it was packed to bursting with hot thirsty shoppers. Rose worked behind the counter dishing out ices and bottles of cola and fizzy lemonade. She had been working there now for over a year, since she left school. Her mother had heard the advertisement for the position of shop girl on the local radio one morning last March and had Rose into the town before she knew what was happening. But as it had turned out, Rose was quite happy with the job. She didn't earn a pile of money but it was a nice shop and the O'Hanlon family were great to work for. During the winter the custom was slow and so the work was nice and easy, but in the tourist season, especially on a hot day like today, Rose was run off her feet. She blew her wet fringe away from her forehead and called over the counter to the endless barrage of customers –

"Who's next please?"

"Two cokes and a ninety nine," a fat lady shouted, elbowing her way to the counter and half knocking a teenage boy off his feet.

"Hey! I was next," the boy complained to Rose, but she hadn't heard him. The room had begun to spin and before she knew it she was lying on the floor in a pool of cola, the bottle smashed into bits.

Iris O'Hanlon was down by her side in a flash and shouting to the customers – "For Christ's sake! Would someone help me get her up?" A middle-aged man came around the end of the counter and before Rose could protest, he had one hand under each of her armpits and was heaving her up off the floor.

"I'm okay, I'm okay," she insisted shakily, "I just need to sit down a bit."

"Bring her into the kitchen here please. Thanks very much sir, that's right, put her down here," Iris fussed, grateful for the man's help.

The helpful customer went back into the shop where he was treated to a free ice-cream for his generosity. "Just a sec please," Iris pleaded with the costumers. She reached for the intercom on the wall at the end of the counter and buzzed upstairs. "Joe," she said into the handset, "I need ya down here now. Rose has just fainted and the shop's stuffed."

"What!" her husband exclaimed loudly, "please don't tell me she's been starving herself again."

"Look Joe, we'll deal with that later okay? Right now I need help." She replaced the handset and began to serve the now irate costumers. The noise of her heavy husband could be heard running down the stairs into the kitchen and then the kitchen door slammed shut behind her. Joe O'Hanlon was a large overweight man in his forties. He had a pleasant demeanour and a round fat face that was often red with being so out of puff all the time. His wife often nagged him about losing weight – "You know what Dr Ellis said. You're putting too much strain on the heart. Look at ya for Christ's sake – ya can't even get yer second wind." Joe would wink at Rose and help himself to a huge cone of chocolate ripple. Rose liked Joe very much and was used to his joking ways, so it was a surprise when he suddenly got all serious with her.

"Rose, I need to ask you somethin' now an' I don't want

ya to get all offended like, y'know?" He had knelt down in front of her and put one hand on her knee in a concerned manner.

"I'll be okay Joe, sorry! It's just so hot out there at the minute. I'll just get a drink of water and then I'll go back," Rose said lethargically. She had thought that Joe was annoyed at her taking an extra break and she wanted to reassure him that she would be working again in just a minute.

Joe got up immediately and left the kitchen scratching his head with frustration. He came back momentarily with a bottle of lemonade and handed it to Rose. Then he leant up against the sink area shaking his head at her. "You've gotta stop this nonsense Rose. No, don't look at me as if I'm stupid. I know you're not eatin' properly." She bit her lip and hung her head, startled at the realisation that Joe knew. She immediately blanked out and was unable to think about her present situation never mind explain herself. Joe was used to Rose's strange ways by now. He had employed her last year straight out of school. She had some qualifications although she had opted out of school right in the middle of further exams. That hadn't really been an issue though as he was looking for someone young and pleasant to do the cleaning, was all. But as the time went on, she proved to be very capable and trustworthy so she was started on the counter and hadn't looked back since. The problem was that there was always this question hanging in the air. Did she ever eat anything? She was desperately thin and she never hung about at lunchtimes so neither he nor Iris could ever say they saw her eating. She had fainted before; last winter it was. It had been a freezing cold morning and he had arrived several minutes late to open up only to find her lying in the shop doorway out cold. Her face had been as white as the snow on which she lay. The O'Hanlons had said nothing at the time regarding their suspicions but surely he had to talk to her, at least now that she was at it again. "I'm sure this isn't easy for ya" he began, "but ya know it's not good to be faintin' like this every turn round. Now Iris has noticed an' I don't want ya comin' back at 'er now, she's only lookin' out for ya. She says you're not eatin'. Are ya eatin' anythin' at all at home?" He beseeched her with his kind eyes, willing her to tell him it was a big mistake, but who was he kidding? He knew there was something major going on with this lovely young woman.

"Aye, course I am. I'm sorry, I'll get myself a packed lunch tomorrow. I normally don't feel hungry during the day ya see," Rose lied through her teeth. She was eating practically nothing to be honest.

"Well, ya know what? Iris and I were thinkin' of getting' one of them microwave thingies for here. It's very easy to just put in last night's leftovers and heat them up. Only takes a few minutes apparently." Joe felt he was on a roll. "What d'ya say to havin' a bite of dinner heated up for ya here?" That wouldn' cramp yer style would it? I know you young ones like these modern coffee bars but it would be handy, eh?"

"Aye, but I couldn't expect you to..." Rose began awkwardly.

"Not at all. That's settled then. Listen now, you stay here an' make yerself a wee cup of tay. I'd better get out there or her nibs will be comin' for me with the ice-scream scoop." Rose giggled. *That's better,* he said to himself, *poor sad wee critter*. No sooner had he left than he popped his head round the door and said – "Her nibs said put two spoonfuls of sugar in it."

That night Rose lay awake, a thousand thoughts going through her mind. She was fearful now that someone had voiced her secret. Not just someone but Joe and Iris who she had to work with every day. *How in under God am I gonna get around this one?* she asked herself. Up until now she never had any interference with what she was doing. Christ! She wasn't even fully aware of what she was doing herself. What *was* she doing? Dieting – losing weight? Was she what was nowadays commonly known as anorexic? No, definitely not. That's where you don't eat anything at all. She did eat – very little mind you and when she'd eaten too much she'd make herself throw it up in the loo. She had watched a TV programme lately that talked about young people committing suicide and it described a new disorder called bulimia. That was more like what she was doing. But the programme talked a lot about psychiatric treatment and people being 'fucked up'. There was nothing wrong with her was there? Nothing... except the fact that she was bad inside. All she knew was that inside her was an evil that meant that no matter what she tried to do or who she tried to be she would never succeed. And God help her if anyone should realise that she was evil. That's why she spent all of her time trying to make people like her and if she had a slim body then she would be more attractive in general, wouldn't she? And a flat belly seemed to be important. It kept the evil showing. So every time her belly showed signs of swelling she would starve herself until it went down again. She'd been doing this for years now, since they came here to live. Her worst nightmare would be if anyone saw that she was evil inside and that's why it was such a torment now that Joe and Iris were asking questions. "They probably know!" she cried into her pillow. "Oh dear God! Please don't let them see the bad stuff." What was she going to do? She'd have to start eating lunch to keep them off her back. Maybe if she skipped dinner instead and she could always drink lots of diet cola… that seemed to stem her appetite. But then Mummy would be on at her. "Oh God," she cried," I hate myself. I wish everyone would just disappear an' leave me alone. Then I could just stay here and die."

Rose had felt like that for a long time now. In fact, she was well aware that a memory she had of when she was a child was of something very akin to wanting to commit suicide. She didn't remember much of when she was a child but she never forgot that. She had been eleven years old and sitting in school thinking about getting a rope and throwing it over a branch of a tree near her house. She couldn't remember how she knew to do that – she must have seen someone being hanged in a film. The thing was, she couldn't remember actually thinking about dying. It was as if the only thing she could remember was a picture of what she was planning. And there was another time just after she'd turned eighteen. She had been out at a dance with Marie and at the end of the night when they were both very drunk. Marie had declared that she was leaving Drumgar to go work in Dublin. Rose had gone home and taken a full bottle of her father's depression pills. As soon as she had taken them she panicked. She hadn't thought about it, she'd just wanted someone to see her sadness, she supposed. She had gone straight upstairs and confessed what she'd done to Caroline who had been sleeping, peacefully dreaming of her forthcoming wedding.

"*You stupid bitch*!" Caroline had screamed at her, "Mummy, Mummy, Rose has gone and done something mad. Mummy, Daddy, wake up quick!"

All hell had broken out. Rose felt that she regretted her actions even more than she would have done had she actually topped herself. Her mother, having jumped out of bed thinking the house was on fire was furious with her. How could ya be so selfish?" she spat, forcing Rose to drink salted water until she threw up. "Selfish …selfish … wee … bitch," she hissed, hitting her on the back of the head with each spiteful word. "What in under God did ya think ya were doin'?"

Rose hadn't been able to answer her. Between bouts of

vomiting, the salt stinging her throat and lips, she was sobbing uncontrollably. With her mother pressing on her back to force her head into the sink, the pain in her chest and throat was agonizing and the tears, along with the mucus from her nose, mixed with the searing vomit spilling forth. When the physical torture was done, the mental torture continued. She sat at the kitchen table and sobbed on and on unable to speak or to think about what had happened. Her mother had sat opposite her. Daddy, Caroline and the boys stared on in shock. "Why?" hissed Mummy her whole body quivering with rage.

"I… I dunno," Rose had stammered, "I can't help it. I'm just so sad."

"Sad? I'll give ya somethin' to be sad about if ya ever pull a stunt like that again."

"She just wants everybody to be thinkin' about her instead of me," accused Caroline, "wants to spoil my wedding. Well, listen to this ya wee witch. I wouldn' feel sorry for you if ya were the last person on earth. If a dog was lying in the middle of the road I'd go to it afore I'd go near you."

"That's enough Caroline," snapped her father, "off to bed now everyone. We'll talk about this in the morning." Thankfully for Rose, in the morning no-one had been prepared to even go there, especially her. She had put it down to being too drunk and had kept a low profile for a while. And after a few days it had been as if it hadn't happened.

That had been almost a year ago now and although Rose thought about it often, she wasn't prepared to go there again and plodded through each week in a constant quest for perfection. But now that Joe and Iris knew about her not eating, she was going to have to shake things up a bit.

As it turned out, things were shaken up quite a bit when a Coca Cola agent waltzed through the shop door, just a few days later. Paul Rooney worked for the Coca Cola Packing Company in Drumgar and although he had been born and raised in Dublin, he had now taken a flat in Richmond Street in the town to begin a career in management. He was fresh out of college and still on his three month trial with the company when he visited O'Hanlon's Ice-Cream Emporium. He was very nervous, but the lovely girl behind the counter made him feel relaxed. He felt an instant attraction between them and it wasn't long before he and Rose McDevit were going steady

October 1987

Rose was now twenty two. Paul was twenty one, and they had been together for over three years. Lately, things had been very difficult. "What d'ya t'ink Jason?" Paul was asking his mate. They were sitting in a pub in O'Connell Street, Dublin. Paul had finished his training in Drumgar and was now back home as manager of a large branch outside the city. Rose had moved in with him just two months ago and she was driving him crazy to say the least.

"Why don't ya' just tell 'er it's not working out an' she

should go back to Drumgar?" Jason replied.

"I can't do that, she's got no job there now. It's not just that she's a clinger but I t'ink there's somethin' badly wrong with 'er, I really do."

"What d'ya mean? What's wrong with 'er? She looks fine to me. I wouldn' kick her outta bed for fartin' anyway." Jason was always crude.

Paul ignored him. Instantly he was aware that if Jason had passed a remark like that about Rose before, he'd have smacked him one. "Don't love 'er anymore mate. Don't t'ink I can be bothered with 'er either. It's like she's suckin' the life outta me." Paul was near in tears.

"Come off it mate, who're trying to kid. It's obvious ya still have some feelings for 'er. But if ya ask me, you're better off well away. Unless ya t'ink she's worth it." Jason had seen his mate like this many a time because of Rose. If she hadn't been so fuckin' sexy he'd have told him to fuck her off ages ago.

"You know what," Paul confided after several minutes silence, "I t'ink she must be psychotic or somethin'."

"What?" Jason blurted out, spitting stout down the front of his shirt.

"I'm serious. You don't know 'er like I do. She gets these really weird moods an' everyt'ing suddenly changes ya know? One minute you're grand and then she starts crying for nothin'." Jason shuffled on his stool and took a long swig of his pint, pretending to be interested in what the barman was doing just then. When he didn't speak Paul went on. "An' the other day like, she goes 'why d'ya not love me anymore? Bet if I'd let ya just hurt me you'd be happy. Is that what ya want, to hurt me? I bet it is.' I mean, for fuck's sake, what's that all about?"

"Jesus man!" grimaced Jason, "Get rid of 'er! That is one mental fuck." He grabbed his cigarettes and lit one up. "No harm to ya man, but get as far away from that one as ya can." Paul was silent. He folded his arms on the bar and rested his head on them. He felt trapped. He did care about her. They'd been in love for over three years after all. How could he just abandon her now that he had insisted she come and live in Dublin with him? If he dumped her she'd have nowhere to go except back home where she had no job, no friends, nothing. But he honestly did think there was something wrong with her and she had become a real drag. Christ! He never knew what end was up with her anymore or where he stood in the whole thing. Sometimes it was as if she hated him. When they made love last night she had actually punched and kicked him and screamed at him to get off her. *That's not the actions of a sane woman*, he thought for the umpteenth time since last night, *I don't need that, I really don't.* He beckoned the barman, shouting – "two pints of Guiness over here please" and he turned his attention towards his mate. "You're right mate, I'm gonna tell 'er it's over." Once he had made the decision he felt heaps lighter.

Rose slammed the front door of the terrace house on Foley's Road where she and Paul had been living for the past two months. It was three in the morning and the street was quiet. The only light came from an occasional window and the odd streetlamp that hadn't been smashed by local kids. The rain was coming down fast and she was drenched by the time she made it to the corner where the bus stop was. She sat down on the wooden bench under the tin shelter. The place stank of cigarettes and old discarded take-aways and tonight there was an overwhelming whiff of stale piss. It wasn't a safe area for a woman to be out by herself in the dead of night but the pub crowd would be gone by now and there would be no-one about to annoy her. Wrapping her arms about herself for warmth and comfort Rose sobbed loudly and rocked back and forth on the bench. She was so lonely and desperately homesick and now Paul had rejected her. She had seen it coming for a long time now but she'd hoped by moving to Dublin where it was so obvious he wanted to be, things would get better. How wrong she was. She was just not cut out for city life. Everyone had the attitude that you were either one of them or not and if you were not then you were alienated. Paul's mates and their women were well used to city ways and the men teased her for being naïve while the women looked down their noses at her. "She's just a *culchie*, you have to make allowances for her." Paul's words seared into her mind now, as she recalled his so-called defence of her from his mates' jibes.

Rose had learned very quickly that 'culchie' was a city

name for someone from the country – someone not slick like them. As she sobbed, she felt a pain in her heart such as she'd never felt before. The only sounds in the night were her sobbing and the relentless clatter of the rain on the tin shelter. After several very long minutes another sound began to rumble from the depths of the lonely girl's pain. It was a deep moanful sound that got louder and louder before it collapsed into a silent throat-wrenching cry. Rose's entire body shook and she let herself fall to her knees on the cold concrete floor. She so badly needed to cry out and release the pain now in her throat but nothing came out but a silent anguish. The rain was pelting in from the front of the shelter and it stung her face as she held herself tightly willing with everything she had not to explode. Suddenly, as if in a flash of lightning, she saw black demonic figures around her, crowding the air from her lungs and restricting her until she was unable to move. And then…nothing. She had slipped into unconsciousness. When she came to she found herself on the concrete floor of the bus shelter, soaked through. She shook with shock and with the icy wetness that seemed to penetrate the very bones of her. Lying still there for a minute she sensed a fear inside her. It seemed to be from long ago. In a daze she got up and sat on the bench again. Her knees hurt from falling onto the hard floor and she had a tear in her new jeans. Staring at the tear she poked a finger into it and pulled hard until the denim material ripped again leaving a huge gaping hole and exposing her bloody knee. She was angry. She was raging with anger and she allowed it to take over as she roared at the top of her voice. The roar became a scream and she stood up and began kicking and thumping at the walls of the bus shelter. When the anger subsided it felt to Rose as if a fog was visible all around her and in that fog she was able to perceive shadows of the past. The fog began to disperse and the now exhausted Rose began to walk.

Rose walked a long way that night. It was to take the fog thirteen years to disperse. She had begun a journey – a process of awakening that was to take her to the depths of hell and back. Eventually she would come back to the beginning where the journey would then take her to the heights of heaven.

Chapter Eight

Born bad – die bad

If someone is born bad then shouldn't it follow that they would be bad all their life? And if someone is bad their whole life then does it not follow that they ought to be punished? Rose was convinced that her judgement day was coming and all that remained was for the devil himself to come for her.

Janey shuffled down the corridor in her worn-out bedroom slippers. It was late in the afternoon and rest-time wouldn't be far off. She decided it was best if she said her prayers now since lately they'd taken to confiscating her rosary beads at rest-time. She knew where she was even if they did think she was going senile. She was very much aware that it had been long, long weeks since they sold her lovely wee cottage from under her very nose and shoved her away in this God-forsaken hole. They had tried before with several places saying – *Now Mammy dear, you'll like it here*.

But she never liked it anywhere except her lovely wee cottage which had been her home for eighty odd years. Then, they'd gone and sold it from under her very nose; or else they'd knocked it down, or worse still they might have the Gormans living in it. The Gormans were her dead husband's family and she and they'd never seen eye to eye since she married John and turned him Catholic. "I'm unhappy," she would say to everyone now. If they thought she was fit for the lunatic asylum then she may as well act like a lunatic. "I'm unhappy, I'm unhappy." That's all she ever said, except for her prayers of course which could never be overlooked even if you were trying to make a point. It was near rest-time now and the prayers would have to be said before they took her beads away so as she wouldn't lie awake praying and keeping the other patients awake. She was on her last Hail Holy Queen when she noticed the young woman sitting on a bed in the top cubicle. *She must be new,* thought Janey, and she shuffled over towards the latest victim. *I wonder have they sold her house out from under her too?* "I'm unhappy" she said aloud.

Rose heard the words.

"Sister, come here! Rose heard 'er… I'm sure she heard 'er!" Annette shouted up to Ward Sister Theresa Coyle who was close by in the office at the top of the ward. Theresa came hurrying down to the first cubicle where Nurse Annette McKinney was assigned to observing young Rose McDevit. The nice-looking wee girl had been brought in two weeks ago and hadn't spoken a word since. At least, not to them she hadn't. At first the doctors had thought she was just refusing to speak but as the days went on it was apparent that she *was* speaking to someone – it was just that it wasn't anyone here. She sat all day long in the high dependency room off the main ward, in total silence mostly. From time to time she would stare ahead as if she was seeing someone there and she would smile and actually converse with the person. Only, no-one was there, no-one real that was. All the staff there at the acute psychiatric ward had tried to reach her, spending long hours talking to her about a thousand different things. She had never once responded to them or her friends and family, which Theresa had noticed was hardly ever there, but then, who was she to judge? When Theresa entered the cubicle Annette was standing with one hand holding the arm of old Janey Gorman as if she didn't want her to leave. Rose was still sitting in the same position as she had left her in an hour before. Theresa had thought that perhaps a change of environment might make a slight bit of difference to the poor girl. And now Annette was shouting that Rose had heard her. Dare she hope for a breakthrough?

"Oh please God, let 'er be coming round at last," she muttered under her breath.

"She heard 'er Sister. I'm sure she did. Janey came right over to 'er, didn't ya Janey pet?" Annette smiled at the old lady. "She said 'I'm unhappy', like she does, and then Rose just turned 'er head and looked right at 'er." Annette was very pleased with herself, as if she had been the one to wake Rose out of wherever she was. She stood, still holding Janey's arm and beaming at Theresa.

Theresa grabbed a chair and pulled it up in front of Rose. She sat down and spoke softly, directly into Rose's face- "Rose dear, did ya hear this lady speak to ya just now? She said she was unhappy. Did you hear 'er dear?" There was no response but Theresa thought she saw a change in the girl's eyes. "Rose dear, could ya look at me please. I want to help ya. Please, can ya tell me if ya heard Janey speak to ya before?" And then came the moment they had all been waiting for since Rose first came into their care. She focused her eyes on Theresa and they filled with tears. Theresa watched, her heart racing as the tears spilled forth and Rose's face began to register what was going on. "Fetch Doctor Pritchard," Theresa ordered Annette, getting up and pulling the curtains around Rose's bed, and keeping a close watch on her at the same time. Rose was still sitting and showing signs of becoming aware of her environment when Theresa put one hand on her arm and said, "You're okay now Rose, you're in hospital. You're goin' to be fine pet." A moment was all it took for Theresa to feel the intensity of the girl's fear. It hit her like a wave sweeping over the gap between them and came crashing into her causing her to catch her breath with its force. In that one moment Theresa knew what was coming and she braced herself for it. Thinking swiftly and professionally she pushed the chair away from her just as Rose sprung up from the edge of the bed and swung one arm upwards in an attempt to push her away. Theresa caught a firm grip of the arm with her left hand and manoeuvred herself behind Rose gripping the other arm with her right hand. The frightened girl screamed and struggled to get away but Theresa had her in a tight hold now, more for her own safety than the girl's. Moments later Doctor Pritchard, Annette and Nurse Cara O'Hagan came dashing around the corner and came to Theresa's aid. Rose attempted to kick and punch free off their grip on her as they moved her onto the bed, strapping her down with large white straps with big silver buckles. All the time the poor frightened creature screamed and yelled in terror. When she was secured to the bed, Theresa let go off her and signalled to the others to do the same. Leaning against the window ledge, she gathered herself together. She had dealt with panic attacks like this before but there was something about this girl's intense fear that shook her badly. She wanted to talk to the girl, console her, but professional experience told her that it would only make matters worse. She had to be sedated before any attempt at talking. Rose began to tire now and as Doctor Pritchard was preparing the shot Theresa moved closer to her again. The poor girl's cries were wearing her down and she soon gave them over to an anguished whine. It was easy to administer the shot as Rose put up no fight at all to Theresa holding her arm. When it was done the doctor and Cara left and Theresa retrieved the chair and sat down thankful that the incident had passed without too much difficulty. She closed her eyes and took several deep breaths feeling all the time that she would burst into tears at any moment. This was so unlike her. She was a professional for goodness sake. The last time she felt like that was trying to get her own child to sleep during a bout of colic and that had been all of twenty years ago. Every instinct in her was crying out to console this poor girl who had been in her care for two weeks and who had as yet, never uttered a word to her. Theresa knew nothing about her other than she had attempted to commit suicide by ingesting almost one hundred painkillers. She and Doctor Pritchard had met with the girl's parents but no-one had any idea as to why such a lovely young thing would want to hurt herself like that. Theresa Coyle had been a psychiatric nurse since 1969 and never until this past year had she ever had to deal with young girls like this in such a bad way. Sadly, Rose was one of many such young things needing help recently, but none of them had affected Theresa like her.

"Are ya alright there sister?"

Theresa was startled out of thoughts - "What? Oh, Annette. Sorry dear, I'm just a little shaken is all. Sure, I'll be grand," she assured the young nurse.

"Shall I stay an' keep an eye on 'er Sister? Looks like she's out cold, poor thing." Annette was assigned to Rose but Theresa wasn't sure that she was able to get up just yet. Her legs felt like jelly and she was still quite emotional. Besides, there was something about this girl that made her want to be there should she wake up.

"No dear, no. I think I'll sit with 'er for a while. You go and do the dinner duty if ya don't mind. Send a plate down to Rose will ya? Just in case she wakes up, she may feel like eatin' somethin'. God knows, the poor wee thing hasn't eaten a morsel hardly this last while. She's skin and bones isn't she? The mother said she eats well enough at home but I don't know. The wee pet looks half starved." Theresa looked up at Annette who was staring at her in wonder. She realised she had been going on a bit which was unlike her usual professional assessment. She said quickly – "Don't mind me dear, I'm just thinkin' out loud is all." She waited for Annette to go and then rested her head against the back of the chair. The girl slept, heavily sedated. Theresa studied her face. The eyes were laden with long dark lashes which looked false against the backdrop of the pallid skin. The lips were slightly apart as the girl breathed slow and gentle and Theresa noticed that even they were the colour of fear. She thought that the girl couldn't have been much older than her own daughter and she felt the maternal pull towards her she had felt just minutes earlier. What really hit her like a bucket of cold water was the fact that even during sleep the girl's face betrayed the inner terror that Theresa had felt so strongly from her. Her Kerry's face was always so peaceful as she slept. There came a small voice from behind the curtain –

"She's unhappy."

"Yes Janey, we know you're…" Theresa began irritated at the old woman's interruption with her constant insistence that she was unhappy. But then Theresa realised that Janey hadn't said '*I'm* unhappy' she had said '*she's* unhappy'. "Thank you Janey, yes I suppose she is. Go back to yer bed now that's a love." Theresa sat upright. Janey had hit the nail on the head. She turned her attention once again to Rose's face, only this time she didn't focus on the obvious fear but looked behind it to the unhappy girl who had found her way into her care crying out for her to help her – to love her. She and all the others had spent so long trying to reach Rose. They had talked and talked for hours about how she ought to come out of wherever she was but to no avail. Theresa knew now that it was never Rose's intention to come back to where she was before but to call on them to come to her – to see her in her reality. Looking at Rose now, Theresa got a glimpse of that reality and what she saw was pain beyond belief. She felt her heart would break as the tears rolled from her eyes and even when she couldn't see any more from behind them she could still feel the compassion pouring from her heart and hurtling towards wherever Rose was, watching and waiting for a sign that someone could see her and was willing to meet her in her world. Ten minutes passed and Theresa never once took her eyes from Rose's face. The tears had dried into her skin and she sniffed absent-mindedly.

Eventually the general activity on the other side of the curtain brought her awareness away from Rose's world and back to the reality of the ward. Annette arrived carrying Rose's dinner tray herself. *I'm not the only one who can't stay away from her,* thought Theresa. She couldn't blame the young nurse. Sure even old Janey Gorman had been affected by her. She made a mental note that it had been a wise move to bring Rose into the main ward. There was something about the girl that shook people up and made them come alive. She would have to keep a close watch on Rose herself and make sure she didn't come to any harm. Just as she thought that, she was reminded of the little swallow she had found as a child. It had a broken wing and couldn't fly. She had cared for it and loved it until one day she found it out of the cardboard box she had kept it in and it was flying around in the back scullery. It was heart-breaking for her to let it go then but she felt blessed that she was given the opportunity to nurse it back to wellness. Theresa remembered the lesson that the little bird had taught her – that by caring unconditionally for the needy in the world, whether it be a bird or a human being, she received back that same love tenfold in her life. That was why she became a nurse in the first place. Somewhere along the line she had lost sight of her true calling and now here was another little wounded creature, totally dependent on her unconditional care and reminding her of her sole reason for being a nurse.

Annette placed the tray on the little table at the foot of Rose's bed. She paused for a moment to look at the girl sleeping with the straps still around her. It seemed an awful injustice for something so fragile to be held down by something so ugly.

"Shall we take the straps off afore she wakes up Sister?

It might frighten 'er all the more if she finds she can't move. Sure, I don't imagine there's any harm in 'er at all."

"No harm in 'er at all," echoed Theresa. She thought though that it was the harm that was done *to* her that they ought to be interested in. The two women silently began to remove the restraints from around Rose and tuck them expertly back under the mattress. All the time the girl slept soundly. When Theresa settled herself back into the chair, Annette knew that she was relieved of her assignment but before she went she wanted to know one thing –

"D'ya think we can help 'er Sister?" she asked.

"Aye, Annette dear. I think we can."

Rose was dreaming. She was on a beach somewhere, in a cave and it reminded her of the cove at the foot of the hills at Granny's old place. In her dream she remembered that she had spent many a precious time at that cove when she was wee and that there was a small copse of trees there at Granny's old place as well… she remembered lying on the ground in among the trees and looking at the sky through the branches… and she knew that she had felt happy there and that happiness had been on short supply when she was wee. There was a lady in the cave. She was familiar to Rose who often dreamed of her. In the dreams the lady showed her photographs of people who had died. She knew that they were her ancestors from both sides of the family and they all wanted Rose to know who she was. Sometimes they would jump out of the photographs and appear like a living person beside the lady. They would talk of joy and peace and places where these qualities could be found. Always they would tell her she had an important place in the world – that she had a destiny. And always, when Rose awoke she would be overwhelmed with grief at being plunged back into the real world where the only things that made sense were pain and fear. She could never remember the words of her ancestors in her wakeful hours. Now the lady was there again in the same cave. She had no photographs with her and no ancestors came to speak to her. Instead, this time the lady showed her a door that Rose had never noticed before. Behind the door a bright light was shining and although Rose was very reluctant to open the door, the lady seemed keen for her to do so. "Trust," the lady said to her with a warm smile. Rose did without hesitation and she took a first step towards the door. Immediately, it opened and there stood a woman. She had a warm smile and bright blue eyes. Her strawberry blonde hair was braided behind her neck and Rose could see that the woman was beautiful. As they looked at each other in silence a wave of love passed between them and Rose was filled with immense courage. She felt as though she could achieve anything she wanted to and she sensed that somewhere was a place for her – a vision of wholeness – of utter peace, and all she had to do was to start moving towards it. From within her mind, Rose heard the ancestors' voice telling her that the woman was the first stepping stone on her way to that vision and as Rose took one more step forward she saw that the woman wore a nurse's uniform.

Rose turned in the bed and hugged her pillow. She was remembering her dream – something about a woman who was kind to her. She remembered a door and the woman had come through the door or something and she was a nurse – that's right, a nurse. Rose wondered what the dream could have meant. She woke a little bit more as she began to hear people talking somewhere nearby. What were people doing in her bedroom? She opened her eyes suddenly to see a flowery curtain. Those weren't her curtains.

"Hello Rose dear." She turned around to see who had spoken and came face to face with a middle-aged nurse sitting by the bed she was lying on. Rose sat up with a jolt and rapidly took in her surroundings. She was in hospital – that was right. She remembered the pills and the cloudiness and the – Oh, God!! Everything was coming back to her now. "You're in hospital Rose. Do you remember why you're here?" the nurse asked her.

"Aye!" Rose replied.

"Well that's grand then. We know you're not well now pet and we're gonna help ya. Is that okay?"

Rose didn't speak. What did anyone know about her? The nurse smiled and Rose was reminded of the woman from her dream. She had been a nurse too.

"Who are you?" she said politely.

"I'm Sister Theresa Coyle but you can call me Theresa. How does that sound pet?"

"Okay … Theresa?"

"What is it dear?"

Rose's face screwed up and she burst into tears – "I don't wanna be here."

"I know dear, but it'll only be for a short while - until we get ya well again, eh?"

"No, I don't wanna be here, ya don't understand. Please, I wanna be gone – I have to be gone." Rose felt the panic rise up inside her and she had an urgent need to get out of there. Scrambling out of the bed she cast the curtain aside and ran. An alarm sounded somewhere and before she knew what was happening several people were surrounding her. She felt terrified that she was trapped and made a desperate attempt at running through the human barrier. Soon she was being held tightly and carried back to the bed she had just got out of. She didn't put up much of a fight since she knew she had no choice but she yelled at her captors and swore that she was going home. As they carried her back she noticed several patients gawping at her and she yelled at them - "What are ya all lookin' at? Get away from me!"

Back behind the curtain Rose settled down and allowed them to put her on the bed. There were two nurses on either side of her – two at the top and two at the bottom – three women and a man. When they began to tie her down with straps she grabbed the nearest one by the arm. It happened to be the Theresa that was here before. "No, please" she begged. "There's no need for that. I'm not goin' anywhere. Just don't put those on me. Please."

Her face was earnest and Theresa knew that she meant what she said. She addressed the others without taking her eyes from Rose's gaze. "No need for this, I believe. Thanks Connor … Cara. Annette, will ya stay here a while please an' help Rose to get comfortable? Aye that's grand now, thanks everybody. She'll be grand now." Rose watched the older woman as she busied herself with tidying the bed covers, plumping up pillows and arranging them behind her back. She let her fuss over her. There was a feel-good factor about the woman that Rose was eager to soak up. Perhaps it was because she reminded her of the woman in her dream. The other nurse had lifted a tray from the table at the bottom of the bed and had disappeared with it but came back moments later with a jug of iced water and a beaker. Rose was amused at all the fuss and was beginning to wonder if things could get a little better if only for a short while.

"Now Rose, I'm afraid the dinner's ruined but I'll get ya a nice cup of tea and a bit of toast if ya like," said the younger nurse to her. Rose didn't answer. She wasn't sure that she wanted to trust this woman. It was enough to deal with the older woman from her dream for the time being. She couldn't cope with two people trying to get her to act normal, besides she was exhausted.

"What d'ya say pet? Would ya let Annette get ya a wee cup of tea and a bit of toast? It'll do ya the power of good, it will," asked Theresa.

"Yes please." Rose smiled slightly at Theresa and was rewarded with the warm smile from the dream. It was not going to be all bad staying here. She wondered if Paul would come in to see her and her mood dropped again, the good feeling from the nurse's care vanished. There was a familiar empty feeling in her stomach and with it came the sense of crowding all around her. That could only mean one thing – *he* was coming to get her - the devil. No time to think – she shook her head repeatedly and waved her hands in front of her. "No, no, no!" she said again and again trying to get the crowding away from her.

Theresa shot up from her chair and reached out a hand to her saying –"Okay Rose, you're safe. Rose, Rose!"

But Rose didn't feel safe. She knew she wasn't safe. Any moment now the devil would be here and she had been terrorized by the thought of this moment for a long time. She acted out of instinct. She had to prevent him from coming. If she could only punish herself just a little it would be enough to keep him at bay. Beating her head with her fists she began to feel less powerless. Someone, it must have been Theresa, grabbed her wrists to stop her so she flung her head backwards violently against the bars of the bed-stead.

"Rose stop it now. Don't do that. Rose!" Theresa continued to attempt to restrain her but Rose was much younger and stronger than her and she was winning the battle. Theresa let go off one arm just long enough to press the alarm button above the bed. The alarm began to sound loudly and in seconds both Annette and Cara were there helping her to restrain Rose.

Rose's fear grew and grew and with each vain struggle to gain control she felt herself slipping into the nets of hell. "No… Mummy…help me! Oh my God, they're demons. I'm goin' to hell. Get them away, get them away!" she roared in sheer terror. The demons were pinning her down, putting huge straps around her. They worked in silence as darkness fell all around them and then, behind the curtain she heard him breathe. The curtain flew to the side and Rose saw him for the first time. His eyes were black, as black as coals, and he had a huge mane of black hair. As he reached out his hands to her she felt the force of his evil sweep over her and she thought she might die at that very moment. She heard her own screams as if from a distance and as they died off she lost sight of him completely. She felt herself being carried down and down into a bottomless pit of incredible, breath-taking fear. Submitting herself to the inevitable, she let go off the fight and began to float in what seemed to be nothingness. The devil and his demons were gone – there was no hospital, no nurse, no bed – nothing at all except a feeling of floating in black space. And there was no fear and no pain, only being. To Rose it felt like utter respite. She was still alive. She knew that thought well. It haunted her every morning she awoke – the mix of shock and disappointment of knowing she was still alive and the relief of knowing that she wasn't in hell – not just yet.

In the tiny office at the top of the ward Sister Theresa

Coyle, nurses Annette McKinney and Cara O'Hagan, and Doctor Connor Pritchard stood in a group drinking coffee and discussing the latest turn of events. "We'll let her sleep that off for now but I suggest she stay on a low dose until Doctor McCavert sees her tomorrow. I can't go over his head." the doctor said. He was annoyed at being called away from his chicken curry which was now a congealed mess in the foil container. "Damn," he complained, "totally inedible." He chucked the curry into the brown paper take-out bag and threw it into the waste paper basket beside the desk. Theresa frowned and the younger nurses both looked to her for their lead. None of the women complained out loud. Connor Pritchard was known to be a bit of a bully and they all tip-toed around him and his volatile temper.

"Right so!" said Theresa, cheerfully rubbing her hands together. "Been a bit of a day indeed. Annette dear, if you could get the patients settled down for the night that'd be grand now, and Cara dear, I'll need ya to get Rose McDevit's admissions for Doctor Pritchard."

"Should we not have to do them again Sister? Now that she's.... well ya' know...erm'... do we have to do them with *her* I mean?" asked Cara who was still in awe of the whole thing and if was totally honest, was a little afraid of Rose. Doctor Pritchard exited the office with a glare at Theresa that said – what kind of muppets do you have working for you?

"Aye, we do dear. But bring them now to his lordship afore he starts all together," Theresa smiled reassuringly at her young charge.

"Rose's wrath might not be the only one we face today, eh?" Annette giggled.

"Ah now there pet, there's no need for that."

"Sorry sister."

In the days and weeks that followed Theresa kept a very watchful eye indeed on Rose. She learned that her initial instinct about Rose was spot on. She certainly conveyed an ability to connect with people on their level. Many of the patients who had chatted with her seemed to come alive in different ways. Where they had been depressed and withdrawn before, they were now sociable and cheerful. Old Janey Gorman had given up the quest to hurt her sons and was now fussing over them like she used to. It wouldn't be long now before she was moved into a nice rest home somewhere where she could have her own space. Theresa had gotten to know Rose herself having chosen to spend her breaks in the ward with a sandwich just so she would have time to talk with her. The girl had a huge sadness within her and her fear was awesome to say the least. Theresa was convinced there was nothing mentally amiss other than the illusions she experienced when she was acting out her fear. The panic attacks became fewer as each week passed, largely due to the drugs and although Rose was clearly in need of psychotherapy, Theresa believed that what she needed most was to be understood. Rose's case had started her thinking again about becoming a counsellor and helping people in that way. Oh, the doctors had all done their tests and discussed their theories about her case but at the end of the day, Rose McDevit was no more insane than she was. Today was Sunday and the visitors were always in good supply on a Sunday. Theresa hoped that maybe today Rose's family might come to see her and offer some encouragement for her to get well but it wasn't to be. It was eight o'clock in the evening now and most of the visitors were gone leaving just the few over-concerned relatives left to fuss about their loved ones. Theresa's shift was over at eight but she decided to stay and have a cup of tea with Rose before she went.

"Here we are dear," she said brightly as she sat two cups of tea down on the little table at the bottom of the bed and wheeled it around to where Rose could reach it. Rose was still on high dependency watch and had to stay in her nightwear all the time so she didn't like to stray too far from the bed. She lifted her cup from the saucer. Theresa had brought her two chocolate biscuits and had once again put sugar in her tea. She took a sip and grimaced at the sweetness. "Drink it up," chirped Theresa, "It'll do ya the power of good." Rose was more concerned about the calories. She took the tea but left the biscuits. "I'm off home in a minute pet. Is there anything ya want afore I go?"

"No, s'pose not … Theresa?"

"Yes dear?"

"Thanks for being so good to me. I mean, ya don't have to."

"Why for ever not dear? You're worth it."

Rose knew that wasn't true but it felt good to hear it. "Theresa?"

"What is it dear?"

"Ya know when I came in first?"

"Aye?"

"Well, what did I say? I mean, I can't remember what I said about...ya'know!"

"About the overdose, dear?"

"Aye," Rose hung her head.

"Ya never said anythin' dear..." Theresa watched Rose's reactions with a hawk's eye and continued "...d'ya remember anythin' at all about those first two weeks?" She knew she was going out on a limb here but the opportunity was ripe to see what had actually been going on for Rose during her 'silence' as Theresa liked to call it. Rose put her cup back on the table and leaned back against a mountain of pillows. She stared for a while at two little birds jumping about from branch to branch of a beautiful crack willow just on the other side of the window. After several minutes during which she seemed to lose herself she turned back to Theresa and said in a whisper -

"I remember you..."

Theresa's heart fluttered in her chest and she smiled warmly at Rose whom she had come to think of as her little wounded bird.

"...I remember yer smile."

Rose hung her head again and Theresa looked at her in silence. She was exuberant. She had made a difference

– a connection. Night after night at home in bed, she had argued with herself that nothing she did or said made any difference to Rose, but here she was, telling her that she had – that she had made a connection. Theresa said a silent thank you to her God in her heart.

"Rose?" She clasped her hand around Rose's fingers tightly so that she wouldn't pull away. She didn't. "Where were you dear? All that time since, ya know… where were ya?"

"I think I was hiding," Rose answered in a way that showed she had given that a lot of thought.

"Who from dear?" Theresa asked her.

Rose took a deep breath. She lifted her head and shook it from side to side, trying to hold back the tears. "The devil!" she whined, and she cried, allowing Theresa's arms to wrap about her. For a long five minutes, the two women remained like that until the tears cried themselves out and they were both exhausted. Theresa got up and busied herself with pulling the curtains around the bed. Instinctively she pulled the curtains across the window as well. It was still light out but she needed to be acting like a nurse to appease the professional conscience niggling at her for getting too attached. Before the two curtains met she saw the crack willow and another little voice told her to leave the curtains open so that Rose could see her tree and take comfort from it. Theresa stood looking at it for a while and the thought came to her that she and that tree were probably the only tangible things Rose had to keep her from slipping further away from sanity.

Where in under God am I getting these ideas from? she asked herself, but although she couldn't explain it and was sure anyone else would say she had lost the plot, she knew that simply being with Rose on her level was revealing something very intense from within herself. It was as if she was coming alive for the first time since she was a child, when everything was simple and the world was a magical place and nothing was impossible. She turned to Rose to say something to her. It would be going against all professional ethics entirely but she was finding it difficult not to say it. She wanted to say that Rose could depend on her to be there for her, that she believed in her and that no matter what she revealed to her, she wouldn't abandon her. Theresa was a great one for believing that God provides the answers when the need comes and just then her God delivered. The cubicle curtain was pulled aside a little from behind and an elderly gentleman popped his head through –

"Hello…Rosie? Can I come in?"

"Gerry!" Rose exclaimed. The elderly man came in and introduced himself to Theresa.

"I'm Rosie's uncle, Gerry McDevit. It's a bit late I know but the missions are on this week ya see. Just come straight from the chapel."

"Yer alright there, Mr McDevit" replied Theresa. "Come on ahead. Sure it's not too late at all now. If that's alright with Rose of course." She looked at Rose and was pleased to see that she was smiling. Rose nodded her head and

Theresa left with a lightness in her heart that said *now then Theresa, no need to get too involved, the old boy will look after her well.* And she knew that it was true.

Gerry McDevit was great for a man in his seventies. 'Even with two plastic hips he gets about in his wee car the very best ya ever seen. An' he never neglects the chapel. A right wee holy man he is' - that was the general word about Gerry in his local town of Drumgar. Everybody knew him and his long-suffering wife Anna. They had lived in Drumgar ever since they wed and had raised five big strong sons in one little three-bedroomed town house. Gerry had four brothers himself, of which the youngest was Sean, Rose's father. He had always been fond of children and wee Rosie had been the apple of his eye. He and Anna had always been very keen to see Sean and Clare coming with the children and although wee Rosie was always quiet and withdrawn, Gerry could tell that there was something very special about the child, despite the dismissive way that mother of hers had treated her.

Gerry pulled back the chair that Theresa had recently vacated and sat down. He plonked a big paper bag bursting with shiny green apples down on his niece's lap.

"Well now young Rosie, there's a wee loch o' apples for ya. They'll soon get ya fightin' fit again."

"Thanks Gerry," smiled Rose, a little apprehensive of what was coming next. Was he going to give her a lecture about what she had done? Anna certainly would. She and Gerry talked politely for a while and it soon became clear that he was not there to give off or to be cross in any way. Rose relaxed and began to enjoy the company as it was a change from the normal routine of the night. It hadn't really bothered her at all, actually, that none of her family had come to see her. Well, not much really, and she supposed it couldn't have been helped since her mum wasn't too well herself and her dad was probably looking after her. She did think that Angela might have come but she had her own life and her babies of course and that took up a lot of time, and the boys… well, she wouldn't expect them to come into a place like this. Caroline wouldn't come for sure, there was no wondering about that. Anyway, she truly was not disappointed, not in the slightest. Gerry stayed until ten o'clock and had to be asked to leave by Annette who was on the night shift and who hadn't seen him come in. She didn't even know he was there until she heard laughter coming from Rose's cubicle and recognized a man's voice. She had been so delighted to see Rose with a visitor that she allowed him to stay on a bit after visiting hours were long over. There was a nice atmosphere among the staff that night as they discussed Rose's visitor and how he was keeping her going with his jokes and stories.

"Bless her, the wee pet," Annette said for the third time grinning at the latest eruption of laughter from the cubicle.

"You'd best be careful Annette," remarked a young student nurse, "You're starting to sound like Sister Coyle."

Aye and that wouldn't be a bad thing, thought Annette happily to herself.

And so Rose stayed in the psychiatric wing of Drumgar Area Hospital for eight weeks during which the devil came for her several times. Each time he came and went without her and Rose clung on to the hope that the good in her would win out in the end.

Chapter Nine

'Back to roots'

Londonderry Airport, Ireland, April 2008

There was quite a queue at the car rental desk. Lissy sat down on a bench beside a European couple and waited for John to come back. The airport was thronged with travellers despite the fact that it was still only April. Lissy could only imagine what the tiny airport would be like in the holiday season. She watched the people for a while, some standing in long lines for check-in desks and some scurrying past pulling large cases or weighed down with back-packs. The couple beside her had a modest sized, bright cerise coloured case with a purple handle around which the girl was now tying an equally bright bandana. She noticed Lissy watching her and smiled politely. "I can see my bag with this," she said, to explain her reason for the bandana. Lissy failed to see how anyone could miss a bright cerise case with a purple handle. She smiled back at the girl and casually enquired as to where she and her companion were travelling to. "We go to Cork," she replied, "in South Ireland. At the bottom of the country I understand. You are not Irish I think, your accent is different?"

"I'm English but I was born in Ireland, in County Mayo. That's in Southern Ireland as well." Lissy felt good to know something about her birth place that the girl didn't know. "Do you live there then, in Cork I mean, or are you just visiting?

"My husband," answered the girl, indicating the man beside her, "he have a job in Cork. He will build houses there."

"Oh, well I wish you both luck."

"The luck of the Irish, yes?" the girl grinned.

"Of course, the luck of the Irish," Lissy echoed and then she added – "You're English is very good."

"Thank you, I learn English when I was a girl. Are you here for holiday?"

"My mother lives here." Lissy told her. Well, that was probably true.

"That is nice," the girl replied and then indicated that she must go and check in.

"Bye!" Lissy smiled as they waved to her. *Well*, she said to herself, *my mother may well live here and I may well be on my way to finding her. Just as soon as John comes back with our transport that is.*

John had been wonderful so far with his research and

endless enquiries into this and that. If it had been left up to her alone she would never have known where to turn, but as it was, they were here in Ireland and about to go to Cloughbeg itself, where she was born. She had purchased a map of Ireland in the airport shop and opened it up now, on the empty bench space beside her. It took a while for her to find Londonderry which was in the North of the country and when she saw how close they were to County Mayo, she began to feel very excited. She traced the main route with her finger down into Mayo where she stopped and circled the map with the same finger, looking for Cloughbeg. For almost ten minutes she scanned the county again and again but there was no Cloughbeg to be found. She was starting to get discouraged when John arrived back.

"What are you doing there Lissy, looking for Cloughbeg?" he asked sitting down on the map.

Lissy thumped his arm playfully and then said rather impatiently - "It's not here. I've looked and looked for ages but I can't find it."

"That's because it's not on the map," stated John getting up and retrieving the map from beneath his bottom.

"What do you mean?"

"Exactly that. It's not on the map. I was talking to an old boy up there in the queue. He's from Galway apparently. So I asked him if he knew of Cloughbeg in County Mayo." John stopped talking and straightened the map out on his lap.

"And?" She gave him another thump on the arm.

"Ow! That hurt!" He grabbed her hand and held it tight so that she couldn't do it again, although it was a good excuse to get holding her hand.

"What did he say?" She liked the feel of his hand on hers. John looked into her eyes intensely and she looked away for fear of what she might feel. Right now the most important thing was to concentrate on where they were going. He let go off her hand and said in a flat tone –

"Cloughbeg is only a town-land he said. It wouldn't be on a map like that. We need a land map of the surrounding area he said."

"Where the hell do we get one of them?" interrupted Lissy.

"Well, I'm sure we'll get one somewhere, when we get closer to the place."

"But we don't know where Cloughbeg is do we? Only that it's in Mayo and that's quite a big area if you look at the map."

"We don't have to. We know exactly where Cloughbeg is," said John triumphantly.

"What?"

"The old boy knows exactly where Cloughbeg is," he said. "He's been there before many times he said. He used to bring his family to a place called Drumgar for their summer holidays. Cloughbeg is right on the coast there and they'd often go and visit little coves around the coast. Apparently there are all these caves that you can get into and the sand is a white as snow."

"Sounds nice, doesn't it? Oh John, we're almost there. Isn't it great?"

"Yea, it's looking good. Cloughbeg is only a few little shops really, the old boy said, and some of the coves are inaccessible from the road but well worth the walk over the hills if one is prepared to climb."

"Wow! Oh, did you ask him if there was a parochial house?"

"Course, silly. I'm not just a good-looking face you know."

Lissy laughed feeling on a high now that they were getting close to their goal. John went on –

"He's not sure about that but he says there is a chapel there just outside the village so he reckons the parochial house wouldn't be too far away."

"And that's where we find Father Sean Murphy," stated Lissy clapping her hands with glee.

"Not exactly, silly. The man's been dead for fifteen years remember."

"You know what I mean. Oh John, we're close. I can feel it." Lissy was practically jumping up and down on the bench. She had a grip of John's arm and she was squeezing it so tight John thought she might cut off the circulation. "Now all we have to do is find the parochial house and this Father Devon guy and then he'll tell us the name of the adoption agency and they'll tell us my mother's name and where we can find her and then, phew! Oh John, I can't wait. I just can't... What?"

John was staring at her half laughing with amusement. Her excitement was infectious and it made him feel happy to see her so enthusiastic. She was being a tad too enthusiastic though since he had spoken to this *Father Devon guy*, as she had called him and it turned out he didn't have as much information as Lissy would like.

"Father *Devlin* honey. The man's name is Father Devlin," he told her with a grin.

"So?"

"So that's his name – Father Devlin – not Devon."

"You told me his name was Devon. Did you not?"

John shook his head, still grinning. "Well, I bet he'd like to be called Devon. It such a beautiful place. I knew a girl once – her name was Elizabeth Dorset. A lot of people knew her as Lizzy Dorset which is almost the same as Lissy isn't it? Anyway, imagine being called Lissy Devon – wouldn't that be gorgeous? Do you think is Devon a common name in Cloughbeg? Wouldn't it be wonderful if my mother's name is Devon too – that would make me Lissy Devon wouldn't it? Well, kinda." Lissy caught her breath and looked at John expectantly.

"Whoa girl, slow down," laughed John, and he brushed a loose curl away from Lissy's eye.

"What?" She said, getting a little impatient with his lack of interest in the fact that they were finally getting there.

"You're going cuckoo on me honey." Lissy hated the way he had taken to calling her that. "The priest is called Devlin – not Devon, and even if he *was* called Devon that wouldn't necessarily mean that just 'cos he's called after a county in England he's gonna pull out all the stops to help us. And…"

"Yeah well," Lissy interrupted, getting up from the bench and gathering her things in a huff, "You would say that. You haven't even met this Father *Devlin* and already you're not even giving him a chance, just as you never gave poor Father Kearns a chance. And while we're on the subject, you never gave Bobby a chance either, did you?"

"Oh here we go. I was wondering when you'd get around to that. For your information honey, we weren't on the subject which is beside the point. The point is the man's a loony."

"I'm not gonna listen to this!" Lissy ranted, "and I don't need you telling me what to do with my own life. If I want past life therapy I'll have past life therapy and no-one can tell me otherwise. Okay? *Honey!"* And with that she stormed off pulling her case behind her and attempting to fold her precious map with one hand.

What the…? John muttered to himself. *Here she goes again*. Why did she have to be so defensive at times? All he was trying to do was protect her from own naiveté really. He grabbed his stuff and caught up with her. "What are you doing Lissy?"

"I'm going to get myself a cup of tea…if that's okay with you of course," she added sarcastically.

There was a small café just to the right of the check-in desks. John guided her towards it in silence. Best to let her calm down for a bit. He thought about Marcus and how he'd called her the ice-maiden. He said to him once – "John, old boy, you just gotta let her get all fired at times. Gets her nice and warmed up if you know what I mean." He would have knocked the stupid smirk right off his bloody face had Lissy not been due to arrive. He was glad he hadn't though because he knew Marcus hadn't meant to be a creep. He was just a bit under the influence after all.

John looked sideways at Lissy now. She was livid, going by the look on her face. He had seen that look several times since they met with Bobby, and Lissy would rant and rave until she burned herself out. And although it may have seemed to be about that situation amongst other equally insignificant things, John knew that Lissy was only finding ways to vent her frustration and passion about herself, albeit unconsciously of course. Her passion was what he loved most about her. Without that she may as well be a nobody. But her passion was intense: it was fiery and screaming with life. It could be seen in her paintings. Take for example *A Mother's Love*. The way that she portrayed the love of the mother for the child was pure genius. Maybe it was because he knew how much her birth mother meant to her but whenever he looked at that painting he could feel the intensity and the sheer ferocity of the mother's love. He saw that same power in Lissy when she raged and he often wondered if he would be able to survive it should she choose to love him. He had made his choice though and wild horses couldn't keep him away from her. If the power of her love should prove too much for him to contain then *bring it on*. Should he be blasted apart with its intensity then he'd die in a million pieces and be eternally ecstatic.

They squeezed their way through a throng of tiny café tables and sat down surrounded by luggage. He watched as she picked up a menu from the table and scanned it over and over, her eyes not really seeing what was written on it. As each moment came and went her face relaxed more and soon she was almost back to being the tired Lissy who got off the plane. He would have preferred to see the enthusiastic Lissy that he had so unintentionally crushed ten minutes ago but a calm, albeit tired, Lissy was enough for now. He would have to find a better way to keep her from getting too disappointed when they reached Cloughbeg. The truth was there shouldn't have been any reason why they had to come to Ireland. He had spoken to Father Devlin on the phone and he was even vaguer than Father Kearns had been. No-one seemed to know what had been the case all those years ago. He would have thought it would be a simple matter of contacting the adoption agency but that was just it – there was no information regarding an adoption agency at all; at least, none that these priests were aware of. If John had been completely honest with Lissy he would have told her of his fears before they came here. He should have told her that things weren't adding up and that although Father Devlin seemed honest enough, he was convinced that the old Kearns boy was hiding something. Instead, he told her that she had to go to Father Devlin in person and prove who she was before he would give her what information he had. She had been so excited and so positive that he couldn't dash her dreams. So he decided that when they got to Ireland, they would try local knowledge to gain the information they needed. As a journalist, John was aware that no amount of research into historical records and so forth was a match for local knowledge. He was convinced that in Cloughbeg, there was a wealth of information waiting for them, as long as they find the right people to ask.

He quietly breathed a sigh of relief when Lissy turned to look at him and said very sheepishly –

"Do you know what I don't understand."

"What?"

"I don't see why Father Devon couldn't just give you directions to Cloughbeg."

"I know. Like I said, I did ask him and he said it was on the map – a straightforward run from the North. That's why we didn't fly to Dublin. He said the road was much more straightforward from here and that we'd be there in no time."

"But it's not on the map."

"Not this one. Anyway, all's well that ends well and we've got the directions we need, so we don't have to call him again until we get there."

"Until we get to Drumgar you mean, and then we need directions to Cloughbeg."

"No problem honey. We'll sort that out when we get the length," John said, smiling warmly hoping to make her feel better.

She smiled back not minding at all that he had called her honey again. John felt that was much better and he took the menu out of her hand saying –

"But first we ought to fill up for the journey. Somehow, I'm not so sure about Father Devlin's idea of no time at all."

"Father Devon!" giggled Lissy, "What *am* I like?" She was feeling much lighter now.

They ordered their food and spent the next hour lazily eating and teasing each other. They had a long journey ahead and God knows how many obstacles they'd find when they got there, but for now it was good just to be in each other's company, laughing and joking and knowing that a full ten days of glorious spring weather and no work stretched ahead.

Lissy threw herself onto the big bed in the tiny little guest house, Hawthorn Cottage. She lay back and surveyed the ceiling. Huge big cracks went along it and Lissy suspected they went the whole way down the walls too though the heavy wallpaper covered them up. The room was tiny and there was a distinct smell of damp and mildew in the air. The bed she lay on was huge, filling almost the entire room. It had a great big mahogany headboard and a patchwork quilt the likes of which Lissy swore she had seen before in a museum somewhere. A threadbare mat lay beside the bed and a little wooden locker with a lamp on top which might have come out of the same museum as the quilt. In the corner of the room stood a wardrobe and chest of drawers – both modern but tiny. Still, she hadn't much stuff with her so they'd do fine. She thought the window and the curtains were the sweetest things ever; the walls of the house must have been at least two feet deep to provide such a deep window sill on which was placed a glass vase of daffodils and a statue of Mary the Mother of Jesus. The curtains were white with little bluebells all over them and pretty bluebell coloured ribbons tying them back with a bow. As she lay on the bed she stared out through the tiny window at the stars in the night sky. She thought of her birth mother and wondered if she was under the same sky right at that moment. Bobby had said that when she found her biological roots it would be a huge healing for her soul. He reckoned that it was important for her to know her true self – the true nature of who she is, he said. By discovering her physical origin in this world she would open the way to knowing her spiritual origin and when she knew that with every part of her being then she would be home and discover that it was all she ever wanted in the first place – to be home. Lissy kind of understood him at the time but now it all seemed so confusing. She thought of her mum and dad back home in England and wondered if they worrying about her. A pang of guilt niggled at her until she decided to call them. She had promised Mum that she'd call as soon as she arrived in Ireland but she had copped out with a text which she did feel very guilty about at the time, since neither Mum nor Dad were keen on the mobile phone she bought them for Christmas and neither of them had a clue how to text back. She fished her mobile from her bag and dialled her home number, then sat back against the giant headboard, looked out the window and waited.

"Hello," it was Mum's voice.

"Hi Mum, it's me."

"Lissy dear, thank God you phoned. Your father and I couldn't make out that message thingy you sent. Are you alright dear? Did you get there alright?"

"I'm fine Mum... we're both fine. We're here anyway. It's been a long day but we're okay."

"And you found the place alright then?"

"Yes, it was easy actually. Well, we're not exactly there yet. We're in a town called Drumgar. We'll go to Cloughbeg in the morning. It's just five miles from here apparently."

"You will be careful now dear, won't you? And keep a close eye on your belongings, you don't know what these small towns are like."

"Mum! How can you say that? You're from a small town in Ireland yourself."

"That's different dear. It was such a long time ago and things change. If your Nan and Grandad were living they'd look after you but as it is there's just Auntie Margaret. Are you sure you don't want me to call her dear? I'm sure she wouldn't mind."

"Mum, I'm not a baby. I can look after myself you know. Besides, John is taking very good care of me. He really has been great, Mum. Anyway, Auntie Margaret lives in Waterford. That's a long way from here."

"Is it dear? Never mind. I'm sure John knows what he's doing? Where is he now dear?"

Lissy shook her head in disbelief – Mum was actually fishing to see if they were sharing a room together. She wasn't sure if she'd be happy or disappointed to learn that they weren't so she decided to leave it open. "He's outside locking the car up for the night." she said.

"I see, give him my love dear. Here, your father wants to speak to you."

"Hello dear."

"Hi Daddy."

"So you got there alright then?"

"We did."

"And when do you intend to see this Father Devon then?"

"We've spoken to him already Daddy and we'll go see him tomorrow morning. Oh, and his name's not Devon as it turns out. It's Devlin. Apparently I heard John wrong."

"Devlin? Is that an Irish name then? I know several people named Devlin as it happens."

"I don't know Daddy. What does it matter anyway?"

"Doesn't matter to me dear, but your mum will be

devastated. She reckons that Devon is actually named after an Irish settler by that name."

"But that's ridiculous Daddy."

"Well, she's got it into her head now that she's right so if you don't mind I'll not tell her about the Devlin bit. No point in disappointing her."

"Oh Daddy, you do encourage her but you are a darling. I shall miss you Daddy."

"We'll miss you too dear. Say hello to John for me and tell him he'd best take good care of my little girl."

"I will." There was a few silent moments after which Lissy said – "I'll give you a ring and let you know how we get on tomorrow."

"You do that dear, bye bye now."

"Bye Daddy, tell Mum I love her."

"Will do."

Lissy hung up. There came a knock on the door – "Lissy, are you decent? I thought we'd go into the town and get some supper. What do you say?"

"Come on in John," shouted Lissy.

John came in and stood at the bottom of the bed. It was the only space for him to stand in actually. He stood with his hands in his pockets like a schoolboy as she sat there on the huge bed. She replaced the mobile in her bag keeping her head down so that he wouldn't see her amusement. "I just called home" she told him. "Mum sends her love and Daddy says you'd best take good care of his little girl."

"So how am I doing so far?" John asked.

"Well enough," she shrugged and then having seen his reaction, laughed.

"Just well enough, is that all I get for moving hell and high water to get you here?"

She looked at him lovingly and added – "I wouldn't want to be with anyone else."

"That's better." John replied staring into her eyes. He made to go before he lost all control of himself and jumped on her then and there. "I'll wait for you in the hall" he added.

"Okay."

She wasn't sure she wanted him to go. The door closed behind him and she stared at it for a while musing over the moment they just had. She suddenly was aware of how tired and dirty she must look after the journey. It had taken all of three and half hours to get here. Jumping up from the bed she opened her case and took out the nice cream trouser suit she was saving for tomorrow and draped it over the museum quilt. In the bathroom across the corridor she washed up and brushed her teeth. Back in the room, she brushed her hair and left it down around her shoulders the way John liked it. Then, having put a full fresh make-up on, she dressed in her new outfit and stood in front of the tiny wardrobe viewing herself in the full length mirror. What a transformation! A quick spray of perfume and she was ready.

"Wow!" exclaimed John when she entered the hall, "you look amazing. We're only going for a quick bite of supper you know."

Typical of a man to take the good out of it, Lissy thought. She tried to concentrate on the wow and gave him one of her melting smiles which was lost on him. If Lissy knew anything about John Brunt so far, it was that when he was hungry he couldn't think about anything else and now he was hungry.

"What kept you so long? I didn't think it would take you the best part of half an hour to look so beautiful" he said. He was forgiven.

"You never know who I might meet tonight. Do we have to walk? These heels will murder me."

"Gosh no, it's a fair bit into the town from here. We'll take the car. I don't feel like drinking anyway. I'm dog tired. Aren't you dog tired?"

"Whacked," admitted Lissy. "Do we need a key to get back in later?"

"Got it."

When Lissy slipped under the museum quilt later that night she was so tired she ought to have been asleep before her head hit the pillow. As it was, she lay wide awake looking at the stars through the tiny window. She was excited about seeing Cloughbeg for the first time, and the clock on the hall had struck three times before she slept. She dreamed of tiny little coves with silver sand and gold-filled caves and when she entered into them expecting to find her mother she found instead John's wide grin and twinkling blue eyes enchanting her with his magic.

They shut the car doors and studied the directions that the guest house owner, Mrs Doyle, had given them which told them exactly how to get to Cloughbeg. No detail was left out, right down to every bend in the road. "It's a wonder she never told us exactly how many trees we pass and how high the hedges are," laughed Lissy, on a high. The sun was well and truly out and by the look of the cloudless sky there was a promise of a glorious spring Monday. They had been up since seven and down the stairs into the breakfast room for seven thirty since their appointment with Father Devlin was for nine and they wanted to give themselves plenty of time should they have difficulty finding him. They ate bacon and eggs with a kind of toasted bread and some sort of flat doughy thing which Mrs Doyle said was called soda farl and purty bread. Mrs Doyle was lovely and both John and Lissy had taken an instant liking to her. They had to listen very carefully to her since she spoke so fast and had strange words for things and they had to stop her several times to ask for a translation.

"Yill heddy watch yoursels on thon road mine," she had said when giving the directions, "meet a sowl on that road an yill be in the shuck afore ya knows it."

"I think she meant to be careful because the local people in Cloughbeg don't take kindly to strangers," Lissy said now as they put the directions down and started on their way.

"Your guess is as good as mine, honey," John replied bewildered.

"What we do know is that we must go into the main street in the town where we were last night and take the road to Lisnablaney" said Lissy going over the directions one last time. "We go about one kilometre on that road passed the white chapel with the green spire, past the two storey farm-house with stone pillars at the end of the lane…"

"Don't forget the pot of daffodils on each pillar," John butted in with amusement.

Lissy shook her head laughing – "Okay, passed the white chapel with the green spire, passed the two storey farmhouse with stone pillars with a pot of daffodils on top, and it's the next on the left. And, if we come to a hawthorn tree that has bits of material hanging on it we've gone too far."

"There it is then, simple!" said John, "Why didn't you say that in the first place?"

That remark earned him a thump on the arm to which he responded – "Well, if you want to get back to your Irish roots then you ought to start thinking like the Irish."

"I'm in too good a mood to be teased today. It won't work, so you may as well give up now."

"I only do it 'cos you're so easy to wind up honey," John admitted. "If you'd only lighten up more you might actually enjoy the ride."

"Listen *honey,*" she retorted, "you're not gonna enjoy this ride if you get us lost, so keep a look out for Lisnablaney Road on your side and I'll look on this side."

"Ha! Very witty! You're learning. Here we are," he said indicating a turn on his right. Lissy stopped chatting and sat up straighter in the car seat eager not to miss the landmarks and feeling more and more excited. They did their best to measure one kilometre as the clock on the car registered miles and they were very pleased with themselves when they both announced that the white chapel with the green spire must be coming into view about now. They were right – Mrs Doyle was right – there was the chapel complete with a green spire and a sweet little white stone wall that separated the grounds from the road. "Now for the farmhouse and the pillars," said John. "She didn't say how far that was from the chapel."

"Bugger!" tutted Lissy.

They found the farmhouse easily enough but the left-hand road was no distance from it as it turned out and they had driven straight passed it and on for another ten minutes when they decided they must have made a mistake. On the way back they chided themselves for not having noticed a hawthorn tree stuck in the middle of a field. On its branches hung hundreds of white rags – they would have to remember to ask Mrs Doyle about that this evening. The road to Cloughbeg was narrow – so narrow that whenever they met another car they had to squeeze into the ditch to allow room to pass. They met a tractor on the road also and had to back up for several yards to find a place wide enough for it to pass. Eventually, they came to a T-junction onto a much wider road. There was a signpost stuck into the ground opposite with 'Tra' written on it.

"Go right here I think," frowned John. "'Tra' is Gaelic

for beach. I'm sure I heard that somewhere."

"I think you're right," replied Lissy just wanting to get off that road and onto one that looked like it went somewhere.

"Yeah, and if the beach is this way then Cloughbeg is this way. Why don't they just say Cloughbeg, left or right?"

They turned off right and were delighted to see that the landscape was getting rather sandy.

"Did you ever see so much stone?" he said in awe of the huge mountains of rock on either side of the road as they drove along. "It's like the Grand Canyon in places."

"That's why there's so many stone walls in Ireland you know, because of all the stone just lying about everywhere," piped up Lissy proudly, "Mum told us that a load of times."

John smiled. She was so innocent and uncomplicated. He was just about to tease her again when some buildings came into view. "Cloughbeg I presume," he announced with a grin.

"We hope," corrected Lissy and then gave a squeal of delight when she read a little white sign on the roadside. "Yes, Cloughbeg."

"That old boy at the airport wasn't wrong," laughed John catching Lissy's giddiness, "Blimey! It's only a few houses really. Where are the shops?"

"I think we just passed them," giggled Lissy, "let's find somewhere to stop."

"Well there's no car-park that I can see. I'm just gonna

abandon her" John giggled pulling the car into the side of the narrow street.

"So what now?" asked Lissy. "Ask someone where the parochial house is? I don't even see a chapel."

"No, it's only just gone eight fifteen. We're too early. Let's have a walk about since it's so sunny and we'll find the chapel ourselves. Besides, I don't really want to disturb anyone this early. The shops probably don't open till nine at least."

"True."

As it turned out Cloughbeg really was only a few dwellings and shops lined along both sides of one very short street. At one end of the street was the road they had come along, stretching out into the rocky countryside, and at the other end of the street was the same road running straight on towards the sea. However, there was another little road at that end that went up to the right of the village. Lissy and John decided to walk that way for a bit. The road was even narrower than the main street, and very sandy. It went up the cliff-side quite steeply until it came to a sharp right turn when it levelled out into a viewpoint. They stopped there and looked around them. They could see for miles out over the bay. The early morning sun splayed its white gold light over the water and highlighted each wave with little sparkling tips as the seagulls swooped above shrieking with sheer delight in the abundance of the silver surf.

"It's beautiful," Lissy sighed.

"Beautiful," John barely whispered with his gaze fixed

on her face lit up with the early morning glory. Lissy heard him and knew that he wasn't talking about the view. A warm feeling filled her, mixing with the tingling awareness of the beauty before her and she thought that she was the most blessed person in all the world. At that very moment she was home. She drank in the loveliness of the surroundings and then turned to face John who opened his arms to allow her to come to him. With their arms around each other tightly and their faces touching, Lissy felt herself softening in the warmth of his body and when she lifted her head to meet his lips with hers, hot tears of release spilled down her cheeks wetting his face with her own. When the kiss ended John wiped her cheeks with his hand and said tenderly – "What is it my love?"

"Oh John, I feel so peaceful… like I'll never be alone again."

"You won't darling. I'll always be here. You know I'd do anything for you, to make you happy. You know that don't you?"

"Yes I do now darling. It's just I feel so alone at times like I'll never really be accepted as who I am. I know Mum and Dad love me and I know you love me but it's never enough. It's as if I'm searching for my birth mother to find out who I am when really inside I know who I am. And I suppose I think that if she could love me, really love me, all of me, then I could feel accepted and love me too. Does that make sense?"

"I think that makes perfect sense," replied John taking

her in his embrace once more.

Lissy began to feel braver than she'd ever been in her life and she continued – "And now that we're here in the place where I was born it feels like, well it feels like I'm home and it's wonderful. But it's not just because I'm here in Cloughbeg. It's because of this beautiful scene and it's you."

"Me?"

"Yes, it's like I can feel you inside of me. You're a part of me and you're a part of this whole wonderful moment. I love you John. I'm so sorry I never told you but I didn't know myself. I guess I was scared but now I'm not. Now, everything is so clear to me. I love you and I never want to let you go."

"Oh darling, I've waited to hear you say that for so long," groaned John as their lips met again. The two lovers remained in each other's embrace until a cold breeze began to blow and they felt chilled. Shivering with cold and excitement they hurried down the road clinging to each other for warmth. They giggled like two schoolchildren who had experienced their first kiss and as they neared the main street of the village they raced each other down the final stretch. A light drizzle had begun to fall and Lissy looked up into the sky. There was a huge black rain cloud blowing towards them and as it passed in front of the sun the morning was transformed into a grey foreboding of a darker day to come.

Lissy shivered –"John, I have a bad feeling. I don't think this is going to be too easy."

"Come on darling," he said in a low voice, "if it's bad news then we'll meet it head on, together."

Chapter Ten

Nightmares and demons

They say that at night when we sleep we pass through the conscious mind into the realm of the unconscious. The dreams we have are sometimes our subconscious making sense of our experiences and sometimes, like Rose, our dream world reflects what our conscious mind dreads to remember.

February 1988, Drumgar Outpatients Clinic

"Were you ever sexually abused?" Dorothy Owens asked Rose.

"No," was the honest reply.

"In my line of work, I get to hear all sorts of things. Did you know that one in four women in Ireland have experienced sexual assault at some time in their life?"

"My God!"

"I know. It's shocking isn't it? But those are the facts

and certainly in my profession one comes across many such cases. I had to ask because it helps me at this stage to rule out possibilities. So, you were saying about your childhood?"

Dorothy Owens was a behavioural therapist. After getting out of the hospital Rose had thought a lot about the things Theresa Coyle had said to her. She had been lovely and she liked Rose which put her high on a pedestal as far as Rose was concerned. She had convinced her to go for counselling, perhaps a little psychotherapy. "It won't do ya any harm pet," she had said, "and if ya don't think it's helpin' any ya can always just stop goin'. Nobody's gonna make ya do somethin' ya don't want to."

"But I'm here aren't I? I can't just go home now if I want, can I?" Rose had replied indignantly.

"D'ya want to go home?"

"Dunno! I'm scared to."

"Well then, ya don't have to. Look dear, I just think it would be a good idea when ya do go home that there's someone ya can talk to…for support y'know."

When Rose did go home she agreed to see a therapist and not just so as to please Theresa but because she had been thinking along those lines herself. If there was something mentally wrong with her then a shrink should know what that was and give her something to make her better.

She didn't want to talk about her childhood but Dorothy kept going back to it all the time.When this hour was over she wouldn't come back. She needed someone to tell her what was wrong with her brain, not talk about stuff that made her feel confused. In her initial interview with Dorothy she had thought she was getting somewhere. Dorothy had asked all sorts of questions about what medication she was taking and all that medical stuff. It had sounded as if she knew what she was talking about.

"Would it not be better if I tell you what way my brain works?" she asked intelligently.

"Of course Rose. That's something we will be discussing and it's very insightful of you to realise that. However, it's helpful for me to get a full background. You don't have to tell me anything you don't wish to, naturally, but it will help if we can be completely open with each other."

"Oh right! What d'ya want to know?"

"What are your earliest memories? That kind of thing."

"Well, I don't really remember a pile" said Rose. "I remember bein' in the back garden in Belfast. I was probably 'bout five or so 'cos I remember my brothers bein' wee then."

"That's great Rose, and how did you feel, do you think… when you were five?"

Rose concentrated on how she must have felt then. She knew it wasn't good but she couldn't make sense of it. Dorothy was waiting for her to speak but she just did not know what to say. She began to feel frightened and was scared that she would take another panic attack. Breathing heavily she looked to Dorothy to help her. Her breathing began to quicken and she shuffled about in her chair in the beginnings of a full blown panic.

Dorothy spoke very matter of factly and with total control - "Okay Rose, let's stop there and we'll get ourselves a drink. Don't know about you but I could do with a coffee."

Rose began to feel ashamed of herself and calmed down a little. "Can I have a cup of tea please?" she asked with tears in her throat. A few minutes later she was sitting drinking her tea and telling Dorothy how that had been the first time she had stopped herself from panicking. She was quite pleased with herself and felt a whole lot brighter.

"Tell me then Rose, how you see yourself," asked Dorothy. "You said your brain doesn't work properly. Tell me how it works."

Rose was keen to answer that question. After all, this was why she was here. "It's not that it doesn't work properly – it's that it works differently. That's what's wrong with me y'see. There's somethin' inside it or I don't know I'm sure you'll know better..." She waited for Dorothy to reply and when she didn't she went on, "It's like I've never really been me – not just me. It's like there's always bin someone else who pretends to be me and that's who everybody sees."

"Who's everybody?" inquired Dorothy.

"Y'know...Mummy and...everybody."

"And who does Mummy see?"

"It's not just Mummy..." Rose felt she had to defend her mother "...it's everybody. When people look at me they see this bad person. There's an evil inside of me that I was born with and it takes over 'cos it's not the only thing. There's good in me as well. It's just that I can't make that seen. It's like the evil always wins and I may as well just accept that's what I am."

"And do you accept that's what you are… if that *is* what you are, which I highly suspect is not the case?" asked Dorothy.

"I don't want to but I'm tired. I just want to close my eyes an' never wake up. I can't stand it any more," Rose cried bitterly. She accepted a box of tissues from Dorothy and wiped her nose.

"Rose? Tell me how your brain works that's different," pressed Dorothy. "So far I haven't heard anything that tells me you are any different from anybody else."

Rose sighed deeply and tried to think of the right words despite the fact that her head was pounding with pain. "I know I imagine things that aren't real. Like for instance there's this Indian…"

"An Indian? like cowboys and Indians you mean?"

"Aye. I've imagined him my whole life I think. He's probably the one thing from my childhood that I do remember."

"And what does he say to you. Who is he?" pursued Dorothy, gently but persistently.

"Dunno. When I was a wee, wee'n…" Rose sat upright to make sure Dorothy understood this right because this was important, "I used to see him but not really. It's like

I go somewhere in my brain only I think I'm goin' away somewhere. I used to actually believe I was goin' away somewhere but I was wrong. It just didn't make any sense. Like for instance, I used to go outside an' play and wouldn' be outside at all. Sometimes" and she lowered her voice for added effect, "I would go up into the sky an' fly about over the houses and everythin'."

"But you know that wasn't really true," stated Dorothy hopefully.

"Oh I know, but I didn't know then. At least I don't think I did."

"Who was the Indian then?"

"He was in one of the places I used to go. There was this woman, right. I always dream about her now but when I was a wee'n I used to see her too. She always brought me to these places and that's when I would see him. I don't know his name but he told it to me loads of times an' I keep forgettin'."

"So when did you last see this Indian and this woman?" asked Dorothy, with great interest.

"I saw the woman when I was in the hospital only I couldn't talk to her. It was like she couldn't hear me and I couldn't hear her, I just could see her. I haven't seen the Indian since I was a wee'n, I don't think – not properly anyway. The thing is y'see, he always was good to me when I was wee but now it's like, because I haven't gone there since, he just shows up like a flash an' scares the wits outta me."

"What do you mean?"

"You know when I was in the hospital and I said that I could see the devil comin' for me?"

"Yes, but you don't see that now do you?" Dorothy was getting more and more concerned about Rose's stability.

"No, I know that can't be true. It's just mad isn't it? I think I really believed he would 'cos, y'know, I was born bad an' so I thought if I died he'd come for me. Och Dorothy, I dunno, I was very confused. I don't know what to think anymore."

"Well you don't have to think about that right now. But you said you saw the Indian in the hospital, is that right? Rose, are you aware that you spent two weeks talking to people that weren't there?"

Rose felt very ashamed. She was well aware of that and she and Theresa had spent many a long evening talking about it. "I didn't mean to mess things up. I dunno really why I did that but I think it was the evil in me made me do it." Rose felt even more ashamed. She knew it was her own doing but that was the nature of the evil. It got her to do things that she could have stopped any time but didn't. She could have come out of that trance if she'd wanted to but the evil had her tricked into thinking she couldn't. "I couldn' stop it. I don't even remember who I was talkin' to. All I remember is feelin' like I wasn't real anymore."

"What did that feel like?"

"Good I suppose, in a way. It didn't feel like anythin' really. It was as if I knew I was there but I couldn' feel myself and... I know I was talking to people but I don't remember them now."

"Were you talking to the Indian?" persisted Dorothy.

"No, at least I don't think so."

"When you were a child and you saw the Indian – did he say anything to you?"

"Oh God, aye! Lots of stuff but I don't remember it. I suppose I do kinda remember what it was about. But you're not gonna believe me."

"It's not about what I think that's important. If you believe it then it's real for you."

"Ah well that's not true is it? Everything I believe is a lie. I imagine it all."

"Who told you that?"

"Mummy."

"Why do you think she told you that?"

"I don't want to talk about Mummy if you don't mind." Rose was feeling extremely uncomfortable again.

"That's fine. Tell me then what the Indian talked to you about."

"Okay! Right, this is gonna sound mad. Are ya sure ya wanna hear it?" Dorothy nodded. "You know the way after we die we go to heaven an' that?" Dorothy didn't respond. "Well, the Indian, y'see, comes from there an' he told me about it. I think that's what he meant. He talked about the universe an' heaven an' hell an' all that stuff. I used to think he came from a place inside me where all the good stuff is hidin' here, y'know." She put her hand on her heart. "The bad stuff is down here," she added indicating her abdomen.

"So the bad stuff isn't in your brain then?" asked Dorothy, stirring up her enthusiasm to describe how she saw herself.

"It is as well. That's the born bad bit. That's the bit that makes me mentally ill an' takes me on all those trips outside myself and makes me do things that are wrong. But at one stage it got down here an' that's when people started to see it. That's why the devil keeps comin' for me – 'cos it was him that put the bad in there."

Dorothy stared at Rose without speaking. She just did not know what to say next. The girl was obviously deluded but what the hell could have happened to her to make her think those mad ideas? Dorothy was pretty sure, after talking to the psychiatrist in charge of her, that she had been sexually abused as a child. Now, she feared that it was much more than that. Along the line somewhere she must have experienced some kind of brainwashing, to put it mildly. Here she was twenty two years old, although Dorothy thought she looked more like eighteen, but she certainly acted as if she was much younger even than that.

"What age are you Rose?" she asked.

"Twenty two."

"And what age were you when the bad stuff got down to your abdomen?"

"Dunno. A long time ago, 'cos I can hardly remember it not bein' there." And then in a flash of inspiration she added excitedly – "D'ya know what? It was about the time that we came here from Belfast."

"What age were you then?"

"Thirteen. Aye, it was 'cos I remember everybody blamin' me for havin' to come here."

"Who blamed you?" asked Dorothy.

"Mostly Caroline I suppose but Angie and Mummy did too. They've never really stopped hatin' me for it."

"And Caroline and Angie are your sisters, is that right?"

"Aye."

"Why do they blame you, do you think?" questioned Dorothy quietly, encouraging Rose to go on.

"Dunno, probably 'cos I did something terrible. That's what it's bin like my whole life y'know – I get blamed for terrible stuff but I never know what it is. I don't remember bein' bad. I know I am 'cos I feel guilty but I can't remember *doing* anything bad. You must think I'm really evil."

"No Rose. No, I don't think that at all," responded Dorothy," What I do think though, is that you need someone to listen to you. I think you've listened to other people your whole life and now it's time to find out what Rose knows to be true."

Rose burst into tears. She was finding it very difficult accepting kindness from people...first Theresa and now Dorothy. She did think that they like all the others would ditch her once they really got to know her but for now it felt good talking about these things. Dorothy was helping her make sense of it all and it felt good, like she was gaining control. She didn't know why she was crying when she was beginning to get somewhere but she didn't feel at all like herself any more. Something was different. She knew what it was – she was angry. She cried even more – she was frightened of being angry.

"Rose," Dorothy said after letting her cry for quite a while, "I think it might be a good idea to leave it there for today. What do you think?"

"Okay," Rose sniffed.

Rose talked to Dorothy Owens for a long time – for three years more or less. They talked about Rose's childhood a lot but as Dorothy found, Rose was by now well and truly unconscious of what had befallen her up until she was thirteen. She remembered all the nice things, like the Indian and the lady in the cave, but although she knew she had been sad her whole life, she never once attributed it to anything other than the fact that she had been born bad. She remembered Granny Doyle's wee cottage by the sea out at Cloughbeg and how she was happier there because of the trees and the cove. In Belfast where she lived, there weren't too many trees to be enjoyed.

Dorothy had introduced her to cognitive therapy and taught her how to challenge her thoughts. Whenever something happened to make her feel bad she would have to write it down in a table along with any thought that she reacted with. Then she would record how the thought made her feel which wasn't always easy because she often cried for hours and then forgot all about the table. However, she had soon got used to doing it so it became easier as time went on and after recording how the thought made her feel she would challenge the thought with something more positive and then write down how she felt after the positive thought. It seemed to work for her because it gave her something to channel her emotions into and she certainly had become all over the place as far as they were concerned. She cried mostly every day and felt that life wasn't worth the pain, but she never tried to kill herself after that time when Paul dumped her.

In the June following the start of the therapy she got another job. Joe and Iris O'Hanlon had asked her to come back and work for them in March but she hadn't felt ready to go back to work just yet. Plus, she was embarrassed, having put them through so much when she was there before and she had left to go live in Dublin with Paul without decent notice. The O'Hanlons were good people no doubt but she couldn't bring herself to go down that road again. She started working for Adair's which was in the main street in Drumgar also. Not too far from O'Hanlon's shop as it was. Adair's was a lovely shop selling children's clothing. Rose loved the work and was well liked by the customers who often remarked to Maggie Adair that her new assistant was such a wonderful help to them in choosing outfits for their wee'ns. Children loved Rose, that was plain for anyone to see and Rose could always relate to them on their level which made entertaining them whilst their mothers browsed both easy and enjoyable. For almost three years she worked there attending to the increasing number of customers. She spent her free time going out with the other shop girl, Anne, to dances and pubs mostly. Anne had a little girl and was a single mother which meant that she didn't bother much with messing around with men and was waiting for Mr Right to come along. That suited Rose down to the ground since she was still reeling from losing Paul who she had been hoping to marry some day. As well as that she believed that all men just wanted one thing anyway and she wasn't prepared to be used by just anyone. She also was hoping and praying I might add for Mr Right to come into her life and make it all seem like a distant nightmare.

Rose was no stranger to nightmares of course. Usually they were few and far between but recently they had gotten more frequent. She would wake up at night shaking with fear. Those were Rose's loneliest moments – in the dead of night with no-one to talk to and with the dread of more nightmares preventing her from sleeping at all. She felt so unloved and she often knelt by her bed in the middle of the night and pleaded with her God to let people see the good in her. Tears would cascade down her face as she begged – "Please Lord, please let them see the good inside. Please forgive me for being born bad. If they could only see the good and You know what I'm talking about. You can see it I'm sure. So please, let this shine outta me instead of the bad stuff."

But the Lord never granted her request for people to see the good in her. Instead, He brought a monster into her life. The monster came in disguise and his name was

Keith Bailey. When Rose first set eyes on Keith she thought he was gorgeous but he wasn't interested in her at all. He seemed more interested in Angie with whom Rose had gone to a disco in the local club. Keith was very clever and didn't tell her that she was his second choice until he had her well and truly trapped. For four fantastic weeks he lured her deeper and deeper under his spell and once he was sure that she wasn't going to turn away from him he began his reign of tyranny. He and Rose had been on a day out at the beach when he delivered the first attack. It had been a beautiful hot sunny day and the beach was thronged with holidaymakers. A group of noisy young people were laughing and cavorting about at the water's edge. Rose and Keith were walking by, Keith bragging about what an excellent surfer he was. As they neared the young people Rose was attracted to the fun they were having and soon became entranced in their joy. It didn't take Keith long to switch from Mr Universe to Mr Nasty. The first indication Rose had that something was wrong was the pain of Keith's grip on her arm as he pulled her around to face him.

"Why don't ya just fuck off now with him an' save me the bother of dumpin' ya?"

"What?" Rose felt a cold shiver go down her spine. She stepped back a bit from him.

"I saw the way you looked at that man. D'ya think I'm stupid?" sneered Keith menacingly.

Rose was trying to figure out what he meant and said in her defence – "I wasn't lookin' at anyone. What's wrong with ya?"

He smiled although Rose wasn't sure it felt like a smile and within seconds she was pulled into his strong grip. He held her tight to him, so tight she could feel his breath on her face. She laughed nervously, still unsure of what was going on.

"I should'a known you were too good to be true. It didn't take ya long comin' across for me did it?" His face was as black as thunder. What had attracted Rose to it originally was gone and in its place was an ugliness that had her losing her breath with fear. At that moment Rose was aware that she had made an enormous mistake.

"But I was just lookin' at them havin' fun. They were laughin'."

What did he mean too good to be true? What was he talking about? When Keith finally let her go the two of them went their separate ways on the beach. Rose walked back in the direction they had come and parked herself on the sand far away from any young men. She loved Keith, or at least she thought she did. She wondered if she really had been looking at one of the men in that way. Maybe she just didn't realise it. When Keith plonked himself down beside her thirty minutes later, she apologised to him and swore she'd never look at another man again. He took some persuading to forgive her but he did and gave her a long lecture on how things were going to be from then on in.

That had been in June nineteen ninety and up until April nineteen ninety one Rose had remained completely under Keith's control. She tried her best to be the girlfriend he deserved but occasionally she slipped up. She would glance at someone in the wrong way or she would talk about things that happened when she was with Paul. That was a big mistake. Keith would go quiet and then his face would go dark and Rose would realise she had messed up. It hadn't been easy, tiptoeing around his moods in that way, but she managed well as time went on. The worst mistake she ever made was to call him Paul. It was out of her mouth before she knew it and there was no taking it back. He had acted true to form and had grabbed her roughly, hissing and spitting into her face before tossing her away from him in disgust.

"You make me sick. You're a filthy slag. You do these things just to annoy me don't ya?" he had said.

Rose had been telling Dorothy about him all along and although Dorothy never once said she should dump him, her whole demeanour spoke it for her. When Rose told her of the night she placed a kitchen knife under the mattress, she was angry and was finding it hard not to show her reaction to Rose. But Rose could sense anger from a person before the person knew themselves that they were angry and normally she reacted with fear. This time however she couldn't prevent her own anger from emerging and when it did it was powerful. Although she was ranting and raving and shaking with sheer rage, Rose began to feel clearer and freer and more in control. By the time the therapy hour was over she was convinced that she should finish it with Keith.

On the night of April the tenth, nineteen ninety one, Rose was alone at home. Her mother was still unwell and was in hospital recovering from an operation. Her father was staying with Caroline who lived near the hospital, and Kevin and Brian were at home in their little flat in Dublin. Rose had just got off the phone from Keith. It had been relatively easy to finish it. Keith was either too proud or too disinterested to even discuss why. He simply said okay and left it at that. There was nothing else that could be said. She had wanted to scream at him from the safety of the distance between them. She would have liked to shout at him all the reasons why she had to leave him but he was too clever. He wasn't going to give her that privilege. She curled up on the sofa and cried, broken-hearted and lonely. In the stillness of the empty house her mournful cries echoed deep with the pain of abandonment. For Rose, time stood still. She was alone and afraid, in a life she never wanted in the first place and all around her was the fog with its shadows and demons taunting her and willing her to end it all. All she had to do was to make the decision. She couldn't be afraid - fear was weak – fear trapped her in this world. Courage was strong, but it was going to take a huge amount of courage to do what she was thinking of right now. She knew she would go to hell. There was no real death, just a different place to be. The devil would come for her and when he did nothing would ever be the same again. She had no idea what it would be like but she did know that she couldn't try any more in this world. Besides, it was as if she was already in hell anyway. The only difference being that when she was there she wouldn't have to try to be something she wasn't. She decided. Scouring the medicine cupboard for painkillers she found a strip of twenty four which she swallowed without thinking. It wasn't enough. "Damn it!" she protested against the injustice of it. Frantically she began to search every cupboard in the kitchen. Under the sink she saw the bottles of cleaning products and her eyes rested on the big bottle of bleach. She took it out slowly and went to her room where she put the bottle on the dressing table beside her bed. She sat down on the bed and stared at it. Could she do it? She had heard of someone who had drunk bleach one time and it had been horrific. The word was that the woman had literally burned from the inside out. Rose thought that maybe it was no more than what she deserved and then with a lurch of her stomach she had another thought. If she died in this way – by burning that was – then maybe it will be enough. Just maybe the devil will stay away long enough for the lady to come and take her instead. She didn't know what to expect after all this time but it was bound to be better than hell. Feeling somewhat braver she began to think of ways she could make this easier for herself. Downstairs, her father kept a cabinet stocked with whiskey and brandy. She thought there even might be a wee taste of vodka there. Ten minutes later Rose was lying on her bed steaming drunk and contemplating drinking a full bottle of household bleach. As she opened the bottle the tears streamed from her eyes and she choked with drunken hiccoughs. With shaking hands she raised the bottle to her mouth and as soon as she smelled the sharp acidity of the bleach she vomited over herself. Despite her drunkenness she managed to get the top back on the bottle and staggered to the bathroom where she attempted to wash the vomit of herself with a wet flannel. She vomited again in the basin and no longer able to physically stand she sat down on the bathroom floor with her back up against the bath and drifted off into a drunken stupor. "This was a big mistake," she heard herself speak as she drifted and then from somewhere she heard the lady's voice saying –

"Rose, get up and get help". Rose had always listened to the lady in the past and even though they hadn't spoken for so long, she was going to listen to her this time. Besides, the lady had only ever made her feel good and her voice now was like someone taking her hand and saying – come on, I'll make everything okay. Rose got up off the floor and went out of the bathroom. Somehow she managed to get down the stairs and to the telephone. She dialled the operator and asked in a very detached voice, for Drumgar Hospital. Soon she was connected to the psychiatric ward and asking for Sister Theresa Coyle.

"I'm afraid Sister Coyle is no longer here. To whom am I speaking please?" came a concerned voice on the telephone.

"My name's Rose McDevit," slurred Rose, "I've bin in there before. Need help. Please, help me?"

"Okay Rose, is there anyone there with you?" The

person on the other end of the telephone spoke to Rose for thirty minutes asking her questions and keeping her alert. At one stage, she asked if Rose was Catholic and began to pray with her to the virgin. The next thing Rose was aware of was a vehicle coming up the drive. The vehicle stopped and two doors were slammed shut. Then came a banging on the front door.

"There's someone at the door," Rose explained to her helper.

"That's an ambulance Rose. They're there to take you to the hospital. Don't worry now Rose, you'll be fine. Best if you let them in." Before long Rose was in the back of an ambulance and was being strapped onto a stretcher by a seemingly kindly man who wouldn't look her in the face. He worked steadily on, ignoring Rose's pleas to leave her where she was. The job done, he shouted to the driver and belted himself into a chair beside the stretcher.

Rose pleaded on and on – "Please mister, leave me alone. I want to die. Please let me die. Don't take me to the hospital mister. Please, let me just stay here an' die."

The whole thing seemed to her like a dream as if she wasn't really there. Any moment now she was going to wake up. The ambulance man wasn't looking at her and she felt sorry for him when she saw that he was crying.

"Don't cry mister" she told him. "I'm okay. I just need to go. There was never gonna be any other way for me ya see. So, there's no need to feel sad. If ya just take me back I won't bother ya again, I promise."

But the man ignored her and sat staring at the floor of the ambulance with tears falling from his face. The ambulance came to a stop and the doors were opened from outside. The kindly man and another pulled the stretcher from the vehicle and wheeled it into the hospital corridor.

Rose connected her gaze with the first man as they went and felt a stab of guilt when she saw the sadness in his eyes. He looked at her and said shakily – "You'll be okay now Rose. These people will look after ya," and with that he went out of her life, weighed down by the burden of his own abandonment.

Rose's previous record was against her and no doctor or nurse in the emergency room was prepared to take her word that she had not taken any drugs other than alcohol. She had to endure the pain and humiliation of having her stomach pumped again. The last time she had taken an overdose the drug had gotten completely into her bloodstream and almost killed her. No-one was taking any risks this time. Her stomach was pumped and she was attached to a drip feeding her with something that made her vomit over and over. Even after several hours she still retched and retched. The pain and humiliation, although traumatic, was nothing to the sense of failure and total abandonment she felt. No-one had any sympathy for her. Nurses came and went, fixing this and doing that but not one of them had a kind word for her. Instead, all she got was endless cold and unaffected questioning. On the second day, a female doctor came to see her and rather sternly informed her of the damage she was doing to her liver by continuing to abuse herself in that way. Rose was almost relieved when she was transferred that afternoon to the psychiatric ward. She was hoping to see Theresa but was disappointed to learn that she didn't work on the ward any longer. She had gone on to be a counsellor and hadn't looked back since. Rose settled into the ward within hours, almost feeling like she was home. However, with the security of the ward came back the need to hurt herself in order to keep the devil away. It wasn't long before she was on constant vigil again to keep her from self-harm. In the first two days she had been there she had grabbed a woman's cigarette, stubbing it out on her own arm and had lit a match and held it to her wrist. When the match spent she lit another and was holding it to her wrist also when she was stopped by a patient. She was bandaged up which she quite liked and although she was in pain she felt a sense of relief that she was safe for a little while. She spent another six weeks in the ward during which time she mostly thought about how she was going to get out so that she could kill herself.

Dorothy came into the ward and they had a meeting with several other officials as to what the future was for Rose. It was decided that she would see a psychologist named Tania Gates for the time being. Tania was an English woman. She wore glasses and was very intelligent looking. Rose liked her immediately. She trusted intelligence. Their first meeting took place inside the ward. It went like this –

"Rose, were you ever sexually abused?"

"No."

"Rose, do you know what constitutes sexual abuse?"

"Of course."

"Do you understand Rose, what you did when you took those painkillers as well as all that alcohol?"

"I do." Rose began to feel very angry.

"And do you realise what the implications of that might have been?"

"I was tryin' to kill myself. There, are ya happy? I wanted to die. I still do. Stop askin' me stupid questions." Rose practically spat at the woman with contempt.

"Rose, we'll get nowhere if you take this attitude. I am here to help you after all and I don't deserve to be spoken to in that manner." Tania remained calm but firm.

Rose backed down a little. She knew she was being unreasonable. "Sorry, but what about what I deserve. Don't I deserve to be happy?"

"Yes! Yes, that's just it. Of course you deserve to be happy but do you really believe that yourself?"

"I don't know," Rose replied, confused and angry still. "I used to think I did but it's gone too far now. I just think that the sooner I'm gone the better for everyone."

"Who's everyone?"

Not another one of those. Dorothy had constantly harped on about everyone being Mummy of course, because Mummy to a child is the whole universe. Rose had resented being likened to a child. She was in her mid-twenties for

Christ sake. "What does it matter?" she said to Tania. "The truth is I'd be better off dead and okay, if ya want to hear it – yes my mother will be better off too. She never wanted me. She hated me or so she said many a time. She wished she hadda' taken the boy."

"What did she mean by that? Who was the boy?" Tania asked. She had pressed a button when she asked who *everyone* was. Like Dorothy Owens, she too had felt that Rose had serious issues with her mother and judging from the way Rose was losing it now, Tania was right.

"I don't know. Nobody. I don't even know why I said that – it just that I'm so angry. I can't think straight." Rose rubbed her forehead with her fingers and began to cry. "I just don't want to think any more. I'm tired, can we just leave it, please?"

"We're almost done Rose. One more question." Tania waited until Rose looked at her before going on. "The last time you were here, well that's... over three years ago now, is that right?" Rose shrugged. "You had a very interesting relationship with Sister Coyle I believe." Rose said nothing, but she became more attentive. "I believe that you confided in her quite a bit. You had little talks?"

"Aye."

"What I would like to know Rose is, why is it you were able to confide in her and not in anyone else? There's obviously stuff you're not saying to me or to Dorothy. I'd just to like to know why, if that's okay."

Rose didn't know why. There had been something

special about Theresa that had made her feel she should trust her. It was because she was like the lady, only not exactly. It was because of the dream she had of her when they met, because of the connection they had. She looked at Tania now and wondered if this intelligent woman was smart enough to get what she meant. "Because she could see me," she said.

In the weeks that followed Rose and Tania had twice-weekly talks. In between times she talked to the consultant psychiatrist of her desire to punish herself for fear of the devil coming. She told him about how she wanted to die and how because she was born bad she was convinced she would go to hell. None of this seemed to sink in with the doctors and nurses but Rose didn't blame them for not understanding. At the end of the day, she was an extraordinary person who was born with an innate evil. Most people could never comprehend that and it wasn't their fault if they constantly tried to tell her that she was wrong. The thing about the ward was this – Rose actually felt a sense of belonging there. As time went on and more and more mentally ill women came and went, she began to understand that there could be a place for her and this might well be it. After all, she had never known this amount of personal care before. She was prescribed drugs to help her – happy pills she called them. Naturally, she wasn't permitted to keep them herself and was administered one every morning along with one sleeping pill at night. Night was not a good time in the ward. Many patients suffered from night terrors and would walk the corridor looking for attention from the nurses. Rose had more than her fair share of nightmares and had taken to sleeping in a sitting position as it made her feel less vulnerable. Her dreams were full of terrifying visions of the demons in the fog around her. Several times during the night she would wake in a fright and sit there silently in sweat chilled skin. Sometimes she would cry out or scream. Very often, she would wake in the morning to find herself under the bed hiding from an unknown assailant. She would describe the dreams to Tania who would get her to attempt to explain them. Quite often the dreams were about herself when she was a child. She would be in her bed and a monster would come to get her. The monster hurt her in ways that were unimaginable to her and then he would leave her to bear the burden of the world on her shoulders. Rose and Tania's seventh meeting went like this –

"Tania?"

"Yes, Rose?"

"You know when you first came here and you asked me if I had been sexually abused?"

Tania swallowed hard. "That's right."

"I was."

"When was this?"

"When I was wee. It was Daddy, Tania … Daddy did it to me."

Consciously, Rose was fighting life with every breath she had.

Unconsciously, she had made a commitment to fight for life. She had begun to remember her first thirteen years. And as she would wake up to the past slowly and painfully, she was to hope for wishes and dreams that she never dared hope for before.

Chapter Eleven

The storm

Lissy and John stood on the gravel drive outside the parochial house. To their right just over a hugely overgrown hawthorn hedge was the little chapel. They had discovered to their immense delight that it was called 'St John The Beloved's'. Lissy had pulled John into a bear hug squealing – "It's a sign, it's a sign! You're John and you're my beloved." John had grinned at her girlish silliness but hadn't felt the need to tease her. He was still reeling with happiness because of what had transpired this morning. Nothing else mattered. She loved him – she said so and she had shown him. She had bared her soul to him – there was no going back from that. He was happier than he'd ever been before and it was all because it was so right – so meant to be. Maybe the chapel's name *was* a sign, who knows. He was so rapt in his pleasure that he forgot that Father Devlin knew nothing of Rose's origin. He forgot that his beloved

Lissy was going to be disappointed. Standing before the big two- storey house now, he wondered if he had been selfish in bringing her here just to have her hopes dashed. But he had agreed with Father Devlin that someone here in Cloughbeg had to know who her parents were.

"Am I doing the right thing?" Lissy looked at him like a little lost girl.

He threw an arm around her shoulder and pulled her to him kissing her on the temple – "You'll be fine," he replied lovingly.

They both walked up to the big front door and knocked loudly with an old fashioned knocker. The door was wooden and had been painted green at one stage but the paint was peeling off and had faded to a whitish green. They waited but no-one came. Lissy looked around her nervously.

"You see the way the salty air has ruined the paintwork on the door?" asked John providing a diversion. Lissy nodded and shivered, wrapping her jacket around her tightly to protect her from the cold breeze. The weather had become much worse and it looked as if a storm was on the agenda. "The cars are all the same. Cars don't last very long at the seaside 'cos of the salt you see. They all rust like hell."

Lissy wasn't interested in the salty air – "What is taking him so long? He did say nine in the morning didn't he?"

Just then they heard the sound of locks being opened on the other side of the door. Lissy let go of her jacket and straightened up. John kept his protective arm around her.

When the door opened a young girl stood there smiling

sweetly. "Sorry there," she said, "I've only just got up. I usually start at eight thirty but Monday morning y'know? You must be Miss Brenning and Mr Brunt. You're down on the book for nine is that right? God aye, it's gone nine now. The Father'll kill me. Come on in now an' make yersells comfy." And with that she stood aside and allowed the visitors to enter. "On in there to yer left now, aye. That's it."

John opened the door to his left and entered a huge front room. Lissy came in behind followed by the young girl.

"Sit yersells down there on the sofa now an' I'll just nip an' let the Father know yous are here" she rattled on to the amused visitors. She hurried out securing her hair behind her neck with a scrunchie.

Lissy looked at John and giggled. "Sixteen going on sixty," she said referring to the girl.

"She does sound remarkably like Mrs Doyle, doesn't she?" whispered John. They both looked around the room they were sitting in. The furniture was old fashioned and worn and the curtains looked like they'd hung there for centuries. There was an overwhelming smell of vanilla and Lissy spotted the culprit sitting on the coffee table in front of them – a huge candle, obviously vanilla scented.

"Why do people buy those vanilla candles?" she said screwing up her nose, "the smell is way too strong. It gives me a headache."

"I've just had a thought," John piped up, taking in the huge crucifix on the mantle. "When your mother first came to Father Murphy about you – she probably sat in this very room."

"On this very sofa too, by the looks of it," added Lissy screwing her nose up again.

"Better watch or you'll stay like that," giggled John and received a thump on the arm.

"This is exciting isn't it?" she said. John started to say something else smart but was silenced by the door opening. It was the girl again.

"The Father'll be down in a minute. Is there anythin' I can get ya? Would ya like a nice cup o' tay?"

"Yes please," they both answered together. The girl smiled. She was a very pretty young thing when she smiled.

"I'm Melissa," she said and left again.

"Wow!" Lissy laughed.

"Another sign?" said John with raised eyebrows.

It was almost nine thirty when Father Jim Devlin finally joined them. He came breezing into the room wearing a pair of royal blue bedroom slippers which looked odd along with the full priest's suit and collar. He was a youngish man. Lissy thought he looked no more than thirty. She wondered how someone so young could be a parish priest. However, Father Devlin was as unlike a parish priest as anyone could imagine. He was so handsome for a start, with pitch-black hair cut in a very up to date style. His brown eyes were captivating and Lissy blushed when he looked at her. He had waltzed in and shook hands, introducing himself almost cockily and plonking himself down on the armchair facing them.

"Well then," he beamed rubbing his palms together, "We've a wee bit of business to sort out now, haven't we?" Lissy was speechless. The good-looking priest was overpowering and she simply could not think what she had to say. He was looking at her expectantly and she began to suspect that he was well aware of his affect on women. Those brown eyes never wandered from hers and his face showed a hidden grin. In the end it was John who spoke.

"Lissy's somewhat nervous Father. I think she's scared that she'll get nowhere with her quest." He beseeched the priest with his face as if to say - please let her down gently.

"Well, as it happens, I've found something that may be of use to you," Father Devlin boomed. John found himself taking to him very quickly. He seemed more like a mate than a priest.

"Do you know who my mother was?" Lissy found her voice.

"Not exactly sweet girl," he replied making Lissy blush again, "but we know a little bit about her, if it *is* her of course."

"What do you mean, if it *is* her? Don't you know who it is?"

"Ah, here we are," he continued, still with his happy booming voice, as he pulled a leather backed journal out from under a pile of newspaper.

He liked the Sunday papers which he read on a Sunday

afternoon. It was usually Wednesday or Thursday by the time Melissa got around to tidying them away. They fell to the floor as he pulled the journal from beneath them and Lissy hurried to help him gather them up.

"Not at all, not at all," he protested, "Melissa will come get them. Of course, they all have to be recycled now don't they. There's probably enough there to save a full rainforest eh?" He laughed at his joke and then said – "You're Melissa as well. Now then, there's a coincidence. I never knew a Melissa until she started here and now I know two. Isn't that grand?"

Lissy smiled – "Most people call me Lissy, Father."

"And you can call me Jim. I don't do with all that Father stuff."

"Gosh, I don't know if I could do that Father," she said, shocked.

"That's because you've grown up with fusty old priests like Father Kearns no doubt. This is the twenty first century. Get with it sweet girl."

Lissy laughed along with John who was thinking that Father Devlin was turning out to be a gift.

"Okay," Lissy joked, going with the flow, "who are you and what have you done with the parish priest?"

"Sent him off to Florida to get a bit of sun about him" replied the priest grinning. "Seriously though, he *is* in Florida…for a month as it happens. So, you thought I was the main man did ya?"

"*I* thought you were too. Come to think of it no-one

said you were. I just assumed, I suppose," John confessed.

"Nah! That's not for me. I like my own space at times. Ya know what I mean? Can't have that if you're in auld Bernard's shoes."

"Are you from Cloughbeg yourself Father?" Lissy felt stupid as soon as she'd asked the question. It was obvious he wasn't."

"I'm from Monaghan, Lissy. That's quite near the north ya know. That's why my accent's a bit muffled. My mum was from Tyrone ya see and Dad was from Sligo. And you're from the south of England. Weather's a bit better there I suppose."

"We're both from Dorset" Lissy replied warmly. "It's nice there but not as nice as Cloughbeg I think."

"I dunno, honey," chipped in John, "the Jurassic Coast is as nice as any. Have you ever been to Dorset, Father?"

"Call me Jim, please. I'm serious. My parishioners have to call me Father but that doesn't mean you have to. No, no I never have John. I've never bin further than the seminary in Dublin. How sad is that, eh?" John and Lissy smiled politely and there were a few moments of silence after which everyone suddenly remembered why they were here. Jim sat back down with the journal and opened it to a page he had marked, before clearing his throat. Lissy held her breath hopefully. "Yeah well, ahem!" Jim began and then suddenly realised something, "Did ya not get tay?"

"Melissa did ask. I guess she's making it right now," replied Lissy in Melissa's defence.

Jim pressed a button on the wall behind his chair and a buzzer was heard going off somewhere in the house and then Melissa stuck her head around the door.

"Yes Father?"

"Melissa, are ya getting our guests some tea today at all, or are ya goin' to China for it?"

"Just back from there actually Father, won't be long now," the cheeky youngster replied.

Lissy was feeling so much at ease. Jim was great and the atmosphere in the house was more in keeping with an audience with Billy Connelly than an audience with a priest. "She's happy at her work," she said to Jim. She couldn't bring herself to call him Jim and opted for nothing instead.

"Oh, she should be" he replied. "She gets away with a lot does that one. Nah, she's grand in fact. She's what people round here might call 'a problem child' for want of a better word. Passed from pillar to post her whole life, poor pet. Grew up in foster care ya see. Apparently, no-one ever gave her a chance. Should be in school really I suppose. She's only sixteen. But, the social people asked us if we'd have her here and here she is."

Lissy felt for the girl. She was shocked that someone as pleasant and pretty as her had such a bad start in life. "You mean she lives here?" she asked.

"Oh yeah, housekeepers have lived here at the parochial house since way back. Of course they used to be middle-aged spinsters but nowadays it's fashionable to have a bit of life in the help."

"Gosh!" exclaimed Lissy whilst John only laughed, "I can't believe you just said that. If my mother could hear you she'd have me out of here in a flash saying that's no priest, it's an imposter."

"Ha ha ha…" he guffawed, "sounds like your mum would get on well with auld Bernard then."

"You've got to admit Jim," John grinned, "you certainly aren't like any priest I've ever known. Mind you I don't know many, but I'm sure they're all more like Father Kearns than you."

"He used to serve here y'know. A right long time ago, when this Father Murphy was PP. This is Father Murphy's journal, by the way, that we haven't even begun to read yet." Jim added indicating the journal he had taken from under the pile of newspapers.

"Oh right, can you read it out to us? Would that be okay?" Lissy wasn't sure if she was taking advantage of Jim's good nature.

"Read it for yourself if ya want. It's obviously your business." He handed the journal to her and pointed out the entry she should read. It wasn't very long. Lissy couldn't believe her luck and she looked at John who appeared equally amused. Melissa came in finally with the tea but was ignored by Lissy who pored over the journal as if her life depended on it. It was headed '20th October 1978' and there was something after that which had been blacked over with a permanent marker. She read on and was both shocked and disappointed at what she read. A huge chunk of the piece was blacked out and what was left told a sad story that held no evidence as to who it was about. She turned to Jim with a scowl and read aloud –

"'"The child's grandmother brought her to see me. I've known the woman for years and I have no concern as to the upstanding of the family. For a child so young to be in such a condition, I can only surmise that she has come to harm outside of the home. I questioned her considerably but she was obviously traumatized by the whole sorry affair and could offer me no satisfactory explanation of what had occurred."'" Lissy didn't understand. This was about a child who was raped or something – not her mother. "Surely this isn't the right one Father?" she said.

"It is sweet girl, I'm afraid. It sounds like he's talking about a little girl doesn't it?

Lissy nodded and John took a deep breath, taking a hold of Lissy's hand and squeezing tight. Jim got up and came over to her. He pointed out a series of numbers scribbled in the margin: '25-08-65'. "Date of birth," he said, "if ya look at the date of the entry she was thirteen years old."

"But that can't be. How could a thirteen year old be pregnant?" Lissy gasped.

"It's not unheard of honey," John answered.

"Oh yeah, now! But not in those days. We're talking thirty years ago. A thirteen year old in those days was just a little child. This poor thing was only a child and she was pregnant. That's what the priest meant by saying she must have come to harm. He thinks she was raped, *a child*!"

"How do we know it's Lissy's mother though?" John asked Jim desperately.

"If ya read on to the bottom it says that the child was sent to Father Peter Kearns in Dorset, England" Jim replied. "He was to provide an adoption for the child.

Lissy scanned the bottom of the piece with John reading it also from the side. He spotted the part first and stabbed a finger on it quoting "'I have told the grandmother that I shall write to my past curate Father Peter Kearns in Dorset, England to arrange a suitable placement. I intend to do so without further delay and I will enclose a copy of the letter with this entry.'"

"Oh my God John!" exclaimed Lissy. "She was only thirteen. How horrible! One can only imagine what could have happened to her. Shit, she's only thirteen years older than me. How weird! Don't you dare tell my mother this."

John would have had no intention of telling Mrs Brenning this news but since he highly suspected she already knew, it wouldn't make any difference if he did. He was beginning to get a better idea of how she must be worrying right now. Christ! It's no wonder she didn't want Lissy doing this. He read the rest of the piece now while Lissy did too. Basically it was about the girl and how she responded to being pregnant. She had a hard time understanding what was happening at all by the sounds of it. It wasn't the easiest thing to read what with all the bits blacked out and that. The worst thing was that there was no name, address or anything. It was most likely that they were the bits blacked out.

"The plot deepens" said John deep in thought.

"What do you mean by that remark?" snapped Lissy.

"Well, don't you think it's odd that there's so much blacked out. It's as if somewhere along the line, someone wanted to get rid of any evidence of who she was. Plus, if you remember, I wasn't entirely convinced that Father Kearns was giving us the full contents of that letter. And where's this copy that was kept with the journal?"

"It may have got lost, I suppose," offered Jim, "but I shouldn't think so. More likely it was never kept in the first place."

"But then, are you really telling us that Lissy's biological mother was only thirteen when she had her, and that it looks like she had been raped?" John asked him. He was finding it difficult getting his head around this revelation. Glancing at Lissy he could see that she too was struggling.

Jim sighed deeply and also checked out how Lissy was reacting – "I'm not telling you anything. All I know is that is Father Sean Murphy's official journal and you read for yourself what it says. I'm as much in the dark as you, I'm afraid."

Lissy got up and went to the window staring out at the heavy rain that had begun to fall. "It was so lovely this morning," she said flatly, "everything was so wonderful but I knew it," she shook her head and turned to face them. "I knew something was wrong. I just knew. It was too good to be true."

"Lissy no," John protested, forgetting about Jim. "You can't say that. It was perfect. Still is. This doesn't mean anything. It doesn't change anything. She's still your mother and I'm still me. I haven't changed. We haven't changed – have we?"

Jim murmured something about Melissa and tactfully slipped out of the room. John looked so forlorn that Lissy felt guilty but she was so angry she couldn't comfort him. She couldn't tell him what he wanted to hear. All she knew was that her dream of the perfect mother had been pulled apart and she wanted to go home and fall into her mum's arms and cry. She wrapped her arms around herself and burst into tears.

"Darling, please don't cry" said John trying to comfort her. "It's not that bad. Really it's not. It just means that she's a little bit younger than we thought she would be, that's all." He went over to her and took her in his arms. What was he to say? He felt powerless to help her. He was thrown sideways by the whole thing himself. He led her back to the sofa and poured her a fresh cup of hot tea. "Here honey, drink this and you'll feel better, yes? And then we'll have a think about where we can go from here. It's not the end of the line you know – there are ways of finding her yet."

Lissy rubbed at her face and sniffed indignantly –"I don't know if I want to know now."

"You don't mean that honey. Look, let's just take our tea

and eat something and then we'll take it from there." She nodded and took a sip of tea.

"Oh John" she whined, "what a mess I've made of everything! And I'm sorry. I... it just hurts."

"I know darling, I know. Look, you know what? It may not be what it looks like at all. Let's get the whole story and then we can make decisions then."

That felt better to Lissy and he was relieved that she was looking a little brighter. Jim opened the door and looked at John questioningly who nodded and smiled at him. He came on into the room brandishing a piece of paper.

"Listen guys," he said, "I was thinkin'. If your mother was a minor then the social would have been involved wouldn't they? This is the name of the social worker who looked out for Melissa. There's a number there too. If she was involved with social services then that woman should be able to help. Tell her I sent you and that'll swing things a bit. She owes me a big favour, that one."

"Gosh yes! That would be a great idea," exclaimed John, happy to get the conversation moving on in a more positive way, "and I was thinking as well – we have her date of birth, which means we could easily get a name from the birth records, couldn't we?

"You could get it from the baptismal records actually. And I could do that for you in a few days, I wouldn't mind."

"What if she wasn't a Catholic? She wouldn't be on the church's records then."

Lissy brightened up and joined the enthusiasm of the two men – "She had to be Catholic if she was brought here. Isn't that right Father?" Jim nodded smiling. "Anyway, mum would never have adopted me if she wasn't" Lissy added.

The atmosphere was changed thanks to Jim's quick thinking and John and Lissy sat and had tea and scones, talking and laughing together with Jim as if they'd known him for years. When the tea was finished Lissy was keen to bring the conversation back to her birth mother – "You know what would really be a bummer? She said – "If she wasn't local at all. Then we might never find her for we won't know where she was from."

Neither Jim nor John had thought of that. It seemed so obvious that she would be from that parish if she was brought to this house. However, it was a possibility and one that no-one was prepared to consider at this stage. No-one except Lissy that was, who seemed convinced that she was never meant to find her mother. "Remember that fortune teller who told me I wouldn't find her but she would find me?" she asked John, a little unsure of what Jim would make of it.

Jim simply laughed. He knew it was a new age thing to consult psychics nowadays and although he didn't believe in all that mumbo jumbo, he didn't take the Church's view that it was the devil's work either. He said so to Lissy to make her feel more at ease. Plus he wanted to know more about what the fortune teller said.

"That's all she said," Lissy told him, "Oh, except that she was a powerful woman."

Jim smiled politely and glanced at John who was smirking. Lissy caught him and thumped his arm. "Ow! She always does that," he said to Jim who laughed.

"You know what Father?" Lissy was serious, "Thank God you're so easy going. It makes things much more pleasant. I want to say thanks, you've been great."

"Ah sweet girl," he replied giving her one of his intense stares, "it's been a pleasure for sure. And I'll give you a ring as soon as I get any more information. I want to help. I really do."

Lissy found herself blushing again and she looked to John to say something for her. "Well, we've taken up enough of your time for today Jim" he said. "I'm sure you've important things to be at. Thanks ever so." He stood up and offered Jim his hand.

"Not at all, my friend," Jim boomed shaking his hand, "and you're welcome to come and visit me again. In fact, why not come for lunch on Thursday? I'm bound to have heard from the records department by then."

John looked at Lissy who nodded eager to accept. "We'd love to, thank you," she said shyly.

She shook hands with Jim and he kissed her on the cheek making her blush again. They said their goodbyes and Jim showed them out the front door. The rain was still coming down hard and they ran to the car holding their jackets over their heads.

John drove right up to the door of Hawthorn Cottage. They had thought that they wouldn't make it back at all. The narrow road to Drumgar had been flooded in parts and meeting traffic had been a nightmare. The driving rain had worsened since they left the parochial house and the wind had picked up to almost a gale. Neither of them had a hood on their jackets so the quick dash to the front porch left them drenched. It was almost noon and Mrs Doyle was in the kitchen baking bread. She called to them to leave their wet coats in the downstairs loo and come on through to the dining room. Lissy opened a door in the hallway and discovered a little bathroom that must have been a cloakroom at one time, for the wall was lined with coat pegs. They hung their dripping coats up and went to the dining room where they were met by the aroma of freshly baked bread and steaming coffee. They stood dripping water from their hair, reluctant to sit down. Mrs Doyle scurried in from the kitchen carrying a platter of warm bread which she put on the best table by the window that looked out over the pretty cottage garden.

"Ah be God! You're soaked through poor pets!" she exclaimed when she saw them, "sit down there now an' I'll just get yous a towel fer yer hair."

"I didn't know lunch was included in the room price, did you?" Lissy asked John.

"No, I was just gonna get dried off and grab a cup of

tea in the room."

"Well let's see what she says."

Mrs Doyle came back carrying a tray with two big steaming mugs of coffee and a dish of curls of butter.

"Mrs Doyle, this if lovely but we thought we'd just have a cuppa in the room." Lissy told her feeling a little ungrateful.

"Not at all, not at all," Mrs Doyle dismissed the very idea of it, "if a body can't treat her guests to a nice bit o' bread and homemade butter then the world's a sorry state. An' I know you yung'ons like this cappuccino coffee. The daughter bought me a cappuccino machine for me birthday. It's nice to get the use o' it. Eat up now an' don't leave a scrap. You're lookin' a wee bit peaky pet, are ya alright? You're not sickenin' for somethin' are ya?"

Lissy and John just about caught the gist of what she had said. "I'm fine, thank you Mrs Doyle" said Lissy. "I'm just a little tired I guess. I might have a nap before we go out this evening. Weather's not good enough to do anything anyway."

"Aye, you do that dear. Sensible girl. Now, is there anythin' else y'd like? A wee bit o' blackberry jam maybe. It's homemade."

"That'd be lovely Mrs Doyle. This is lovely, thank you. You're very kind," Lissy replied. John was stuffing his face with homemade bread thickly spread with butter.

"Delicious!" he mumbled giving Mrs Doyle the thumbs up. Mrs Doyle went to fetch the jam, beaming with pleasure. When she came back Lissy had an idea -

"Doyle, that's a common Irish name is it?" she asked MrsDoyle.

"Oh aye, very common dear. In fact, Drumgar is comin' down with Doyles as it happens."

"And what about Devlin?"

"Not many Devlins about here dear. Why d'ya ask?"

"We were visiting Father Devlin in Cloughbeg this morning," Lissy wasn't sure if she should go on.

"Were ya dear? That's nice but what would a couple o' English youngsters like yersells want wi' Father Devlin?"

Lissy looked at John and he seemed to be in agreement. "Well I was born there you know" she told Mrs Doyle. "I was adopted – that's why I grew up in England. I'm trying to trace my birth mother and apparently she may have been from that parish."

"Well, what was 'er name dear? Maybe I can help? There's not many I don't know these parts or in Cloughbeg either for that matter" Mrs Doyle replied.

"I don't know her name unfortunately. There doesn't seem to be any information about her except that..." Lissy paused. Should she go any further? She looked at John and almost burst into tears at that very moment.

"Except that it looks like she was only a minor when she had Lissy," continued John, "that's all we know about her I'm afraid."

Mrs Doyle tried to hide her fascination -"I see dear. That makes a big difference then don't it. If a wee'n was in trouble round these parts then it'd be round the town in no time. How long ago?"

"Nineteen seventy eight."

"No,no, no, I don't think so dear. Are ya sure she was from here? There's not much I don't mind about those days. Everybody knew each other's business in those days." John suspected that Mrs Doyle knew everyone's business nowadays as well and he was beginning to regret telling her at all.

"Never mind, it was a long shot" he said. He wanted to close the conversation especially since Lissy was looking very upset.

Mrs Doyle however never let a good story go when she heard one – " 'Cept of course if she had family here. That'd explain it."

"What do you mean?" asked Lissy. John was staring at her as if to say drop it, but she had to know what Mrs Doyle meant.

"Well, let's say she had a grandmother here. In those days the grandmother would take charge o' any business as delicate as that, and the shame woulda bin tarra fer the parents ya know. Makes sense to take 'er to the grandmother's parish."

"Oh my God!" exclaimed Lissy, "Then...do you think you might know her grandmother? It was the grandmother who brought her to the priest in the first place you know?"

"Goodness, I'm not sure. Coulda bin anyone. I know one thing. If it hadda bin *my* grandchild I would'n a towl anyone anyways. No, afraid I'm not much use to ya dear after all."

Lissy was dismayed. What Mrs Doyle said made perfect sense. *Fuck it!* she thought, *it's useless... Damn!*

John tried to get both women to drop the subject but both for their own reasons were not going to give up. "It was a Father Sean Murphy. Do you remember him?" Lissy asked, grasping at straws.

Mrs Doyle loved an opportunity to talk about the *auld days*, as she called them. "Oh God aye, a lovely priest was Father Murphy, very holy man. Passed away years ago, God rest 'im. He had a yunger sister y'know – still living in the village. Let me see now, there was Father Murphy an' auld Father Mullan an' that yung'on – what's this ya called him now? ... Aye, Father Kearns. God, he was a sharp one an' no mistake."

"Father Kearns had left by that time" added Lissy. "He went to England. It was him who arranged my adoption as it happens. He's still sharp by the way. We spoke to him before we came over here."

"Is that right now? Well, I never. Fancy you knowing wee Father Kearns. Ye'll tell 'im I said hello, will ya?" Lissy only nodded. She wasn't gonna get any joy from Mrs Doyle. By the looks of it, she wouldn't get any joy at all. It all rested on the social records. She didn't hold out much hope for Jim's investigation. Suddenly, she was very tired and she hadn't eaten a bite. John had scoffed a lot of the bread and although he had left her two nice pieces, she didn't at all feel like eating. Mrs Doyle noticed the change in her and scurried off to the kitchen to make a fresh mug of coffee.

"Are you okay honey?" John asked.

"Oh John, I'm not feeling very well. I think I'll go and lie down if you don't mind."

"Come on," he said offering her his arm which she refused. He felt deflated. He had a good idea what was coming next. "Honey," he said stupidly, "don't go off on one of your huffs now. It's not that bad. Anyway I warned you not to tell her any more."

"What! You didn't say that" Lissy huffed. "Anyway, we know the truth now don't we? There isn't a snowball's chance in hell of finding her now. We should have stayed in bloody England." She stormed out of the dining room with angry tears in her eyes and all John could do was to follow after her like a lost puppy. The day was turning out to be a real rollercoaster of emotion and he was second guessing her mood all the time. She tried to open the door of her room but couldn't get the key to go into the lock. "Fuck it!" she spat and burst into tears. John took the key from her and opened the door. He wondered should he come in with her?

When she flung the door wide open and ran in throwing herself on the bed, he entered quietly and closing the door behind him very softly he said – "Darling? Don't push me away, please. I want to help you – make you feel better. Will you let me make you feel better?" She sobbed into the pillow and said nothing. "Darling, where is all that enthusiasm from this morning? You were so happy and sure that this was what you wanted. You said you loved me. Do you love me? Have you changed your mind?"

She sat up and wiped her face with her sleeve. "Oh John – darling – of course I still love you. I can't help feeling like this. I get so angry and it looks so hopeless and I can't *allow* myself to love you. It's like, if I let you in then I'll start crying and I don't think I'll ever stop. I don't want to feel that way, I don't," she wailed as John rushed to her and took her in his arms.

He let her cry whilst he held her and he felt his heart would break in two. The tears rolled silently down his own face and he pressed her closer and closer to him, willing with all his heart for the love he felt for her to go from his heart straight into hers.

"I'm so scared John," she wailed, "what if I never find her? I don't want to feel like this the rest of my life. Oh John, I need to know. I need to know that she loves me because if I don't ever know that, then I'll always feel like this – I'll always feel alone and I'm scared that I'll never know who I am."

He made her face him and he said – "You listen to me now. You're Lissy Brenning, that's who you are, and I love you. Your mother loves you, not the person who gave birth to you but the one who loved you from you were a helpless infant – your mother, Lissy, your *real* mother. Don't ever say that you're alone. You're never alone. I'm here and I love you so much darling. I wish you could know how much I love you. I'd die for you. I would. And when you say those awful things about not feeling loved, it hurts me too. Here! Feel this." He took her hand and put it on his heart. "Feel how my heart is pounding? That's because I'm scared too darling. I'm scared that you'll never let me love you and that I will die longing for you."

"Oh John!" she cried cupping his face in her hands, "I'm sorry, please, I don't want you to hurt. I do love you, I've always loved you. I'm so sorry I've hurt you. I won't do it again my love, I promise. Please say you forgive me."

She searched his face with her eyes and as he grabbed her head and pushed his lips hard against hers she groaned with both pain and pleasure. They fell back on the mattress kissing and crying and holding each other with such an intense passion that they exhausted themselves and they fell asleep in each other's arms clinging to each other's heart for survival. When the storm outside had blown itself out it was five in the afternoon and the two indoors woke amidst the sweetness and freshness that always comes at the end of a storm. Without a word, their lips met again and their bodies embraced expressing the months of passion that had never been acknowledged until now.

Chapter Twelve

Who is Rose?

As time went on and Rose began to deal with her inner conflict she began to discover a strength within her that willed her to hope for a better life. She had made that choice to live – that brave choice that was all the difference between being a victim or a survivor. The question she had to ask herself now was – who is Rose?

Spain, June 1993

The sun was about to go down beyond the horizon and the ocean was glistening a bright red. Rose watched the heavenly display in complete silence, not once turning her gaze from the spectacular sight. The sky had gone from orange to red and now was aglow with crimson and violet as the sun pulsed on into the night. Sitting on the rocks beside her, her companion let out a low whistle, marvelling at the wonder of the sunset as he had done so many times in his life. Each time though, for Carlos, it seemed a brand new experience. He turned to Rose who was rapt in awe by the beauty of the sky.

"Every sunset is different from the one before," he said, in perfect English, "and it shall never be again."

Rose didn't reply. She didn't even acknowledge that he had spoken. He felt a little deflated and getting up off the rocks he sauntered off towards his car to fetch the bottle of red wine he had stashed under the seat. He had never met anyone like Rose before. Not only was she Irish, and he simply loved Irish women, but she was so mysterious and deep. All his life he had been a deep thinker. Men jeered at him because of it and women loved him for it but always he was so very alone. He was extremely attractive to the opposite sex – he knew that, and he had never been without one or two sexy senoritas hanging onto his every sensitive word, but not until now had he known a woman to whom he could truly relate. With Rose he was himself and nothing else. She understood him when he talked about his thoughts and dreams and how he saw the world. She hadn't wanted to change the subject or talk about silly girl things or prance about on his arm showing off to the other tourists. She had listened to his deep philosophies on life and they had connected – him talking and her reflecting his words - she had mirrored his inner soul. As he carried the wine and goblets back towards her now, he thought about the moment they met. He had been working by the hotel pool as a lifeguard.

She had smiled at him as he stood nearby and he was already captivated. Seven days on and he was completely entranced by her gorgeous blue eyes and wavy chestnut coloured hair. Her skin was a light golden brown and when she smiled his heart lit up with a warm glow. She was beautiful, not only on the surface but also on the inside. She had a radiant glow inside her that shone when he looked at her and when she laughed his whole world seemed to laugh with her. Even more amazing was the uncanny way she seemed to reach into his heart and pull out all the years of loneliness he had known. The silence in those moments said more about the two of them than any amount of words could define.

Rose was spellbound by the beauty of the sunset. She knew her eyes were streaming with water but they didn't hurt. She wasn't seeing with them. It felt as if she was seeing the sunset from deep within her mind and as if the sunset was connected with her in that way. She didn't have the words to define what was happening just then but she knew what it felt like and that it was good. It was all of those things that she was longing for and didn't know it – love, security, acceptance, unity, joy and a deep knowing of what was real. The sun pulsated with all the colours of the rainbow and as she watched Rose was aware of nothing other than her connectedness with it.

The final amazing pulse of colour gave way to a whitish glow as the sun dropped down below the horizon and Rose's heartbeat had slowed to almost a stop when something within her said, *'Remember Mexico!'*

When Carlos jumped down from the rocks behind her she barely reacted. He laughed at his own antics for a moment before he was struck silent by the power she was radiating. She seemed to be looking at him but her eyes displayed the distance between them and as he looked he became entranced. Her eyes pulled him closer and closer to her until he was no longer aware of where he stopped and she began. Suddenly, a wave of fear swept through Carlos and he gasped loudly as a picture flashed in his mind blocking out all sight of anything else. He saw a little girl lying on a bed and the girl was dying. She was physically paralyzed from the neck down and Carlos knew in an instant that she was paralyzed with fear and that he was looking at a scene in Mexico. He didn't know how he knew, but he was sure it was Mexico. The picture flashed off as quickly as it had come and Carlos dropped to his knees on the sand in front of Rose. The spell was broken and they both came slowly back to conscious awareness.

They said nothing for five minutes, just staring at each other as if they were trying to figure out who they each were. The night was very rapidly becoming dark and a warm breeze picked up from the direction of the sea. The sound of the water lapping up the sand could be heard directly behind Carlos. He was wet before either of them noticed that the tide had come in. It was Rose who broke the silence –

"Have you ever been to Mexico, Carlos?" she asked.

Carlos was shocked both with disbelief at the mention of Mexico and the unmistakable sadness in her voice.

"*Who are you*?" he whispered.

"I'm Rose." She spoke clearly for his benefit but she didn't sound convinced.

"Who is Rose?"

She looked away from him towards the sea and then up into the sky. She thought of the lady and the Indian and she smiled, putting her hand on her heart. She thought of her father and mother and her life back in Ireland and she frowned. But looking back at Carlos she suddenly realised with certainty that she didn't belong here. Not just here in Spain but here on this planet. She now knew she was much more than Rose McDevit. The good inside – the part of her that knew that her life wasn't meant to be this way – that was who she was, but who exactly *was* that? She got up and ran into the water, crying out loud.

Carlos ran after her and grabbed her pulling her into his embrace and insisting over and over – "Who are you? Who are you?"

"I dunno!" she cried, "I dunno who I am any more."

"Come," he whispered in her ear, "sit down and tell me. Tell me what makes you so sad my beautiful one."

They climbed over the rocks to the boardwalk and sat down on a bench. Carlos put an arm around Rose's shoulders and pulled her close to him. She rested her head on his shoulder and began to feel better. Should she trust this man she had only met a week ago or should she run the other way as fast as she could? He was very intense and she knew he was falling in love with her but she could never allow herself to be hurt again. She would be going home in a few days and life would go on. No Carlos, no romantic night strolls along the beach, just her sad, confused existence and the memory of something much more wonderful to remind her of how she had it perfect for a while. Then she thought of the feeling the setting sun had given her and she smiled inside. *That's* who she was - but what *was* that? What had it to do with Mexico?

"The wine!" exclaimed Carlos, running back over the rocks and rescuing the bottle of wine from the incoming tide. He had to search for the goblets which thankfully weren't broken. Rose laughed as he came back to her grasping the bottle and goblets to his chest and soaked to the thighs. He was grinning from ear to ear, not caring at all that his designer jeans were ruined with salt water. Putting the wine and goblets very carefully down on the boardwalk he stripped off his jeans revealing a pair of dazzling white boxers which glowed against the bronzed wet skin. Rose diverted her eyes for fear of losing a grip of her senses. She laughed to free the awkwardness and as he laughed too he lifted the wine and held it to the sky giving a loud whoop of delight.

"You're so full of life. You make me dizzy," she laughed.

He pulled her to her feet and began to dance with her swinging her around and about. "I'm just happy I've saved our wine" he told her. "I cannot have moonlight and a beautiful woman without wine."

He began to sing in his native tongue and as they danced and he sang Rose was enveloped with such joy and sheer pleasure at being alive in this moment with this wonderful man. His words filled her heart and although her ears did not understand them, her soul recognized them and it was singing also.

"This is who I am!" she cried with delight, her arms spread wide indicating her entire surroundings.

"What? You are dancing, *si*?"

"Yes, I am! And I am this language and this beautiful song and everything about this moment. This is who I am. It feels like I belong here in this moment."

"Wow, Rose! You are amazing, *si*?" He stopped dancing and flung himself on the bench with his arms over the back of it and his head flung backwards to gaze at the sky. "I feel I never want tomorrow to come. I am alive in this moment. I love you Rose. I want you to stay here with me in this moment forever."

It was fortunate for Rose that he couldn't see her face as she reacted to his words because, beautiful as they were, she knew she could never give her heart to this man. Besides the obvious reasons, there was an even greater reason and that was that somehow she now knew that her heart belonged to another. She didn't know who that was but she knew he wasn't too far away and that when she met him she would know him. But it wasn't Carlos - gorgeous, deep, wonderful

Carlos. He didn't realise that they were not meant to be together, that she was destined to be with another, but *she* knew. She sat beside him and opened the bottle of wine.

"Carlos, have you ever been to Mexico?" she suddenly asked.

Carlos sat up straight and looked at her bewildered. "Why do you ask about Mexico Rose?"

She was busy pouring the wine into a goblet which she handed to him and began on the second. She kept her eyes down the whole time avoiding his reaction to what she was about to say. "When I was watching the sunset a voice spoke to me inside and it said – *'remember Mexico'*."

There was a silence during which she could hear Carlos's breathing quicken and then he told her what he had experienced when she had looked into his eyes. He said "Your eyes, they looked deep inside me and I saw a picture of a time long ago. I saw a little girl. She was paralysed and she was dying. She was only four or five years old. And she was in Mexico."

Instantly Rose realised something and looked him in the eyes softly. "That was me," She said quietly.

"But I don't understand..." he began, and she interrupted with –

"I don't understand either. I just know, somehow, that before I was born I was that little girl in Mexico and I died like that."

"But this is..oh, how do you say?...lives before?

"Reincarnation."

"*Si*. I always think…yes, this is true…but I never remember. How do you know this is true?" He wanted to believe her because he had always believed this was possible, and how otherwise could she explain the way he had seen her like that?

"I don't have all the answers Carlos. I just knew when you told me what you saw, I knew that was me. And I believe you were in that life also, in Mexico. Somehow I know we were meant to be in love in that life but it never happened because I never grew up. I wasn't meant to die that way. I was paralyzed with fear."

"That is true because I felt it."

"And now I am in Ireland and I am destined to love someone else. He is waiting for me."

"And it is not me," he stated with a sigh.

"No, it is not you. Our time has passed, but we have this time together now and maybe this was meant to be so that we can say goodbye."

"How do you know this my beautiful Rose?"

"I just know. When I was a child, I knew things like that. I thought I had forgotten how to do it but I guess you never forget. And when you sang that beautiful song in that beautiful language, the words spoke to my soul and reminded me of how we were supposed to be together like this a long time ago."

"Wow! I think I shall never be the same Carlos ever again. I will always be the Carlos who loved and lost you two lifetimes in a row. But now, it is very strange, because

I feel I know now why I feel so sad all my life. It is because I was longing for you."

"We never had the chance to say goodbye."

"*Si*, that is right. I think I was your little friend and I was not permitted to be by your side as you were dying."

"And now we say goodbye." She searched his face and deep within it she could see her childhood friend from Mexico – the boy she had loved since they were born and that had been lost to her when she died. "Carlos?"

"Yes my love?"

"What did the words mean – the song - what was it about?"

"It is about a man who loves a woman and how he crosses a great distance to be with her."

The two soul-mates spent the entire night holding each other under the boardwalk. They made love secure in the knowledge that their love was for this moment and when Rose would go back to Ireland they would say goodbye and know that it was right. They talked about their past lives and this life and what it all meant, and they told each other secrets that they held fast to their hearts. Rose told Carlos about her sad childhood and about the lady and the Indian, and he told her about the little village where he grew up in the North of Spain and how he'd always longed to leave Spain some day and travel around the world. Maybe now his first destination would be Mexico. For the following three days they spent every minute in each other's company, not wanting to waste a single moment. When the time came for them to part they were both ready to say goodbye but they clung to each other for one final kiss and promised to meet again in another lifetime. That had been the most perfect time in Rose's life to date, for one miraculous night she knew who she was and why she was there. And although it was the end of her beautiful relationship with Carlos… it was not the end of Mexico, as she later discovered.

Tania Gates had been delighted to hear about Rose's brief holiday romance, for that is the way in which Rose had described it to her. She hadn't felt the need to share her wonderful experience or indeed allow Tania to get an insight into the private world of Rose McDevit. She didn't think Tania would understand anyway – about past lives, about Mexico. Tania was as unlike Carlos as could be. Come to think of it, most people were unlike Carlos. Most people were unlike her, of course. Carlos had been an exception, but then, he had been special to her and it was always going to be that way with him. She hugged the memory of him close to herself now as she sat opposite Tania.

"I must admit," confessed Tania, "I am a little jealous."

"I'm a little jealous of myself. Y'know, of the Rose that was on holiday."

"And is that Rose going to see Carlos again?" askedTania.

"No, I didn't give him my telephone number or my

address and I didn't get his either."

"Why not?" pressed Tania.

"It was perfect while I was there. But here, well it wouldn' be the same. I'm not *that* Rose here."

"So what Rose are you here?" Tania continued to probe.

"I'm just the crap that's left, aren't I?" said Rose disconsolately, because things had gone back to being the same as soon as she got home.

"What about the good that you say is in you? Isn't that still there?"

"Oh aye, but it doesn't work very well here" sighed Rose. "In Spain I was happy for a while. I've never laughed so much in my life and I felt sort of peaceful, I s'pose, for a while… whenever I was with him, anyway. But the thing is – the good stuff worked for me 'cos I was feeling happy. Here, I always feel sad, so it doesn't work."

"So feeling happy is the key," affirmed Tania. Rose nodded. "So, what makes you happy?"

She shrugged – "Dunno."

"Put it this way. If I ask you to say one word that means happiness, what would it be?"

Rose thought for a while. "*Being real*," she said emphatically, "In Spain I was being real."

Tania simply smiled. She always found it hard understanding Rose. In fact, she was beginning to think that Rose was so complex and intelligent that she could probably counsel herself. As it was, she had already learned a great deal about herself just by trying to figure out Rose. She decided to wing it: "And if I asked you to break down *being real* into smaller parts – what words come to mind?"

"*Erm*…acceptance…truth….justice."

"These things are important yes, but what about love and friendship and relationships; are they important?"

"Of course, but I don't have many friends…not real friends anyway." Rose thought about Carlos – *he* was real, and although she could not tell Tania this, the link with him went back to another world, another time.

"You've no real friends at all?" queried Tania.

"I've got Anne," reflected Rose, "an' she's always good for a laugh. And then there's Diane. She's the one with the two wee boys, y'know? She and I get on great together 'cos we have so much in common, don't we? But it's like…I can't explain it…they're not bein' *real*. It's like we're all playin' different parts in a massive TV show. No-one talks about reality, we all just play our parts an' we believe that's who we are."

"And are you playing a part?" asked Tania.

"Aye," Rose replied sadly.

"What part are you playing?"

"I'm playin' the part of Rose McDevit aren't I? But as well as that I'm pretendin' that even she is somethin' she's not."

"What are you pretending?" asked Tania intrigued.

"Well, I'm pretendin' all the time. When I was a wee'n, I pretended to play 'cos that's what wee'ns do, and when I was older I pretended that I was the same as everyone else when I never was and never will be. Tania, I think people pretend all the time. They pretend that they're happy when they're not. They pretend they want what's best for the people they love – well, that's just bullshit. They just want what's best for them, never mind about me. Then they have you pretendin' that it's okay when it's not." Rose was beginning to feel angry and she didn't like that. The best thing to do was to shut up and pretend like everyone else.

"If you pretend all the time Rose, then what are you pretending at the moment?" Tania asked gently.

Rose was shaking. She hadn't meant to say so much. The TV show feeling took over and before she was aware of having said any more, it was out of her mouth and done and dusted – too late to take it back. God forgive her if it was her imagination or worse still, if she was lying. She had said "I'm pretendin' Daddy's not tryin' to kiss me."

Rose could see that Tania was being very good and trying not to react badly to what she had heard, but she could tell that she was disgusted with her. Kevin and Brian had been disgusted too. She had told them about it just as they had set off for the airport last month to go on holiday to Spain together. Of course, they hadn't believed her. Why would they? They were completely innocent of the whole thing. Thank God they hadn't held it against her and snubbed her the whole time they were away. Meeting Carlos had been a godsend in that way too since it had freed her from the awkwardness between her and her brothers. She had sworn to herself that she would never repeat it and now here she was saying it to Tania. *I've told her that much I may as well tell her it all*, she thought to herself now.

"I want to remind you Rose, that whatever is said in this room stays in this room unless you wish otherwise" Tania reiterated, and then added wisely, "Speaking something out does not make it real. If it is real then it is real. Speaking it out just allows me to know it as well."

"And what if it's not real?" asked Rose, terrified.

Tania wanted to scream at her. How the hell could anyone be so unsure of what was real or not? If the dammed man was at it again, surely she could tell her exactly what was happening without questioning her sanity like that? Rose McDevit was far from crazy, of that she was sure – or was she?

"You've gotta stop questioning your perception Rose. Do you really believe that you're making whatever it is up?"

"No," she said, although her heart felt crushed.

There was a silence during which Tania seemed to have trouble remaining calm herself, then Rose told her. She told her everything that had been going on. She told her how every night her father had been coming into her bedroom to say goodnight – how he would say that he was terrified of losing her and how much he loved her. She told her about how he would hug her and rub his hand over her breasts and about how he would kiss her on the cheek and let the kiss linger with his lips moving closer and closer to hers.

She told her about all these things but most of all she told her of how they made her feel. She felt sick and scared and guilty and perverted and most of all, she felt powerless to stop him.

"There was one night," she said, "I was almost asleep and he'd bin in. He was wearing his pyjamas and it made me think about years ago y'know? Anyway, as I said, I was near sleepin' an' I just saw this thing on the other bed in the room. I looked at it for a while an' then it just appeared to be his clothes from long ago. It was as if I was in their bedroom when I was a wee'n. It was like one of them flashbacks I get. And that's not all. The weirdest thing happened. There was this big word too on the bed…just a big giant word. It said 'baby'. It seems stupid but it's like I know it's important and when I saw it I was scared stiff."

"What were you scared of?" Tania asked.

"I dunno. It was like somethin' terrible would happen but like it had already happened, y'know. Oh God! I feel sick!" She got up and began pacing around the room breathing heavily and shaking her head. She didn't want to think about being in her parents' room, never mind allow herself to remember what 'baby' meant.

"It's okay, Rose," Tania was thankful for the breakthrough, "it was a long time ago and it can't harm you now. You're perfectly safe here and now."

Rose looked at her, wanting her to say it was all her imagination. She felt safe with that, but Tania didn't tell her that – she told her, "These are your memories Rose. Trust them and know that they are only memories. They can't hurt you now."

Rose sat down and began crying. Tania went on, "Sometimes memories are much worse than the actual event you know. We keep them locked away in our sub-conscious for years because we can't look at them. Then, when it's safe and we're stronger and more able to deal with them, we let them out. The problem is we're remembering them as a child when things seem much more frightening but actually, as an adult, we are more able to cope with them."

Rose picked up. "And y'know, as well as that…" she began, getting into her self-counselling mode, "I couldn' possibly have bin able to understand what was happenin' when I was a child. Children don't know about sex an' all that. That's why it was so scary for me. Of course it was painful 'cos I was after all, only small an' well…y'know. But now, I'm an adult an' I know about sex and I can deal with it as an adult an' not a wee scared wee'n that doesn't know what's goin' on."

Before the end of that session, Rose had talked herself around from being frightened and unsure of what she was going to do about her father's recent advances to being angry and motivated into putting a stop to it for good. She was going to tell him *no* and make sure he was aware that it was not acceptable – not *now*, not *then*. As well as that, she was going to get out of that house and find somewhere to live by herself where she could protect herself for sure. She didn't realise it then, but she had made a decision that was to bring about huge changes and propel her closer towards not only surviving but towards recovery. Spain and Carlos now seemed a long way away.

November 1993

Rose had been in her new home for five months now. It was a one-bedroom flat on the other side of town, on the second floor of an old building and it had no central heating. Plus, the windows were draughty and did very little to keep out the noise from the busy street below. There was a tiny kitchen that was crying out to be re-furbished and a pokey little bathroom that had been painted black by the previous tenant. With her brother Brian's help, Rose didn't waste any time in slapping several coats of brilliant white emulsion on walls, ceiling and bath panel. On the floor she placed a bright pink mat and on the window sill – a vase of silk roses. The kitchen cupboards were given a new lease of life with white paint and new shiny black knobs and Rose splashed out on a brand new piece of linoleum for the floor. In the sitting room a settee and a television had been left, which were both in reasonably good condition. Angela and her husband Paddy had a little table and two kitchen chairs in their garage which Paddy had helped her to carry up the two flights of stairs. They were placed in front of the sitting room window. Rose found a beautiful pair of pink curtains in a charity shop and with another vase of silk roses placed on the little table, the room was looking good. The bedroom was just about big enough to hold Rose's bed and with one small wardrobe squeezed into the corner it was barely tolerable, but tolerable none the less. When all was done Rose cooked for the first time in her new home and Brian was invited for dinner to say thank you for all his hard work. Rose was still very fond of him and although he had his own life in Dublin with Kevin and his job as a nurse in the city's main hospital, she knew that she need only ask and he would help her out with whatever she may need. Kevin, on the other hand was more of the thoughtless type and spent all of his time pursuing women and having a good time outside of his work as a brickie. Rose admired Brian. He was intelligent like her and no doubt had loads of her sensitivity but he had been wanted and loved and he had deserved it. The two of them got along together pretty well unless Kevin was about and then Brian treated her with indifference so as not to lose face with his big brother. Rose understood though – it wasn't easy going against the group belief that she was strange. Plus, there was by now a new group belief that said that she was mentally sick and that she ought to be tolerated but not indulged.

Brian was watching a documentary about package holidays abroad. It was one of those programmes that talked about people's disastrous holidays – cockroaches in the beds, dirty pools, that sort of thing. He shouted to Rose who was still busy in the kitchen – "Rosie, come here a minute."

Rose had always liked the way Brian called her Rosie. He was the only one who did except for Daddy and Auntie Lett. She remembered that Lett had said to Mum that she'd call in on Rose some day this week.

"Lett's supposed to be calling in some day this week, probably tomorrow, I'd say" she called back to Brian. She came into the sitting room and handed him a can of lager. "What d'ya think she wants? Sure we never see her anymore since she had the wee'ns." Lett had married ten years back and had four children by now, all girls.

"Och! Y'know what Lett's like," replied Brian, more interested in the documentary, "at Mum's beck an' call. Look, d'ya think that's where we were. It looks like it don't it?" Rose looked at the scene on the television. It showed the pool area of a hotel on the Costa Del Sol.

"Aye, it does look like it. D'ya remember what it's called?" she asked.

"*El pueblo del Ingles*," said Brian with a Spanish accent.

"You sounded just like Carlos there" laughed Rose.

"Good craic if we see him standing beside the pool" said Brian studying the screen intensely. "Nah, it's not it. That bar wasn't there."

Rose was disappointed. It would have been a long shot to spot Carlos there but it wasn't even the same hotel. She went back to her cooking.

"Beats me why ya didn't get Carlos' phone number," Brian told her later whilst digging into his bowl of spaghetti Bolognese.

"I told ya. We both agreed that it was best left the way it was."

"But he was mad about ya and there's no point in denying it – you were mad about him too."

"Yea but..." she wondered how much Brian would understand now that there was no Kevin to make fun of it. "Do you believe in fate Brian?"

He sat back in his chair and watched his sister intently as she flustered, avoiding his gaze. "Aye, I think so. What do you think?"

Rose played with her food. "I think everyone has a destiny and it doesn't matter what way you go in life – you're always gonna end up with your destiny."

"So what's that got to do with Carlos then?" he was almost reluctant to ask. The last thing he wanted was her going off on one and acting all loony.

"He's not my destiny. Well, he was at one stage, but he's not now. Someone else is."

What the fuck? Brian thought. He knew he shouldn't have indulged her. Now she'd gone all weird on him again. He decided to ride this one out for a while just to give her a chance. God knows, she might say something that would help him understand what was going on with her. "Okay then, go on, tell me who it is" he asked her.

Rose wasn't thick. She knew Brian was acting all – *I don't really believe you but I'll listen anyway* – but to her, the reality was that deep down he wanted to believe her and wanted to talk about these things that were lurking beneath his surface

– he just was afraid to go there. And Rose couldn't blame him, could she? He knew the way she'd been teased and tormented because of the way she was. There was no way he would openly say that he was the same. She looked at him with compassion and shook her head but said nothing. Moments passed in silence. He felt very uncomfortable. He had never forgotten the time when he was eight years old, when they still lived in Belfast. The way she had looked at him, very much like she was looking at him now. Back then he had thought she was putting a spell on him but now he knew that the strangeness had been something that he had yet to encounter with anyone else in his life but when all was said and done, it was something that ought to be present throughout everyone's life, and that was integrity. Rose had looked at him with complete integrity.

After several moments she said –"Bottom line Brian… Carlos would only be a distraction from the real thing. The man I'm destined to marry is out there somewhere. I'm ready for him and I really do think I have to go out tonight 'cos I'm gonna meet him really soon."

"Aye well, you'd better hurry up. What age are ya? Pushin' thirty? If ya don't meet him soon no-one will want ya." Brian dodged a feigned slap from his sister and the both of them laughed, the atmosphere lightened a great deal.

"Better get one of them beers," Rose laughed as she dashed to the fridge, "got a big night ahead of me." She reached into the fridge to grab a can and a vivid memory of that night with Carlos washed over her filling her with the same certainty she had felt then – "I *am* gonna meet him tonight," she smiled to herself.

Later, at eleven thirty pm when all the pubs were shut, Rose and her friend Diane were staggering along the promenade in Drumgar looking for somewhere to get a final beer before calling it a night. They had been out since seven thirty that evening and had had more than enough to drink as it was but neither of them wished to go home to their lonely lives, not while people were still having fun in the dancehall. At one am everyone would come spilling out onto the promenade and the craic would be great. Rose and Diane wanted to hang around till then and make the most of their night out. Money was in short supply for both of them, that was the reason they didn't go to the dance, it cost ten punts just to get in and then the drinks were two prices as well. It wouldn't have been a big one anyway since the tourist season was over and the really big bands only played then. Passing Farley's bar they almost collided with a man as he exited the pub.

"Larry Burns, how's it goin'?" Rose knew Larry Burns from when she worked for O'Hanlons.

"Well, if it isn't wee Rose. How are ya there? I haven't seen you in yonks." Larry was even drunker than she was and he swayed as he spoke. Rose was reminded of her father back when he would have had *too many wee ones*, as she had called it. The bitch was that now she remembered what happened to her when Daddy had had too many wee ones.

She ignored the urge to cry and pretended that all was rosy in the garden.

"Grand, Larry" she said and turned to Diane, "Larry delivered coca cola to O'Hanlons years ago" she told her. "What ya doin' now Larry?"

"Oh, mostly about Dublin now. Just come down for the weekend with me mates. Tell me this, whatever happened to yer man, Paul Rooney?"

"God knows for I certainly don't" replied Rose acting cool. "Why?"

"He left Coca Cola after you and him split up ya know. There was a rumour goin' round the plant that he came after ya, put ya in hospital."

Rose could see that Larry would not have been saying those things should he have been sober. So, people in Dublin knew she had been in hospital? That means that Paul must have known something. What was it to her now though? She didn't care what he thought any more. "Never seen him since we split up," she said. Best to change the subject – "What's goin' on in there tonight? Sounds like a lock in."

"Yep" hiccoughed Larry. "I can get ya in if ya want. Owner's a friend o' mine."

"Happy days," said Diane, "hurry up though, I'm foundered."

Larry disappeared back into the bar and a couple of minutes later reappeared to pull them in through the door. There weren't too many people there. Just a few of the regulars propping up the bar and some lucky ones like themselves that had been in the right place at the right time. Mickey Farley was behind the bar serving as usual. Rose knew who he was but outside of the bar she wouldn't know him from Adam. Larry managed to get them a couple of beers and invited them to join him and his mates. Neither Rose nor Diane knew any of them at all. They were all from Dublin and thankfully no-one bar Larry knew Paul Rooney. The craic was going great when Larry took Rose to the side and told her that a guy he knew up at the bar had been asking who the woman in the red jersey was, meaning her of course. He pointed the guy out to Rose who took quick stock of what she would be dealing with. The man wasn't bad looking but then again he wasn't exactly Carlos standard. He had brown hair cut tight to his head and he wore a plain shirt and jeans.

"He's Jack Farley, Mickey's brother," Larry told her, "A quiet lad ya know, not like Mickey. Jack's okay. Go on up an' say hello, ya'd wait all night for *him* to do it."

Rose was feeling brave, plus she was drunk and it seemed that Jack Farley was drunk too by the way he was teetering on the edge of his bar stool. She had nothing to lose and since Diane was deeply engrossed with one of Larry's mates, she thought *why not*? "Hi, I'm Rose" she said to Jack. "Who are you?"

Jack Farley looked at her, eyes flashing with amusement. He grinned and slurred drunkenly – "Jack…who are you?"

Another wise guy. She and Diane had had their fill

of that kind tonight. She couldn't be bothered with that. "Look, Larry Burns just said to say hello and I did, so…" Rose turned to go and Jack caught a hold of her arm.

"Sorry... Jack Farley….how are ya?" He held out his hand and Rose shook it.

"Okay," she said beginning to like the look of his smile, "how are *you*?"

"Oh, I'm just fine and dandyo," he grinned, "now that you're here."

"I know what ya mean," she laughed. Jack Farley was a funny guy and she liked him immediately. The thing was, she really did know exactly what he meant. He really was fine and dandyo and so was she…now that he was there.

Jack was her destiny - another crucial piece of the jigsaw had suddenly fallen into place.

Chapter Thirteen

The little white cross

Cloughbeg, April 2008

Lissy was having such a wonderful time. She had never been so relaxed. For at least a year now she had been feeling restless, like she needed to be somewhere but didn't know where that was. Now, she felt as if she had packed her case and was well on her way. John was terrific. He loved her very much and she was very much in love with him. To think that she had kept him at arm's length all that time, she must have been mad. It was wonderful spending so much time together. They had been to the promenade in Drumgar and had walked the length of the beach. It was still too cold to take their shoes off for a paddle but they enjoyed the brisk sea air and the general buzz of the early spring holiday feeling. Last night they had dinner in The Sea Front, a fantastic seafood restaurant on the promenade and then they had a couple of drinks nearby in a cosy little pub called Farleys. Today was Wednesday and they were going back to Cloughbeg to have lunch with Father Jim, as Lissy had taken to calling him. Actually, they were meant to go there on Thursday but Father Jim had called early to say that he had heard back from the social worker and that since he now had to help out with a bit of a tricky situation in Drumgar tomorrow, could they please come today instead?

They had spent the morning browsing the shops in the town. Lissy bought some nice trinkets for her parents and for Lynn. She rang her parents whilst sitting in a cute little ice cream parlour on the main street. John was ordering two banana splits with all the trimmings and the big fat jovial owner was keeping him entertained with stories about the locals. Every now and then he would give a loud guffaw and Lissy had to keep asking her mum to repeat herself. "Bye then, bye," she said over the loud laughter. She put her phone away and joined John at the counter.

"Ah now, who is this lovely vision?" the owner almost shouted.

Lissy offered her hand – "Lissy Brenning, how do you do?" She smiled sweetly and shook his hand.

"Lissy, eh? That's not a name ya hear every day. Joe O'Hanlon's the name sweetheart. John here says you're off to Cloughbeg, that right?"

"Yes, we've been there already but we didn't have time to get a good look round."

"Ah well, yer talkin' to the right man. From that neck o'

the woods meself y'know."

"Oh really, how nice. We would love to explore some of those little coves along there you know, but it's finding the access roads. I don't suppose you could…"

"Are no access roads me dear," he butted in, "ya can get the car as far as the hills then ya heddy walk from there."

"That's too bad," John said, "but Lissy and I don't mind a bit of hill climbing. Do we honey?"

"No, not at all. I'd love it. If you would be so kind as to give us general directions, Mr O'Hanlon."

"I'll go one better than that me dear. As I say, the auld home place is out there, so it is. Bin ages since I went to see me auld ma. What d'ya say I take ya out there meself?"

Lissy looked at John questioningly. What did he think about the idea? Certainly seemed like fun to her.

"That's not a bad idea" John stated seeing how enthusiastic she was, "If you don't mind Mr O'Hanlon."

"Not at all, not at all, what time would ya want to go then?"

"Well, we have a lunch date in Cloughbeg for twelve. Shall we meet there, say one thirty?"

"No problem, great. I'll just tell the missus." He waddled off, shouting for Iris and forgetting totally about their banana splits.

At five minutes to twelve Lissy and John knocked on the big green door of Cloughbeg Parochial House. Melissa opened it, promptly this time and gave them one of her wide smiles – "How are ya?" she shrilled and once again Lissy and John were reminded of Mrs Doyle, the guest house owner.

Lissy was fond of the young girl - "Hello again Melissa, how are you dear?" John thought she sounded like her mother then and made a mental note to warn her about it.

"Ah, sure I'm grand thanks" repliedMelissa. "Come on in now, the Father's in the study." She stood aside and grinned like a Cheshire cat as they passed her and went on into the hall. "Just go on on down to the kitchen there. 'Fraid there's no big fancy dining room in this house. The house in Drumgar has the poshest one ya ever seen."

She ushered them down the long hallway and through a door into a huge kitchen. It wasn't old-fashioned like the front room but, to Lissy's surprise, it was extremely modern and very clean. Every surface, including the tiled floor, shone like polished silver and great big bunches of daffodils and tulips were displayed wherever you looked.

"Melissa!" exclaimed Lissy, "this is absolutely beautiful, and you keep it so marvellously clean. Aren't you the gem?"

Melissa beamed broadly with pleasure and pride. She liked this woman with the same name as her, and her partner was alright too. She busied herself with checking the food in the oven stating in her grown-up voice "Sure it's not hard to do a lock o' dishes. Sit down now an' I'll tell the father you're here."

"Will you be joining us for lunch then?" Lissy enquired

both to be polite and to please Melissa by treating her as an adult.

"Good gracious no!" she exclaimed, "It wouldn' be proper, but yer real nice fer askin' Miss Brenning, and you too of course Mr… erm…"

"Brunt," said John, "but it's Lissy and John to you."

"And Lissy's short for Melissa, isn't that right? I'd love people to call me Lissy, it's far nicer, but me ma always says that ya use the name ya were christened by and be grateful fer it."

"She must have liked Melissa though or she wouldn't have named you that," said Lissy.

"Oh no, Theresa's not me real ma. She fostered me when I was five. Me real ma couldn' look after me an' me sister. But Theresa's bin more of a mother to me, so she has."

Lissy had forgotten that she grew up in foster care – "And did she foster your sister as well?" she asked awkwardly.

"Nah, we were separated ages ago. She was only a baby, probably 'bout ten or eleven now. She lives in Lisnablaney. We see each other sometimes y'know but I hardly know 'er so it doesn't really matter."

Lissy couldn't believe how flippant the girl was being about her real family. She felt sorry for her and instinctively felt all maternal over her. "Melissa, how would you like to come with us this afternoon? We're going to visit some of the little coves round here. I know it's a bit cold and that but if you wrap up warm. Well, you'd be very welcome and we'd enjoy your company."

John looked at Lissy as if she'd gone mad. He didn't want anyone else joining him. The big guy was enough. When Melissa left to fetch Father Jim, delighted with the prospect at spending an entire afternoon with her new friends, Lissy wasted no time in explaining her actions to John. "Think about it John" she whispered to him, "Mr O'Hanlon may be able to show us where to go but he can't very well lead us over the hills now can he? The poor man is hardly fit to walk as it is. Did you see the way he puffed and wheezed. Too heavy I suppose. Melissa is bound to know the way down to the coves, she's from round here."

John put his arms around her and pulled her close kissing her neck. "Our own personal guide, eh? How do you know she lives round here though?"

"Father Jim said so on Monday, don't you remember?" replied Lissy in disgust. "I don't know, you men never pay attention to anything. Oh, watch out, there's the priest coming." She pushed him away from her as she felt he was being a little too familiar for the eyes of a priest.

"Well now," boomed Jim, "How are we all?" He shook hands with John and kissed Lissy. They were both happy to see him again. He certainly did have a happy demeanour about him.

"Good, Father, I mean Jim, and how are you?" John replied, grinning broadly.

"Ah now, can't complain. There'd be nobody listenin' if I did. Hope you're hungry folks – Melissa's made a quiche."

"Oh lovely, my favourite," answered Lissy, "is that it in

the oven? Shall I dish it out?"

"Ya can if ya want sweet girl. Melissa's gone to run an errand in the village and I'm not what ya might call domesticated, I'm afraid." The three friends had a very pleasant lunch of salmon quiche and salad washed down with a glass of white wine and finished off with fruit pavlova and fresh whipped cream. John made instant coffee as Lissy and Jim continued to discuss the issue of her birth mother. Lissy had prepared herself for the worst and she hadn't been wrong.

"Do you mean there was no social involvement at all?" she moaned.

"If there was it wasn't from that department" said Jim.

"But what about other departments? Surely, there had to be some level of involvement somewhere," she folded her arms and scolded. Every bloody time she got a break, something buggered it up. Jim had come up with nothing on the baptismal records as well. He just shrugged now in response to her question. "Did the social worker put in Father Murphy's name?" Lissy asked him.

"She did everythin' she could think off. Father Murphy came up a few times for different reasons but none of them about a thirteen year old girl. She did suggest that the situation may have been recorded under the girl's mother's name or indeed another relative such as an older sister."

"Is that legal?" shouted John from the far end of the kitchen.

"I suppose it must be, to a certain extent perhaps."

Lissy was deep in thought. An idea was coming to her.

"I know," she piped up excitedly, "What if she puts in Father Kearns' details in Dorset? I know we have no name but we might just get an address."

"Wouldn't think so," Jim answered her, "that kind of information on adoption records can't be given out unless the birth mother gives her permission."

"I have thought about that," said John, setting the coffee mugs down on the table. He sat down again at his chair. "What it boils down to is this – an adopted person can enter their details into a search that should find their adoption records. They may be given the adoption agency's name but not any personal information about the adoption unless the birth mother agrees to it."

"So why haven't we done that?" asked Lissy indignantly.

"Just wait a minute," John held up his hands at her, "I *have* done it, remember? – in February just after your exhibition? Remember I said I'd do some investigation at work? It was one of the first things I did – I entered your details but nothing - absolutely nothing." Lissy was looking at him as if he was her worst enemy. "Honey, listen to me" he told her, "I said before we came here that this was our only hope."

Lissy wasn't sure he had been straightforward but then, why would he not be? Suddenly it occurred to her – "You knew we would find nothing here" she accused him. "Why did you drag me all the way here when you knew it was hopeless?"

"I didn't know it was hopeless."

"Yea, but you knew if you got me here on our own I'd not say no to you."

John leapt up off his chair and poor Jim had to make his excuses and disappear once again.

"Fuck sake Lissy, if that's what you think of me there's not much point is there?" said John defending himself, though he felt guilty – it was not entirely untrue.

Lissy was sorry - "Sorry, I didn't mean that. But why come here in the first place? It's hopeless."

"It's not hopeless darling, there's still ways of finding out who she was and then we can take it from there. Look, we'd best not talk like this here, it's not fair on poor Jim."

"I know, but he'll be the first to tell you, we've practically zero information to go on."

Jim must not have been too far away because he came back just then and had obviously heard what Lissy had just said because he replied to her - "Not exactly zero, sweet girl. We know several things. We know her date of birth and we know that there were no Catholic baby girls born on that day in Cloughbeg or in Drumgar, so we know she wasn't from this parish. We know her grandmother was though." He waited for Lissy to respond but she said nothing. "Don't you get it sweet girl? Find out who the grandmother was and you find her."

"And we find the grandmother by asking the local villagers. Someone is bound to know something. It's a close community. For all we know, the grandmother might still be about," added John, thankful that Jim had defused the situation. "Maybe Joe O'Hanlon will know something, or his old mother."

"Or..." Lissy almost squealed with excitement, "Father Murphy's sister. Mrs Doyle said she still lived in the village. The priest's own sister, she must have known a lot of what was going on in the village." John and Jim said nothing. They were both trying to take in Lissy's sudden transformation. She had a point though, the priest's sister, still living in Cloughbeg.

"It's worth a try, well done honey, nobody thought of that," said John hugging her.

But Jim wasn't so optimistic. "I don't wish to be a wet blanket or anything folks but I don't really think she would know any more than any other villager" he told them. "I'm quite sure the priest didn't tell her all of his parishioner's business." Jim wasn't sure he could witness another mood swing like the last two and didn't wish for Lissy to get her hopes up again. *What a roller coaster,* he thought.

"Well, she's a good place to start" said John brightly. "Hey, maybe you know where she lives?" he realised suddenly.

"That I do. She lives in the village," replied Jim a little flatly. Was he beginning to feel differently about the whole thing? Maybe it wasn't such a good idea to get so involved. Auld Bernard might not be too happy should he compromise his parishioners. Nevertheless, he said he would help and help he would. "Give me a minute, please," he said and went to his office. Having found the telephone number he required he dialled and waited.

Mrs Sarah Scallon lived in the main street in the village, beside the post office. Her husband had been the post master for years but had died some ten years ago now. She still lived there on her own – never had any children – with only her cats for company. Jim often visited her on a Saturday to give her Holy Communion and hear her confession. He waited now as the phone rang on and on with no answer. She was probably asleep in her armchair this time of the afternoon. He'd call back later. When he went back into the kitchen Lissy was chatting excitedly whilst John was up to his elbows in suddy water.

"Leave them John," Jim insisted, "Melissa will be back soon." Lissy and John noticed the decline in Jim's usually bubbly manner.

"Lunch was great Jim," Lissy told him, "you must let us treat you in the town before we go home."

"That'd be nice, thanks Lissy. When do you go home anyways?" Lissy noticed he hadn't called her 'sweet girl'.

"Not till next Wednesday, a whole week yet" she told him. "Oh, by the way, I asked Melissa if she would like to join us this afternoon. We're going to visit the coves if that's okay? Mr O'Hanlon will be guiding us so she'll be well looked after."

"Mr O'Hanlon...?" Jim looked puzzled.

"He owns the ice cream parlour in Drumgar. A big fat fellow, very jolly."

"Ah yes, I know *him*...Joe!"

"That's him. Would that be okay then?"

"Don't see why not. She doesn't do much outside of here the poor pet. No, it'll be more than okay, it'll be grand. Are ya sure ya don't mind havin' a wee'n taggin' along though?"

"A wee'n, what's that?" laughed John, he was trying to lighten the atmosphere. Father Jim had gone all priest-like on them.

"A wee'n – that's what we call a child round here. Well, not just round here, I suppose everyone in Ireland calls it that. A wee'n – *wee one*, get it?"

"Granny and Grandad used to call me that and sometimes Mum talks about the wee'ns when she means Auntie Margaret's children. Mind you, they're not children any more but she still thinks they are."

"She still thinks *you* are," added John mischievously. Lissy dipped her hand in the washing up basin and planted some bubbles on his nose. Everyone laughed and pretty soon things were lightened up.

When Melissa knocked on the kitchen door no-one heard her over the laughter. She came right in and grabbed a tea towel to dry up. Jim, who was feeling more himself, told her to leave it and go and get ready for the hillwalk. "You're all havin' a good time I see," she smiled at Lissy, "is it still okay... to come with ya that is?"

"Certainly dear, we're looking forward to it. Have you eaten? There's some of your scrummy quiche left if you want it?"

"No ta, I dropped in on me ma. Gotta go, see ya in a minute." She left the kitchen and could be heard running up the stairs. Everyone laughed.

"Her ma lives in the village. She usually makes dinner at this time and wee Melissa never says no to her ma's dinners," Jim told them.

"She's so sweet. I never had a little sister but if I did I would like to think she'd be just like her." Lissy was feeling high now that they had another plan, plus the weather was lovely and they were going to spend the day at the seaside with this delightful teenager. Jim was keen to put an even bigger smile on her face and told them that he had rung Sarah Scallon, Father Murphy's sister.

"She was likely napping beside the fire but I'll call back in an hour or so an' I'll let ya know what she says."

"Great! Got a good feeling about her," replied Lissy, "we could call and see her tonight couldn't we John?"

"As long as it's okay. Don't see why not."

"Don't see why not what?" asked Melissa excitedly as she came back wrapped up in a padded jacket and woolly hat and with a wide grin from ear to ear.

"Melissa!" exclaimed Jim shocked at her cheek.

"Sorry Father," she apologised but never once did the smile fade.

"She's fine Jim," said John. "We were just planning to visit Sarah Scallon down in the village," he told Melissa.

"Auld Sarah? Sure what would ya want wi' her? She lives beside me ma and da y'know. I'll take ya down there meself if ya want." She was keen to do anything for lovely Lissy.

"Thank you Melissa, I'm sure that John and Lissy can find their own way to the village though," said Jim ushering her out to the hall. "Off ya go now an' wait outside. Our guests will be along in a minute."

After summing up the day's developments with Jim, Lissy and John closed the green door as they left and climbed into the car with a grinning Melissa behind them. It was twenty past one, just in time to meet Mr O'Hanlon.

Joe O'Hanlon took off his shop apron and hung it on its peg on the back of the kitchen door. It was twelve o'clock, just enough time to grab a sandwich and wee cup of tay and then have a half-hour nap before meeting that nice young English couple in Cloughbeg. Iris, his wife, had been glad to see him taking time off work for a change, although she wasn't too keen on him traipsing over hills.

"By all means," said she, "go and enjoy yerself and keep them right, but no traipsing over them hills. You're in no fit state for that carry on."

Joe had no such intention. He thought he might go a little ways down though just so as the wee critters didn't get lost. Then he might pop in to see his ma and have a wee cup of tay with her and a couple of bits of scone bread with some homemade butter and his ma's best gooseberry jelly. His ma was famous round these parts for her gooseberry jelly. She was eighty three years of age this month and wasn't much able to look after the place so well anymore but she still loved to make her jams.

Joe put the electric kettle on and sat down at the table for a moment. He wasn't feeling so good today. He was tired. Thirty four years he'd had this wee shop. When he was younger, he was fit to do his share on the farm and run his own business at the same time. Then his younger brother Tom took over the farm work completely which left him and Iris off the hook and was a good thing because he never would have described himself as a land person – no, he was more of a people person. The kettle clicked off but he sat a while longer. *Just til I get me second wind*, he said to himself. His chest was paining but Dr Ellis had assured him it was only a wee bit of angina, nothing to worry about and he had given him a bottle of pills which he was very reluctant to take. The pain got worse – *ah damn it*, he thought. He shouted loudly for Iris to hear - "*Where's them damn pills?*" There was no answer. *Ah be God, I'll heddy get them meself*. He got up to look for them, *Jesus, the sweat's lickin' off ma*! He was about to reach into the top cabinet when the pain gripped him hard across the chest and down his arm. He opened his mouth to shout for Iris again but the words never came. He was dead before he hit the floor.

They had waited for twenty minutes for Mr O'Hanlon but he didn't arrive and when they phoned the ice cream parlour there had been no answer so they decided to press on with their plans without him. They had Melissa after all. The road out of Cloughbeg was no wider than the road to there from Drumgar. They passed hedgerow after hedgerow and stone wall after stone wall as the car climbed steadily upwards. When there was a break in the hedge the views were fantastic. There weren't many houses about but Melissa knew which lane led to which particular farmhouse, which sheep belonged to which farmer, and just who had built that particular wall.

"You certainly know a lot about this place," John had said.

"Me ma grew up here. She knows everyone an' she tells me every time we go fer a visit out here."

As the road began to even out high up on the mountainside Lissy could see for miles out to sea. The hills fell away sharply in some places and more undulating in others where juts of land reached outwards. Around the edges of these were tiny little whitecaps that were likely not so tiny up close. Each jut of land had one or two little cottages on them. Lissy stretched to see if there were any modern houses but there didn't seem to be. "Can we stop here for a bit?" she asked, "I want to get a proper look."

John stopped the car where it was as there was nowhere to pull in anyway. They all got out and gasped with the icy wind that threatened to toss them off their feet.

"Nice with the sun shining into the car," Melissa giggled, turning her back to the wind. Lissy pointed down to one of the jutting out bits of lands.

"Look, down there" she said. "See that little cottage with the red roof?" John and Melissa tried to see where she was pointing. "There, do you see that group of trees, like a little wood. Just behind that. See it now?" John nodded, grimacing with the cold wind biting his face. "Isn't it adorable?"

"That's me ma's auld house," Melissa stated proudly. "Her ma still lived there up till she died nine years ago. I can take ya down there if ya want. There's a wee walk down to one of the coves from there. See the trees there? Just behind them is the way down to the cove."

"Gosh, yes, that'd be great." Lissy wasted no time in getting back into the car. As it turned out they were very near to the tiny road that ran down the mountainside. Melissa proudly gave them a running commentary the whole way, which was longer than Lissy or John would have thought. The road twisted and turned as it went down. They passed two other little cottages that were deserted also, they each had tiny little windows with smashed glass out of which flapped torn net curtains. Lissy thought they were like little ghost houses with the wind howling through them as they waved at the visitors to stop and take a look. She wanted to but John said that time was moving on and they had already wasted half an hour waiting for Mr O'Hanlon.

"That's the Bradleys' auld place. She's in the auld people's home in Drumgar now, that wee woman," offered Melissa as they passed on by the second cottage without stopping. "There's a wee lane on yer right just comin' up about...now," she said, and they immediately turned right, down an even narrower lane. It was so pretty. The tall hedgerows on either side were absolutely festooned with rhododendrons. Soon, the car pulled into a yard and there was the little white-washed cottage right beside them. On their other side was the group of trees – it really was more like a small wood.

"It is okay to leave the car here isn't it?" asked John.

"No bother," answered Melissa. She hopped out and ran to the door of the cottage. She tried the latch but it was locked. She peered in through one of the tiny windows that had been smeared with window cleaner. "It looks different from I remember, smaller" she remarked.

"That's because you're bigger," John told her. He looked in through the window as well. The room was empty except for an old range cooker. He went to the second little window and looked. "There's a couple of old bedsteads in here."

"Where did Lissy go?" Melissa asked him looking around for her. She was no-where to be seen.

"Round back I suppose," said John casually. He walked around to the back of the house and found two old sheds almost toppled to the ground but no Lissy. "Lissy, where are you?" he shouted. Lissy didn't reply. He walked around the other side of the house looking about all the time but he didn't see her. In the front yard Melissa was pointing to the wood.

"She's in there." John followed Melissa in. Lissy was kneeling down in front of something. When John got closer he saw it was a little white wooden cross.

"What have you found there?" he asked.

"I think it's a little grave," answered Lissy forlornly. It certainly did look like a grave, although maybe a bit too small even for a baby coffin. Scraped into the wooden cross was a single name – 'GRACE'. "It feels so sad, doesn't it?"

"It may be a pet," suggested John.

Melissa shook her head –"No way, nobody in our family has a pet called Grace. There's just me ma and her two sisters lived here – Aunty Collette and Aunty Clare an' none of them have any pets at all. Besides, this is new. It wasn't here when Granny died."

Lissy was reluctant to leave the little grave. *It could be a pet's grave*, she was thinking, *but somehow I don't think so. It feels so significant, like it's marking something – something major in someone's life*.

Melissa was keen to get showing them the cove. She had only been a few times when visiting Granny Doyle but she remembered the way. Of course Granny Doyle wasn't her real Granny but she had been really nice in telling Melissa that she could call her Granny. Besides, Melissa could hardly remember her real family at all and Theresa and Pat McGuiness had been the best parents she could have hoped for. "Let's go, I'll show ya how to get down to the cove," she offered almost jumping with excitement.

Lissy was picking dead leaves and twigs off the little

grave. "Give me a minute will you. I think I might say a little something here. I know it seems silly but well....I don't know...I just want to."

"I'll ask me ma if ya like. See what it is in there" offered Melissa.

"No, don't do that dear. Whoever put this here obviously went to a lot of trouble and I think they put it here for a very important reason. I don't think they would have wanted anyone to know about it." She looked up at John – "I say we just leave it be and tell no-one."

"Agreed," said John, "Melissa, you're on no account to tell anyone of the whereabouts of this little white cross." Lissy knew he was teasing her. "Now, let's go" he insisted.

"You go on – I'll be out in a minute," said Lissy. The others left the little wood and went back into the yard to wait for her. She finished tidying the grave and then looked about her till she found some crocuses growing beneath a large pine. The earth was dry and so it was easy for Lissy to dig in with her fingers and pull the crocuses up, bulbs and all. She brought them over to the grave and re-planted them at the foot of the little white cross. Then she self-consciously muttered a few words – *bless this little white cross and bless the hand that made it.*

It was almost five pm when the group made their way back to the cottage. Lissy had been unusually quiet the whole time they were away. John had wondered if she was feeling disheartened about the search again but actually, she just couldn't stop thinking about the little white cross. It had pulled on her heart strings so much that she found herself wondering who Grace was. Was she a cat or a dog or was she indeed someone's little baby? The funny thing was, she didn't think it was any of the three. *I guess I'll never know*, she relented as they neared the top of the hill and the red tin roof of the cottage could be seen coming into view.

Chapter Fourteen

The meetings

The fog was still there – thick and murky with demons lurking in every corner. The jigsaw was started and the first few pieces were in place but the fog was hiding pieces that Rose knew were crucial, in order for her to see the whole picture.

January 1994

Rose was head over heels in love with Jack Farley. Each minute they spent together emphasised the feeling they had that they had known each other a long time. For Rose it went even deeper than that – she was convinced they had been together for lifetimes.

"The soul comes back again and again meeting the same other souls until they have fulfilled their reason for being together," she told Jack, because she knew that now. It was something she had known since the re-encounter with

Carlos, which had been destined. Jack wasn't convinced that she knew what she was talking about but he loved the idea that she and he were soulmates so he smiled and let her jabber away about her belief in reincarnation. They spent their time talking into the wee hours of the mornings. Jack stayed in the flat almost every night, went to work in the mornings at nine am, thought about Rose all day long and then hurried back to her in the evenings. They couldn't bear to be apart. Jack worked as a car mechanic for a local firm. He had thought about going into the family business but in the end his younger brother Mickey seemed keener to take over the running of the pub than he was, so Jack stuck with the mechanics. He was also an avid biker. Motorbikes were his life and Rose was quickly becoming a fan as well. Sitting on the back of a bike going seventy miles an hour with her arms wrapped around Jack, she got such a sense of freedom and release. Jack Farley was good for her – there was no denying that. She was good for him too it seemed – she gave him her respect, made him feel worthy and appreciated.

"That was what I needed," he would say to her many times – "to be appreciated." One day he showed her a snapshot of his little daughter. "This is my Emma. She's four years old."

"She's gorgeous," Rose told him, "like her daddy."

"I told her mum Kelly about you," said Jack. "We never married y'know. I always knew it wasn't to be – not like us.

"How did she take the news? that you're with me now?" asked Rose.

"Not good but she'll be fine. It's just that we were together an awful long time – eight years really. I get to see Emma on Wednesdays and Sundays. I was wondering if like...ya wanted to meet her...maybe this Sunday?"

"Jack," Rose spoke very seriously, "I need to tell ya somethin'. It's important and ya might not want to know, but...here goes."

Jack couldn't imagine what she could tell her that would be bigger than - *I have a four year old daughter. How do ya feel about takin' on the two of us?* But what she said was big without a shadow of a doubt. Rose told him how she had been in the psychiatric hospital and how she had tried to kill herself twice. She told him about the psychotherapy with Tania Gates and she even told him about her father and how he had sexually abused her as a child, and that she had had to leave the family home because he had started it again when she was grown up. She told him all these things, but she never once mentioned that she spoke to dead people. That was a chapter of her life she wished to shut tight and never go to again. The lady and the Indian she would never talk about to anyone ever again – not to Tania Gates and certainly not to Jack Farley. It made people think she was mad. She had learnt her lesson.

As it was, Jack had known about her mental illness. Kelly, in a last desperate attempt to keep him, had told him everything that her friend who knew Rose McDevit had told her. His response told Rose all she needed to know. He listened to her silently, taking in every word, his heart grieving with her, crying with her, raging with her and then he quite simply said –"I love you Rose."

It was now the second month they were together and they fitted into each other's life with ease – each one an invaluable piece of the jigsaw. Emma was a darling – huge blue eyes and strawberry blonde hair that fell onto her shoulders in ringlets. Her milky complexion complemented the soft colour of her hair and her cheeks and lips had a healthy red glow. She was a confident, bossy little madam who on the first day she met Rose asked her father why that woman seemed to be following them. She was smart, that was sure; she questioned who Rose was and why Daddy was living at her house. On many occasions she suggested to her father that he 'stick it back together' with her mother. What was incredibly amazing about the child was that although all these thoughts were going on in her head she was as fond of Rose as Rose was of her and she never once said *I don't like her* or *I want her to go away*. Rose simply adored her but at times she had to admit it was difficult to share Jack with her. She had discussed this at length with Tania Gates and chided herself often. How could she be jealous of a four year old? The thing was, as Tania explained, Rose had never had a healthy relationship with her father. She had no understanding of what that was and judged all such relationships on her relationship with her own father. However, she was the adult and Emma was the child so she swallowed her difficulties, swearing that no child would ever feel unloved or unwelcomed by her.

Now that Jack was present, Rose began to feel more and more that her life was less hopeless. He was her rock, her crutch to help her through the nightmares and the flashbacks. He spent hours listening to her tear herself apart with outlandish accusations of guilt and self-hate. Often she screamed at him to leave her alone and let her wither away all by herself. During love-making she kicked and scratched at him petrified with sudden panic. Those hours in the dark of night were the test of his commitment to her but he bravely and lovingly stuck through it all holding her long into the night, willing his own heart not to break so that he could be strong for her. He loved her with an oath that came from deep within his soul – he would shield her from all harm – from herself if need be and if he never achieved anything else in his life – he would have her know that she was safe and wanted and loved – that she was love itself in all its beauty.

But Rose knew there was still something from her childhood that she was not remembering and that she needed to remember if she was going to get well. She was discussing it with Jack one evening when they were curled up on the sofa in front of the fire. She told him that she had been thinking for some time of trying hypnotherapy, so that she could safely remember what was so buried. She was beginning to feel sure this was the right thing to do. "There's somethin' I'm not remembering," she told him, "I do kind of remember but it's so scary that I'm afraid to remember. Does that make sense?"

"I suppose so," reluctantly agreed Jack, who was worried about the idea of this, "Are ya sure though? What if ya remember somethin' and ya can't cope with it?"

"It's not like that" reassured Rose. She explained to him that someone had already given her a hypnotherapy expert's number and that a little while ago she had rung him. "He said I would have complete control at all times…if I'm not ready to remember somethin' then I won't remember it."

"So what's the point then?"

"The point is the therapy helps ya to relax enough to allow yerself to remember. It makes it easier. It's about lettin' the subconscious memories ease out gently," she explained.

"Well what d'ya think?"

"I think I should do it. At least see the man an' see what he says."

Rose found the scrap of paper with the man's name and number scribbled on it at the bottom of her handbag. Robert Peterson was his name. In a matter of minutes an appointment had been made.

Robert Peterson lived in Balina, a huge town in Mayo. It was only a thirty minute drive to get there and they found the house easily enough. Robert was a huge man in his fifties – six foot tall and with a girth that almost equalled his height. With greying dark hair, a fuzzy beard and a red bulbous nose, Rose thought he looked like a giant gnome. She and Jack sat on Robert's sofa whilst they discussed Rose's progress so far. Robert had agreed that Rose could come for a consultation but he hadn't said he'd definitely take her case. After forty minutes Robert cleared his throat and delivered his verdict.

"Ahem – well Rose, I like you. You've got integrity and I think you've been through a rough time. What do say we start now and see if we can get to the bottom of that wall?" He had likened Rose's situation to a brick wall. Behind the wall was whatever it was she felt she was unable to cope with. As time went on she had built more and more bricks into the wall in order to keep herself from remembering whatever that was. What she had to do now was to take the wall apart brick by brick – reverse the situation.

"Well I have to admit that I'm scared stiff but I'm determined so, yes let's get on with it," said Rose, bravely.

The hypnotherapy had been gentle enough for the first few sessions, but as time went on and Rose became more relaxed with it she managed to tear down quite a few of those bricks from the wall. The thing was, as the wall became thinner the *thing* on the other side of it had started to become clearer. During the sessions it was as if she was a child again and re-experiencing the things she had experienced then. She was surprised at how much she remembered. Three things began to filter through to her conscious mind. The first was that she realised she had forgotten about the boy who grew up with her – the ghost boy that always said nothing but, as she now remembered, was connected with Auntie Lett in some way. She remembered him in the garden and in the cupboard. She remembered him at different ages and she even remembered him before she was born. She remembered being in the womb and feeling his presence and then he would be gone. She even remembered the strangeness and the force of being born – how she was so warm and safe and then was forcibly expelled into a huge cold bright space. All security had left her then and she had never felt the boy's physical presence again. She was able to describe how she had felt when Auntie Lett had held her, nursed her. Then the security came back and the boy's energy was there. When Clare had held her, her little arms and legs had flayed about with fear. It was cold – she was unwanted.

That had been the first thing, and then after some time Rose began to remember something that she must have completely blotted out of her mind… that once she had been told by the adults that Auntie Lett was her real mother. It had happened when she was about ten or eleven and the adults had been arguing in the sitting room, and everyone was upset. She had been sitting on the stairs listening whilst her brothers and sisters slept and she was hearing something like – '*I shoulda' kept the boy – I never wanted 'er in the first place.*' That night had been terrible and she had been in a right state. She remembered her father giving her a bath and how she was put to bed still wet with her red nylon nightie on her. She remembered her parents sitting at the bottom of the bed and telling her that Auntie Lett was really her mother and that she had felt over the moon after that. It had felt *real* to her and real felt good. She remembered that on what seemed like the next day, she had been taken to see a woman and left there alone in the woman's house. The woman had asked her questions about her parents and said that she was going to be a kind of mummy to Rose for a while and had asked her if that would be okay. Rose hadn't known if that was okay or not but she had known that she liked the woman. She had felt a kindness from her that she had never known at home. But she didn't get to stay with her because her parents and Auntie Lett had come back that evening and taken her home. The next thing she could remember was sitting in the shed trying to figure the whole thing out – *Okay, so Mummy is my mummy but Lett is my real mummy and now this woman is gonna be my pretend mummy* she remembered thinking.

Then faces began to filter into Rose's conscious mind; lots of faces. There was Daddy's face as it turned from being Daddy into a monster and there was the other monster's face that turned out to be Mummy when she was extra specially cross or when she went mad and thought Rose was Auntie Lett. The face of the devil flashed into her awareness just as he had come for her in the hospital but this time he turned into a snake that hissed and bit at her legs. In the hypnotherapy sessions the Indian's face flashed often but now she backed away from him in defiance – *I don't trust you anymore – go away* she said to him.

The third thing that filtered through was the memory of the 'meetings'. Rose had at last begun to remember meetings that had taken place at her home while she was a child, and she spent terrifying hour after hour on Robert's sofa enduring the same torturous memories over and over for months on end whilst Jack sat in the car outside waiting for her to come back to him. She would run to the car like a hunted rabbit, her face chalk white and the smell of fear on her breath would turn his stomach so much he couldn't look at her. There were days she begged and pleaded with him not to make her go there – *don't make me go in. Take me home. I give up. I can't do it. I'm better off dead. I'm a liar, I made the whole thing up. Please don't make me go.* She tried every trick in the book to get him to turn around and go straight back home but he would sit there outside Robert's house until she gave in. Clients would come and go and often Robert found himself receiving her well after his cut off time, but he had already told himself that he would never let Rose go without helping her.

"It's when she puts up the most resistance," he told Jack, "that she's on the verge of a breakthrough."

Jack was a patient man by nature – gentle, wise and understanding, with a wit that came close to insults but never did anyone any harm. He would spend hours standing on a riverbank, fishing rod in his hands, listening to the sound of the water and the birds. Many an evening he would go to the river and lose all track of time, suddenly finding himself up to the top of his waders in water with the darkness of night closing in around him. He was at peace with himself when he only had the river for company. His father fished and had taught him the value of the river bank. But Jack had a frustration within him that he had never understood. Perhaps it came from the time he was bullied at college? He didn't know for sure because even as a teenager he had been known to suddenly 'lose the plot' and lash out. He would exercise his great patience for so long and then snap. He was a complex man, though, for despite his quietude, he had a need for speed, catered for completely by his love of biking. As a young man he had raced motorbikes like his grandfather had before him – and the bikes gave him the respite needed to cope with any difficult situations in his life. Like the river but in a very different way, bikes allowed Jack to emotionally switch off. And never until now did he need to switch off so badly.

Rose had continued seeing Robert every week for two and a half years and each day Rose talked and talked about her past. She was remembering so much of what happened then and she needed to offload it somewhere now that she didn't have Tania Gates to talk to. Robert wasn't a counsellor and he didn't believe in going over old ground anyway. It was best to bring awareness of the experience to the fore and then cast it away like old clothing. Rose on the other hand, felt she dealt with things best when she could talk it out and make sense of it all. She was to learn many years later that there were some things you could never make sense of, however hard you tried.

Now Jack was listening to her talking it out again. She was lying on the floor with her back to him staring at the fire so she couldn't see that he had his head bowed, his face cupped in his hands.

"I was at the meeting again," she was saying, "the same people were there – Mummy and Daddy, Michael and Anne Donnelly and Mr and Mrs O'Hare. I don't remember all their names. Sometimes when I go there seems to be even more people."

Oh God, please stop, Jack was thinking, *I can't take much more of this*. But he would never have said this to Rose for she needed him to listen. How could he not listen? If he refused her he would just be one more person in a long line of people who denied her the right to speak her truth. He could feel the anger boiling up inside him as she went on to describe in horrid detail the memories she had uncovered.

"Everyone was wearing white robes and masks. Y'know the way I always freak out when we see white robes on the telly?

"Yeah," he said despondently.

"I can't help it – it's so fuckin' scary. Everyone had white robes on but there was this one man and I think that definitely was Michael Donnelly. He was like a kind of leader, like the main man. Actually, it was more like he was a kind of priest. One minute he would be Michael Donnelly an' the next he would be this priest. Then it was like some kind of play. Y'know the way them monks in Tibet and places pray? It's like a murmuring, a chanting. Well, that's what they do. Sounds weird doesn't it?" She didn't pause to get confirmation that he knew what she meant. She was on a roll and the quicker she spoke it out the more she felt the truth of it. Sometimes, lying awake at night, she would wonder if she *was* mad and this was all part of being born bad, but then she told herself that it was crazy to think that she was remembering this from nothing. Even the whole notion of being born bad was beginning to sound crazy to her. As she lay on the floor now she knew without a shadow of a doubt that the crazy things she was remembering were completely and utterly real.

She went on - "And there was this symbol on the priest's robes like a cross but with a circle on it." Then she lowered her voice and whispered – "Darling, it had to be somethin' to do with the occult 'cos I can feel it!"

Jack had to say it – he had to keep a rein on her – stop her from jumping to mad conclusions. He said – "Rose, please don't get carried away. How would you know what the occult was like?"

"Jack," she scrambled up on her knees and faced him. He looked terrible. "I told ya that black magic was goin' around Belfast at that time. Besides that, it's like," ... she thought for a moment ... "y'know when we met and it was like we recognized each other? Well, it's like that – like I know it was the occult 'cos I have a deep recognition of it."

Jack got up and went to the kitchen. He took a can of cider from the fridge and opened it. "D'ya want one?" he asked with a slight air of being pissed off.

"No." She knew she had said too much – she wouldn't say any more. She knew he couldn't cope with it, not tonight. She wouldn't tell him the rest. She wouldn't tell him how she was held up high whist the priest came towards her and hurt her between her legs. No, she would never tell him these things now she could see that he couldn't cope with them. She would keep them a secret from him, write them down in a journal. That was a better idea all round. At least that way he wouldn't have to listen to how they had almost destroyed her. He wouldn't have to listen to how the evil got into her and then burst out in a deluge of blood. He wouldn't understand how she had survived that, no-one would but if she wrote it down in a journal maybe some day someone would understand. Maybe some day someone would understand how the lady would come for her in the mad throes of it all and take her away in her mind to a green place, an apple tree and the Indian who once loved her.

One day Rose was on Robert's sofa. "Do you think I'm mad?" she asked Robert who was sitting quietly waiting for her to get into a relaxing position.

"Do you think you're mad?" he said throwing her question back at her.

"No."

"I think you've been messed with big time," said Robert, "and I think you have a vivid imagination." It was the truth, he knew that. She said nothing but hung her head and sobbed into an already soaked tissue. "Look Rose..." he said, not wanting to get into a full conversation but nevertheless, she needed to hear this, "One thing about you that I saw on your first day here and you have proved to me over and over, is that you have integrity. All this stuff that you're remembering it may seem a bit mad at times but you know and I know that the truth is there. It might be mixed up and a bit crazy at times but it's there all the same. Trust your memories Rose."

"Tania Gates said that to me too," said Rose. "The thing is I don't think the way I remember it is too mixed up – a little bit maybe and bunched together maybe but not completely false." Still she sometimes felt uncertain.

"Okay, so let's get started then, shall we? Now," he said when she was relaxed and ready to remember again, "I want you to go back to a time when something significant happened. Something that made you feel the way you do now."

As she was now used to doing, Rose started to go back and within seconds she was back in her parents' bedroom, sitting on her parents' bed and her mother was sitting in front of her. *"It's all your fault,"* she was hissing at Rose, "*you're a filthy bitch*." Her mother's face was pale and her eyes appeared to be looking right through Rose. Rose knew she had been smoking that weird cigarette again. *"I should never have allowed ya into the house, Lett. Both of ya are just pure evil. Born bad – that's what's wrong wi' ya. You and him going at it together – ya should be ashamed of yerself. Now look at the mess we're in. Didn't want her in the first place. Shoulda' kept the boy. It's all your fault. If ya hadn't come here."*

Rose was listening to all this being said, hiding behind

the TV show feeling that she used to get… if she couldn't feel it then she could believe it wasn't happening...that her mother wasn't going mad…that she wasn't swaying about in front of Rose's eyes calling her Lett and accusing her of ruining everything.

Then she jumped to a memory of the 'meetings', and although this time the lady hadn't taken her away, she was still out of her body, floating up near the ceiling and watching all that transpired. There was chanting and a circle of people, with her in the middle on the floor, her arms and legs spread-eagled and when the priest came to her he was black like the devil. As she watched herself from above, from out of her body, he was covering her as everyone chanted louder and when he arose there was the devil inside her and the priest was white again. Then she was watching on as the women held her under her arms and the devil came out of her again. There was a lot of blood and the devil was burned in a fire.

Coming back to the present with a shudder of horror, Rose felt as she lay on Robert's sofa that she would never want to go back into her body again. Of course, she did, she had to. She had to live mostly because the alternative was to go to hell but she also wanted to live because now that she had Jack, she had a life worth staying alive for.

The months went on and Rose's life was bitter-sweet. She was madly in love with Jack and he with her. Emma was becoming increasingly adorable and Rose was smitten with the child to Jack's immense delight. They were the only two people in the world that Rose felt real with though. Carlos seemed a lifetime away and the few friends she had drifted off into the background. Her family were getting more and more difficult to cope with as she remembered the past. Rose found that she couldn't keep up the pretence that everything was okay when it wasn't, but any time she spoke out the truth of what had happened she was browbeaten with - *you're not well dear. We don't know what you're talking about dear.* This now became so difficult for Rose that she began to feel she would prefer the company of dead people to the living; at least the lady and the Indian had always been real with her. But now they were gone and, apart from the momentary flashes during hypnotherapy when she saw the Indian's face, it had been years since she'd seen them. They most likely wouldn't want to know any more. The memory of them was fading and she was now rapidly finding that she could hardly remember them at all. The good memories were fading away and the bad ones were getting stronger. At night, the nightmares were getting worse. Rose constantly fought off the devil as he lay like a snake between her legs. She would wake up with him standing over her bed watching her, and poor Jack always had the job of calming her down after being startled from his sleep by blood curdling screams.

"Why don't ya tell you're parents just to fuck off and leave ya alone?" Jack was at a loss as to why she couldn't do that. But the truth was she was too frightened to speak out to them. It seemed to her like an insurmountable wall – not one that she could take apart brick by brick, and she went back to self-doubt.

"Oh Jack, what if I'm just pure evil and I've made the whole thing up?" She knew that was just an excuse. "Besides I don't want anyone to get hurt."

"Hello! Someone has already got hurt. They deserve everything that's comin' to them" he almost sreamed at her.

"I don't work that way, darling. I can't hurt a fly let alone my family – no matter what they've done to me. I just want them to admit the truth… that I'm not lyin'"

"Well, that's not gonna happen. They'll never admit to it," insisted Jack. "Christ sake, they probably can't even admit it to themselves! Ya know what that generation's like. If ya don't think about it – it's not real."

"I know that only too well," said Rose sorrowfully.

By the start of nineteen ninety six Rose had disposed of so many bricks from the wall that she was beginning to see daylight behind it but the thing that she was hiding there was becoming more solid, more alive and Rose withdrew her gaze from it, choosing instead to go around in circles, dealing with each brick again and again for fear that she may just have to look at what was staring her in the face. The sessions with Robert continued until Rose and Jack got married and went on honeymoon and returned pregnant with their first child. On the day of the wedding, as she danced with her husband, Rose looked up into his face and said – "I'm ready to let myself be happy."

Jack Farley held her tight to his body and murmered in her ear –"I'll make sure of that Mrs Farley."

Rose McDevit was now Rose Farley. Rose McDevit had been a girl who was lost – who had been abandoned in hell but she had found the key to unlock that. She was scrambling out, clinging on to the edge and reaching out for her unseen friends to come back and fetch her. Rose Farley now had her husband's love and her unborn child giving her the strength to reach out even further.

Chapter Fifteen

Behind the wall

Salvation comes in many different guises. For some it may be the support of a good friend or a loving partner – for others it may be the promise of a reward that equals the task. For Rose it was to be the divine love within reflected in the innocence of two little boys.

March 1998

Rose was in a deep dark pit. She had fallen in as she wandered about on the hillside just above the little cove at Granny Doyle's old place. She had gone there hoping to find the lady again, to rekindle their connection, but to no avail. Oh, the lady was there alright, Rose could sense her in the cave. She could smell her lovely home-baked bread smell. The warm aroma of hot apple pie filled her nostrils and she knew that the lady had been baking, but she didn't show herself or speak to Rose in the beautiful kind loving way that she had used to. Rose called out for her but she remained elusive and finally, as the night fell, Rose was forced to give up. She had tried to make her way from memory over the hill. When she neared the cottage the light in its windows glowed like beacons in the dark and she moved towards them, but as each step brought her closer to her destination she began to feel apprehensive. Apprehension turned into reluctance and reluctance into fear. She panicked, running around in circles in the dark, stumbling on rabbit holes and running into prickly gorse. All scratched up and miserable she dropped herself onto the ground and wept. All was hopeless. She was trapped. There was nothing left for her back at the cove but rejection and loneliness and if she went forward she would meet with the monster of monsters – because down in the dip ahead the cottage sat, hiding the one thing she had spent most of her life avoiding – in the cottage the devil was waiting to destroy her. That's when she found herself at the bottom of the pit. She was crawling with all manner of creeping creatures and the air was so thick she found it difficult to breathe. Clinging onto roots in the earth she managed to scramble to the top where to her surprise she saw the little ghost boy of her childhood reaching down to her with his small hand.

"Hold onto me!" she cried out, "Don't let me fall."

A voice answered, booming out all around her but it wasn't the voice of a child but the voice of a man – a man she knew – it was unmistakably the voice of her favourite uncle – Gerry McDevit. *"Listen to me Rose. You must go forward. Follow me and I'll show you the way."*

Rose awoke with the vibrating voice filling her senses. She sat up in bed. She knew she had been dreaming again. Beside her Jack lay in a peaceful slumber. *Thank God I didn't wake him*, she thought. The dream had been so real and she was aware by how wet her face was and how stressed her throat was that she had been crying out in her sleep. The bedroom door was ajar. She was grateful for the artificial light from the hall keeping the dark away. She hadn't slept in the dark for years, not since she was little. Sitting there in the semi-darkness she listened for noises in the house. They had rented this old country house near Lisnablaney after they married. It had been wonderful to get away from the noise of town life and into the country with its fresh air and open spaces but the country had its own noises, especially in the dead of night. Rose could hear the cattle lowing in the field beyond her bedroom window and the walls and floorboards creaking in the stillness. An owl screeched somewhere nearby and Rose's skin prickled making her suddenly cold even though she had been sweating because of the dream. In the bedroom across the hall her son moved in his cot. She heard him blow bubbles with his little mouth and *'ga ga'* over the baby monitor on the bedside table. *I must have woken him*, she thought guiltily. The dream faded away as Rose pricked up her ears and listened for her child. He wasn't crying for her so she knew it was unnecessary to disturb him in the middle of the night but she craved to be near him, to cuddle him close to her and to feel his little heart beat against her body. Inside her womb his baby brother shifted his position digging his little foot against her diaphragm uncomfortably. Getting out of bed she pushed against his foot with her hand which always made him move it away.

"That's it my darling, now let's go check on your big brother," she whispered rubbing his tiny back which he loved, and putting a shawl around her shoulders she went to her son's room. Oliver waved his little arms and legs with excitement when she looked over his cot and talked to him in a low gentle voice. "Shhh now Olly, Daddy's sleeping. Come on my darling – sit down here with mummy, that's a good boy." She sat on the nursing chair she'd had placed in his room and cushioned her back and sides with pillows. Resting Olly beside her she held him close and hummed to him. It was just her and her two precious babies in the safety of their own home. Her husband – their father was asleep just across the hall from them should they need him. She had so much love to give them. All through the years she had been so terrified of herself, of what was inside her, but she hadn't banked on the little glimmer of good she contained. She hadn't realised all that time that she was capable of such huge love and that these tiny little people would make such a vast difference to her life. She loved their father madly, deeply – deeper and deeper every day; but it wasn't the kind of love that she gave her children.

That kind of love was innate, unconditional and wholesome. It was divine, pure and infinite.

As Rose hummed, Olly fixed his gaze on her face with total trust. She was overwhelmed with the innocence and purity of him and, as if an angel had swept through her mind washing it with healing clarity, she realised that no child is ever born bad. In every tiny infant throughout the history of the world was nothing but purity and godliness. *The world pollutes children with its evil*, she thought. "Olly my precious, I love you," she told the child, "and I love *you*," she said patting her bump, "I'll always love you both, more than anything ever in this world. Trust me darlings, if there's one thing you will know for sure when you're big it's that your mummy loved you and did everything in her power to make you safe and happy."

Olly's little brother took an age to come out into the world. Oliver had been born within a few hours and Rose had sailed through that delivery but not with Jerimiah – his delivery was difficult at best and Rose was exhausted by the time she heard his first cries. It had been different this time, though, for she had dreaded it coming for weeks. As the time came closer she was more and more anxious and Jack was concerned that if she didn't relax she would do herself and the baby some harm.

"One more final big push Rose," the midwife said. Jack was holding her hand and mopping her forehead with a wet cloth. Her face was almost purple, bruised with pushing and screaming so much. He thanked God she had calmed down enough to finish the delivery without further help. Minutes earlier she had screamed so much that the midwife had been disgusted –

"Ah now Rose, let's not get so dramatic," she said, which was a perfectly excusable response to Rose's behaviour. But Rose hadn't been screaming because of the pain – she had been screaming in terror, and she was terrified because she was at last remembering what was behind the wall. Flashback after flashback swept in and out of her mind – memories of pain and terror – of blood and drugs – memories of a snake-like demon between her legs. She saw faces she knew and heard things that she was now remembering and all the time her son was being born. When he finally came out into the world Rose was aware that he was not her second born, but her third. All she wanted to do was sleep and never wake up. She lay back on the hospital bed... or was it Granny's sofa? She wasn't sure where she was.

"Rose, don't you want to nurse your son? You can sleep later pet. Here he is, nice an' clean." The mid-wife was a little concerned about the mother's lack of interest.

Jack spoke lovingly to his wife – "Rose, Jerimiah's here. He wants his mother."

"Go away!" she yelled, and then she said something that puzzled them greatly – in a child-like voice she said, "Don't look - you're not allowed to look."

"I think she doesn't know where she is," Jack told the

mid-wife, "she takes panic attacks ya see, it'll have bin one of those." He wasn't going to start explaining his wife's behaviour right then and anyway he felt he shouldn't have to.

"She'll be fine in the morning" said the midwife, "Let her sleep tonight and we'll feed the baby. Here, give him to me and I'll look after him. You see to Rose, Mr Farley."

"Thank you…thank you," said Jack gratefully, carefully handing his son over to the midwife. He stroked his wife's head. She was sound asleep. "What in under God did they do to ya?" he whispered. He knew something major had been going on with her just now. She had remembered something, it had to be that. Unfortunately, whatever that something was, it had obviously frightened the life out of her. Jack rested his head on her arm – *Please God, let her be alright*, he prayed.

Rose hadn't been for hypnotherapy since she was five months pregnant with Jerimiah and now she had no intention of going back. Now she knew what had happened to her when she was thirteen and she had told Jack that there had been a baby. Somehow she knew it had been a girl. The wall was down now – and she had to survive amidst the dust and rubble. Jeremiah cried almost all the time and she clung to him for fear that someone would come and take him away. She held him next to her in bed and only let go when Jack took him out of her arms, placing him in a cradle beside their bed.

"He's fine darling. He's not going anywhere."

"Oh Jack!" she'd cry, thinking about the baby she now knew she had had when she was thirteen, "I can't stop thinkin' about her. What happened to her? D'ya think she died?"

"Shh darling," he'd say, "you'll be fine. Let's concentrate on these two for now an' then we can deal with that later."

The health visitor called at the house to see Rose and the newborn. Jack was staying at home instead of going to work because he didn't want to leave Rose alone with the two babies. "I just can't leave her like this," he told the health visitor, "she gets more and more depressed each day. Oh, she's seeing to the wee'ns alright, but it's her I'm worried about. It's like they are the only reason she's surviving."

He had sat the health visitor down as Rose slept and told her the whole story of how Rose had been abused all her life and forced to have a baby when she was only thirteen. "I've spoken to her therapist," he added, "and he says that back then she coped the only way she could – by shutting down – the only thing that's keeping her from shutting down again is the wee'ns."

"Don't worry Jack," the health visitor had said, "there's plenty of help out there. You won't have to cope with this on your own."

The health visitor was true to her word and soon a very capable young woman called Laura was calling at the house every morning to help Rose with the babies. Laura was a godsend and she and Rose got on like a house on fire. The days went by in a cloud of nappies, baths and feeding times and Laura could clearly see that Rose was more than willing and capable of looking after her children's needs. If anything, she seemed to be running for 'mother of the year'. According to Laura, the thing was that Rose herself needed the looking after. It was obvious she was neglecting herself. In the short time Laura had been coming to Rose's home Rose had become painfully thin and withdrawn. She had a history of depression and anxiety – Laura knew that and she could see that Rose was lonely.

Maybe she just needs a friend she can talk to, she thought and arranged for Rose to have an interview with the co-ordinator of 'Blue Skies', a local charity she knew about that befriended young families. And that was how Sam Morris came into Rose's life. Samantha Morris - charity worker, mother of five and wife to a local farmer was, as it turned out, a crucial stepping stone to the future.

It had all started one afternoon when Rose received an unexpected visitor. She and Laura had just got Olly down for his afternoon nap and were preparing a feed for Jerimiah when a car pulled up in front of the house. "Wonder who that might be?" Rose said, "I'm not expecting anyone."

It was a beautiful sunny May afternoon and the back door had been left open to let the fresh air into the kitchen. Rose could hear a car door shut and a single set of footsteps crunching on the gravel yard and then someone called out –"Hello, is the lady of the house at home?"

"Gerry!" Rose called, shooting a grin at Laura that told

her it was a welcome visitor.

Uncle Gerry appeared at the back door his arms laden as usual with gifts of food and drink. Rose noticed how old he looked. His face was etched with deep lines and under his yellow-tinged eyes were heavy, shadowy bags. He seemed a little thinner than usual and it seemed he was having trouble clearing the steps up into the kitchen. He puffed, wheezing as he did so, and took a fit of coughing as Rose sat him down on a chair. She ran to fetch a glass of water.

"Ahh, this auld chest," he croaked patting his chest. "Have to cut down on the auld pipe, don't I?"

"Well, it's not doin' ya much good now is it Gerry?" Rose answered concerned to see him so ill. "What about the hips – are ya in pain?"

"Not at all, not at all, young Rosie. Just a wee bit stiff is all. Sure there's life in me yet."

"I should hope so. It's nice to see ya. Did ya come to see the baby? He's in the living room."

"Aye well, I come to see you did I not? Sure do I have to have an excuse to see me favourite niece?" He started coughing again and Rose frowned. He didn't sound too good.

"I'll just give this to Jeremiah and then I'll go," said Laura, "give you two peace to chat."

"Thanks Laura," smiled Rose. It was plain to see that Rose was very fond of the old man. She stood smiling at him thinking what a godsend he had been when she had needed him most.

Gerry was no fool – he knew she was glad he was there but would she be when she found out *why* he was there? He wasn't even sure himself that he was altogether happy with his mission. His wife Anne had told him to intervene on Sean and Clare's behalf…"Go and tell that young madam that what she's doin' to her mammy and daddy is a sin. Not lettin' them see their own grandchildren – sure it's an utter disgrace. Go and talk some sense into her Gerry. She listens to you."

Gerry wasn't entirely convinced that his wife's opinion was warranted. She hadn't seen Rose in the hospital terrified out of her wits. "Somethin' has happened to that child," he had told Anne way back then, "God forbid if our Sean has anythin' to do with it."

Now, as he sat in Rose's kitchen, he still hadn't purged the horrible thought that his little brother had interfered with the child. But how could he think such a thing? In his defence, he allowed that he was doing what was best for everyone regardless of what had passed. "What are ya standin' there fer with yer mouth hangin' open? Get the tay on?" he said jokingly, "Anne sent ya some biscuits and there's a wee lock o' apples fer ya."

Rose smiled as she put the kettle on to boil and busied herself with teacups and saucers. Auntie Anne always used the best of china in her house.

Gerry decided not to talk some sense into Rose that afternoon, as it happened. He allowed that Rose was quite sensible enough. What he did do though was leave his paper bag containing the wee lock o' apples on the sideboard behind him. Also in the bag, unknown to Rose, was a leaflet about a charity that offered counselling to 'survivors' of rape and incest.

She found the leaflet later that evening when she went to put the apples in her fruit bowl. "Jack!" she had shouted, "come and see this!"

Jack had been out in the yard, kneeling down beside a motorbike, tools all around him on the ground. "Do this one thing for me first darling," he had said as Rose stepped into the yard, "when I say go, I want ya to squeeze the brake gently, okay?"

Rose put her hand on the handle and reached for the break. "Gerry left this for me to see. He obviously didn't want to discuss it. Look, it's a..."

"*Go*," said Jack. She squeezed the brake. "Let go," said Jack.

"It's about counselling for abuse," she continued. "It's a charity called 'The Alison Project'."

"Go again," said Jack. She pulled the brake again. Jack was lost in what he was doing. She waited until he put down his tool.

"Jack, what d'ya think about this Alison Project?"

He stood up and took the leaflet from her hand. Having perused it briefly he handed it back saying "I suppose it looks like the thing but are ya sure ya want to drag it all up again? Are we not doin' alright as we are?"

"What?" she suddenly yelled, throwing her arms in the air and storming off across the yard towards the house. Changing her mind she turned and stormed back to face him – "How is this doin' alright? My whole world's falling apart an' no-one wants to know. I've been pissed on from a great height but oh no, just keep takin' the tablets an' ya'll be grand." She cried hysterically, leaning against Jack for support. He wrapped his arms around her and let her cry.

He had known this was coming. She had been coping too well lately, but listening to her cry and whine in her sleep at night, he had known it was only a matter of time before she would break down. She was trembling in his arms. She was terrified of anger - he knew that. She was even more terrified when it was her own anger. He said nothing, just held her tight.

"Oh darling," she wept, "it's not fair. I have a twenty year old daughter out there somewhere and I'm just expected to say nothing an' pretend everything's alright, well it's not alright. Fuckin' sure it's not alright. I have a right to know where she is and she has a right to know me." She tensed even more in his arms and pushed herself free. She kicked the garage wall seething with rage – "How dare they? I hate them, I hate them." Finally, having spent her energy, she fell into Jack's safe arms and sobbed until she could sob no more.

As it turned out, it was Sam Morris who had a great idea: "Instead of coming to see you on a Monday morning why don't I come on an evening?" she suggested. "My husband can watch my lot and you and I can go to Balina to The Alison Project. My boss can get ya a place in no time, 'cos normally y'know, you would have to wait for a place."

"Gosh, that'd be fantastic," replied Rose, "an' Jack can stay here an' watch the wee'ns. That'd be the very thing. But are you sure ya don't mind? You'd have to sit an' wait for me, probably an hour even."

"Not at all, leave it with me an' I'll see what can be done."

Sam had it all sorted out within a week and the following Wednesday she and Rose were on their way to Balina to begin what was to be the next phase of Rose's recovery. Sam had insisted on driving. "You'll have enough to deal with," she said sympathetically.

Sam Morris was a rescuer and Rose Farley needed rescuing. But Sam also knew that Rose was a fighter and that she possessed qualities that few others did. She was honest and genuine and she was a loving, passionate woman who was dedicated to being the best that she could be, not only for herself but so that her children would have the best mother they could possibly have. Sam Morris was going to do her utmost to ensure that Rose had the very best help available and The Alison Project was apparently the best there was – experts in the field of childhood sexual abuse.

"Want to hear somethin' interestin'?" Rose asked Sam on the way to Balina. "I had a dream just before Jerimiah was born. It was one of those dreams that seem real y'know?"

Sam said she knew the kind. "Anyway, in the dream I was lost and I had fallen into a pit. Someone pulled me out and he had my Uncle Gerry's voice. Y'know…the one that gave me the leaflet about The Alison Project?" Sam said she didn't know but was that right? Rose nodded - "He said 'listen to me – I will show you the way'."

Sam agreed that that was very interesting – "It's like you're *psychic,*" she added innocently.

Rose said nothing, the *psychic* chapter of her life was well and truly closed; the lady and the Indian had made it quite clear a long time ago that they were no longer available to her. Rose felt a twinge in her middle. That didn't feel altogether true but it was what she knew for now. She fixed her thoughts on the meeting ahead of her and let Sam chat away about how she had seen this fortune teller once who knew everything about her and had predicted her charity work and all.

"We should go see her some time, you and me. What d'ya say?"

"Yep, maybe she can tell me where my daughter is?" Rose answered half-heartedly. As she said it, she thought she could smell the aroma of home baked bread. She shook the notion away and fell silently into a sombre mood.

Janice Golding, the counsellor, had told Rose during their second meeting that as a rule The Alison Project could only take clients for six months at any one time, but that she had spoken to her supervisors about her case and they had agreed that Rose should stay with them indefinitely. She now knew the full story of Rose's history, about the abuse and the baby.

"There's a lot there, Rose, that needs to be dealt with," she had told Rose. "We're not dealing with something that just happened yesterday. We're talking about changing a lifetime of dealing with this situation in a particular way. That way doesn't work for you anymore and now you must find a new way, one that will mean you actually deal with the situation and not simply repress it again."

Rose had told her that now she wanted to deal with it and to get to the truth, that she hated living with lies and secrets. She knew now that she only felt okay when she was being real, no matter how much the truth hurt. Janice told her that it might mean going to the police and asked Rose how she felt about that.

"Why would we go to the police unless I want to press charges, which I don't?" Rose asked and Janice told her that it wasn't just about her and that it was because a crime had been committed involving a third party.

"If you won't speak for the baby then I'll have to," she said, explaining that they were obliged by law to report any births that may have occurred as a result of rape or abuse, if they hadn't already been reported and that in this case it looked very much like there had been a false registration of birth to say nothing else. Rose had been terrified that someone would find out, but Janice had reassured her that it would be quite confidential and had made an appointment with the Sergeant in charge of such cases; the Alison Project had used him often and she knew he was very sympathetic. Rose had agreed to it when she understood that Janice would have to report it anyway and that her cooperation would make a difference.

"Okay, I guess I'd rather be there," she said.

"Rose, you're doing the right thing," said Janice warmly, and went on to tell her that this same Sergeant had dealt with another client of The Alison Project that had been the worst case on record, the Waterford Case. Rose had never heard of the Waterford Case and Janice went on to tell her that about ten years ago a fifteen year old girl from Waterford had had a baby – in a hospital but she had still had no idea what sex was or how she had come to be pregnant. It had been her uncle who had abused her and she had written a book about it. She had been on the telly talking about it. "Have you never heard about it? The Waterford Case?" she asked Rose.

"No, never," said Rose. "You know what *is* a coincidence, though? I've been thinkin' about writin' a book about my story as well."

"Why not? You do have a story to tell and people should hear about stuff like this, that it goes on," said Janice, and she told Rose that her supervisors wanted to offer her help indefinitely. They thought her case was even worse than the Waterford Case and they wanted her permission to use her notes for training so that others could be helped. Rose didn't see why not, she was feeling stronger now that someone was taking her case seriously. As far as she was concerned it was extremely important that she tell the world the kind of things that happen to children behind closed doors. She knew that anybody will tut and say 'isn't that terrible' when it comes to child abuse, but they're always ready to blame the stepfather or the uncle. No-one wanted to believe that a father could do that to his own child. It was time people listened and realised that fathers were just as much to blame as anyone else. After all, Janice had told her that a child is in more danger of abuse in its own home than anywhere else.

After that, every Wednesday for almost three years, Rose had gone to see Janice Golding whilst Sam Morris sat outside in her car waiting for Rose to come out, just as Jack had waited all those years outside Robert Peterson's house. During the sessions she told Janice about the lady and the Indian, how they had taken her away and helped her, and eventually she remembered most of what had happened on the night she had given birth to a baby.

"Grace, I've decided to call her," she told Janice one evening. "I remember thinkin' about her before she was born, but I'm convinced I was pretendin' that she was a doll and I remember thinkin' about the name Grace. Although I really believed she was the devil growing inside me and that I would burst and the devil would come out an' take me to hell. Remember I told ya all that stuff about the time I thought he was comin' for me?"

"When you were having hallucinations?" asked Janice.

"Aye. But I have this memory in my head. It's like it's just a picture but it really happened, only not exactly like in the picture, do ya know what I mean?" Janice explained that it was something called a 'screen memory'. "I'm sitting in the wood at Granny's auld place in Cloughbeg," Rose continued, "and Auntie Lett is sitting with me. She's telling me about how she had a doll once that she had to give away and that there's a doll inside me. I know that it's the devil but I don't want to tell her. And then I turn to her and say *– you had two dolls Auntie Lett – a boy doll and a girl doll.*"

Janice had found herself enthralled with the way that Rose had dealt with her childhood experiences. It was as if she had catalogued them into little boxes and hidden them away neatly so that when she came to recollect them she knew she could safely retrieve them in the order she wanted them. She even had a label on everything so that she knew exactly what went with what and what to do with it as soon as she had looked at it. She was obviously very intelligent. "The likes of Freud and Jung would have been ecstatic to have a case like Rose for their work," she had stated to her supervisors, "what makes her even more intriguing is the way she imagined herself flying and leaving her body to go someplace else away from the abuse. These are actually real experiences for her and if you really want to hear something weird then listen to this – sometimes I'm not exactly sure she was imagining them at all."

"You mean you believe she did those things? That there

was a house where this woman took her to see an Indian? You really believe that?" one supervisor had asked Janice.

"If you were listening to her talk about it you'd nearly believe her yourself. To her that was the case. That's what she remembers."

"My God, I've heard it all now."

"That's just it. I don't think we have," said Janice.

"How did it go then?" Sam asked Rose one evening, as they sat in the little café across the street from The Alison Project. They had taken to treating themselves to a plate of chips and a mug of tea after Rose's sessions with Janice. Rose found it gave her time to make sense of things and Sam was a willing listener. It meant taking up another half hour of her time but she would have done anything for Rose if it made a difference. It was the evening that Rose and Janice had been to see Sergeant Mitchell about Grace's birth.

"It wasn't easy Sam," replied Rose, "but it was informative that's for sure."

"What d'ya mean?"

"The policeman is well used to cases like this an' he was tellin' me that quite often when a child is born, someone in the family or close to the family takes the child to England for adoption. Apparently, the Catholic church is famous for arranging adoptions out of the country without askin' any awkward questions."

"That sounds about right. Do ya think that's what happened then?"

"I tell ya what. I remember that priest out at Granny's place. He asked a lot of questions and if I'm not mistaken, he arranged somethin' with Granny to do with the baby. For Christ's sake Sam, he even prayed for the devil to come out of me," said Rose, who could now remember all these terrible details.

"What?"

"Aye. He put his hand on my head and blessed me an' all with holy water. Then he prayed for the evil to come out. I remember that like it was yesterday. I'm so fuckin' angry."

"Maybe he was just doin' what he thought was best. He wouldn't have known the truth I'd imagine," said Sam. She was a devout Catholic and she wasn't comfortable with Rose dissing the Church like that. "What else did the policeman say?"

"That he would interview some of my family. He's not gonna go to my parents or my sisters or brothers but he *is* gonna ask my Auntie Theresa and her family 'cos I stayed there for a while after it happened. He won't annoy Granny though since she's too frail. In fact, I'd say she's hasn't long to go now."

"God Rose, how do ya feel about all that?"

"I don't even wanna think about it," she replied, tucking into her chips. "Oh, and there's no counselling next week. Janice is away on holiday."

"Tell ya what," suggested Sam, "why don't we keep our time as usual an' go to see that fortune teller I told ya about?"

"Good enough. Sergeant Mitchell needs all the help he can get," Rose laughed and for the rest of the evening the two women laughed and joked about all the mad things the fortune teller could possibly tell them.

Imelda Crown, the fortune teller, had married an Irish man thirty years ago and come to live in Ireland but she had been born and raised in Canada. After her husband died, she had lived on in their little white-washed cottage on the northern outskirts of Drumgar. She had two daughters, now both in the States and neither of them eager to come home to the Irish countryside.

As she drove up the long lane to the cottage in Jack's car, Rose was reminded of Granny Doyle's cottage, only without the trees. Imelda's cottage stood isolated from all other human habitation and bog land stretched as far as the eye could see all around it. Rose wondered how anyone could survive out there on their own, without even a tree for company.

"I had an aunt once who lived like this," Sam told her. "She never saw a sinner from one end of the month til the other."

"How did she manage for food an' that?" enquired Rose, thinking that there was a lot to be said for having this much peace and quiet.

"Oh, she was mostly self-sufficient y'know – kept goats and hens an' that, and as far as I know there was a neighbour came out an' took her to the town every so often."

Rose pulled the car up outside the cottage door. They were twenty minutes early but Imelda Crown was already standing on the doorstep waiting for them. Imelda wasn't the old wizened crone that Rose had visualized. She was in her fifties perhaps, although her complexion was a fresh as a twenty year old's, with rosy cheeks and bright eyes. Her brown hair was tied behind her neck in one long plait and almost reached to her waist. She was a tall, plump woman with a huge bosom. She wore a blue skirt that brushed the ground, the hem dusty and torn, and a white v-neck sweater. There was an aura of calm about her and Rose couldn't help but compare her to the lady. Sam was out of the car and giving Imelda a hug before Rose had a chance to compose her thoughts. She got out and joined them, introducing herself to the big woman who was rapidly seeming very familiar to her.

"Hello Mrs Crown, it's nice to meet you. I'm Rose Farley."

"Yes, I know who you are Rose, indeed I do." She gave Rose a look that sent a wave of energy right through her. Rose instantly knew that feeling, it was akin to what she felt as a child when the lady used to come for her.

"I feel I should know you too but I can't quite place ya," she replied. She held on to the woman's hand and she didn't seem to be in a hurry to let go either. She felt suspended in time. The only other time she remembered feeling like this was when she was with Carlos in Spain six years ago. Sam and the cottage faded away into the background and the only thing that felt real to Rose was the feel of her hand in Imelda's and the warm rush of energy that now engulfed the two of them. *This is another piece of the jigsaw*, thought Rose with certainty.

"Okay, let's go inside and we'll commence," Imelda insisted, ushering them in through the little door. Inside, the cottage was even more like Granny Doyle's than outside. There was the range with the huge chimney and the tiny little suite of furniture. In front of the window sat a small table with two chairs. Rose saw a set of tarot cards on the table and her thoughts flew back to the 'meetings' as a trickle of fear threatened to unsettle her.

"Don't worry about what's past, Rose," Imelda said. She was busy at the range, her back to Rose the whole time. How could she possibly have known what Rose had been thinking? She picked up the cards from the table and put them in Rose's hands. Rose's heart beat fast in her chest and she felt as if she might run if Imelda hadn't had a hold of her wrists.

"There's nothing to be afraid of here Rose. They're just a pack of cards – nothing sinister. The lady that came in with you…" Rose looked towards Sam, "No, not her dear… the lady that's always with you…she used to read the cards. You can too if you wanted to. In fact…" she smirked and shook her head, "Oh my word…you'll do much more than that."

Rose was submerged in the warm energy again. Her

heartbeat slowed and she found herself relaxing. She recognized what Imelda had said. She knew she spoke the truth and that although she had so often felt alone, the lady had never really gone away. She knew she had a connection to Imelda – the kind of connection she had with Carlos and Jack. *This is one of those moments*, she thought, *when I'm exactly in the right place at the right time, like it's part of reality, not the pretence.*

Imelda let go off her wrists and took the cards from her, placing them back on the table. "Now, normally I don't chatter much before the reading," she began in a business-like voice, "but sometimes, like with you Rose, the reading starts before the cards are laid. So if you want to sit there, dear, and we'll continue." Rose sat on one of the chairs at the table and Imelda sat opposite her. "Okay, if you want to wait in there Sam dear, that would be good."

Sam and Rose didn't leave Imelda's cottage until nine o'clock that night. They had fully expected to be home by then but Imelda had insisted that they stay and have a cup of tea and a slice of cake. Rose understood that she had felt the connection as well and that she obviously knew something that Rose didn't. That being the case, Rose was more than willing to stay and listen to what she had to say.

"How d'ya know about the lady?" Rose had cautiously asked her during the reading.

"I can see her dear. Those people that were around you when you were a little girl…You know who I'm talking about....they haven't gone away. What's more they will be working very closely with you in the future. You have a long way to go Rose."

Rose swallowed hard. Her throat felt as if there was a stone in it. She glanced at the door of the room wherein Sam sat waiting and Imelda understood.

"She can't hear us dear, don't worry. It can be a secret as long as you want but if you ask me...you'll never be happy unless you embrace it."

"Embrace what?" Rose wasn't sure she wanted to hear any more, but she knew that Imelda was talking about the picture people of her childhood.

"It will be revealed." Rose relaxed. "Have you any questions?"

"Two."

"Okay, fire away."

"Do you know where Grace is?"

"Grace, dear?"

"Maybe that is her real name, or maybe she wasn't born at all," Rose was still subject to her old doubt.

"Oh, she was born alright. Let's see now. I see a lot of water. Could be the sea I'm not sure. The south of England dear. Have you any connections with the south of England?"

"No, none at all."

"That may be where she is dear. I can't be more specific than that. What was the other question?"

Rose didn't quite know what to feel now. It was all

coming so fast and she knew it was all true. That is why she was here in this present moment with this woman. It was a part of the jigsaw – of the real story – the real Rose. Bravely, she asked her second question – "There was a boy when I was growing up. He always was the same age as me but he was one of *those* people…y'know."

"Ah yes" replied Imelda looking intensely into Rose's eyes, "you will see him again Rose, and he *is* your brother. Don't doubt that."

Rose's head was swimming with thoughts on the drive home. Sam had her own tales to tell of how Imelda read her like a book and what she said about this and about that. "It was weird the way she seemed to pounce on you like that, wasn't it?" she said to Rose.

"In a way."

"Did ya know what she was talking about?"

"Kinda."

"You're not giving much away are ya?"

"Nope." Rose laughed to make light of her secrecy.

"She knew a hell of a lot about ya, did she not?"

"Aye."

"She knew important stuff anyway like your past an' that?"

"She did."

Sam gave up. Rose clearly did not want to talk about her reading. She went back to chatting about the things Imelda had told her. Rose was only half listening. She was trying to figure Imelda out. Who was she and what had been their connection? Imelda had certainly known a lot of things about her. She knew about Grace and the lady and she knew about the picture people, but she didn't know the one thing that Rose now felt was somehow the keystone to who she *really* was, even though she had shut him out of her mind for years. Imelda hadn't known the most stand out – wave a flag above your head – look at me I'm different thing. She hadn't known about the Indian.

But the wall was down and the fog had lifted. Rose was beginning to see where she was going. All she had to do now was turn on the light.

Chapter Sixteen

Endings

Drumgar, April 2008

Mrs Doyle told them the news. She hadn't been aware that they had met Joe O'Hanlon so when she discovered they had she was very pleased to have been the one to tell them the latest. Mrs Doyle knew most people about Drumgar and anyone she didn't know she knew someone who did. She went to every wake, every funeral and never missed a single iota of news which she re-told at the drop of a hat and added to – naturally of course. I suppose one could call her the town gossip but she saw it as her duty to inform her neighbours of that which they ought to know. Today, she wasn't too happy at all – auld Mary Kerr had rang almost a full day after it happened to tell her that big Joe O'Hanlon from the ice-cream parlour had dropped dead yesterday with a heart attack.

"Right there in his own shop. Poor wee Iris had to come in an' find him lyin' in a heap. Must 'a give'er an awful shock, the critter."

"Ah well Mary dear, thanks very much fer lettin' us know. Paddy will be right upset, he will. I s'pose they'll be waking 'im the night?" Mrs Doyle had said, wondering if her Paddy knew 'im at all.

Lissy and John had been quite distressed at hearing the news. "To think I was annoyed at him for standing us up," Lissy said to John when they had finally got shot of Mrs Doyle at breakfast.

John had to admit, he was feeling somewhat guilty too. Still, they weren't to know and anyway, it had been all his idea. "Good job he didn't come with us. What if he had died out on the hills?"

"Gosh, I couldn't bear to think about it," answered Lissy, worried now that she had told Mrs Doyle of their original plans yesterday. As it was, Mrs Doyle was in her element that she knew something of Joe O'Hanlon's business that day that no-one else knew except maybe Mrs O'Hanlon. She had to get telling someone. Before the breakfast things were cleared up she had rung Sissy Scallon, Pat Carlin from the chemist and Seamus and Kate McKeown who went to every wake and every funeral and always were a good source of who was related to such and such. Now that the word would get round that Mrs Doyle's English guests had been scheduled to meet Joe just as the Lord had taken him, she applied herself to the dishes with smug satisfaction.

"I thought I might buy some art materials," Lissy said as they got ready to go out that day. They hadn't anything special planned to do. Lissy wanted to hang about in case Father Jim would finally manage to contact Sarah Scallon. They had sent him a text on his mobile last night after not receiving his promised call should he speak to Sarah. He had quite tersely replied that Sarah appeared to be unavailable at the moment.

"I hope she's not ill" Lissy had said. She was beginning to feel afraid that they had all the information they were going to get and that was that.

John, on the other hand, was feeling more and more suspicious of the entire situation. It was plain to him that people knew more than they wished to admit. Could it be that he had totally mis-judged Jim Devlin? Had the priest changed his mind about helping them out? Perhaps he had learned something he didn't want them to know. John knew he was being paranoid but as time went on he felt he had good cause to feel so. Perhaps they should start asking questions now instead of waiting for Jim's go ahead. *No point in telling Lissy my fears*, he decided, *best just put ourselves out there and see what we come up with.* "You're gonna start painting? – here?" he asked her when she told him about her thoughts of buying art materials.

"Not paints no. I thought I might like to go back out to that wee cottage and sketch it. I can always paint it when we go home."

"If you're gonna do that then best do it today when the weather's fine. It gives more storms for tomorrow to last for days."

"What a bummer!" she moaned, glancing through the window.

"Hurry up and make your phone call and then we can get going." said John.

Lissy had promised she'd phone home last night but they were having such a lovely evening out she'd put off the call until the morning. She finished brushing her hair and then flung herself across the bed to speak to her parents. John watched her as she talked excitedly about the previous day's events, twisting her auburn hair around her fingers, her eyes shining brightly. She really was beautiful and he adored her. He was still getting his head around the fact that she loved him too. The past few days had been magical. Their love-making had been incredible. For the first time in his life, John Brunt knew what it felt like to be utterly and blissfully happy. If only he could give her everything she ever wanted. Here he was in the back end of nowhere looking for a woman he had barely a snowball's chance in hell of finding, but he'd do it ten times over if it meant getting one tiny step closer to making Lissy's life complete. Oh, to have her turn to him like she did on that first day up on the cliffside, and to hear her say again that she was at peace and that he was a part of her that she never wanted to lose. If he could give her that peace she so needed, his happiness would be even more complete because she would be right there with him.

"Oh dear, that is terrible," Lissy was saying. John listened intensely. "Yesterday lunchtime you say? Isn't that weird? – Mr O'Hanlon died about that time too – a heart attack. What a coincidence!" When she finally came off the phone she told John what her mum had told her. Apparently, yesterday lunchtime Father Kearns had keeled over in the street – a heart attack. "How's that for a coincidence?" she asked the gob-smacked John.

"Would you believe it? I don't suppose he left your mother's name and address for us before he died?" John received a thump for that remark. "Hey, I'm serious. That old boy knew more than he was letting on."

"John Brunt, some things in life are more important than proving you're right. Father Kearns happens to be highly thought of in the community. Mum and Dad are right upset by his death. Have some respect." John nodded his head with nonchalance. He looked at Lissy, his head down, eyes raised – she was trying not to laugh.

"Can I still call him a fusty old fart?" he pleaded. That remark got him another thump. "Okay, okay, I'll shut up… before I'm black and blue."

They were still discussing the coincidence of the two deaths as they browsed the craft shop on the main street in Drumgar. It was directly across the street from the ice-cream parlour as it was and they could see that the shutters of the shop were still shut tight. Lissy chose some pastel chalks and a large sketch pad. She was eager to get to work on the cottage. They had been the only customers in the shop for the full twenty minutes they were there and they couldn't have missed the strange looks the shop keeper was giving them. When they sat their chosen merchandise on the counter the elderly lady asked them –

"Are you the couple staying at Doyle's place then?" John knew they were about to get the Spanish Inquisition and Lissy walked right into it.

"Yes, we are. We were very sorry to hear about poor Mr O'Hanlon. Did you know him well?"

"Oh God aye! Me and Joe go way back. Went to school together, we did. Never knew her much though, mixed marriage if ya know what I mean. Not that I have anythin' against that sort of thing, mind you." The old woman suddenly realised her customers could be from the other side of the house as well. She went on – "I believe ya knew auld Joe?"

"Oh, we didn't know him really. We just met him yesterday morning. We happened to be in the shop and he offered to show us the way to the coves out by Cloughbeg." Lissy was beginning to feel awkward and wished the woman would take their money and let them go.

"If you'll excuse us, we're in a bit of a hurry. How much is that please?" John asked assertively. It did the trick. The woman rang their things through without another word and John shuffled Lissy out of the shop and around the corner out of sight. "That old biddy should be ashamed of herself," he scowled.

"Whatever for?" asked Lissy a little out of puff for having been pulled along so hastily.

"Lissy! Do you not see what she was trying to do back there?" Lissy looked bewildered, "God darling, you can be so naïve. She wanted to find out as much as she could about us so that she could spread it around the whole town."

"But that's okay, is it not? We want people to take an interest in us. How else are we gonna get them to help us?"

"Not that kind of interest silly. You never hear the truth from a bunch of gossips. I should know, I've interviewed enough of them. No, all you'll get from trusting that woman is a load of heartache, believe me." Lissy seemed crestfallen. Nothing was turning out right. "Let's go," John said putting his arm around her waist, "we can grab a sandwich in Cloughbeg and then call in with Father Jim and let him know about Father Kearns. I suspect he'll know anyway but it'd do no harm to put the pressure on about Sarah Scallon."

"Oh but he's not gonna be there today remember." An idea was coming to Lissy. She turned around to face him and bit her lip wondering if she should say or not.

"What? Spit it out" said John.

"I was thinking – what if we call anyway to see Melissa say, and we could ask her to ask Sarah for us. Her foster parents live beside her don't they? If Father Jim asks us about it we can always say we were just chatting and it came out."

"Or we could simply call at the woman's house."

"No, we shouldn't do that. It would be rude. We're supposed to wait for Jim to talk to her first."

"Says who?" John was becoming a little agitated with Father Jim's silence.

"Well, says he."

"That's just it isn't it? Why should we wait for him to ask if it's okay to talk with her when we could ask ourselves?"

"I dunno darling…it doesn't feel right. Maybe we should wait. I'm sure it won't be long. Anyway, I'm sure Melissa knows lots of folk around here who might know something."

"That means telling her why we're here. How do you feel about that?"

"Aha…I see what you mean. She *can* be excitable…. But then again, why not? She may surprise us." They had reached the car and John dug in his pocket for the key.

"Okay then" he said when they were in the car, "let's do that then."

"Now?"

"No time like the present."

Lissy had been right about Father Jim not being there but that was fine since it was Melissa they wanted to see. Unfortunately, she wasn't there either. John and Lissy had knocked four times but there was no answer. They decided to go down to the village and look for her. The village was quite a busy place. People obviously wanted to make the most of the sunshine while it was here.

John parked the car outside the little post office and they got out.

"What now?" asked Lissy.

"Let's get a sandwich first. I'm hungry. We can keep an eye out for her while we eat."

"Good plan. There's a café down at that end of the street. I saw it yesterday when we were waiting for Mr O'Hanlon."

They walked to the end of the street and entered a tiny little café. It was like coming into an oven from the cold air outside. The only light came from the tiny little windows with lace curtains and a dark lampshade hanging from the ceiling. An open turf fire was burning and the smoke filled the room making it darker than it should be and tickling their nostrils. The floor was made of stone slabs and there were four little tables placed evenly about the room. They took the nearest one to the window so that they could look out for a glimpse of Melissa. A young boy came over to them, pencil and notepad in his hand. He smiled at them shyly. He couldn't have been more than ten.

"Hi," said Lissy smiling warmly at the child.

"Hello missus, may I take your order please?" the boy asked in a very proper manner. John and Lissy warmed to him immediately. They both continued to smile at the boy who added that his name was Sean and his ma said to take their order and she'll be out in two shakes of a lamb's tail.

"Okay then Sean," said John giving the boy a cheeky

wink. Sean giggled. "We'll have two rounds of egg salad sandwiches to go please." They watched with pleasure as the determined child wrote the order down on his little notepad, his tongue sticking out with concentration and then trotted off to the kitchen proud of his accomplishment.

"What a darling!" Lissy's eyes were twinkling with joy and John thought what a wonderful mother she would make.

When Sean came out with their sandwiches in a paper bag they gave him the money and added a generous tip for him. His eyes opened wide as he looked at the two euro coin John placed in his hand. As they turned to go John asked him – "Do you know where Melissa lives by any chance?"

Sean did. "Aye, Missy lives just down there," he pointed down the street, "two down from the post office."

Melissa hadn't been at home either but her foster mother was in and seemed delighted to meet them.

"Melissa has told us all about ya," she said, "she's very taken with ya."

"We're quite taken with her too Mrs… erm…"

"McGuiness, Theresa M'Guiness. It's nice of ya to say so but I know our Melissa can be a bit of a handful."

"No, she's lovely, Mrs McGuiness. I'm Lissy by the way, Melissa really as well, and this is John. It's very nice to meet you."

"We were hoping to see you actually," said John thinking quickly, "we have some questions and we thought maybe you might be able to help us."

"My goodness, I don't know what I can do to answer yer questions but sure ask away. Come in, come in now. Don't be a stranger standin' there in the street."

Theresa had been very decent in inviting them into her home and giving them a glass of cranberry juice to drink. It was plain to see how Melissa had turned out so well. However, things turned around so quickly they were left reeling from the force of it. They had told her all they knew so far about Lissy's birth mother. At first, Theresa had listened sympathetically. She knew what it was like for Melissa with *her* birth mother. But then she suddenly changed. She became not only dismissive of Lissy but almost defensive it seemed.

"I think you're barking up the wrong tree dear. If ya ask me, the person you're lookin' for isn't from around these parts. Sure, she could be from anywhere in the country," she had said quite crossly. Lissy told her that the grandmother was obviously from Cloughbeg but Theresa didn't seem to want to acknowledge that at all. "I wouldn't go bothering poor auld Sissy – she's not the best these days and sure her mind's not what it used to be the poor dear. No, you just leave well alone there m'dear."

Theresa had ushered them out the front door and back onto the street before they had a chance to reason with her. John was feeling well pissed off with their sudden dismissal.

"You'll let Melissa know we called won't you?" he asked

wondering if this had anything to do with her. The answer he received left him even more suspicious but determined to stay in Ireland until they had some satisfaction.

Theresa had said – "I will indeed, although she's off to Lisnablaney this evening so I doubt ya'll see her afore ya go."

"Well…" said Lissy when they were back in the car, "what do you make of all that?"

"It's obvious isn't it? She doesn't want us anywhere near Melissa, or Sarah Scallon for that matter. I'd be very surprised if Melissa was scheduled to go away at all. Now she'll likely be packed off to Lisnablaney against her will."

"Poor Melissa, and it's all thanks to us. But she'll get to see her little sister won't she? She's in Lisnablaney, isn't that what she said?"

"Yea..." John was beginning to wonder, "…know what I think? I think that Mrs McGuiness knows exactly who the grandmother is. She's protecting her. Maybe, she's still alive."

"Maybe it's Sarah Scallon." Lissy stared at John…"Well, it could be."

John was worried - "I think we need to speak to Sarah Scallon and before Mrs McGuiness does."

"Oh John, this is exciting. It's like one of those mystery novels." Lissy was on the edge of her seat. She loved a good drama.

"The only problem is, we don't want to upset the whole village do we? So we can't just go disturbing Sarah now that we've been warned off. I think we ought to leave it for at least a day. Maybe Jim will arrange it after all."

Lissy understood John's sudden change of heart. She didn't want to upset anyone either. "But in the mean time, Mrs McGuiness will have got to her and told her not to say anything."

"We'll just have to take a chance on that. Besides, we may be jumping to conclusions here. Let's not assume anything until we know better, eh?" His experience as a journalist had told John that his suspicions were almost always correct but also that you never tread on peoples' toes or it could backfire on you.

As the day went on it became clear that Jim wasn't going to phone, either because he had changed his mind or because Sarah Scallon really was unavailable. They had gone out to the white-washed cottage again. It felt a little like trespassing actually since Melissa wasn't with them and because Theresa McGuiness, whose family owned the place, had made it quite clear that she didn't want them sniffing around. Nevertheless, no-one said they couldn't go there and there was no sign saying no trespassing. John had sat in the woods with a rug around his shoulders and read a book whilst Lissy sketched her picture. At three o'clock in the afternoon the sun was beginning to get low in the sky leaving them feeling rather chilly. John had read several chapters of his whodunit novel glad for the escape from their own mystery. He got up to stretch his legs and he spent some time looking at the little white wooden cross wondering who Grace was. A story of mystique began to form in his mind. He shook himself out of his daydream – *Gosh John old boy, all this 'who is the grandmother' business has you suspicious of everything*, he thought to himself.

Lissy was just about finished her sketch. She was very pleased with the result and had decided to call it *Endings*. "Because," she explained to John, "today has been a day of endings. First we hear about poor Mr O'Hanlon and then Father Kearns. Then it seems we've lost Melissa – we'll not see her again, and now here we are at this lovely cottage that has seen its best years and has been left here to fall away … no use to anyone ever again. It's quite sad really."

"And there's the white cross with its little grave, if that's what it is," John reminded her, "that's a kind of ending."

"Yes it is and that's why I've included it in the picture… see?" John looked and there in one of the windows in the picture was the reflection of the little white cross.

"Genuis!" he exclaimed.

"Why thank you kind sir," she laughed. "Hey, let's have a try to see if we can get in." She looked in through the first little window. Then she tried the door again but it was locked. Making her way around the back of the house she began to hum happily. John followed, content that she was content. There were the old toppled down sheds. The door of one of them was gone completely and the tin roof was hanging down into the shed. As they went to take a look where the door had been they stood on something under the grass. It was old rusty tin.

"Probably the door," suggested John, "be careful honey. Don't touch anything. It's very precarious, could fall in at any moment." She stood at the door and watched him go on in.

"It smells a bit whiffy," he screwed up his nose. Heaps of old magazines and papers lay rotting. What looked like old hen boxes sat at one end and there were feathers all over the ground. John picked his steps carefully and stood in the middle of the shed. "Gosh, look at this," he approached a wooden box in the corner. It had a hole in the top and a lid that was left open against what was left of the tin wall. In the box was a tin bucket. "I think this was a toilet…Yuk!" He pinched his nose – the bucket was filled with dank rusty water. "Come here and see this," he said motioning to her to come in, "this is crazy."

Lissy stayed where she was. She didn't like the feel of the old shed at all. The smell was overpowering yes but it was more than that. "Just come out of there," she pleaded, "it feels horrible. Let's go." She went back to the front of the cottage very quickly and waited for John to catch up. A couple of minutes later he came around the side of the cottage breathing the fresh air in a showy manner. He found Lissy leaning against the car sobbing, her face deathly white. He dropped the fooling around and became very serious.

"You're as white as a ghost. Are you okay?" he put his arms around her and she dropped her head onto his shoulder.

"I dunno. I just came over all funny. I don't like that place. It feels horrible. I came over all panicky and had to get away."

John was surprised at how it had affected her and wanted to get her back to the guest house as soon as he could. "Let's go honey. It's been an upsetting day all round. Let's get you back and get a rest. It'll do you good."

On the drive back to Drumgar John chatted merrily about his plans to see a bit of Ireland since they had almost a week left. He talked about going down to Galway to see the famous Dingle Dolphin because she loved dolphins. She was only half listening though. She knew he was trying to take her mind of that nasty place but she couldn't stop thinking about it - *How can a place be so lovely in one way and in another be so horrible?* The old shed had shaken her up and left her wondering what might have happened there that was so awful. She interrupted John who was talking about dolphins. "Something happened in that shed – something horrible. I never want to go back there as long as I live."

"You won't have to honey" he assured her.

"Good, because someone died in that shed. Someone was terrified. I felt it darling and I never want to feel like that again."

"You won't, honey."

Lissy began to cry and she cried the whole way home.

Chapter Seventeen

Shocking news

Drumgar, April 2008

It was the day of the funeral. The main street of Drumgar was quiet, most of its trade at a standstill for the afternoon. On almost every door were hung various sizes of paper with the same message written on each – 'closed for the funeral'. It was Sunday. Day trippers from neighbouring towns usually filled the streets on a spring Sunday afternoon but since the weather was atrocious most of the shopkeepers reckoned there wouldn't be too many about today.

"Anyway," stated Maggie Adair from the children's clothes shop, "poor auld Joe was well thought of by all of us. I'd say there's not a soul open the day."

"Aye you're right there Maggie. Be a big one no doubt," agreed Pat Scallon from the fish 'n' chip shop.

"Oh God aye! And I'd say there'll be a fair wee crowd

from Cloughbeg an'all. What about yer aunt Sissy, how's she doin'?"

"Och she's rightly thank God. Her an' me ma were away to Knock there during the week."

"Ah now isn't that nice fer 'er?"

"Oh aye, stayed over in the hotel an' all. Had a great time so I hear."

"My God, isn't she the great one? Let's hope we're all that great when we're her age, what. And yer ma's good to her, is she not?"

"The salt o' the earth, Maggie. But then, we're all auld Sissy's got left. She'd be on 'er own if it weren't for us Scallons."

"She never had any of a family at all then?"

"None at'al. The Murphys are all gone an' sure even the Scallons are gone now. There's only me ma and me and me brother left."

"She'd a brother a priest hadn't she? What's this ya called him?"

"Aye - Father Sean Murphy. That's goin' back a bit. Never really knew 'im meself but I often heard tell o' im. He was right an' popular was Father Murphy I believe. Not like that new one now – Devlin. I can't be doin' with all these new fangled ideas o' his."

"Can't say as I know 'im'," said Maggie, "anyways I'd best be off. Got a funeral to go to. See ya."

"See ya Maggie." Pat Scallon went back to fixing his message on the door. He would best be off too. He had to lift his aunt in Cloughbeg at eleven fifteen and be back here in time for the mass at twelve. He thought about Father Devlin. No, he wasn't too keen on him at all. He had too loose an attitude for a priest. He had wanted to speak to auld Sissy too last night, about something to do with that English couple that had been asking questions around the village. *Ya ijit Pat*, Pat said to himself now, *ya should'a went out there last night – found out fer yerself what's goin' on.*

John and Lissy had decided that they ought to go to Joe O'Hanlon's funeral. They did know him after all. The weather had been awful since they went to Galway on Friday. It had rained the entire time they were gone, and it was chilly for April.

"We would have been better off spending the time around Cloughbeg," moaned Lissy on the way back to Drumgar, "at least we might have learned something."

"You enjoyed the nightclub did you not?" John asked cautiously. Lissy was in one of her dark moods.

"It was okay, but it's not why we came here is it?"

"That's why I think it'd be a good move to attend this funeral. With Mr O'Hanlon being from Cloughbeg, there's bound to be lots of the older villagers there. Plus, Mrs Doyle did say that Sarah Scallon might be there. It'd be a good opportunity to talk to her. I say let's go and spark off some interest in our quest."

As it was John was spot on – many of the funeral goers were interested in who they were and why they were there. Kate O'Donnell who owned the café was talking to Theresa M'Guiness as they sat in the hotel lounge after the funeral.

"Pat Scallon said that Father Devlin had been talking to auld Sissy to do with them" she told Theresa, "and last week he had them round at the parochial house for lunch. They've even befriended young Melissa."

"I know, I had them round at the house meself. Called at the door bold as brass, lookin' for Melissa. God knows what business they're up to but I sent my Melissa away out of it for a bit. She's too innocent for her own good, that one."

"You know they were in the café. Oh aye, chattin' away to our Sean when I wasn't there to keep an eye on them. Gave him two euro to tell them where Melissa lived, they did." Mrs O'Donnell folded her arms and shook her head in disgust. "If ya ask me Theresa dear, ya did the right thing getting your lass as far away as possible."

"What d'ya suppose they want with Sissy?" Theresa wasn't stupid – she knew exactly who Lissy Brenning was but she wanted to see how much other people knew about why she was there.

"God knows dear" replied Kate, "but as I said, I was chatting to Pat and he reckons they must be some relation o' hers come out of the woodwork now that the wee critter's on 'er last legs. Well that's as may be but they may as well have stayed where they were. Sure, hasn't Pat's ma bin a godsend to poor Sissy all these years? As if she'd pass her by and leave it all to strangers, the very idea."

"You're not wrong there Kate. I must speak to Sissy about somethin' anyway. Where is she I wonder?" Theresa scanned the lounge and spotted Sissy sitting with Pat Scallon and his mother. She said a quick bye to Kate and made her way through the crowded room towards Sissy. She spotted the English couple sitting in a corner booth with Father Devlin and it looked like they were deep in conversation with him. "*Thank God our Clare's not here*, she thought to herself and then she had the most dreadful thought – *Christ! Rose used to work for Joe and Iris way back. Please God she's not here. That poor girl's had a lifetime of trouble as it is.* When she reached the Scallons she saw that they were not alone in the booth. Joe O'Hanlon's poor auld mother was there with her daughter-in-law, Iris.

Sissy was the first to see Theresa approach them –"Ah well, there ya are Theresa dear. I was just sayin' to Mrs O'Hanlon here what a good job you've done with that young Melissa. The Father says she's doin' a right good job up there at the house."

"Aye, she's a great one now. How are ya Sissy?...Mrs O'Hanlon...Iris...How are ya bearing up?" Iris O'Hanlon said that she was doin' alright and the doctor had given her somethin' for her nerves." She motioned for Theresa to sit down which she did.

"Aye well, it'll take time dear. You'll be closing the shop for a while I suppose."

"Not at all, sure we haven't done much in the shop ourselves this long time. I dare say things will go on as usual."

Theresa saw the opportunity. "Our Rose used to work for ya didn't she?" she asked Iris.

"Oh aye, grand one that. It's a pity she wasn't too well now." Iris said nothing else. Everyone at the table knew that Theresa's niece had a few marbles loose.

"She's here is she?" asked Theresa praying she wasn't.

"Aye, didn't she come over to us in the graveyard?" Iris asked her mother-in-law who replied that she wouldn't know – all Mrs Doyle's grandchildren were grown up now. She wouldn't know her from Eve. Theresa was wondering should she keep a look out for Rose – make sure she didn't come face to face with the wee English one.

"Och aye Theresa dear," Sissy said to her, "You left a wee message on me phone. We just got back last night dear. What was it ya wanted?"

Theresa was glad it was her that brought the subject up - "Do ya know what it was Sissy, and I'm sure you'll agree with me Pat – it's about that young English couple that's bin hangin' about. I don't think it'd be a good idea to let them over the door now. Ya never know these days with people. Best be on your guard eh?"

"Hear hear!" agreed Pat, "I just got done tellin' her not to entertain them at all."

But Sissy argued her point again - "Father Devlin was round last night and he's gonna be there to see what it is they want. Don't worry about me dears, I'll be grand. Sure the Father won't see anyone do me any harm." Sissy Scallon was as stubborn as a mule at times and if she wanted to do something she would do it and that's that. "Anyway, I haven't said I'll see them yet. Maybe I won't."

"You see that you don't, mind Auntie Sissy. Let them go on there," insisted Pat.

That was the wrong thing for anyone to say to Sissy. The old woman made up her mind then and there that she would see the English ones with or without Father Devlin. *The poor wee girl hasn't done anyone any harm*, she thought, *all she wants is to find out a wee bit about her mother. If I can help the poor wee critter, then I will.* She had racked her brains last night. She hadn't been able to fall asleep because of thinking so much but as hard as she tried, she couldn't remember any thirteen year old being pregnant all those years ago and she didn't think she'd ever heard anything about someone's grandchild being in that predicament either. If her brother Sean had seen the girl at the time then she was in no doubt that he had kept the whole thing as secret as possible. He had a right good heart had their Sean. That's why she liked Father Devlin, he reminded her so much of her brother.

A bell was rung at the bar and a voice shouted – "The O'Hanlon Funeral please. Refreshments are now being served in the O'Connell Suite." John and Lissy waited for most of the lounge to empty. Father Jim had gone on having spotted a man he wanted to see about a dog. They had been chatting to him for the last fifteen minutes. They had talked about everything that had happened since they last spoke with him and they told him all about the cottage on the hills and the little white cross in the wood. Fortunately, it seemed that either John had been wrong about him or he had had a sudden change of heart because he was very interested in continuing the search and he had, he told them, managed to talk to Sarah Scallon about them. He even pointed her out to them. She was sitting at the back of the lounge facing their way so they were able to get a good look at her.

"Finally," muttered Lissy when Jim had left, "something is going right for us. Let's introduce ourselves. Maybe we could see her tonight."

"Did you see who she was talking to just now?" Lissy shook her head. "Melissa's foster mother, Mrs M'Guiness.

"Shit!"

"Never mind, Jim will vouch for us I'm sure" said John. He watched the last of the people disappear into the O'Connell Suite. "Don't know about you honey but I'm beginning to feel as welcome as a fart in a spacesuit. I'll be glad to get home."

Lissy giggled and agreed that it did feel like they were prisoners on trial here. "So will I darling, back to normality. This is so fucking stressful and probably a whole bloody waste of time."

"Not entirely," argued John, "it got us together didn't it?" Lissy gave him one of her best smiles. The kind that lit up her face.

"True." The smile left her face and she looked down at the glass of wine in her hand. "But…"

"What?" John held his breath. Since it all began he had been dreading that she'd suddenly realise she didn't want him after all.

She looked up at him, tears filling her eyes –"What if we go home with nothing? How can I face people knowing that my mother was only a kid and that's all I know about her? I came here to find her John, and so far I've found absolutely sweet fuck all. I dunno if I can go back to the way it was."

"You'll have me."

"Yes darling, but to be out there in Cloughbeg and so close to my origin – it's changed something in me. It's weird but in a way I feel like I belong here and since I haven't found her and it all seems so hush hush, I feel even more rejected than I did before. I've just made things worse by coming here, haven't I?"

John moved closer to her and put an arm around her –"Let's see what Sarah Scallon comes up with. I have a good feeling about this."

"Yeah," she decided getting up off her seat, "let's go find her."

"Lissy" he said holding on to her hand, "I love you."

She smiled though her heart was heavy – "I love you too." Her eyes glistened with tears again.

In the O'Connell Suite were lots of round tables scattered

around the room. On one side of them was a small bar and on the other side was a long table covered with white tablecloths. Hotel staff was pouring cups of tea and coffee for the funeral goers. John and Lissy busied themselves with fetching two coffees whilst all the time scanning the room discretely to see where old Sarah Scallon was sitting. They spied her in one corner just as a familiar voice called their names –

"Lissy, John." It was Mrs Doyle from the guest house. She sped through the crowd towards them waving like they were old friends.

"Oh, here we go," John complained to Lissy.

Mrs Doyle was making such a show that lots of people were looking in their direction. She caught them up and with a voice loud enough for most to hear she said – "There you are me dears. I want you to come and say hello to a good friend of mine. She's lives in England too. This way dears." And off she went grinning from ear to ear, pleased that anyone who mattered had their eyes firmly fixed on her and her guests. "Here we are dears, let me introduce ya to Bunty Gordon. Bunty is from London y'know. We've bin friends ever since we were wee'ns at school, isn't that right Bunty dear?"

"That's right Breda. So, you're from Dorset I believe?" Bunty asked them.

"Yes, Lanesworth. Do you know it?" asked Lissy politely.

"Indeed I do dear. Such a quaint little place. I have

business there in June as it happens. One of my many clients will be appearing in The King's Arms , do you know it dear?" Lissy knew it. The King's Arms was the most upmarket hotel in Dorset. It was where the psychic fair had been held last year.

"I do, it's quite something," she replied.

"It's satisfactory I suppose but then my client isn't too fussy."

"Bunty is a big entertainments manager in London dear. She manages big celebrities an'all," Mrs Doyle told Lissy and John proudly.

Bunty silenced her with a raised hand. "Yes of course, however my client is from here you know. She's showing promise of greatness though. A few more months in London and then she'll be off to the States – with my help, naturally."

Lissy felt that Bunty Gordan was a bit of a wannabe, a fake it till you make it kind – only the worst possible version of that with the inflated ego to go with it. Lissy wasn't going to hang around just so that Mrs Doyle could impress her superficial friend. "Isn't it a small world indeed," she said with her mother's best air of grandeur. "Anyway, we must dash. I do apologise but someone is waiting for us. It was nice meeting you Ms Gordon. Goodbye then. Bye Mrs Doyle, we shall speak later." She walked away without a second glance, John on her heels in total admiration for the ease with which she managed the situation.

He caught her up and took her arm. "You amaze me.

You really do," he said with a grin. "Look, there's Sarah Scallon with Jim. Perfect." They made their way over to the old lady and the priest.

"Ah, speak of the devil and he's sure to appear," grinned Jim offering them a seat. "This is Mrs Scallon. Sarah, this is Miss Lissy Brenning and Mr John Brunt."

They all shook hands and sat down. For the next twenty minutes John and Lissy sat drinking coffee after coffee and having a great time chatting casually with Sarah Scallon. It turned out she was a great person to chat to. She had a bright mind with a fantastic memory and she was more than willing to meet with them later that evening. "In fact," she said, "In my airing cupboard is a box of my brother's things. I'm pretty sure there's an old journal there y'know. Och, Sean was a great one fer keepin' a journal. Used to write everything down he did, even when he was wee."

"But Mrs Scallon, that is exactly the kind of thing we're looking for," said John excitedly. He could see that Lissy was on the edge of her seat. "Are you sure it would be okay for us to see that?"

"Well, what's the use in me tellin' ya it's there for if you're not gonna look at it?" said Sarah sharply which made everyone smile since it was obvious she was just messing with them.

"I think we're gonna get along just fine Mrs Scallon," said Lissy, "aren't we John?"

"Like a house on fire," he said, pleased as punch.

"So you think your grandmother may have been from the village then?" Mrs Scallon asked Lissy that evening as they drank tea and ate scones in her little kitchen.

"Not *my* grandmother Mrs Scallon – my mother's grandmother. It was her that took my mother to see Father Murphy all that time ago."

"I do wish ya would call me Sissy dear. Everyone else does with the exception of the good Father here. The only time he calls me Sissy is when he's mooching me cherry scones, isn't that right Father?" Jim smiled. He was very fond of old Mrs Scallon and her cherry scones.

"John's quite partial to a cherry scone as well. Mum bakes them for him. I think she's been trying to get us two together for some time now," laughed Lissy.

"Your mum's not so slow then dear. You make a lovely couple. Any fool could see that. John dear, I'm sure those aren't a patch on what you're used to but I hope they're alright for ya."

"No no, they're very tasty actually," John replied tactfully. He wanted to steer the conversation back to Father Murphy. The sweet old woman had a habit of drifting off to another topic entirely. At this rate they'd be here until midnight before they saw that journal. "You were saying before Mrs Scallon...sorry, Sissy... You were saying before about a journal that Father Murphy had kept."

"Och aye, dear, Sean's stuff. It's up in the airing cupboard

I think. I'm sure that's where I last saw it." She got up off her chair with some difficulty. "Maybe ya can fetch it down fer me Father, me old bones aren't what they were."

"Not a problem," Jim jumped up from his chair, "You sit where you are now an' I'll fetch it myself. Just tell me which room it's in."

"In the wee room at the back, Father, in the airing cupboard. It'll be on the top shelf way in at the back I think. Ya might have to look hard." She waved a strict hand at John – "Go on, lad, give the Father a hand now." John obediently followed Father Jim out of the kitchen and up the stairs.

In the kitchen Lissy smiled at the old woman – "I can't tell you how grateful I am, I really can't. This could mean the difference in going home with nothing and actually discovering who my mother really is."

"You worry me though dear," Sissy told her, "what is it that you hope to gain from all this? Ya obviously have a good mother at home. Why do ya need to go diggin' up the past? Y'know dear, I've lived a long time, and if there's one thing I can say to you it's that there's never anythin' to be gained by diggin' up the past. Let sleepin' dogs lie – that's my motto."

"Oh Mrs Scallon, I understand what you're saying, I do, but well…it's kinda hard for me to explain…I need to know who she is so that I can know who *I* am…does that make sense?"

"None at all dear I'm afraid, but it's clear it means a lot to you and I'm sure you've thought it over long an' hard…"

"I have...for months."

"Then that's good enough fer me dear. What does your poor mother think of all this?"

"She was against it at first but she knows I need this so she gave me her blessing, and my dad too. They're okay and they know no matter what happens I'll always be grateful for what they gave me."

"I don't think it's yer gratitude they want dear."

Lissy felt like a chastised child – "No, but they know I love them too. Nothing will ever change that. It's just... well, Mum is so controlling." She thought twice about saying anymore. She was beginning to feel like an ungrateful teenager.

Sissy had heard all she needed to hear. When *she* was a young girl she had wanted to go to America to her aunt's family. She had longed to be a nanny and live in a big house in New York or Chicago with some modern family. She had a dream, she supposed, but her mother wouldn't hear of it. She'd been poorly for years and Sissy's father had died of cholera when Sissy was only twelve. She had to stay at home and look after her mother even though her two brothers were old enough to look after her *and* themselves. Still, she hadn't held it against them, but when Sean announced that he wanted to be a priest and go off to Dublin their mother was so pleased and proud of him that Sissy couldn't help but feel a little bitter about it.

"It's okay dear, ya don't need to explain yerself to me," she told Lissy. *I understand what mothers can be like, only too well* – she thought.

"Here we are now." Father Jim plonked a large cardboard box taped up with parcel tape on the table in front of Sissy, "Just where ya said it would be." Sissy picked at the tape.

"Here Lissy dear, you can get this off, with those nails, quicker than me." Lissy pulled at the tape nervously. "Listen wee'ns," the old woman said to them. "Enjoy yer young years while ya can. You'll be old an' useless afore ya know it."

"Ah now, you're never old an' useless Sarah," boomed Jim, "You're only as old as ya feel eh?"

"These take me back a bit that's fer sure. Let me see, what's this now?" Sissy was taking objects very carefully out of the opened box. "Och aye, that's me ma's auld medal collection. Look at these Father, there's holy medals there that even you will not have seen." She passed a small paper bag to Jim who took it with amusement, not one bit interested in the medals. He, like John and Lissy was dying to know what was written in the journal, if anything, about Lissy's mother. Object after object was taken out carefully and examined by Sissy. They had to listen to a story about each one before going on to the next. "And this is me mammy and daddy on their wedding day. Some age that photo." She showed them a yellowed photograph of a smiling couple. It was covered with cling film in an attempt to preserve it but the corners were curled up and it had one long crease right through the bride's head.

"You ought to get that copied. It's very easy to get a good copy nowadays and they should be able to take that crease out as well," John told the old woman who was stroking the photograph, a far away look in her eyes.

"Aye that'd be done on computers now wouldn't it?" asked Jim. John nodded saying a quick yep. He had spotted a leather backed book just like the one they had read in the parochial house.

"Is this the journal do you think?" he asked as he lifted it out. Sissy put down the photograph and took the journal from him.

"That's the very one I believe," she said. She opened the cover and read aloud from the first page – "The Professional Chronicles of Father Sean Francis Murphy." Everyone was quiet for a few moments as the spoken words seem to enforce silence taking centre stage. Lissy's chair made a scraping noise on the tiled floor as she practically lay over the table in an attempt to read the journal upside down.

"Why don't we take this into the front room and have a good look at it?" suggested Jim. They got up to go. "Here, let me take that for ya Sarah. It looks heavy." The journal *was* heavy, and very thick with added pages and notes. They followed Jim into the front room where a fire was blazing brightly giving a welcome warmth and feeling of hope to Lissy as she sat down beside Jim on the sofa. Sissy sat in her armchair beside the fire and John remained standing.

"Sit down John," said Lissy, "you're making me nervous." She patted the sofa on her right hand side. He danced about on the spot and then perched himself on the arm of the sofa beside Jim.

"I'll sit here honey. Can't settle til I've seen this," he muttered not taking his eyes off the journal on Jim's lap. He waited impatiently for him to open it. "Come on then," he said to a hesitant Jim.

"I don't think we should look at everything," Jim said a little red-faced. He was feeling somewhat forward at not handing the journal back to Sissy. "Maybe you should read it Sarah? Just the part that relates to Lissy."

"If it's there," added Lissy.

Sissy was thinking that she was too old to be flapping about the issue like this. When you get to her age, she reckoned, you don't waste a single moment by holding back. "Oh fer the Lord's sake, would ya just read it Father. Open it up an' let's see what's there. Sure isn't Sean dead an' gone this long time – he's hardly gonna be fretting in his grave about you reading his book. In fact, he'd be right pleased it's come to some use."

Everyone smiled and Jim opened the journal at the first page. He read aloud the title again and a bit underneath which said – '*Cloughbeg parish 1970*'. On the next page the first entry was dated May 1970 and was headed – '*John James McElroy, farmer, 24-03-36*'.

"That would be wee JJ McElroy. He had a farm out on the hills. Well, I say a farm – it was just a wee lock o' sheep really, but he made a right honest living, so he did. He would'a wanted them big lads of his to take it over but they went to England an' I don't' think there's any hope of them comin' home now. Och no, the wee farm's just gone to rack an' ruin, so it is." Sissy was carried away in her memory of the old days and began to talk about folk giving up the old traditions and so on. John had to bring her tactfully back to the present task – finding the entry they needed.

"Flick through til you come to the year 1978," he suggested to Jim who did so very carefully as quite a lot of pages were loose and added sheets kept threatening to slip out. There was more written in the early seventies than any other time, it seemed, since more than half the journal was filled by the time they came to 1978.

"Here we are," said Jim at last.

Lissy saw that the date at the top of the opened page was August 1978. She read the heading out loud – "The third of August, nineteen seventy eight – Miss Kathleen Caldwell – 13-05-59." Jim, Lissy and John all scanned the entry which was obviously not about Lissy's mother. Lissy continued – "Nineteen year old girl pregnant…bla bla bla… sent to St.Mary's in Belfast…oh my God! ...girl's father, Mr Peter Caldwell, gave permission for the baby to be adopted. Oh how sad, the poor girl probably didn't have a choice."

"That's the way it was done in those days dear," said Sissy, "nowadays it's so different. Young girls havin' babies without as much as a ring on their finger. There's far too many children these days bein' dragged from pillar to post, not a look-out on them. Take that young Melissa for example Father, if it wasn't for Theresa and Tommy God knows what the poor wee critter would'a turned out like."

"Yes Sarah, that's true indeed, although there are two arguments to every story, eh?" Jim answered her, "but we shouldn't be reading anything that does not relate to Lissy." He turned the next page which was about a trip to Lourdes in September of 1978, and on to the next which was dated October 1978 – a young newly married couple seemed to be in difficulties of some kind. The next entry was dated January 1979. Jim flicked over to the next entry which was the following June and then he flicked backwards to the first 1978 entry. "It's not here," he said disappointedly.

Lissy was gutted. She threw herself back on the sofa and sighed – "Ah frigg it!" she muttered angrily.

John wasn't so quick to despair. He took the journal from Jim's lap and getting down on his knees on the floor, he spread the journal flat on the carpet. Carefully turning to the back, he scanned the last page. "Let's see if it was added later." He began reading the dates from the last entries. "*March 1992...November 1991....April 1991...* Yes!" he exclaimed excitedly, "This is it! *October 1978.*" Lissy leapt onto the floor beside him. He took a loose sheet of paper out of the journal and gave it to her. "Look, it's a copy of the entry in the other journal. You know, the one you have Jim. Take a look at this. This one hasn't been blacked over. It's all here, the woman's name and everything."

"Oh John, how brilliant...wow, you're right. 'The twentieth of October nineteen seventy eight – *Miss Rose Collette McDevit – 25-08-65'*. Rose, what a lovely name, isn't that a lovely name?"

"Calm down honey," John told her, hardly able to contain his own excitement. He was grinning from ear to ear. "Give it to me. I'll read it. You'll not do it right."

"What!" Lissy exclaimed laughing, but she gave the paper to him anyway.

She stood up and began moving about the room her hands to her mouth as if she might say something that would change their luck entirely and the whole journal would never have been there in the first place. Jim read the entry slowly and precisely so as not to miss a single important word. The rest of the group listened carefully as they learned that the grandmother's name was Mary Doyle of Upper Cairn, Cloughbeg. Again they heard that the child was to be sent to Dorset England to the care of Father Peter Kearns who would arrange the adoption. They shook their heads when it said about the child being harmed outside of the home and that she appeared to be terrified and unaware of what was happening to her. They had known this but it was the bits that had been blacked over in the original copy that had them on the edge of their seats. Lissy listened with growing disbelief as Father Sean Murphy had gone on to say that the child had talked about apparently illicit meetings and what he feared where issues of sexual abuse. He had written that he had contacted the child's own parish in Belfast and had spoken to a Father Corrigan who reassured him that the family was of good moral conduct and that although there had been rumours of anti-church goings on, he was certain that it was unfounded and most probably fabricated from previous events of that nature in Donegal.

'There is very little doubt in my mind Father Murphy had written, *from what young Rose has related to me, that what she has been subjected to is evil in nature. I fear we are talking about black magic and I stress the urgency for a full investigation to be instigated. However my elders are quite confident that they shall deal with the situation sufficiently and that my suspicions are unfounded, based purely on the testimony of a very disturbed young girl.'*

Lissy was in shock. Jim wished he'd never got involved in the first place, and little old Sissy was beside herself with grief. How did her poor brother keep such a secret to himself all those years? Oh, the nature of it. She knew exactly what her brother had hinted at. *Good Lord in Heaven*, she prayed silently, *grant him peace and poor Mary Doyle too.* What *the poor woman would have gone through. It doesn't bear thinkin' about.* Sissy knew Mary Doyle well, she had bought eggs from her for years. *That's right*, she said to herself, *Mary's eldest married a McDevit from Drumgar and they lived in Belfast for quite a few years I believe. Well, it has to be wrong. How could one of Mary's girls be involved with that nonsense? And sure there's poor Theresa next door. She'd disown her family if she even thought they'd be up to that carry on. No, it has to be wrong.* Still, Sissy said nothing about knowing Mary Doyle at all. These things were best left alone.

John was the only person in the room who found a voice. After several minutes of anguishing silence he said – "Now we know what all the secrecy was about."

Lissy remained quiet. She couldn't quite understand what Father Murphy had actually concluded but she didn't feel she could cope with whatever it was. Could it be that her mother, this thirteen year old, was involved in some kind of cultish crap, maybe even a child sex scam? Lissy preferred not to think about it. Suddenly, all she wanted was to be at home with her mum and dad stressing about silly things like where Dad had left his glasses. John took her hand in his and studied her face. He had seen her like this before. It usually came at the beginning of a long silence between them but this time it seemed she was further away from him than ever.

"Are you okay honey?" he asked. She looked at him forlornly and shook her head. "Aren't you pleased that we know her name?" Lissy got up off the floor and walked out of the room. John could hear the kitchen door shut noisily. He got up to go to her.

"Leave her John," Jim told him, "give her time. She's not goin' anywhere." John sat down quietly on the sofa. No-one spoke. They all stared at the journal lying on the carpet, the dreadful entry still clutched in John's hand. Jim took it from him and read it through silently to himself. Sissy stoked the fire and threw on three large clods of turf. Then she settled back in her chair muttering a prayer under her breath for the poor child that was sitting in her kitchen trying to cope with the realisation that she was the product of some dark wicked devilry.

For the first time in his life John Brunt couldn't think of

anything to say. The ever ready, take anything on journalist had finally been struck dumb. He felt useless. Lissy needed him and he was useless. He couldn't even blame anyone – who would he be angry at? – Rose McDevit? – The perpetrators? They were just words on a sheet of paper. What use would that be? If he ought to be angry at anyone then he ought to be angry at himself. He could have talked her out of this but he had encouraged her – and for what? If he was truly honest with himself he did it because he wanted to be near her. Well, he won didn't he? He finally broke the ice lady down and won her heart, but it didn't feel so great now that her heart had been broken. *Oh, why did I bring her here? She was better off not knowing this…this crap*, he thought to himself bitterly.

In the kitchen Lissy poured herself a glass of water from the tap. She wandered over to the back door and opened it stepping outside into the garden. It was still raining. It hadn't stopped all day. She thought about the first day they were here – up on the cliff side. Was that only six days ago? It felt like a lifetime. It had rained that night – the night she made love to John for the first time. Oh, he was so good to her. He loved her so much. She thought about the moment she had realised how much she loved him too. Everything seemed magical. The sun was shining on the ocean and to her it was also shining in her heart. He had held her tight and kissed her and the whole world stood still in one perfect moment. She had known without a doubt in her whole being that he was the one for her.

"Oh John," she sighed sitting down on a low stone wall at the bottom of the garden. She could see the ocean from there just between two hills. It was grey and heavy like the sky, like her heart. "You fooled me," she spoke out loud to the ocean, her tears falling onto the stones beneath her. "You let me believe I could be complete here; that all I needed to do was find her and I would find myself. And now I have, I've found her but I haven't found myself. You said I would but you were wrong. I've lost everything I thought I was about. I'm nothing but a…a freak – someone's dirty little secret." She cried until she could no longer see the ocean through her tears and she was soaked through and shivering with cold. The back door opened and John stood there bewildered and alone. "Oh John," she cried running to his arms.

"It's okay darling," he said hugging her neck, "we'll sort this out. Trust me." She relaxed in his arms wiping the tears from her face with her hand. John noticed a box of tissues on the table and offered them to her. "Honey, come back inside. There's something else you should see."

"I don't think I want to know any more," she sniffed.

"You'll want to know this, trust me. Maybe you should take that wet jumper off?"

"No, I'm okay, just show me what you've found." They went back to the front room.

Sissy was glad to see Lissy. "Thank the Lord, you're in one piece," she said fussing over her. "Here child, get upstairs and take those wet clothes off. You'll find some old jumpers in the back bedroom."

"No, I'm fine, honestly. What have you found?"

"Well first of all we've found that copy of the letter sent to Father Kearns," said John, "It says all about Father Murphy's fears. I knew there was a reason why old Kearns wouldn't let us see it. Honey, it even states her name and everything. No offence to your church Jim, but if he wasn't already dead I'd make sure of it."

"No offence taken now" said Jim, "Here Lissy, that's not all. Sit here and read this."

Lissy sat beside him and looked at the journal on his lap. It was opened at the date April 1991. A pain shot through her forehead and she sat back in the sofa with a sigh. "You read it...please. My head is throbbing."

Jim squeezed her hand sympathetically. "You'll be grand sweet girl. It's just a bit of a shock is all" he told her. Then he began to read – "'Twenty first of April nineteen ninety one - Mary Doyle – the first of the twelfth, nineteen twelve. Mrs Doyle came to see me about her granddaughter Miss Rose McDevit'."

"Nineteen ninety one?" asked Lissy, "What age was she then...twenty six? I would have been thirteen then?"

"That's about right," said John, "but listen to this."

Jim read on. The entry stated that Mary Doyle had been concerned about Rose's well-being. She had wanted Father Murphy to pray for her. She had told him that Rose had been trying to commit suicide and that she was in the mental institution in Drumgar. She was at her wits end worrying because the girl seemed hell bent on destroying herself and her family. She was having hallucinations and violent outbreaks and her parents were increasingly concerned that she was mentally insane. Father Murphy had written that he had relayed Mrs Doyle's concerns to the parish priest in Drumgar where Rose lived and he trusted that the priest would visit Rose and give her the Blessing for the Sick.

When Jim finished reading Lissy threw her arms up in the air in a gesture of dismissal. "That's it then, she's insane – a loony bin."

"Honey, don't you get it. She lived in Drumgar then. For all we know she's still there." John was sure Lissy would be excited about that but he couldn't have been more wrong.

"For all we know, she's still in that mental institution. Or worse, has managed to kill herself. No, no thank you. I'm not having anything to do with it."

"But aren't you even the least bit curious in seeing her – finding out what she knows about you?"

"Most likely she doesn't even know who *she* is let alone who I am. No John, I'm not curious at all. I just want to go home to my nice sane mother and father and live my life. If you're part of that life, then good. Are you?"

John was worried. He knew her attitude would change and it would be too late to do anything about it. Furthermore, it was futile trying to reason with her. He would just have to let her ride it out. "Of course I am." he said.

"Y'know....Rose may not be insane at all. She could

very well be a normal woman with a normal life. She could very well be married and have children for all we know," said Jim in an effort to bring some hope back into the room.

Sissy piped up and stated categorically – "That woman is mad alright. I knew Mary Doyle an' a better family ya couldn't meet. If that Rose led our Sean to believe what he did, then she had to be crazy – a bad 'un I'd say."

"You knew Mary Doyle?" asked John wondering how long she had kept that a secret from them. Did she know who Lissy's mother was all along? *No, she's just realised*, he told himself.

"I did dear. She was a good holy wee woman an' all. Lived out by the coves on the coast. Lived there her whole life, so she did, in a wee cottage hardly big enough to swing a cat in. Reared three daughters there an' all. Aye, Mary was a good 'un an' no mistake. Didn't deserve that misery thrust upon 'er that's fer sure." Sissy shook her head in disbelief. "She'd turn in 'er grave if she could hear us talkin' now."

Both John and Lissy had it worked out in a trice. The tin-roofed cottage with the little wood and the cove down below – it had to be it. Melissa had said that her granny had lived there all her life and that she'd had three daughters, Theresa and two others.

"That's right!" Lissy exclaimed loudly. "Melissa said that her Granny's name was Doyle. John!"

"I know…the cottage…it was Mary Doyle's. Sissy, the cottage that you said she lived in her whole life – did it have a red tin roof and a little copse of trees nearby?"

"Well, yes dear. It did."

"And were there two tin sheds behind it? ...and a long lane up to it? You have to climb over the hills to get to the cove."

"Aye dear. Mary Doyle. Her daughter lives next door."

John addressed Lissy – "Theresa M'Guiness." He turned back to Sissy – "Sissy, did Theresa have a daughter called Rose?"

Sissy thought for a while – "No dear, I think she may be one of Clare's girls. Clare was the one that went to Belfast."

"That means that Theresa McGuiness next door is my great aunt," said Lissy as if she didn't quite believe it. "Oh John, to think the whole time…no wonder she was defensive."

"She was trying to protect her sick niece," added John.

"I don't understand," said Sissy, "how do you know where Mary lived?"

"We went out there a few days ago Sissy, with Melissa. Didn't we Jim?"

Jim nodded - "I said she could go. She was so excited. What would she make of all this, eh?"

"Don't you dare tell her Father," warned Sissy, "that one would have it round the village in no time an' poor Theresa doesn't need that now."

"I don't think it'd be a good idea to tell anyone," Lissy assured her. "I for one just want to go home and leave this as it is. I know my mother's name and that she's not a well person and I know more about my birth family than I had ever thought I might. What do you say John, we just go home and leave it at that?"

"It's entirely up to you honey. It's your life and you know I'll support you whatever you wish to do." Lissy looked at him lovingly. Dear, dependable John, where would she be without him?

"You can't say fairer than that sweet girl" said Jim. That being settled, the three friends said goodbye to a rather tired Sissy and walked down the street of Cloughbeg, Lissy with an arm linked in each of her best men.

"Do you know what I'm thinking about?" she asked them. "I'm thinking about the little wood at Mary Doyle's cottage. I'm thinking about that little white cross at the tiny grave and I'm thinking – do you suppose it has anything to do with Rose McDevit?"

"I suppose it could have," replied John.

"Then do you know what I think?" she went on - "In her madness, she thought her baby was dead. Maybe that even drove her to madness but whichever way it was, I think she put that cross there."

"Perhaps she did. When you think about it, it's not really all that mad is it? Especially if she really thought you were dead."

"If it was her and that's why she did it, then you know what that means, don't you?"

"No, what?"

"It means that I'm Grace."

"That's all as maybe though," said Jim, "what if it wasn't her at all?"

"What if it was?" asked John, "we'll never know now, will we honey?"

"Maybe, maybe not."

Part Two

The Good Red Road

Chapter Eighteen

Into the light

Our abilities, our talents, our gifts in life are what make us special. Rose had begun to wonder if indeed what she had attempted to purge herself of since she was thirteen was actually what made her special. What would happen if she should embrace her differences?

Lisnablaney, September 2001

Rose and Jack watched the two little boys play with their big sister Emma. It had been raining all weekend and the yard in front of the house was muddy and covered in puddles. Rose had bundled four year old Olly and three year old Jerimiah up in warm waterproof clothing and had put cute little red wellington boots on their feet. The boys were having heaps of fun splashing in the puddles and getting all wet and muddy. Olly had had a habit since he was a toddler of sticking his head in the puddles. He loved to feel the muddy water running down his face when he stood up and true to form he did it again. Jerimiah copied him squealing with delight – "Look at me Mummy, I'm washing my hair."

"Ha ha ha!" laughed Jack. Emma ran to wipe the muddy water away from Jerry's eyes but the excited child ran away giggling. Before she could catch him he plopped himself down bottom first in a deep puddle. Jack laughed louder. Not to be outdone, Olly found the deepest puddle he could and plopped down into it with a splash.

"Come and get me Mummy!" he yelled getting up and running with his mother after him.

"I'm the tickle fairy an' I'm coming to get ya!"she sang. She grabbed the child and picked him up swinging him around by the arms. They twirled and twirled and then they both fell onto the muddy ground giggling and hugging. Jerry came running to them and joined in a big group hug.

"Come on Emma," squealed Olly, "a big huggle."

Emma was twelve years old and a real muck magnet as her daddy often said, but even she wasn't prepared to roll about on the wet muddy ground with two mud-drenched little boys. "No way! Rose, you're flippin' mental!" she laughed.

"Oh well we all know that don't we Daddy?" Rose grinned at her husband. "Okay everybody inside – into the bathroom now." Olly and Jerry followed their mother obediently into the house and to the bathroom. Rose and Emma stripped them of their wet clothes and ran a warm bath. Emma added a huge dose of strawberry scented bubble bath and soon the boys were having just as much fun splashing in the bubbly water as they had had in the puddles.

"May I have a bubble bath?" asked Emma as she wrapped a soft towel around Jerry and dried his blonde curls. She planted a kiss on the tip of his nose and the child giggled with glee.

"Of course pet," replied Rose, "and for being such a great help I'll have some hot chocolate and marsh mallows ready for ya when you're done." She watched her step-daughter dry her son as she knelt on the floor, Olly wrapped up in a towel on her lap. She hugged him to her and smelled his damp hair. *What a difference from when I was a wee'n,* she mused, *bath times then were a necessary evil, not all fun and laughter like this*.

Ten minutes later, the boys were curled up on the sofa asleep, worn out from all the excitement. Emma was in the bath, Rose and Jack could hear her merrily singing a song she had learned at school. "We'll just pick them up and put them straight into their beds," Rose said to Jack as she picked Jerry up trying not to wake him. She carried him to his bed and tucked the covers up to his chin. Jack put Olly in his bed as well. His little face was flushed pink and his mouth turned up at the corners into a smile. "He's having a nice dream," said Rose.

"He's a happy child," said Jack, "they both are." They looked at Jerry. He looked so peaceful, so safe and warm in his little world. Tears sprang to Rose's eyes. She didn't even notice them as her mind drifted back to when she was a small child about Jerry's age and in the bath when all of a sudden she was submerged in the water. Her mother was scowling at her, her face dark and twisted like a monster. She had frozen, shut down just as she had when she had sat in the coal bunker one time, just as she had after Grace had been born.

Only that time I didn't wake up again… until now, she thought sadly to herself.

"Come on darling," Jack said kissing the top of her head, "don't let Emma see you like this." Rose gathered herself together and went to the kitchen with Jack.

"I told her I'd make her some hot chocolate."

"You spoil her. She just had a shower this morning before I picked her up from Kelly's. It wasn't as if she got dirty too."

"Well, she may act all grown up but she's still a wee wee'n – wanted a bubbly bath just like the boys, didn't she?" said Rose. She stirred the mug of hot chocolate and added five marshmallows to it. "There that should be to madam's requirements I think."

"You're too good to her."

"She's a good kid and I love her, don't I?"

"She's a lucky girl – two mothers to spoil her rotten."

"Y'know," said Rose, tears stinging her eyes again, "I

used to love getting' all dirty like that when I was a wee'n. I used to lie down in the sand at Granny's and I'd rub the sand into my scalp to get as dirty as possible."

"Didn't your ma get cross at ya for that? Thought you always tried to be good so she wouldn't get cross?"

"She never noticed really or if she did she never mentioned it." Rose blew her nose with a tissue and composed herself. "I don't really know why I did that. It felt good. Do ya know what it was like? When I used to lie down on the grass and hold on with my hands, pressing myself against the ground. It stopped me from flyin' away somewhere and when I got really dirty and rubbed the sand into my scalp and skin it made me feel like I was stuck to the ground."

"It's because it made ya feel earthy. You were grounded instead of havin' your head up in the sky all the time. It's what most people feel all the time" said Jack kindly.

"Normal people ya mean. I was far from normal," said Rose bitterly.

Jack was concerned that she was going to get too upset. He could hear the anger in her voice. "Emma will be here soon. Don't let her see ya like this darling," he said. "Here, why don't you have a hot chocolate as well? I'll put the boys' things in the washing machine an' clean up the bathroom."

Rose looked at him fondly. She was grateful. It had been a long day and she hadn't stopped since she got up this morning. "Thanks darling. I'm beat," she replied.

At nine thirty that night she had dried Emma's long red hair with the hairdryer and painted her finger nails and toe nails bright pink. Her father tucked her into bed and kissed her goodnight. Rose was in the living room, content that all the children were safe and happy. Jack joined her with two glasses of wine in his hands. "Ta love," she said taking a glass.

"Feeling better?" he asked.

"Not really. I'm not angry if that's what ya mean, but I'm just tired y'know?"

"Yea, it's bin some day."

"It has, but I mean I'm tired generally y'know? I'm tired of the whole business of feeling like a freak and wondering who my mother really is. No point in talking to them, they'll deny everythin' till they're blue in the face. Got too much to lose." She rubbed her forehead and sighed heavily. Years of talking and crying had worn her out and she was mentally exhausted. "Och, darlin', I'm just tired of secrets and lies and havin' to hide away all the time. I just wish I could flick a switch and not have to think anymore," she moaned.

"Well, what about what Davy suggested?" asked Jack.

Davy Smith had worked with Jack for years and was now freelance with his own handyman business. He had been practicing an ancient Chinese form of energy healing called Reiki for a couple of years now and was convinced that it really did help people. Reiki worked on an invisible field of energy around the body, and, as Davy had explained to Rose one evening a few months ago, was about channelling pure lifeforce or *chi* as the Chinese call it, through the healer to the person being healed. It worked by breaking down the emotional blocks that keep people from being well and Davy had felt that it would definitely make a difference to Rose. But Rose hadn't been too sure. It sounded a bit too close for comfort for her. She remembered when she was a child she used to see shadowy shapes around people that were ill and that with her mind she could manipulate those shapes until they disappeared and a bright blue light would fill the space instead. It was just one more thing that made her a freak. One more thing she preferred to forget.

"Why not give that woman a try..." Jack continued, "y'know the woman that Davy went to at the beginning? He swears that she has a natural ability to heal people."

Rose thought about it again. She hadn't thought much about it since she last saw Davy, but she had been so tired lately that she had basically given up all resistance towards anything. In fact, in her prayers at night she talked to the divine spark that she knew was the good within her and she would say – *I'm tired trying to sort my head out. I'm tired hurting so much. I've tried everything I can and now I am handing it over to you. It's in your hands, I can't try any longer.*

Very soon after starting to pray like that, Rose's pain shifted so phenomenally that she was left with no doubt that a higher force was taking control of her life – that her prayers had been answered. It all began when she decided to take Davy's advice and give Reiki a chance. She had made an appointment with Peggy Greer, a Reiki Master. Peggy turned out to be lovely, about fifty five years old she was a small thin woman with a broad smile and a huge heart.

"Were you sexually abused as a child?" she asked when Rose had gone to see her and was lying on a kind of treatment bed. Peggy had her hands on her head and there was a heat radiating from them that was comforting to her and she didn't flinch when Peggy asked her the question.

"Yes, I was. How can ya tell?" she asked.

"It's all there in your energy field," Peggy said, "when I tuned in with ya I felt like I was being held down and the pain was incredible."

Rose couldn't speak. She was overwhelmed with sadness and she couldn't prevent herself from crying – hot, heart wrenching tears. She cried like she had never cried before. When she stopped it was as if a weight had been lifted off her chest. She remained speechless. Peggy was making specific movements with her arms above her abdomen and she felt her body tighten with resistance.

"Relax Rose. You're perfectly safe here," Peggy told her.

But Rose felt she would never relax. To let go meant that something terrible would happen to her. It felt as if she was back in Granny's shed and she was having Grace all over again.

"Take a deep breath and let your tension go," said Peggy. "You're holding on to somethin' here that is doin' ya harm."

Rose couldn't let go. How did she know *Peggy* wasn't doing her harm?

Peggy then held one of her hands and put another hand on her chest. "Rose, how many children do ya have?"

Rose began to feel the heat coming from Peggy's hand. It helped her relax a bit. "Two boys" she muttered sadly.

"Did ya have a wee girl before that? Did ya miscarry?" A wave of the heat flooded into her heart and Rose was aware of a wonderful loving energy all around her and within her. Tears fell from her eyes again and tumbled down the sides of her face. Taking courage from the wonderful energy she told Peggy about Grace.

"So then, what we're gonna do is remove that old energy from your womb. You've held on to her ya see Rose. It's as if she's still there. By letting that energy go it can be transmuted into pure lifeforce which can be used for well-being instead of a bundle of negativity which it is now."

Rose was feeling more and more relaxed and she found that she understood Peggy's theory, regardless of the fact that she'd never heard anything of the sort before. Peggy worked on for a few minutes above her womb and when she was finished Rose did indeed feel as if something had shifted from her. She had a strange sense of freedom around her as if she were floating in mid air but with her feet touching the ground. "I've never felt like this before," she told Peggy in a voice that didn't sound like herself.

"It's because you've always bin surrounded by so much dark heavy energy. This is probably the first time you've felt what it's like to be free of that."

"Can I come back please?" asked Rose.

"I recommend that ya come at least twice more," said Peggy. "We've done a lot this time but we've only just touched the surface really. There's a lot more there to clear," she told her.

"For years y'know, I felt like there was a fog around me," explained Rose. "It was filled with shadows of my past, memories y'know and fears an' that. I finally feel like it's gone completely."

"Well, I feel that you have certainly cleared a lot. It's like this, Rose," Peggy explained, "we are all made up of three… erm…parts if ya like – mind, body and spirit. What you've done til now is work on the healing of the mind which is vital for well-being. What we do here is work on the spirit which is just as important and as a result of that the body is healed. Do ya see the natural order of it all? – everything begins with the mind – with a thought – then that thought creates emotion which is held as energy in the spirit, in the spiritual bodies – that is the energy field or the aura – then it finally becomes manifest in the physical – in the body, in the form of some illness or other."

"I understand that. I'm not sure I could repeat it but I feel I do understand it," replied Rose, excitement rising within her.

"Then you'll understand that by changing our thoughts to happy positive ones, we can experience well being instead of illness?" suggested Peggy.

"Of course…oh my God," she gasped, "this is important." She realised that Peggy would understand what she was about to say. "For years now Peggy, I've bin tryin' to work out who I really am and why all that crap happened to me. This is important. This has got to do with who I am. I know it has." Her mind was working overtime and she began to feel a little light headed. "Oh, I don't feel so well. I need to sit down."

"You've gone straight back into your mind again," Peggy informed her, "and ya need to be in your body, grounded. Here let me do this." She stood behind Rose and did something and then Rose felt better again. "What ya need to practice is bringing yourself down into your body and staying there. Imagine ya have a great big pair of heavy wellies on and feel your feet being pulled down to the ground."

"Oh my God," Rose told her, "that's just what I've bin talkin' about this last week or so – being grounded."

"There ya go ya see, ya know yourself what's best for ya. You're not so slow Rose. It's my sense that you're well on your way to knowing yourself. In fact, my sense is that you're very gifted when it comes to matters like this."

"I always felt different but I never liked it."

"Well, like it, 'cos I think not only are you gifted but you're very special indeed. I think you'll do great things Rose."

Rose drove home to Lisnablaney with lightness in her heart. She sang at the top of her voice – "*Give me joy in my heart, keep me singing. Give me joy in my heart I pray. Give me joy in my heart, keep me singing. Keep me singing till the break of day.*" What a feeling! She had never felt this good about herself before. All her life she knew there was something specific she was here to do but that feeling had been buried under all the horror. But she had known all the time that she was something specific – special – not like anyone else. "Yes," she said out loud to herself, "not like anyone else 'cos I do have a gift. It's not evil at all. It wasn't the reason why all the crap happened. It was the thing that saved me."

She pulled the car into a lay by and got out. It was a clear night and the moon was shining brightly, lighting up the fields and trees at the side of the road. Rose leaned against the trunk of a mountain ash. She loved trees. Ever since she was a child lying among the trees at Granny's place she had felt an affinity with them. They had been her friends when she had no-one to hear her. When she was a small child they had listened to her, witnessing her pain and providing a safe haven for her to fly off with the lady to see the Indian. They had always been there when she needed them, them and the cave at the cove. She remembered how when she couldn't get to them she would sit in a cupboard and close her eyes and then the first thing she would see would be a huge tree or the cave, ready and willing to be of service to her. They had been her gateway into the spiritual realms where the lady and the Indian were waiting for her. As she leaned against the ash tree now, the memory of the ancestors came softly back into her mind. She smiled as she remembered how they would come in her dreams and talk to her gently about who she was and why she was here on earth. With tears of joy this time filling her eyes, she spoke to the tree.

"I have a purpose – I'm not a freak or a witch …I'm not born bad… I was born for a very special reason and that is to seek the truth in all matters. That is what the Indian is about and that is why he came to me – 'cos I have to help him – we have to tell the world about the truth." She astounded herself at the knowledge she had just spoken out. *Knowledge, that's what it's all about*, she thought. She didn't know what that knowledge was – what the truth was that she had to bring to the world but she could feel it. It felt like God. It was as if it was about the true nature of God and the universe. "It's not just about telling the truth," she told the tree, "it's about helping people to realise the difference between truth and error." *But first of all*, she thought, *I have to realise that myself. That is what the next piece of the jigsaw is all about.*

She was in a very pensive mood when she arrived home. It was late. She had stood with her back to the tree for a long time. Minutes had flown by like seconds. Jack was waiting for her, keen to hear how she got on with Peggy. "Oh Jack I feel wonderful - like I've emerged from a long dark tunnel," she told him quietly and relaxedly.

Jack was beginning to see a side of his wife he had never seen before and he liked it. She was softer, more alive. Her eyes shone like diamonds. Many a time she had walked into a room and lit it up as if she had turned on a light and Jack was aware that people's gaze followed her wherever she went. Now, as he studied her he could see that there was a light within her that shone like a beacon, bright and warm like a welcoming fire on a cold night.

<u>January 2002</u>

Sitting in Peggy's front room with four other women there for the same reason, Rose could see that the blonde haired woman had a spirit with her. Ever since she first had a healing session with Peggy, Rose had begun to see the picture people again. Like when she was a child, they would tell her things in her head only this time it was as if she could feel what they were feeling as well. A spirit man called Arthur had been appearing to her for days and he was there again standing behind the blonde woman, with a hand on her shoulder.

"What's your name again?" Rose asked the woman.

"Kathy."

"Kathy, do ya know you have the spirit of a man with ya?"

Kathy wasn't surprised. "Yes, it's my grandfather. Peggy told me ages ago. He won't go away apparently and I'm not sure I want him to anyway." Kathy smiled widely. She had a beautiful face, with her grandfather's smile.

"His name is Arthur is it?" asked Rose.

"Aye... you obviously have the gift...like Peggy."

"Like more than you'd think," Rose found herself saying. Was that true? Was it more common than she had thought, as well? There was something about Kathy that told her yes. "Arthur has been coming to me for a while now" she told her. "I was surprised to see him with you."

"I think he wants us to be friends. Perhaps we need to learn something of each other." Kathy also was saying things she didn't know she knew, but there was something about Rose that was intriguing and she seemed to bring her alive in new ways.

Peggy spoke to Rose – "Can ya see the person I have here at the moment?"

Rose looked at Peggy for a while and then could suddenly see, as if she had come from nowhere, that there was a tiny woman sitting beside her. "I see her now," said Rose. "She's quite old and small. Long, long grey hair. The way she's dressed she looks like a gipsy woman."

Peggy was delighted – "That's her. That's my aunt Bella. She always wore long flowing skirts, kinda like gipsy skirts alright. Hardly ever wore shoes. Well done Rose. You're really opening up."

Peggy had meant that Rose was clearing her energy field well and was beginning to open up to the way of being that she was destined for. Rose, like the other women, was there to be initiated with Reiki energy. She wanted to become a Reiki practitioner and at the end of the day she had had an amazing time as she had begun to practice the ancient art of Reiki healing. It felt as natural to her as breathing and ... as she had suspected...it was very much akin to what she had been doing with her mind when she was a kid and saw those shapes around people. She was now feeling all those things she had been longing for – acceptance of who she was, knowledge of what she was about, and joy and hope in knowing that she was following her heart's desire. The other women all had their stories to tell of who they were and what they wanted from life, some of them had fascinating tales of survival. Rose, however, felt she couldn't talk about herself openly quite yet. They all could see that she was a medium but she drew the line at exposing her ability to leave her body and transcend to the realms of spirit. Even *she* wasn't convinced that she wasn't a tad loopy when it came to that. She wondered what her daughter Grace would make of her if she knew. She wondered if Grace knew that she was adopted. She wondered if Grace was alive. She would be twenty three years old.

Peggy had told them that they ought to practice the healing on themselves each night for four weeks. Rose would lie on her bed, cushions all around her for comfort and to support her arms as she pressed her hands to specific parts of her body for a few minutes at a time, clearing her chakras - her energy centres. Peggy had taught her that according to the ancient art of Reiki, these invisible centres take in energy from the universe and use it for specific parts of the body.

"It's different from just getting energy from our food,"

said Peggy, "it is a spiritual energy that permeates all things including food. It is the lifeforce essential to us, the breath of life. In fact, breathing is one way in which we can receive this energy. Through the healthy functioning of the chakras is another way."

It was Rose's third week and she was really beginning to feel the benefit of the practice. Besides feeling more alive and less anxious, she was beginning to feel the way she did as a child when it came to freeing herself from her body. On one particular practice session, the spirit of a man came to see her. He was there only briefly but Rose was sure that he had been the spirit boy who grew up with her – who she now knew was the twin brother that she had heard her mother referring to, who had not survived the birth in body, but whose spirit had stayed close to her all those early years. He wanted to give her a message and so she took a pencil and found herself writing in her diary – *'In order for me to do this work more successfully I need to come out of my body and enter the spirit world again'*.

What did her brother mean by making her write that? It was a long, long time since she had left her body, and the lady had been with her then. How could she possibly do it now without the lady? Did she even want to? It wasn't something she had thought she would ever go back to. Nevertheless, she decided that she would do what had been working for her these past few months and that was to leave it up to the divine spark within her, and one week from that day, on the eighth of February two thousand and two, Rose once more left her body and travelled into the spirit world – into the light; and from that moment she was never to look back. She had come full circle on her journey. She had walked willingly into the fires of hell and clambered out by the skin of her nails. Then she had begun to piece together the little shards of truth, her shattered consciousness, and now at last she had arrived back at the beginning. Now, she was to climb to the heights of heaven where she was always meant to be. Now she was being real.

This is how it came to pass. She was driving along the busy road from Drumgar to Lisnablaney after spending the morning shopping. Jerry was chatting merrily to her from his little car seat in the back but she wasn't really listening; she had to concentrate on the road. There was a great big bus ahead of her on the road and it was travelling very slowly. It was late and she had to get back in time to lift Olly from school. After some time of watching she felt it was safe to pull out and pass the bus, but immediately it became apparent that it wasn't safe at all. It had seemed to Rose to be several minutes but it was actually only seconds before the car speeding towards her met her own. When it did, she didn't feel it or hear anything. She was high above the car, rising higher and higher until she saw before her a spiral of light. Dreamlike and emotionless, she felt her body moving effortlessly into the spiral and on and on as if through a long, light-ribbed tunnel. At the end of the tunnel stood a man. He appeared to be dressed in pure white light. Rose stopped in front of him and, in the same way that the Indian had used to speak to her, he said – *"Rose, it is not time. You must go back. You have work to do."* Rose could feel herself say that she wanted to stay here with him but he repeated his words. She felt her body move back and then suddenly she opened her eyes. She was being lifted out of the top of the car.

"My legs!" she groaned from behind an oxygen mask.

"You're alright, love," a voice said just before she lost consciousness.

As it turned out, Rose had collided with an oncoming vehicle. She hadn't seen it coming, for whatever reason - it still eluded her. It remained in her mind though that she had a message one week before, that she was to re-enter the spirit world. That message, and the fact that there had been a paramedic in the car following the vehicle that hit her, and that in the car following him there had been a doctor, left her wondering if this *was* the hand of destiny. Just how much control did we have over our lives? Both medical men had been on the scene of the accident immediately and thanks to their professional action Rose had survived. Little Jerry not only survived but was carried away with just a few scrapes and scratches. He was to become quite angry with his mother in the months to come, often telling her – 'You should'a waked up'. The poor little mite had had to endure thirty minutes sitting in the back of the car with all sorts of strange people and noises surrounding him. The one person who could have consoled him was unconscious.

Rose remained drifting in and out of consciousness for a week. When she finally was able to stay awake for long enough, Jack told her that her beloved uncle Gerry had passed away peacefully the day after the accident.

Three months in hospital and two operations on her legs later, Rose came home to Lisnablaney in a wheelchair. If anyone was expecting her to anguish over what happened they could not have been more wrong. From the moment she opened her eyes in hospital she had told everyone that would listen – *This has happened! Now let's see where it takes me.*

What a transformation! Jack was amazed at how far she had come in such a short time. Sometimes he wondered if the miraculous transformation in Rose's attitude was a result of the Reiki healing she had had with Peggy. Later, Rose was to tell him that although she believed that the healing had been a major turning point in her well-being, it was the accident - or rather what happened to her in the accident, that was the real miracle. According to her, something had changed in her when she travelled into the light that day. She told Jack all about it three weeks after the event. She told him it wasn't the first time something of that nature had happened.

"There's so much you don't know about me Jack," she told him. "I've bin to places like that in my mind many times. One time when I was small…I don't remember why, but I think I was propelled out of my body and into the spirit world just like this time. Only, I was only a toddler y'know? I don't remember it much...in my child's way I thought I flew up into the sky where I saw a big white light and it guided me down to my cot. There was a blue ball of light that got bigger and filled the room and a voice said that I had to stay there or somethin' to that effect. I don't even know if I'm remembering it correctly but that's all I have."

Jack asked her - "Well then, what's the difference between that time and this time? How come you were left in the shit then, and now it's like it has all bin lifted off ya?" He was puzzled. Surely if it was divine intervention then all that terrible stuff could have been prevented? She could have had a normal childhood.

"I think I was always going to go through experiences of that kind. I think that it was all part of the plan that I know that stuff so that I can change it."

"But it happens all over the world. One person can't change the entire world, darling, as much as you might want to," said Jack gently.

"I don't mean change the world. I mean that I was always meant to change that knowledge within myself. Do ya remember I told ya once that it was as if I already had an awareness of the occult and black magic an' that?"

Jack nodded. He was beginning to realise that his wife's intelligence stretched far beyond what most of us would see as natural. He was beginning to wonder if his wife did indeed possess paranormal awareness.

Rose continued – "I think I need to alter my awareness of

that. I think my whole attitude towards it wasn't healthy."

Jack really was in difficulty now as to what his wife was about. Was she unwell? She did get a right knock on the head. He took her hand and said gently – "Rose, try not to think so much. You've bin through a rough time. Try and get some sleep now, you look shattered."

She *was* tired. It was hard for her to stay awake for more than an hour at a time. Jack kissed her forehead and she closed her eyes. She was asleep within seconds. Her husband watched her sleep. She seemed so peaceful and of course, he was thankful for that, but how could he ever break the news to her? It would devastate her. Everyone knew that Rose had a heart the size of the sun. The truth would be too much for her to bear but she had a right to know. She seemed to suspect already that something was amiss, but she had by now stopped asking awkward questions and had seemed to accept that there was nothing to tell on the matter.

Rose had been aware that no-one would give her a satisfactory report on the well-being of the people in the second car. They all said how the male driver had been lucky and was absolutely fine but that his wife had been hurt, but that as far as they knew she was okay too. Rose hadn't been convinced they were telling the truth. Nurses and doctors skirted around the issue, telling her nothing concrete. That evening, when she woke, Jack was still sitting by her bed. Her brother Brian was in the corridor talking to a nurse. "My parents aren't here?" gasped Rose in panic when she discovered that Brian was there.

Jack reached for her hand – "No, no darlin'. Just Brian. He wanted to see that you were okay. He'll report back to them I'm sure."

"That's okay but I don't want them here, not yet." She hadn't seen them in four years. There was no way she could cope with them now, like this.

"Don't worry they won't be here. Brian and Angie have pleaded on their behalf but I said no and I mean to stick to that. I thought that's what you would want."

"It is, for now."

The nurse came in with two cups of tea and a plate of digestive biscuits. She looked at Jack in a funny way, Rose thought, and when he rose and followed the nurse out to the corridor she was sure there was something afoot. Jack came back and the look in his face spoke volumes to her. "What d'ya have to tell me?" she said, then it dawned on her – "It's the woman in the other car, isn't it?" Jack said that it was but he wouldn't look at her. "She's dead, isn't she? She's been dead all along."

"Darling…it…" He was going to say that it was one of those things that seemed to fall into place. That the poor woman had been very ill for months and that her family had been relieved, in a way, that she was out of pain, but the words wouldn't come. The woman was dead and nothing could explain why her family had to live without her just as nothing could tell him why his Rose, who had suffered so much in her life, now had to live with the knowledge that she was responsible for another's death. Rose was the colour of snowdrops against the frozen earth of winter. Even in her weakened state she shone like hope in the darkest of times. She was deathly silent but the strength she so abundantly possessed announced loudly that she was fine. She would cope with this too. Jack relaxed somewhat and managed a smile which brought a glimmer of colour back to Rose's complexion. He babbled away now about who and why and what, but Rose had shut herself off from the knowledge. She would deal with it but in her own time and in her own way. And she did. When she slipped back into sleep that night she dreamed of Uncle Gerry. He came to her as a young man again and she was a little girl. He sat her on his lap and he told her that everything was going to be okay. He told her that he had to go but that he had fulfilled his part of the plan and that the Indian would come back into her life and she would never feel alone again.

"He loves you with a love that is so much a part of who you are. Never forget who you are Rosie."

Rose opened her eyes. "Uncle Gerry!" she whined. The realisation that Gerry had died hit her suddenly and she grieved her loss in the middle of the night in the hospital ward. Jack had gone and the only people to witness her pain were the many spirits that visited their loved ones as they lay ill in their hospital beds.

Jonathan Kane was a spiritual healer. He had the gift all

his life as did his mother before that. He was what people called 'a seventh son of a seventh son'. From a very early age Jonathan had felt drawn to put his hands on people. If one of his young siblings complained of tummy ache Jonathan would place his hand on their tummy and the pain would go. He didn't know how it worked but as he grew older and his mother taught him everything she knew, he fell into the calling naturally. He counted himself blessed that he had a team of spirit guides and helpers with him that knew exactly what they were doing and made sure that he knew what he was doing. He was a Kildare man, but he was prepared to travel around the country if someone should need his help enough, so he wasn't surprised when he got a phone call from a friend in Mayo to say that his friend had a friend whose wife was in a bad way. She had had an accident in February and she was now out of the hospital in a wheelchair. Would Jonathan be able to fit her into his busy schedule as the poor woman apparently had had a tough life and was in need of healing on all levels? As it was, Lisnablaney in Mayo was quite a bit off Jonathan's current route but he had a strong urge to find out more about this woman.

"Go to her," his spirit guides had told him, "it is for the greater good of all on earth."

"Jonathan, can I tell ya somethin'? It's a bit mad and I'm not sure that I'm not imagining it." Rose was lying on her bed at home. Jonathan Kane had been doing what he did for about twenty minutes now and she was very relaxed and comfortable. He nodded yes without stopping what he was doing. Rose could see that he was seeing from within, the way she did at times. She knew enough about it now to know that he was seeing with his 'third eye', his inner spiritual eye. "What you're doin'…I can see." she told him.

"Tell me what you see?" he encouraged her.

"I see a long line of blue light comin' from your right hand into my body and a black line goin' from my body to your left hand."

"That's right. What else do you see?"

"There's a woman near ya. I feel I've known her always. I recognize her although I can't place her. I recognize you too, like I've known you forever."

Jonathan stopped what he was doing and sat down on the bed beside her. He smiled joyfully. He knew there was something about Rose that was significant to him. The woman with him was his late mother. Now as he felt his mother's presence, she relayed to him the real identity of Rose. "It's my mother you see" said Jonathan. "Her name's Mary."

"How come I recognize her?"

"We're all connected Rose," Jonathan told her. "There is no separation between any of us. You and I have worked together like this so many times." This is something he had felt sure of as soon as he saw her.

Just as he said that Rose began to have a vision of Jonathan and herself in an Egyptian temple working just as they were now, but in a different life – they were two different people but with the same souls. She told him this. He had seen it as well, at the same time and Rose immediately felt she didn't have to ask – that she already knew that Mary, Jonathan's mother, was making sure they both saw their connection to each other. But what was her connection to Mary? It all felt so natural. "It all seems perfectly natural to me," she said to Jonathan. "It feels great to be able to be so *real* like this with someone." She explored her feelings further. "Do ya understand when I say that I feel like Mary is *my* mother too and maybe we were brother and sister? But no, it's like I *am* you. Oh this is crazy, I'm sorry. I didn't mean to sound so crazy."

"It's not crazy," reassured Jonathan, explaining what he already knew. "In the basic reality of things you are me and I am you. You are Mary and Mary is you. Do you understand?"

Rose was a little confused as to what he meant but she could feel the truth of it and that was enough for her. "No," she said, "but I know it's right. I can feel it."

"And that's how you discern the truth in anything Rose. You feel it. You know that inner gut feeling you get? Your intuition?"

Rose nodded, deep in thought. A million tiny realisations were opening up within her at that very moment and she felt as if she were waking up from a dream – a dream that had lasted her entire life. And it turned out that Jonathan knew about the dream – the long sleep he called it. It was as if human beings were asleep, he said, and their lives were their dreams. People think they are awake and when they sleep they dream but in reality they are sleeping and when they go to bed at night and they dream, their spirit is free from the restraints of the sleeping body and is really awake. "Do you ever have flying dreams?" he asked Rose.

"All the time," she told him, "and sometimes when I'm awake, it's as if I go out of my body and fly. I haven't done that much since I was a wee'n though."

"You know how you feel when you are out of your body?" said Jonathan. He knew that feeling too.

Rose thought about it. It wasn't too hard to remember. She was beginning to feel like that right now. She nodded quietly, soft tears falling down her cheeks. The one thing that would prevent her from welcoming that feeling was fear of being out of control. Jonathan lovingly wiped the tears with his hands. Rose could feel that he was a godly man. She softened more and cried more.

"That's what it feels like to be awake," said Jonathan, "the trick is to stay awake when you're in your body. It's not advisable to fly out all the time. You need to stay grounded."

"I think I always knew that," replied Rose, feeling herself beginning to panic at the sensation of going out of her body. "Jonathan…I feel now like I'm going to float out and I'm scared. What shall I do?"

"Come to me Rose," he said, "you'll be safe."

Rose allowed the feeling to wash over her and then felt she was moving forwards. Instead of flying away, however, she felt grounded; but not in her own body - she was now in Jonathan's. Jonathan knew what he was doing. He had to keep her safe. He saw at once that it had been too late to send her back into her body – that she was already out so he had said *come to me*. Her spirit was pure – so there was no danger.

As Rose experienced awareness of being Jonathan she knew herself as the little boy he had been, with an overwhelming desire to heal people of their pain. Rose was experiencing it as if it had been her childhood. Then she found herself moving back, feeling again the free feeling of being ungrounded and then she was back in her own body. Jonathan had guided her back safely. He stared at her and she at him for a while and they both had tears in their eyes. They were tears of release – of aliveness. They both were aware at that moment of the oneness of life. *There is no separation* – Jonathan had said. Rose knew now, through her own experience, exactly what he meant.

"Who am I Jonathan?" she asked in a small voice. As if in answer, the spirit of a man now appeared beside her. She felt him before he was there – and it was as if he had come from her heart. To her immense joy, it was the Indian.

Jonathan gestured towards him and said – "I see a Native American Indian here."

"I know," said Rose, smiling happily. "He's my friend. He's bin away for a while but I knew he was comin' back," she said.

"He hasn't been gone at all," Jonathan told her. "You

were in too much darkness to see him. He is part of who you are. The rest you will get to know as he guides you."

Rose could see the Indian with complete clarity, but she could not hear him. "How come I can't hear him now? He's just a moving picture," she queried.

"You will as you heal," said Jonathan. "You're a lucky woman Rose. Not everyone can see their spirit guide."

Suddenly Rose could see that there were people standing behind Jonathan. "There are a load of people behind you. Are they *your* guides?" she asked – she could see them quite clearly.

"What do you see? What do they look like?" pressed Jonathan.

Rose described them - "They're small for men and they look kinda like monks and kinda eastern looking."

"That's right. They're Tibetan."

Rose pulled herself up by her arms into a sitting position on the bed. She felt like she was ready to begin business. Now that the Indian was back, she was determined to be the Rose she was always meant to be. She wouldn't let him down.

"You know what?" she sighed, "All my life I've struggled through the crap. There's bin many a time I wanted to fall asleep and never wake up again. Even when I had Jack and the boys I still would have preferred to die rather than go on with life. But now, well it's like I've finally come out the other end and I actually want to live. D'ya know what's even more amazing? I actually like who I am and I'm proud of myself for what I've achieved. From now on my life is good and I feel truly happy for the first time – not that ecstatic top of the world happy like when somethin' great happens but really truly happy deep down within myself." She looked at Jonathan. He was smiling broadly – he understood.

"Yes, and you will do *this*..." he said, indicating the healing process with his hands, "and you will teach." He also showed her how to take a pencil and paper and 'channel' from her guides. "This is called automatic writing," he told her. "This is something you can do. Just connect with your guides and start writing. You will be amazed at what you are writing without thinking about it."

"I think I've done a bit of that already," Rose replied, remembering the message she had written down in her diary before her accident. She took several deep breaths. The truth in what Jonathan was telling her was swelling her heart with emotion and an overwhelming feeling of homecoming. Beside her bed and in her heart she could see and feel that the Indian was now beaming with pleasure.

The Indian was joyful. He knew that the song would soon be sung – he knew that the prophecy would soon be fulfilled – and all this would be revealed when Rose finally returns home to him.

Chapter Nineteen

Developments

Lanesworth, Dorset, England May 2008

Lissy looked at the tiny white window on the plastic stick – pregnant. "Crikey!" she gasped. She checked again. It was definitely positive – she was going to be a mother. She smiled and closed her eyes, relishing the wonderful news. Ever since she got back from Ireland it had been slowly dawning on her that something was different. Oh, she had stormed and stomped about alright, true to form. Why wouldn't she? Wouldn't anyone if they had just learned that they were the product of such a dark disgusting thing? She could get over that though if her birth mother hadn't been left mentally looped as a result. She was probably cooped up in some hospital somewhere, maybe in a straitjacket. Lissy supposed she could easily find out but what was the point? If she was then she obviously wouldn't know who Lissy was anyway, and if she wasn't then she wouldn't want to be reminded of what happened to her. Either way, Lissy wasn't prepared to meet rejection face to face. Besides, she was much more at ease now. Whether it was just because of John or because she had found out so much about her birth mother she wasn't sure. All she knew was she no longer felt so restless. Maybe it was because she was to become a mother. Something was beginning to fill the gap. Maybe, all along, she contained the divine mother's love within herself. That holy, pure, unconditional love that she portrayed in her painting was her all along and the child on the woman's lap was her unborn child that right at that very moment was growing in her womb. She hugged herself with happiness. She couldn't wait to tell John. He would be ecstatic. She would move in with him now that they were going to be parents. He had wanted her to. He talked about nothing else since they left Drumgar, but she wasn't sure which end was up at that time and since then she'd been distracted with the notion that she might be pregnant. Mum would be the problem though. She was raised with the belief that children should come after marriage and not before. Oh, she was worldly wise enough now to know that shacking up together wasn't a cardinal sin after all, but she would draw the line at babies. Still, nothing could spoil Lissy's happiness now. *I'm going to be a mum*, she thought squeezing herself with glee.

"Darling," she said to John that evening as they lounged on his sofa with a pizza, watching a romantic movie. He never tired of hearing her calling him that. His chest swelled with happiness as he looked into her blue eyes and he noticed that they were the exact colour of his own. How come he hadn't realised that before? It was a sign, as she would love to say, that they were soul-mates – always meant to be together. She was wearing her hair down over her shoulders just as he liked it. It was so beautiful with its soft auburn highlights that glowed in the light from the fire and her cheeks and lips were flushed pink with the warmth. He bent his head to kiss her lips and she pulled back from him grinning from ear to ear.

"What?" he asked grinning back.

"Guess."

He studied her face intrigued. She could hardly contain her excitement. "You've realised you can't live without me and you want me to marry you, right here, right now, for ever and ever til death do us part," he said.

She laughed and said that it wasn't that, but she had heard crazier things than that in her time. John thought he couldn't get any happier. He was wrong.

"Oh John, my darling, my love, my life! I have the most wonderful news. We're going to have a baby – I'm pregnant."

John scrambled to his feet and stared at her for a moment.

"It's true, we're going to be parents," she said.

He jumped around the room whooping with joy and thrusting his fist in the air. This was better than winning the rugby final. Lissy laughed at his antics, overjoyed that he was overjoyed. He threw himself in front of her on the mat and with his hands joined in a praying manner he begged her – "Honey, please now will you move in with me? You can't say no now. We're gonna be a family."

She laughed on and cried out a resounding yes! He flung himself on her kissing her face and hair and neck. Wrapping her arms around him she felt so emotional she cried. Big fat tears cascaded down her face and as he held his head back to look at her he found that he was crying also. "Oh Lissy," he croaked, his throat full of emotion, "my heart is pounding so much I think it will come out of my throat."

"Mine too," she giggled tearfully.

"Darling, marry me. Let's do this properly. I love you so much. I'd die for you. Please, marry me and make me the happiest dad on the planet."

If Lissy had ever known anything in her life to be right, she knew what her answer should be. Without a moment's hesitation she cried out – "Yes! Yes please."

Brenda and Russell Brenning were more excited it seemed than the parents-to-be. "I'm going to be a grandma!" Brenda kept saying, shaking her head in disbelief. "I never thought the day would come. Oh, Russell you must be excited. You're going to be a granddad."

"Of course dear, I'm very pleased. John's a good lad. He'll do right by our girl."

"And a wedding too! Oh, I think I shall burst with excitement. It'll have to be proper mind you. Lissy shall have the best of everything."

"When did she not?" Russell was wishing that the whole thing was over already and he could get some peace to read his paper.

"I was telling Lissy that she ought to have an engagement party and do you know, she has already decided she will. They have booked The King's Arms and all. Did you ever know that our Lissy was so organized?" Russell wondered how she could not have been, with Brenda for a mother. "Anyway, it's booked for the twentieth of this month and the guest list is already made out and all. I just couldn't contain my delight when she told me. They're inviting a long list of people apparently. Everyone's invited, even that Father Devon from Ireland is invited."

"I told you dear, it's Devlin. If the good Father does come, I don't want you calling him Devon."

"I wouldn't dream of calling him anything but Father, dear. Did you know that Lissy and John have been referring to him by his Christian name? It's Jim as it happens but I never…what is the world coming to when people start calling priests by their Christian names?"

"I'm sure you will keep them right dear."

Brenda sat down on the pouffe in front of her husband and took the newspaper out of his hands. "I'm so glad that woman didn't get her hands into our Lissy," she told him with a frown. "Thank God she saw sense before she got in too deep. I knew it would end in tears. I told her it would but would she listen? Oh no, our Lissy listens to no-one."

Russell was not prepared to get into this conversation again. Lissy was home and in one piece and that was all that mattered. It was the future they ought to concentrate on now, not the past. "For Goodness sake Brenda" he said impatiently, "will you stop going on about that woman. Hasn't Lissy suffered enough? Let her forget about it and look to the future. Now, I won't say any more on the subject and neither should you."

Brenda got up in a huff and went to the kitchen were she began to prepare tea, banging cups and saucers loudly so that her husband knew she was offended. Russell shook his head hopelessly and went back to his paper. "Like mother like daughter," he muttered under his breath.

It was the nineteenth of May and John had wrapped up his work for the day. He was about to leave the main office when Julie, the editor's assistant, called to him. "John, John wait up! There's a call for you from Ireland."

From Ireland? It could only be Jim. Maybe he could come after all. He and Lissy had invited Jim to the party but unfortunately he wasn't able to get the time off his parish duties. John rushed back to the phone. "Hello."

"John, hello there. It's Jim. I'm glad I caught ya. Lissy doesn't seem to have her phone switched on and I wanted to leave a message before I left."

"Left for here?" asked John hopefully. Lissy would be made up if Jim could make it.

"Aye. Auld Bernard says he can manage an' I'm due a bit of fun anyway. Think he might be feeling guilty about stayin' in Florida an extra week. Anyways I'm on me way. The plane lands in Exeter at ten twenty five. I wonder can ya still pick me up? Would that be okay?"

"No problem Jim. It'll be great to see you. Lissy will be made up. Tell you what…if I can't be there at ten twenty five I'll send Lissy's dad. I think Lissy has a list of things for me to do tonight. How does that sound? We won't see you stuck anyway."

"Aye sure that's grand John. Looking forward to it. Gotta run now though or I'll miss the check-in. Oh, Melissa's wavin' at me here. Will ya say hello? I'll be off now. See ya later."

"Hi John, how are ya?" came Melissa's excited voice over the phone. John grinned. He had forgotten how nice it was to witness her girlish excitability.

"Hi Melissa, we're good. How are you?"

"Och sure I'm grand now," she answered in the manner that reminded one of Breda Doyle. "I wanted to come. I asked me ma but she wouldn't hear tell o' me leavin' Father McGirr in the lurch. Will ya tell Lissy I said congratulations and it's over the moon I am, fer the both of ya?"

"I will Melissa. She'll be pleased to hear from you. She's very fond of you. Maybe your ma will let you go to the wedding?"

"I doubt it John," said Melissa in disgust, "she's taken a right hump wi' me lately."

"Never mind. We'll work something out."

"I'd better go. Father McGirr doesn't like me usin' the phone."

"Fair enough, bye then."

"See ya."

John hung up and threw the phone onto his desk. *Pity*, he thought, *but at least Jim's coming*. Lissy hadn't said so but John knew she would like some connection from Ireland at the wedding and young Melissa was the closest thing to her Irish roots she was ever likely to have a relationship with. He had wondered if he should track down Rose McDevit on his own but decided that it would be deceitful to go against Lissy's wishes like that. Besides, should she change her mind it wouldn't be too difficult to do. He glanced at his watch. He wanted to pick up his suit at the dry cleaners before it shut. Five fifteen – he would just about make it.

Twenty minutes later he closed the front door of his house behind him. "A Mother's Love" stared at him from the focal point in the hall. At least Lissy had said that's why it ought to go there. John had replied that she read too many interior design magazines and had received the habitual thump on the arm. She would be here soon. John stood looking at the painting, marvelling again at the passion it portrayed. He began to study it more this time, taking in the trees in the background and the little doll lying on the red blanket. He had to go closer to make out what was on the cover of the little black book – it was a tiny white cross. "Blimey!" he muttered. The mother, the child, the trees and the white cross; they were all there, just as they were at Mary Doyle's little cottage in Cloughbeg. What a coincidence! Was it possible that Lissy had had some kind of insight into what they were going to find? "I wonder where the doll comes in?" John said aloud.

"What do you mean?" He jumped as Lissy spoke behind him.

"How long have you been here honey?"

"All day. I didn't go in today – threw a sickie."

"Why, are you okay? Is the baby ok?" John grabbed hold of her suddenly as if she were about to collapse.

She laughed –"I'm fine silly. No I just didn't feel like facing work today. Anne's being such a bitch to me and anyway I felt exhausted. It's normal – don't worry." John wasn't going to relax though until she was seated on the sofa, a cup of tea in her hand. He ushered her into the sitting room and ordered her to put her feet up. "Darling, I'm not an invalid," she laughed, "I'm only nine weeks pregnant not nine months."

But John was worried. "That's precious cargo you're carrying there honey. You'll do as you're told."

"What did you mean…about the doll?" asked Lissy. John looked puzzled. "You were saying – 'I wonder where the doll comes in?'"

"Oh! Nothing important."

"I put a doll in the painting 'cos I always had a rag doll

like that and the child was supposed to be me in a way. I've still got that doll in my room. I always called her Meg but now I like to call her Grace cos…well, you know."

"I just wondered why you put her in the painting," he explained, and thinking quickly he added – "and a black book with a white cross on it."

Lissy laughed knowingly – "Ha ha! You noticed it too did you...the synchronicity with the wood at my great grandmother's cottage?"

"Yea, isn't that weird?

"I was talking to Linn," Lissy began and John rolled his eyes at the mention of Linn's name. "Oh here we go" he teased.

Lissy threw a cushion at him. "Linn reckons that it is a powerful synchronicity. She reckons that it indicates that I ought to stay with the search for Rose and she says that it was my inner knowing that painted those things."

John tried not to laugh. He knew she was into all that new age jargon. "Your inner knowing?"

"Yea, my intuition. Call it what you like but that's how I knew that there was a white cross in a wood somewhere that was connected with my mother and me."

John couldn't hide his amusement. He burst into giggles and made a dramatic show of feeling Lissy's forehead for a high temperature. "Crikey!" he gasped in feigned horror, "you're burning up. Call for the men in white coats – quick." That remark didn't have the effect he would have liked. Lissy was furious – how could he joke about such a thing? John knew the signs that meant that she was huffing with him. When would she ever grow up? "Honey, lighten up. It was a joke, that's all."

"That's all? John, how could you? My mother's in a loony bin in case it escaped your notice. Do you really think it's something I would laugh about?" Lissy's face was red with frustration and she was close to tears, her voice breaking.

In a way John was glad that he had messed up. She hadn't referred to Rose's state of mind since they left Ireland with the search completely cut off at a crucial point. Should they make contact or not? At least now she might be prepared to face that question head on instead of burying it with all the rest of the hurt inside her."Your *birth* mother, honey," he stressed, "who you have never even seen before let alone have had anything to do with. Your *mother* is a hundred percent sane. And anyway, we don't know that Rose *is* insane. She may be fine now. She may never have been crazy at all."

He could see that her temper had cooled and he took her hand talking calmly and assertively – "Darling, it has occurred to me that if Rose had really been the victim of some terrible crime then those that had something to hide would obviously declare her insane should she try to tell of her experience." John breathed apprehensively while she pondered his words. Her face gave her thoughts away completely and John could see that she was processing the idea looking for a window of hope that would give her a reason to follow through. "Honey, let me trace her for you" he said hopefully.

"No, I couldn't face it," she resorted to her anger again. "Whether she's in a loony bin or not, I don't want to know. I'm not getting involved with all that horribleness."

"Don't be scared darling. It's in the past. That's if it actually is true."

"I said I don't want to know, it would only bring more heartache."

"You already know it might have happened. Knowing it for definite won't change anything." John was convinced she would come to regret her decision but she wasn't going to budge. He wouldn't push her. She was stressed enough as it was and he had to think about the baby. Stress wouldn't be good for the baby. "Tell you what Honey" … he decided to lighten up himself … "I've got some really good news for you."

"What?" she sniffed trying to look like she wasn't interested.

"Jim phoned. He's coming…tonight. He rang me at the office." She brightened up immediately. "I'll ask Russell to pick him up" John added, pleased to see her smiling.

It was almost midnight when the front door bell rang. Lissy ran to the door and opened it. "Look who I found," Russell grinned knowing that his daughter would be delighted to see the priest. She had spoken about him non-stop when she got home from Ireland.

"Jim!" she cried, "You're here. How lovely!"

"Jim mate," came John's delighted cry from behind her.

Jim was ushered into the hall by a rather embarrassed Russell. He was sure the priest must be offended by the casual use of his Christian name. He was even more surprised at the intimate way Lissy was greeting him. She had thrown her arms around the priest's neck and had squealed into his ear – "You had to come. You just had to. It wouldn't be the same without you."

The priest laughed – a great big guffaw and answered – "how could I not come sweet girl?" and kissed her on both cheeks like they were long lost pals.

Thank the good Lord Brenda isn't here to see this, Russell thought to himself disgusted with his daughter's familiarity.

"John, how are ya?" The priest asked in a booming voice, shaking John's hand and pulling him into an embrace also.

"Er… I'll just nip off then," Russell said embarrassed. He didn't wait for a response in case the priest should hug him as well. When he was halfway down the front path Lissy shouted after him –

"Bye Daddy, see you tomorrow and thanks a bunch for tonight." Russell waved without turning and almost ran down the street to his own house.

"Come on through Jim and sit down. I'm sure you're tired," Lissy said, feeling quite the hostess in her new home.

"Aye, I am that now," he replied. "Get the tay on woman." John gasped and laughed as Jim got one of Lissy's predictable thumps.

"I hadn't got you down as one of them male chauvinist pigs," she told Jim with a grin. She was so pleased to see him, she couldn't stop grinning.

The three friends laughed and chatted until two am when Lissy admitted that she couldn't stay awake any longer. After she had gone upstairs to bed Jim turned to John and said in a serious voice "I have something to tell ya John, but I wasn't sure I should say it in front of Lissy"

John sprang to attention – "I'm all ears," he said.

"I've been doin' some investigating about Rose McDevit," said Jim, waiting for John's reaction before continuing. He got the reaction he was hoping for thankfully.

"Good for you mate. What have you found?" John didn't feel deceitful since it hadn't been him who had done the investigating.

Jim continued – "Well, first I asked the parish priest in Drumgar and he knows the family. Wasn't it Clare was the name of Rose's mother?" John nodded in eager silence. "Father Morrison says that Clare and Sean McDevit are in his parish. They've been there since 1978 when they moved to Drumgar from Belfast. He gave me loads of information. Apparently they have three daughters and two sons. Only one of the daughters still lives in the parish and her name is Angela. The eldest daughter whose name is Caroline lives in Dublin and so do the boys, Kevin and Brian. The other daughter Rose, he says was a strange one."

"Strange in what way? Loony?" asked John his heart racing.

"Aye. According to Father Morrison she had acted strange ever since he could remember her. Wait til I tell ya this." Jim sat forward in his chair and listened for signs of Lissy before going on – "She used to work for Joe O'Hanlon. Y'know the man whose funeral we were at?"

John could not have been more gob-smacked. To think that Joe O'Hanlon knew Rose. They could have been talking to any amount of people that knew her. The idea that they come that close to her was unbelievable. He shook his head – "I wonder did he know about Lissy?" he thought out loud.

"Dunno" replied Jim. "But apparently he had a quiet word with Father Morrison one time. He was worried about Rose 'cos she was very withdrawn and sad he said to the father. He wanted the father's advice as to how to deal with her."

"Well she would be withdrawn and sad wouldn't she?"

"Of course she would. Stands to reason don't it? Anyways the Father reckons she went to Dublin for a while and when she came back she tried to commit suicide."

John couldn't believe what he was hearing –"How did you manage to get that information out of him?"

Jim smiled a little abashed and replied – "Ah now, there's means an' ways."

John was none the wiser but he didn't hesitate to ask

the next question – "And did she succeed? In committing suicide that is?"

"No, she's alive and well as far as Father Morrison knows. But she wasn't the same since that, he said. She tried a second time and was talking all sorts of rubbish, he said, about the devil and stuff. She wasn't making sense. Everyone assumed she'd lost the plot but then she came alright again."

"I bet there wasn't anything wrong her at all. I bet they put her away in case she'd say again what she said to Father Murphy," John said, enraged. Obviously, he didn't know what the truth was but he had a gut feeling that Father Murphy's conclusion of child abuse was the truth. "Did she say anything about Lissy?"

"That's just it, John. As far as Father Morrison is aware she never once mentioned having had a baby."

The two men looked at each other quietly. The truth came to John in a flash - "Exactly!" he exclaimed. Jim looked bewildered. "Father Murphy said that Rose had no idea that she was pregnant even though she must have been at least seven months. What if she had the baby and still was unaware of it? Or what if she had the baby and was so distressed she didn't want to think about it? That would explain why she never mentioned it."

Jim thought about the theory for a while. "But how does that explain Lissy's theory about the grave in the wood?"

"Rose could have done that years later. It didn't look like it'd been there for that many years, come to think of it." Suddenly it struck him. His thoughts were racing -

something Lissy had said about the doll in the painting. She called it Grace. What if Rose put a doll in the grave to represent Grace. She was burying the past. That's what she was doing. That's why the grave's so tiny – it's a doll. He put his hand to his mouth as his thoughts raced on.

"What?" Jim pressed.

John shook his head and thinking quickly said – "Nothing, I was just thinking that she must have put the grave there in an attempt to bury the past. She must have been saying goodbye to the baby she never knew – letting go. You know that sort of thing. It's something Lissy might have been up to herself." The more he thought about it the more he was convinced that the little white cross and the tiny grave in the wood was indeed put there by Rose and for that very reason.

"What way is Lissy with all this now?" asked Jim. It suddenly dawned on him that Lissy wouldn't welcome this information. Rose after all, hadn't shown any concern about her at that time. However, years had passed since Father Morrison last heard of her – anything could have happened.

"She doesn't want to know. Doesn't even want to find out where she is," replied John.

"Well, that's another thing…I *know* where she is." John stared open mouthed as Jim went on to say what he had discovered. "Father Morrison mentioned that she had got married quite a few years back. He had done the wedding himself. Anyways, he found the information he wanted and got back to me with it." Jim paused and took a deep breath. He wondered would John tell Lissy what he was about to relate. How would she cope with it? Would she be pleased like he thought she might be or would she be angry at him for interfering?

"And?" encouraged John.

Jim decided he had come so far, he may as well go the whole hog. "And she married a fella called Jack Farley from Drumgar in nineteen ninety six. I know of the Farley family as it happens. They own a wee pub down at the promenade. It's very popular with tourists as it happens. It's all done up like one of those Irish bars in Spain an' that. Anyways, I went to the bar an' spoke to Jack's brother Michael. He told me that Jack and Rose live out by Cloughbeg."

"Cloughbeg? What? She was there the whole time?"

"We wouldn't have known. She lives way outside the village near the forest park. I don't know whether you saw it or not. It's inland from Cloughbeg but on the other side not the Drumgar side."

"I didn't see any forest but Mrs Doyle at the guest house mentioned it to us one day when we were at a loss for something to occupy us. What's this you called it?"

"Carrick Glen Forest Park," said Jim.

"Yeah, that's it. So that's where she lives. Blimey man, I'm telling you – it's weird to think we were so close to her all that time. It was the secrecy of course. No-one knew about Lissy except the priest and her family I suppose."

"She has a family too," Jim said to John's growing

astonishment. "She and Jack have two little boys – ten and eleven. And she has a step-daughter of eighteen. I even know their names."

"Blimey!"

"Oliver and Jerimiah who they call Jerry, after one of Rose's uncles – Gerry McDevit. The girl is called Emma."

"But how come you never knew this before if she's in your parish. Surely, you would have come across her?" asked John.

"No, never. I asked Michael Farley the same question and he told me that they didn't class themselves as Catholics any more. What's more he said that Rose hadn't been all that well before she met Jack but that she was fine now."

"Did he not wonder why you were asking him so many questions about Rose? It's a wonder he told you all that."

"Not really, people tell priests anything. They trust the dog collar don't they?" Jim grimaced not feeling entirely worthy of that trust.

"Did he ask why you wanted to know?"

"I told him I needed to trace her for a friend an' that was that. It's the truth." *At least I was honest*, he told himself.

"You know what?" John began suddenly feeling rather tired and subdued, "Lissy and I were in that Farleys' pub." He shook his head with a heavy sigh. "I don't believe it."

Jim yawned loudly.

"Hey, you must be exhausted" said John suddenly

realising the time. "Come on, I'll show you your room."

After the two men had gone to bed John lay awake beside Lissy, watching her sleeping. He wondered should he tell her. The party would be on tomorrow night. It was probably best to wait until after that at least – and perhaps give her a chance to settle down to some normality first. She was painting that picture from the sketch of Mary Doyle's cottage. She wanted to get up early to finish it before the party. He wouldn't give her this whopper to think about – not for a while yet. *When she's ready*, he decided.

Chapter Twenty

Reconnecting

Rose now knew that the key to her happiness was being real – being true to her self – to who she was, and as she uncovered more and more of her identity she firstly had to learn to accept and love who she was...and she was finding that the perfect teacher always came at the perfect time.

Lisnablaney, October 2003

Jonathan Kane was on his second year coming to see Rose Farley. She had made such good progress both physically and spiritually. Jonathan was pretty sure she would do great work in years to come. *But not yet*, he thought, *she still has a long way to go. She has yet to come to know herself in her spiritual identity. She must reconnect with her soul's journey in order to fulfil her purpose for being.* Often when he spoke with her he would be amazed at the level of knowledge she contained. Many times she came out with knowledge and wisdom that took most people years to comprehend. "You're a genius," he often told her.

Today they were going on an outing. Rose and Jack had found a house for sale some twenty miles or so away and Rose wanted Jonathan to go there and feel the energy of the place and tell her what he thought about them purchasing it.

"I've phoned the owners an' they're not going to be there but they said we could look about anyway," she told him on the drive out to it. It was near to Cloughbeg, where Rose's granny had lived before she died four years ago. There was a beautiful forest there and the house was just on the edge of the forest. Near enough for Rose to walk to it and enjoy the company of the trees.

"And you say you had a vision of the place before you found it?" asked Jonathan.

"Aye, as I said I was meditating and suddenly I began to see this place. Beside the place was an alternative, self-sufficient community. I began to rise up into the air and then it was as if hundreds of people followed me up. I knew every single one of them."

"Have you seen this place yet?"

"Oh aye, course we have, and it's just like the vision. There's a spot in the south east corner of the garden where the energy is so strong and when you stand there the view is exactly like that of the vision. There's also a caravan and chalet park beside it and I'm convinced that's where the community will be."

"Seems to me that you are meant to buy this place," Jonathan told her. He was listening carefully to his inner knowing and the signals he was getting were thumbs up all the way. "You'll find that it's for your soul healing," he said.

Rose smiled to herself. Inside she had a feeling of peace and everything being in its rightful place – "That's exactly why I must be there," she confirmed. She thought about what a psychic, Francie Connor, had said to her – that she would be in a community before the end of the year. She remembered that Imelda Crown had warned her about Francie one day when she had gone back for a second tarot card reading. Imelda had said that she saw a man who was influencing Rose to her detriment…if she ever wanted to be free of his hold on her she had to release his energy completely and protect herself psychically from him.

Rose had first met Francie Connor while she was still confined to the wheelchair. The guy who put Jonathan in touch with her – Rose called him the *Networker* – had also put her in touch with Francie. The Networker had said that Francie was amazingly psychic and knew a lot about that kind of phenomena. It had turned out to be a very deep and powerful relationship for Rose – having both a positive and a negative effect on her, and as time went on she had no doubt that it was a relationship that she was destined to encounter in order to see the finished picture of the jigsaw. The moment she had first laid eyes on him she had known he was a piece of the jigsaw – a man from her past lives. She recognized his spirit instantly and had felt a tiny inkling of dread but as the relationship developed she encountered much joy and reunion. However, the gut feeling of dread was always there underneath it all and it was that initial impression that Imelda had obviously picked up on and that Rose was to listen to in the end. Francie had mirrored her innermost knowledge, often acknowledging the truth in what she said with the effect of great joy and acceptance. It was as if he could reach into her mind and pull out anything she had ever known to be true. He told her many amazing things – he told her that she was a clear channel who would one day channel the wisdom of her guide. He told her that she was what was known as a *shaman* – someone who could transcend other realms at will for reasons of gaining knowledge and healing for others. She told him that shamanism, then, was a core part of who she was; that when she was a child she had practiced travelling to other realms on a regular basis and that is where she had met the Indian.

"Tell me about Black Elk," he had said as they sat with his partner Selena. They had been sitting at a table, hands held to form a circle.

"Black Elk is the name of the Indian – my guide," Rose was amazed at how she felt as if she had never forgotten his name. "My other guide is a woman who says she is a friend of my Granny. I just call her *the lady* for I don't know her name."

"You will," replied Francie, "they are both working very

closely with ya as will many more spirits of all kinds. Rose, do ya know you're a clear channel and Black Elk will speak through you?"

Rose had a fair idea what he meant – Black Elk would send her thoughts to her mind and heart the way he did when she was a child. "Aye, he has done that before" she told Francie.

"But just you wait till you're speaking with a man's voice. Then you'll know he's speaking through ya."

Rose went quiet. What Francie had implied was pretty heavy stuff but she could feel the truth of it and she knew the truth of it as if she had never forgotten it. Francie had told her many things that she knew inside. He spoke of the earth and humanity's relationship with it. He spoke of how there is a change of consciousness taking place in this new Aquarian age and that 'lightworkers' all over the world were working to raise their consciousness in order to bring about peace and harmony on earth. Rose told him how Black Elk called the earth 'our Sacred Mother' and that he had taught her all this stuff when she was a child.

"That is how you so easily grasp the knowledge…" Francie said, "…'cos he has already imparted it to you."

"Not only that, but it feels as if I knew it always. He just reminded me of it."

"That's true Rose. We all have that knowledge stored in our DNA. As we raise our consciousness our spiritual DNA opens up and the knowledge is remembered or released or whatever way ya choose to put it."

"This feels so good to me, to be talking like this," said Rose, "it feels like I want to sing for joy. All these things I thought about when I was a kid. I could feel them in my very core. But they aren't things one can talk about. I was always called a witch when I was a kid 'cos I knew these things and other things about people that they didn't even know themselves until later. I had a really shitty time when I was a kid. If it hadn't been for Black Elk and the lady, I wouldn't have survived."

Francie had said something to Rose then that empowered her to accept and understand her past, and her present as it turned out. He had said – "When a child is born into the world and like you has a great light within them that they intend to use for the greater good – does it not make sense that the powers of darkness would make an attack on that child in order to block her from fulfilling her purpose?"

"It makes perfect sense," answered Rose. *Not only in my past but right here and now*, she added in her mind. She could tell that Francie Connor was a good man but the dark shadow within him was doing all in its power to control her and manipulate her just as she knew it had done many lifetimes before. She knew that Francie Connor's shadow self was an old adversary of hers and here he was again. She wondered if he was consciously aware of their connection – she knew she shouldn't underestimate him – he was a powerful spirit and the warning signals of dread were screaming at her to *watch out – don't get drawn away from your path*. Eventually, she stopped going to see him, feeling that she was too vulnerable. She missed him, though, for he was also a kind man who showed her acceptance and encouragement. But for now at least, she had had to cut all ties to his energy.

Jonathan and Rose were coming close to the place she and Jack were hoping to buy and the terrain was beginning to look less like farmland and more mountainous. The forest stretched out across the hills in front of them and its ethereal beauty shone like a beacon to them leading them on down the road and to Rose's place of belonging. When the car pulled up beside the house they got out and admired the view. Mountains rose high on all sides and the forest stretched around them. It felt like the house was nestled in a dip with giant sentries standing guard. Across the field to the left of the house stood an old monastery tower and the area was bathed in a prayerful energy.

"Come down here," said Rose leading the way to the south east corner of the garden. She stopped there and spread her arms wide. "Feel this."

Jonathan copied her and smiled. "It certainly is a very light energy," he agreed. He knew that Rose was experiencing her own power and that this spot was intrinsically linked to her because she had wanted it that way. "Tell me what kind of energy it is," he probed.

"Well, it's not exactly a healing energy like we're used to workin' with," she replied. "It feels cooler. It's more like awareness…it's knowledge – aye, knowledge."

"Sometimes Rose," he said to her, "it's easier to externalize our power rather than own it within ourselves. Think about that for a while, but don't answer me now. It is something that you will come to know through time."

"Let's walk around the place," suggested Rose. She didn't know what Jonathan meant but once again she knew he spoke the truth. Why would she be afraid to own her power? She knew she was but she didn't know why. They walked around the garden examining the trees and shrubs there. It was very beautiful. They didn't look into any windows or indeed talk about the house much except to discuss the possibility of using one of the rooms as a healing centre. Jonathan felt pretty sure that he could foresee lots of people coming and going. Rose was in her element. She didn't stop grinning from when they arrived there till they got back to Lisnablaney.

February 2004

The telephone rang in the Farleys' new front hall. It was Marjorie Armstrong, an international psychic medium from Wales. The Networker had given Rose the contact for Marjorie's manager, Bunty Gordon from London. Apparently Ms Gordon was originally from Dublin and managed people from up and down Ireland as well as the United Kingdom. The Networker had thought that she might be interested in Rose and would be able to put her in touch with people that might be of help to her. That was why Marjorie Armstrong was on the phone right now from Wales, asking to speak with Rose Farley. Jack handed Rose the receiver.

"Hello, this is Rose."

"Rose, this is Marjorie Armstrong. Bunty gave me your number. I'm a medium dear if you didn't know."

"I know of you, yes," replied Rose.

"We need to talk dear. I've been talking to them upstairs, if you know what I mean. I must tell you that you are a trance channel dear. You need to work. I have a woman here in spirit dear – she says she is a friend of Granny's."

Rose's heart was thumping so loud she was afraid Marjorie would hear it on the other end of the phone. "She's a woman that has been with me ever since I was a child," she said. "I don't know any of Granny's friends. Especially ones that have been dead for over thirty years, but I am familiar with her. She's always kept me right."

"Her name's May, dear. She says she loved to bake. Do you understand?"

"Very much so, it's how I know her. I smell baking first and then she comes." Rose didn't want to tell Marjorie that she and May baked together in the spirit world.

"She read playing cards for people. She was quite good at it and she intends to work with you in that manner. There are a lot of things you will learn to do. You had an accident did you dear?"

"Yes, two years ago now – a car accident."

"You died my love, did you know?"

"Yes."

"Who is Paul?"

In an instant Rose knew who the man in white had been. "It's Saint Paul. He met me on the other side. He sent me back."

"He intends to work closely with you in the future as will May and…who is this now…a Native American…is he your guide? You have many I believe."

"That's right. At least it's beginning to look that way. What will the work be?"

"Well, I have to teach you dear. There's a lot you need to know. Do you think you could come to Wales?"

"I don't see why not."

"I'll be in touch dear. Leave it with me."

Rose spoke to Marjorie for a while longer about how she had come this far and what Marjorie's work involved. By the time she put down the receiver Rose was over the moon. "Oh Jack, I knew it - I knew it," she told him crying with relief. "The lady and Black Elk are going to work with me. That medium was definitely communicating with the lady. She told her she would work with me and Black Elk and I know exactly how that's going to be. She's even gonna teach me how to read cards. That's something that Imelda Crown said once y'know – that I'd read the cards like the lady. Marjorie said her name's May. I must ask my mother."

When Rose asked her mother about May she confirmed

that Granny had a sister-in-law called May who did psychic readings with playing cards. *Of course*, realised Rose, *that is what May meant when she said she was a friend of Granny's*. Granny always called her relatives friends. She would often say that such an' such is a friend of such an' such when she meant that such an' such was related to such an' such.

"Well I should have known you were a medium" was Clare McDevit's reply. "It makes perfect sense to me."

Why the fuck didn't ya say that to me when I was a wee'n instead of puttin' me down, thought Rose, *it's too little too late.* Still, she forgave her and moved on. Rose McDevit had come into this world with a huge capacity for forgiveness and a higher intelligence that spelled a recipe for success. There was never gonna be any other way.

September 2004

Rose and Jack were in the garden planting more trees. "There can never be enough trees about the place," Rose said dreamily looking up towards the forest. Jack simply grinned to himself without lifting his head. He had dug twelve holes already and that was only for the orchard. She wanted a row of mountain ash along one side and a rhododendron shrub between each. He straightened up, his back was killing him.

"Christ Rose, don't be planning any more. I've still got the stones to do." In the eight months since they moved here they had transformed the marshy ground beside the house into a well drained garden. Jack had made a little winding pathway bordered with logs that opened out into a sitting area that would eventually be nestled in a small orchard. He was going to put a layer of gravel on the path, keeping with the natural look Rose insisted on.

"Through time," she said. This will be a little private place where I can sit and commune with the trees and nature. I shall be disturbed by no-one. It isn't exactly the wood I knew as a child but it will be more special 'cos I raised it."

"You're not the one breakin' your back over it," moaned Jack.

"I appreciate it darling, and you'll be glad next spring when all the daffodils come up. It will be a spectacular sight."

Jack plopped himself down on the grass and took a swig from his bottle of water. He looked around him and as goodness knows how many times before, he muttered a prayer of gratitude for the blessings in his life. "God Rose, we are truly blessed to live here aren't we? he said. "To think of all the people stuck in high-rise flats, frightened to send their kids out to play for fear of who their neighbour might be. We don't know we're living. By the way, what time do I have to pick the boys up from the party?"

"Five thirty" Rose told him. "Then I have to be in Drumgar for the singing group at seven so we may as well stay in the town. We can go to your mum's and get our tea."

Last year Rose had been introduced to a local singing group. They met on a Tuesday evening in Drumgar and sang songs from all over the world, in many languages – mostly folk songs but also some gospel and a little African call and response songs that they sang whilst drumming with tribal hand drums. Rose loved it and she had met some lovely friends through it. She liked to think of it as a catalyst for other activities and groups that inspired her and helped her to grow in confidence and self worth. She was already involved with a local art group and a writing group. She loved to write. Before long she was writing the most amazing poetry and short stories. She began to seriously think about the book she had always thought she would write - *the* book – her story. But she reckoned the story had really only begun and until she had the complete jigsaw she wouldn't have the complete book. The singing group had taken a break for the summer months but was re-commencing this evening at seven. Jack wasn't so sure that Rose should go this evening. She hadn't slept much last night. Her legs pained her most of the time but especially when she was tired and her resistance was low. She had tossed and turned all night murmuring about him going off and leaving her on her own by the riverside with the children. She was dreaming of course.

"Why didn't ya come back?" she murmured over and over. Eventually Jack had to wake her. Rose often confounded him in the middle of the night by coming out with talk in her sleep that even he could understand was about things that hadn't happened in this lifetime. Often she spoke in different languages although during the day she knew only a little Spanish. The night of all nights was when she began to talk in a very strange language and with a deep male voice. She woke both of them by doing so and proceeded to tell him an amazing tale of how she was on a stage and Black Elk was speaking using her voice box. She had understood every word he had said but upon wakening found that she had forgotten it. Another time she woke him up again with the male voice but in English this time. Again, upon wakening, neither of them could recollect the words.

Sitting in the garden, Jack stared at her with deep concern. "What were ya dreamin' about last night?" he asked.

She sat on the grass beside him. "It's very strange," she told him, giving him the chance to withdraw the question.

"When is it not? Go on, tell me. Ya know ya want to."

She laughed. Jack knew her so well. "I had that dream loads of times, even before I met you" she told him. "Even during the day when I meditate I see it in a vision. It's a memory of a past life when we were married like now."

Jack lay back on the grass and covered his face with his hands –"Hit me with it" he said.

"It's in France in the year thirteen hundred and six and we're standin' beside the river Seine with our two kids – a boy and a girl," explained Rose. "There is a fracas kickin' off in the city – Paris. You go off to fetch someone and ya don't come back. I think ya got shot in the chest. There's a doctor in a buggy at the end of the riverside path and he tells me and the kids to get into his buggy and he will help us but instead he brings about my death."

"And what? You think I'm gonna go off an' leave ya in this life? Is that it?" Jack wanted to know more. He was very curious. A strange feeling of *déjà vu* had come over him and he knew – he had a gut knowing that what Rose had told him was actually true. He rubbed his chest absent-mindedly. A slight ache had begun to irritate him.

"No, I don't think that's why I remember it" said Rose. "It's more about what had happened to me - why I was killed and what was goin' on in the city. In fact, I know what that was – I know quite a bit about it as it happens, thanks to Black Elk and Hilarion."

"Hilarion? Who the hell is that?"

"He's my higher guide – my master guide," Rose told Jack. "He used to be Saint Paul in the life before Hilarion. Do ya remember the man I said met me when I died in the accident? – Him – He's the ascended master. He presides over a temple in the etheric realms above Crete. It's called The Temple of Truth. In the temple is the Green Flame of Truth. Lots of souls go there between embodiments to learn the truth of all teachings. Lots of souls like me go there in meditation or at night in their sleep for the same reason. When I go there, I meet with Black Elk and we learn side by side."

Jack was flabbergasted. As long as he lived he would

never grasp who Rose was. Was all this stuff that was obviously true to her really the God's honest truth? It wasn't the kind of thing he was comfortable with. What he did feel to be true though, was that he was a deeply grounded person and for a very good reason – so that he could keep Rose on the ground and protect her from her own natural tendency to fly away and be spaced out all of the time. She agreed with him on that matter at least. He rolled over and pulled her down on top of him. "Ok then, Shaman Rose…" he began.

"White Buffalo!" she said smiling at him.

"What?"

"Black Elk calls me White Buffalo Woman – White Buffalo for short."

Jack scratched his head – "Why? What's wrong with Rose?"

"Nothing's wrong with Rose. It's a beautiful name and by the way I wouldn't mind some more rose shrubs just over there." She pointed to a little corner of the garden that was ideal for roses. Jack rolled her over so that he was lying on top of her. "Watch my legs," she cried. He shifted his weight but didn't release her.

"Ok then, *White Buffalo,*" he went on, "if ya go to them places so easily, how's about taking me and you off the earth right here and now. Come on gorgeous, make the earth move."

"Christ! Do you ever think about anything else?" She struggled underneath him but he held her firmly. "Get off me ya big sex maniac," she laughed, "someone will see us."

"So what? Isn't a shaman supposed to love nature? There's nothing more natural than sex outdoors." He kissed her and released her. *She may be an enigma*, he thought to himself, *but God how I love her.* He laughed as she scolded him light- heartedly and in his usual slagging manner he said – "Maybe I should go back to Paris and get myself a big blonde French woman."

She shook her head trying not to laugh. "You wouldn't be slagging if I told ya I could prove it?"

"Aye, surely," he teased.

Rose explained that Black Elk had told her to look it up on the internet and that she had found that in Paris, in the year thirteen hundred and six, there had been a huge revolt which had been something to do with the whole crusade to capture and kill Cathers. When she had read this Rose had known that she had been one of them… *Of course,* she thought, *how could I have been anything else*? "Anyway," she said to Jack, "to cut a long story short, many women were murdered that night – burned as witches. I was one of them and *you* – you had gone and got yourself shot. Now tell me Jack Farley, that I'm imagining things."

Jack was gob-smacked – "*I've* never told ya you're imaginin' things. That was your mother."

"Well, she can't say that anymore can she? 'Cos I'm not listenin'."

"That woman's gonna be here tonight," Rose stated as a matter of fact, later when they were getting ready to leave for the singing group.

"What woman?" asked Jack.

"The woman we saw last week. Do ya remember – at the stone circles? The Romany lookin' woman."

"Oh aye, that big tall woman with the wee girls?"

"Her, aye. She's gonna be here at the singing."

"How do ya know?"

"I keep seeing her today in my third eye. I think she and I are goin' to be good friends."

"As if you need another friend. There was a time you had none practically. I was the one with all the mates, but now you're comin' down with friends," commented Jack.

"Well, friends are like trees – ya can never have too many," Rose smiled. She was happy. Jack was right – she made friends so easily now and they were mostly good positive colourful people who Rose loved to spend time with. There was Vicky, an English woman who was married to a local man. She was a fantastic singer. It was she who had founded the singing group several years ago. Not only was she a wonderful singer and teacher but she was also a talented artist and had had several exhibitions up and down the country. Then there was Kate who was younger than most at the group and who was so sweet and refreshing that Rose took to her immediately. Kate was, in Rose's book, a real person – not someone living a dream like the many that were walking the long sleep that Jonathan referred to.

Kate was a great singer as well as Vicky. Between the two of them the singing group was a roaring success. Rose smiled as she thought of her many friends. There was Bea, short for Beatrice, who was a yoga teacher in her spare time and brought a distinct energy of the east to their little circle of friends. Then there was Majella and Hazel, Stacey and Rona and little Simone who was French and was married to Hazel and Stacey's brother Warren. All these friends loved to drum and sing and generally have a good time together. The singing group itself had many other members whom Rose liked and who liked her in return. *If only they could see how I was just four years ago*, she often thought, *they wouldn't believe it's the same person.* Well, Vicky, Kate and Bea knew of her past. They had become such close intimate friends that she felt she could tell them anything. "Everyone has their own stuff," they had said, "it's up to us to support each other as we heal."

Rose took herself out of her thoughts and noticed that they were at their destination. She got out of the car – "I'll ring ya when I'm ready," she told Jack – "bye, love you. Love ya boys – bye bye. Be good for daddy."

When she opened the door to the singing group there was the tall Romany looking woman surrounded by interested welcomes. She smiled at Rose who went straight over to her and shook her hand. "Hi, I'm Rose. I saw you before at the stone circle last week."

"I remember," the woman said, "I'm Gertge."

"Where are ya from?" asked Rose. The woman's accent

was quite strange although her English was excellent.

"I'm from Holland. I've lived here for many years now – out at The Willow community outside Drumgar. You know it?"

"Yes, I do actually, but only recently." Willow was a community that cared for people with learning disabilities. It turned out that Gertge was what they called a house mother – someone who ran the day to day household and was responsible for the villagers and the many workers who stayed there for one or two years training before moving on to other jobs in the same field.

"Do you do readings?" Gertge asked Rose one evening.

"Ya mean mediumship readings? I do card readings which my great aunt May taught me how to do and I do some shamanic healing. Nearly always, spirits will come through when I'm doing healing but I always have to ask the healee if it's okay to pass on messages. A lot of people don't want to know about that sort of thing ya know."

"I mean can you do a mediumship reading for me? There is no reason why I ask – only that I feel it is the right thing to do."

"Well there are some spirits already coming through for you," Rose told her. Just then a heat surrounded Gertge. Rose felt it. "Did ya feel that?"

"Yes. Maybe, we make a date for a reading – yes?"

Gertge's reading was very successful although there

seemed to be no other reason for it than to give Rose confidence that she could do it. Gertge had listened to her intuition and had, in her wisdom, given Rose the much needed self-belief she was lacking. As time went on their friendship grew closer and was woven into the huge outer circle of friends and associates made up of artists and writers, singers and dancers, drummers and chanters – all wonderful creative and joyful people. Such a diverse group of contacts allowed Rose to experience many various ways of expressing her self. Gertge, Bea, Kate and Vicky in particular provided her with a safe and accepting environment in which to heal on an emotional level as she painted, wrote, sang and voiced her innermost truths. Surrounding her self with a support network like that taught her to trust others which was valuable for the next stage of her journey to wholeness – she was to discover her self not only as a member of an inspirational group of friends but also as a member of a separate group of souls dedicated to a common purpose. It first began to transpire when Rose started feeling an overwhelming sense of guilt. She had expressed and transformed many aspects of this massively destructive emotion for years during talking therapies and so on but this overwhelming feeling was of a guilt that seemed to be an ancient part of her being and that was probably the festering wound that attracted countless other wounds of blame and guilt. She had to know where this feeling was coming from – she had to connect with it – understand it.

Black Elk had told her –*"When you observe and understand*

the enemy, you conquer it."

"Tell me how I can unlock the core wound?" she had asked him. He showed her many pictures – screens of past lives where she had manifested this guilt in various ways. She began to feel it in a very raw manner – the more she felt it the less its power seemed.

Eventually, Black Elk said – *"Say yes to Glenda, the wound shall be revealed."*

Rose had come across only one Glenda, to her knowledge, and that was recently. A friend, Liz had invited a London Astrologist, Glenda Hoffman over to her home. "She will do out your birth chart and talk you through it. Apparently the planetary alignment at the time of your birth can tell a lot about who you are and how your life will generally pan out," Liz had informed a somewhat intrigued Rose. Now that Black Elk had encouraged her, she was happy to make an appointment with Glenda.

When the day arrived and Rose entered Liz's home and came face to face with Glenda, she knew something significant would reveal itself. She recognized Glenda's spirit immediately and felt terribly uncomfortable. The feeling seemed to be mutual because Glenda could barely look her in the eye.

"Now Rose, if you could move into the area marked with the Libra symbol please," said Glenda. The birth chart, about three metres diameter was laid out on the floor. Rose stood in the place for Libra.

"Why Libra?" asked Rose.

"Libra brings balance to all aspects of our being. You need to bring about balance between your feminine and masculine energies. It also suggests that you will work for Truth and Justice. These are very important to you. It is opposite Aquarius which represents your spiritual lineage. My guide, Little Wolf, tells me that you are contracted to find your spiritual family and that this will be reflected in your earthly family."

"That makes sense," said Rose thinking of her confusion as to her birth mother and her thoughts as to whether or not she will ever find her daughter, Grace. "And by my spiritual family you mean my soul group?" Rose asked, wondering where that question came from. She had an inkling that a soul group was souls like her and Jack who came together over many embodiments, in order to fulfil a certain purpose.

"That's right," answered Glenda.

"And how many souls are in this group exactly?"

"It's generally thought seven, I believe."

"That makes sense," replied Rose. She had a faint memory of Black Elk telling her of seven rays – seven colours – seven aspects of the mind of God. *It stands to reason*, she thought now, *that each of the seven souls represents a certain aspect of the whole.*

Glenda began to indicate a shape on the birth chart. "If you make a triangle which is a sacred geometric shape..." she began and was interrupted by Rose -

"Aye, I know that. Black Elk taught me about sacred

geometry. The triangle represents higher truth, he said."

Glenda looked irritated and ignored the interruption -"You can see that the triangle's third point is at Cancer" she continued. "This suggests that the way in which you will express yourself is through teaching and counselling. Now, and this is very important, so listen carefully..."

Rose felt a tingling fear and began to feel quite hostile towards Glenda who was clearly having difficulty with her too. *Stand back and observe*, Rose reminded herself of Black Elk's guidance.

Glenda continued. "You see this here in Capricorn?" She picked up a strange looking symbol that Rose couldn't quite catch the name of. "This suggests that there is a major resistance with you." Rose stiffened. "Little Wolf tells me that you have a contract here to experience the unknown but you have a resistance to that. It is as if you have stated firmly that you will not go there again."

"The unknown, what exactly does Little Wolf mean by that?" asked Rose her body tingling with dread.

"The Occult."

Rose sat down on the spot and took several deep breaths. She found that her mind was racing and she couldn't settle on one thought. She became very ungrounded and felt dizzy and high. Sweat glistened on her face.

"Are you okay Rose?" came Glenda's distant voice. She came over to her and placed her hands on her feet. "You're spinning out. You need to come down into your body. Wait! I have a grounding crystal here that can help. As

Glenda placed a huge crystal between Rose's feet and began to work to help her ground, Rose began to come down into her body where she felt the massive guilt once again only this time she understood it. She knew exactly why she had a resistance to the occult. She knew why she didn't want to go there again but she certainly was not going to reveal that here to Glenda. After several minutes she felt well enough again to stand.

"Look," Glenda said lifting a symbol that Rose had been sitting on. "This is the symbol for Venus – representative of the heart – the divine feminine. This suggests that your mind is saying no to going there again but your heart is saying yes, and your heart is always right." Rose looked at the symbol and the colour drained from her face – it was a kind of cross with a circle on top – the very symbol on the robes of Michael Donnelly in the meetings.

It's about helping people to realise the difference between truth and error – she had said to the tree that wonderful night when she first opened her heart to who she was – but first of all I must realise that myself. She knew now what her greatest error had been and why she had felt so guilty. Could she accept her self now knowing what she had done? Could she forgive her self and bring compassion to quash the guilt?

Chapter Twenty One

The Shaman

"As I have danced upon the earth – so shall you"

Cloughbeg, spring 1975

Nine year old Rose McDevit was playing and chatting merrily with her playmates. They had their own special language. It was a language of nature, a universal language that Mother Earth had taught to all her beloved children eons ago. In Granny Doyle's wood were many of Mother Earth's children. Rose knew every one of them and they knew her. The trees swayed and the grasses and wild flowers danced merrily as their sister the wind sang, her sweet dulcet tones reaching into every nook and cranny of the wood. Rose was hiding from Wind behind the trees' huge bodies – skipping from one to another giggling with sheer exhilaration. Wind would discover her hiding place each time and tickle her face and neck with her hair. "You always find me," laughed Rose. This was her favourite game. She skipped to yet another tree and waited – Wind didn't come – she stopped playing. Her brother the sun had come out from his hiding place behind the clouds and was beaming down through the high reaching fingers of the trees searching for Rose and calling to her –

"Come, he is waiting."

As Rose lay down on the soft warm mossy earth she was joined by the lady, smiling and saying "You were having fun with your friends Rose. Your joy is a ladder to the higher realms." She took Rose by the hand and they spiralled off to *The Green* where the Indian was waiting for them.

"Shall we bake a cake today?" Rose asked the Lady.

"Not today. He wishes to show you something."

"I know. He's gonna show me the vision – the prophecy."

"What do you know of the vision Rose?" asked the Lady wondering how much she understood about who she was.

"Not much," Rose replied, "just that there's a tepee like what Indian's live in. It's on a white cloud and it is has a rainbow over it."

"Anything else?"

"The Grandfathers are sittin' inside it."

"Do you know who the Grandfathers are Rose?"

"Don't think so."

Black Elk was waiting on the doorstep, his little black book on the grass at his feet. He opened his arms to welcome Rose and she ran to him. "I liked your game Little White Buffalo," he told her, "Sister Wind and Brother Sun love to play with you. They are closer than you would know, my little calf. They are part of you – they are your breath and your spirit. Rose thought about this, furrowing her brow and biting her lip. The Lady and Black Elk watched her amused. When she smiled broadly, looking into his eyes with understanding, the Indian said – "*Mitakuye oyasin…*" meaning 'all my relatives'.

Rose picked up the little black book. It had a white cross on the front cover. "Tell me about the two roads," she asked. She loved to hear Black Elk talk about the two roads that met in a cross.

"This one that goes up and down," he told her, "is the good red road. It goes from the North where the white giant lives and from whence came White Buffalo Calf Pipe Woman to bring the pipe of peace and harmony to our people – to the south from whence the little nature beings come that bring the gift of life to all things like your friends the standing ones."

"The trees," interpreted Rose. He smiled and touched her face and she felt as if he had touched her heart.

"Yes, the trees. And this is the fearful black road. He traced his finger from left to right. It goes from the place in the West from where the thunder beings live to the place in the East where Brother Sun is always shining."

"And that is the road we must walk so that we can bring destruction to our foes." Rose had learned that power comes from knowledge of the fearful road.

"And what power do we get from the good red road?" asked Black Elk.

"The power to make live."

"Good."

"Tell me about the middle bit. Tell me about the flowering tree," requested Rose wanting to hear again about the tree which was her favourite thing of all.

Black Elk grinned. "Where the two roads meet is the centre of all things" he told her. "It is the centre of you and it is the centre of me. It is the centre of a great people – a great nation. When I was on the earth and this knowledge was given to me I thought the nation was my Lakota people only but I came to know that it meant all manner of peoples, not just the Lakota, for all peoples are my relatives. When I walk the good red road the tree in the centre is blooming and healthy and the nation shall live, but if I only walk the black road the nation shall suffer."

"I like it when I walk the good red road," said Rose.

"But you must also walk the fearful road my little calf." Black Elk knew that her fear was great and that she was learning great things, and now it was good to show her the vision. "Come, I shall show to you the knowledge that was given to me when I was your age upon the earth."

He took Rose's hands and they closed their eyes. In a moment they found themselves on a high mountain. "This is the top of the world," Black Elk told her. "What you shall see now is the great vision that was given to me." And when he had said that he turned into a spotted eagle and flew off the mountain. He came to a stop some distance away in the sky and he was a little boy standing on a white cloud. There was the rainbow tepee before him with the Grandfathers in it. As Rose watched many horses of all colours appeared and there was a great noise from them. There were buffalo and geese and elk and men with spears. She saw the two roads – the good red road and the fearful black road. Down below her the world began to change and it was sick. Rose watched as Black Elk swooped down and made it green and well again. She saw many things pass and she understood it all.

When Black Elk swooped back as the eagle he told her – "There is a time to destroy and a time to make live." Then he said – "Look to where I go – As I have danced upon the earth – so shall you."

He swooped off to a village of tepees down below and he began to dance with the people there. Round and round they danced in a circle and as each one fell upon the ground they changed into birds of all manner and followed Black Elk into the invisible realms where they were happy. The spotted eagle flew to the top of the world again and there he was the Indian once more. He took Rose's hand and they began to come down. When they were close to the ground Black Elk pointed to a tepee. A little boy had come out of the tepee and was lying sick on the ground. Rose could see that it was Black Elk as a little boy. As their feet touched the ground the child stood up and took them into the tepee. Many people were crowded around a bed where a sick child lay on animal skins. Rose looked and saw that many of them were Indians but two of them were not. A man and a woman stood crying as they watched the little girl on the skins. They were Mexican and the child was their daughter and she was paralysed.

Rose looked to Black Elk who said – "There is no separation." And when Rose looked back she saw that the child was her.

"Look again" said Black Elk, and when she looked again the child was him as a little boy.

Then the child opened his eyes and a Grandfather said – "Welcome back my child – you were gone a long time."

Little White Buffalo Woman understood how she should dance upon the earth. She understood that she should walk the fearful road and that in the place where the two roads meet she would find balance between heaven and earth – between spirit and body. That would be her respite – her place of rest from the awesome task that lay ahead. The fear was great and the challenge at times would seem insurmountable but as long as she kept her attention on that centre of power then she would be dancing the good dance and the prophecy would be fulfilled – the tree would blossom and the nation would live. She also understood that should she walk the fearful road without remembering to come to the centre thus neglecting the tree then it would wither and she and the nation would suffer. For three more years Little White Buffalo Woman danced the good dance. Black Elk continued to teach her and although the black road was difficult and for most of the time she flew above it to avoid the pain and anguish she was learning valuable lessons and gaining great power. When the overwhelming moment came and Grace was born, Little White Buffalo Woman had ceased to dance and had shut herself down. The lessons ceased and Black Elk seemed a distant memory but he was never far from her. In fact, he was very close, in her heart, a deep ancient part of her. But of course, the heart was a place Rose refused to go to for a very long time

Spring 2005, Carrick Glen

Rose opened her eyes and brought her awareness back to where she was sitting in the garden – on the bench amongst all the young trees. She had been meditating. The garden was the best place for her to do so. The lady, May, had said to her so many times that the joy created from being with nature was a ladder to the higher realms. Rose would sit and watch the trees and other plants. She would feel the sun on her face and the breeze touching her and she would feel love for all her relatives and they in turn filled her with a love and a joy that lifted her up and allowed her to access the higher realms. She had been to a place where Black Elk had taken her many years ago when she was nine years old. She had forgotten the experience until now when she went there again. It was the highest peak at the top of the world. Black Elk showed her as before the great vision he had when *he* was nine years old and he showed her how he had danced upon the earth. His words came back to her now and she cried as she remembered the tender way he had lifted her up and spoke to her saying – *'As I have danced upon the earth – so shall you'*. She was already practicing shamanic healing as he had done, attracting and working with many spirit helpers as she came into her power. He had been a teacher particularly when the last of the great Indian tribes, the Sioux came to stay at the reservations. Black Elk told Rose how he had taught the Christian way then as well as the Lakota way using a map of the two roads and likening it to the symbol of the cross. Rose loved the Lakota way and she longed to be Indian. She wore her hair in braids and practiced all the Lakota ways that Black Elk had taught her and although she was still a believer and follower of Christ she had given up the Catholic ways years ago. It seemed curious to her that she seemed to be a mirror image of Black Elk in so many ways including the fact that he had chosen the Catholic way whilst being rooted in the Lakota truths. Being Indian gave Rose the sense of identity and belonging that she had always yearned for but she knew she was living a fantasy – wrapping her self up in a nice safe identity was not being real – it was living the dream – the long sleep - reaching outside of her self for confirmation on who she was instead of having the courage to go within her heart to the divine spark within her that she knew was her source – her real self. That was where she would find her self in her wholeness - the only place she would find the hidden pieces of the jigsaw. Black Elk said to her – *"White Buffalo, it is only when we have the courage to stand naked before the source and declare that this is who we are that we find our selves in our wholeness."*

Summer solstice 2005, Lisnablaney Stone Circles

It was four am. Rose and Gertge were sitting in the middle of one of the enormous stone circles just outside Drumgar. They sat in silence waiting for the others to get there so that they could celebrate the solstice sunrise together. Rose was thinking about the dream she had had the previous night - she had come before a Grandmother – a keeper of wisdom, and she had asked her for her wise words. The Grandmother had taken a comb and given it to Rose saying – "Take this comb and comb through your hair. When you wish to fight you braid your hair. You are hiding behind your braids saying – this is who I am. You are obstinate and will resist the picture behind the braids. Let your hair down and walk with the wind – she will clear the path for you. Remain centred and open to receiving. You may braid your hair – yes, but remember to look behind the braids."

Rose lay back on the grass and watched the sky. It was beginning to lighten in the east. It would soon be dawn. Rose was mindful that this morning's sunrise would mirror the dawn of her return to wholeness. She could feel it coming within her. Black Elk called the sun Wakan Tanka and had said to her before – *"White Buffalo, Wakan Tanka represents the source of all things but you must remember that He is but a reflection of the true centre which is within each and every one of us."*

She put her hand over her heart and felt its strong beat. As she focused more within the beat became louder and slower – *b'boom... b'boom... b'boom.*

Suddenly there was a flash of colour and the world was filled with white golden light. A circle appeared and from it came a figure of an Indian. He wore a headdress of white feathers and his heart was ablaze with golden flames. He came down to Rose and said to her – "*My child, I am so proud of you.*" She knew Him to be the spirit within – what she called the Christ Energy – what Black Elk called Wakan Tanka. He came right before her and touched her face with his hands and His love was greater than greatest. "*You will always find me in your heart*," He said.

Rose sat up and saw that the others were approaching. She said nothing to Gertge of her vision.

"Good morning everyone. You all could come. That is good," said Gertge greeting her friends. "I think we shall have a nice experience this morning."

When the sun came up they were all sitting on the grass

in a circular fashion and deep in meditation. Rose was facing the sunrise and as she communed with the inner centre she lifted her arms in praise to the outer. The Grandmother's wisdom came to her thoughts and she opened her braids combing her hair out with her fingers and as she sat like that before Wakan Tanka she was mindful that she was stripped off all identity except for that which she now felt so very powerfully – her true self – pure spirit in an earthly body.

Rose was experiencing what she called an alignment. It was when she was in a shamanic trance and her guides would lift her up to a higher realm. As she danced further upon the earth she raised her awareness to a higher and higher level and an alignment was necessary for her to access the higher knowledge and wisdom she needed to fulfil the prophecy – the balance of heaven on earth. This time she and her guides formed a large circle and there was much celebrating. After a while Rose was invited to enter the circle and as she stood there she could feel the knowledge and wisdom coming from the minds and hearts of her guides to her mind and heart.

Black Elk came forth and stood before her. "*And now you shall see how the prophecy will be performed on earth*." He took Rose's hands and he became part of her. They were no longer two, they were one. They were in a meadow with warm sweet air all around. "*This is how it is for me*," said Black Elk in her heart. She lifted her eyes to a high mountain peak. The voice continued – "*See the top of that mountain*." In a breath they were there, standing at the peak of the mountain. Rose began to feel her throat opening up as if she were about to speak but she had nothing to say. Black Elk continued to speak but this time it was through her – using her voice box to project his voice. Suddenly he was before her again and was smiling. "You have done well White Buffalo. Soon the prophecy will be fulfilled but first you must be master over your fear. You will come to see and understand this as you trust more."

There is a shaman in each and every one of us capable of transforming our lives from pain and suffering into peace and harmony. If only we remember when we walk the fearful black road to come into the centre of power where all things are in balance. It is from there that the shaman rises from its wounds like a phoenix from the ashes.

Chapter Twenty Two

A mother's love and a daughter's grief

Lissy put the finishing touches to her painting and stood back to admire her work. She had decided to name it *Mary Doyle's Cottage*. Upstairs her mum could be heard humming as she happily prepared more party food. Lissy smiled and held her hand to her womb. "Nanna's happy," she said. Rose McDevit came into her thoughts and she pushed her out along with the resentment she now felt for her. Resentment and anger were probably the main feelings she had for her birth mother lately, suffocating any desire she may have had to know her and love her. "You never have to worry. I will never abandon you," she said to her baby. She lifted *Mary Doyle's Cottage* off the easel and carried it up the stairs to the kitchen. Just then the door bell rang and she ran to answer it. It was John and Jim.

"Are you ready then?" John asked her before he noticed the paint stains on her hands. "Go and get cleaned up… now, go."

She ran up to the bathroom on the first floor to get ready. They were going to meet Linn and Mark for lunch at The King's Arms.

"Oh, my painting is in the kitchen. It's still wet, be careful with it!" she shouted down to them. John and Jim grinned at each other and went to the kitchen.

"Oh John dear, and Father. How are you today Father. I trust you slept okay?" Brenda fussed about them like a mother hen. "You'll take a cup of tea Father."

Jim said that he was fine thank you and he had slept very well as it was. He was about to refuse the tea since they were on their way out to lunch when John piped up.

"You may as well have a cup. Lissy will be at least ten minutes" he said.

Jim nodded pulling out a stool for himself. "Tay it is then Mrs Brenning. This must be the painting then," he said picking up the canvas. "That's pretty good isn't it? She's quite the artist."

"Oh yes, our Lissy can paint," replied Brenda. "You must get her to show you her work. They're all down in the cellar."

"That's excellent actually," remarked John looking at the painting in Jim's hands. "That's exactly what the place looks like."

"I've seen the one in John's hall. Beautiful – *A Mother's*

Love is it called?" Jim asked Brenda who didn't remark on it at all. John gave Jim a look that said – don't even go there.

"Are we ready then?" asked Lissy when she burst into the kitchen fifteen minutes later. She looked fantastic. She wore a lavender cotton shirt and a pair of white jeans. She wore no make-up and in her hair was a band with little white flowers along it. Her cheeks were glowing and her eyes glistened with excitement. John whistled, much to Brenda's disgust. Soon they were on their way to The King's Arms. Linn and Mark were waiting for them in the foyer.

When the introductions were done and the pleasantries over Linn asked Lissy.

"Have you seen this poster?"

She led her to a large poster on the foyer notice board. It was advertising an audience with an alternative writer and psychic. The poster read: – *'Bunty Gordon presents an audience with best selling author of 'The Wounds of The Shaman' Eliza White Buffalo, Friday 27th June 2008, 7-9pm, book signing at 9.30pm.'*

"Bunty Gordon – where have I heard that name before?" asked Lissy. Linn shrugged. "And *The Wounds of the Shaman*," Lissy added, "that's that book you were telling me about, isn't it?"

"Yeah. It's four or five weeks away yet. When do you and John get back from Mexico? We have to go Lissy. She's supposed to be amazing."

"We'll be back on the twenty first. What does she do?"

"She's a shaman. She channels a spirit called Black Elk.

He was a famous Native American – Sioux I think. Anyway he had this famous vision once about a new, higher way of life for all who live in a sacred manner. Eliza White Buffalo channels his wisdom and teaches how each of us can actively raise our own consciousness, so that we can live this new life. She talks about the journey of the soul and the oneness of life and all that stuff."

"What do you mean, she channels his wisdom?"

"He speaks through her using her voice box an' that. It's his voice that you hear. Well, something like it. I heard that it sounds really eerie especially since it's coming out of a woman's mouth."

"God, I dunno Linn," said Lissy, "it's a bit out there."

"Read the book. Look, it's for sale in the lobby shop."

"What's it about?"

"It's about her isn't it? Eliza White Buffalo – about her life. Crikey Lissy, You're not a boring old housewife yet. Read it and find out. You'll love it. I promise. You won't be able to put it down."

"Are you two coming or are you waiting for dinner?" yelled John.

"You go on. I'll pop into the shop now before I forget," Lissy said to Linn.

"Bobby has seen her you know – in Cardiff. He reckons she's a must see" Linn added.

"Gosh yes, Bobby phoned me yesterday about the party. I forgot to tell you – I made an appointment with him for the past life therapy."

"Good for you babes," said Linn throwing an arm around Lissy's shoulders, "good move."

The lobby shop was cool and spacious with various stands of gifts and souvenirs. Just at the entrance was a large display laden with copies of the one book – *The Wounds of the Shaman*. Lissy spotted it straight away. On the bottom of the display was the same poster as was in the lobby and beside it was a picture of Eliza White Buffalo herself. Lissy studied the picture. The woman looked vaguely familiar. She read the words underneath. They read –

Irish born Eliza White Buffalo was chosen and taught by the spirits since childhood to follow her shamanic calling. She works very closely with the famous Sioux Shaman and Holy Man Black Elk. 'The Wounds of the Shaman' tells the story of this amazing woman's life. An inspiring and sometimes heart- wrenching tale of survival and transformation – Eliza White Buffalo invites us into the deep mystical world of the shaman which she believes dwells within each and every one of us.

Lissy picked up a book and flicked open the cover. Inside was the same picture of Eliza White Buffalo. She had dark brown plaits of hair and wore a large ruby gemstone necklace which sat on her chest like a name plate. She also wore around her neck a long string carrying a four inch white cross which gleamed against the dark red of her shirt. *Well there's a sign if I ever saw one,* thought Lissy, *okay Eliza White Buffalo – you look normal enough. Let's see what you have to say.* Feeling very much decided on the book and the audience, Lissy made the purchase and joined her friends for lunch.

It was the Monday after the party. Lissy was feeling rather tired but she kept her appointment with Bobby and was now lying down in his therapy room trying desperately not to fall asleep. Jim had gone home last night and she and John hadn't got back from the airport until gone eleven. The weekend had been hectic. No-one could have known that a Catholic priest could have partied so much. He had kept them up until three in the morning entertaining them with jokes and tales of journeys to far off lands, which was all poppycock really since he'd never even been out of Ireland. Still he seemed to know a lot about other countries.

"Discovery channel," he had told Lissy to the side when he had everyone hanging on his every word. Lissy thought that the Catholic church could do with a few more charismatic characters like Jim.

"John and I are going to Mexico next week," she'd told him. "Mum and Dad surprised us with it as an engagement present. Mum thought I looked a bit peaky when I got home from Ireland. She reckons the sun will do me good."

Jim of course, had then entranced everyone with his fictitious adventures at the ancient Aztec ruins of Chichen Itza and Tula. Lissy hadn't laughed so much in a long time.

Life hadn't been this good since well, ever. She was in love with John Brunt and they were going to get married. But the best thing was that she was going to be a mother. She had smiled to herself all weekend when she thought of how lucky she was. Underneath it all though, there was a growing feeling of apprehension that she was trying very hard to ignore. It was a fear of something happening to ruin it all. She couldn't quite put her finger on it but it felt like she was afraid that one day it would all be taken away from her and she would be abandoned – lonely and insignificant.

Now, lying on Bobby's couch she drifted off into that feeling…soon she began to have a clear memory of a life she lived before…

It was wartime Britain. She stood on the platform and studied her mother's face as she hung the label around her neck. On it was written her name and where she was to go. She was frightened, there was no use in pretending she wasn't and by the look on her mother's face she was frightened too. Her mother had that look most of the time when her father went off to war but when the telegram came to say that he had been killed in the line of duty her face had taken on a blankness. Not until now had she seen that frightened look come back on her mother's face. "Promise me you'll be good for the Spencers my darling," Mother said.

"I'm frightened Mother," she replied, "what if the Spencers don't like me?"

"They'll love you precious. Just like me."

"But what if I don't like it in the country? Why can't I stay with you?" Mother couldn't help it. Huge big tears spilled from her eyes. "Why are you crying Mother? I will be back soon won't I? It's just for a little while – didn't you say?"

"Yes darling. It's just for a little while and then I shall come and fetch you."

"Promise?"

"I promise. Look out for me. I shall be coming to take you home."

She waved goodbye from the window and watched Mother getting smaller and smaller as the train pulled out of the station. She clutched her little suitcase in her arms along with Mr Ted and prepared herself for the long journey to the country. The Spencers were supposed to meet her at the other end. She wondered what they were like. She had never known country people before. What if they were mean to her? What if they ate little children for their dinner? Father used to read to her at bedtime. She loved the story about Hansel and Gretel who were sent out to the wilderness. They came across a house made of sweets but the old woman who lived there was a witch and ate little children for her dinner. She hugged Mr Ted to her and said – "It's okay Mr Ted. Please don't be frightened. I'll look after you."

She spent the entire summer with the Spencers and each day she looked out for her mother coming to fetch her but she never came. The Spencers were okay, she guessed, but they were a bit cross and they made her do chores. She never had to do chores at home. They had Miss Agnes who did all the cooking and cleaning so that Mother never had to do any nasty chores. Mrs Spencer had made her brush the floors and wash up and she had to make her bed every morning. Mr Spencer made her help him on the farm and her hands were sore and chaffed from the hard work.

"These are hard times," Mrs Spencer would say to her. "We all have to do our bit – even you. You've had it too easy, that's what's wrong with you. Spoiled little rich kid. Well, there'll be no spoiling here. It's hard graft and if ya don't like it then tough."

After the summer, autumn and winter came and went and Mother didn't come for her. She often asked the Spencers when she could go home but she always got the same answer – "These are hard times and no-one knows what end is up anymore. You're poor mother is likely doing her bit for her country God bless her. She doesn't need to worry about the likes of you."

Lissy opened her eyes. 'Hard times' – that phrase cut through her like the sharpest blade. "How come those words hurt so much?" she asked Bobby. She had been in a trance, remembering a time when she was a little war refugee. She told him all about it and how she waited and waited for her mother to come for her and she never came.

"I dunno. I suppose it *was* hard times really. Everyone suffered in those days," replied Bobby not wanting to say too much.

"She never came you know – my mother. I think I remember something about looking for her when I was grown up but I think she had died in the blitz."

"Rotten luck."

"Yeah." Lissy shook her head and sighed.

"How do you feel?"

"Pretty shitty actually. I feel lonely and abandoned. That's what I feel – abandoned."

"Remind you of anything?"

"You know what? I think that's why I've been looking for my birth mother. I was never reconciled with my mother in that life so I tried to find her in this."

"Do you think that's why you chose to be adopted?"

"Do you think I *chose* to be adopted?"

"Maybe. How do you feel now that you know what you've been looking for?"

"That's just it isn't it? I was looking for my mother then and I am now this time but, I don't know why I was abandoned in the first place."

"Because it was wartime and lots of children were sent to the country away from their parents and because your current mother couldn't look after you."

"Yes, but there has to be more to it than that. There's a reason why I chose that abandonment in the first place. You're always saying that we choose our lives to learn about ourselves. Well, I have this feeling of guilt now that I don't understand. Do you suppose it could be connected to that?"

"Very possible. Maybe you abandoned your daughter in one lifetime. It could be a simple case of karma," suggested Bobby.

"I don't believe in that. It's more about balancing experience than revenge."

Lissy was glad she had done this but she could feel the old restlessness and need for answers rising to the surface once more. She had thought she had dealt with that but here it was again and now she had this guilt to shake as well. However, she had gone looking for answers before and it only brought her more grief. *Fuck it,* she told herself, *the answers can come looking for me.*

"Maybe there's a little bit of both going on," said Bobby, "we are responsible for creating our experience but at the same time there's an element of destiny as well."

"Yeah. I'll tell you one thing though," said Lissy jumping off the treatment table and grabbing her shoes, "I never would have thought much to this past life stuff until now. That was so real it was as if I had never forgotten it."

"You hadn't – not really," replied Bobby, "we hold all that stuff in our spiritual bodies."

"Our what?"

"Our aura. There are different layers of energy surrounding us all the time and all our soul's information is imprinted on them. Some psychics can read the energy field or aura and tell what past lives you have had that are significant to this one."

"Like a book?" laughed Lissy.

"Exactly! That woman, Eliza White Buffalo, who's at The King's Arms next month – she could probably tell you all about why you chose to be abandoned for a second time. I think she does private readings but you would have to book months in advance to get an appointment with her."

"Fuck it Bobby. I've had it hard enough dealing with this life without taking on past crap as well. The answers will just have to find me," Lissy insisted. She simply wished to leave all feelings of abandonment aside and get on with becoming a mother herself. At least her child would never have any cause to feel like that. She put a protective hand on her womb but instead of the familiar wave of love she had gotten used to there was a very different feeling – an overwhelming fear of loss. *You're being irrational*, she told herself shaking it off but she couldn't shake the stabbing guilt that was growing with every breath she took.

6th June 2008

It had been a busy morning at work and Lissy was tired as usual. She and Anne were closing up for lunch. "I thought it was supposed to get easier at this stage," she moaned to Anne who had been doing the lion's share all morning and wasn't feeling in the least bit sympathetic. "I'm twelve weeks today and I'm still throwing up. God, I hope I'm not gonna be one of those women who are sick the whole time. How am I gonna cope in Mexico? We go tomorrow."

"For fuck's sake Lissy," said Anne disbelievingly, "why can't you just for once be thankful for what you have and stop moaning. I swear, it's like a broken record with you."

"Huh…what?" Lissy was taken aback. What was up with Anne this last while? She was being even more of a bitch than usual.

"I mean you've got John haven't you? He's crazy about you. *And*, you've got a little baby on the way. Anyone would think you'd be happy but oh no, you're still moaning and going on about how hard done by you are. Well, let me tell you this you spoiled bitch – you don't know you're born." Anne spat it out like a bad taste in her mouth she had had too long.

Lissy watched her gob-smacked. Anne was near to tears she was that angry. What on earth could have provoked her to be so horrible? And a spoiled bitch? *Do I really come across like that?* Lissy wondered. "Anne I…" she began. She didn't quite know how to deal with it, "…I never meant to upset anyone. It's just I've been feeling so shitty and …"

"That's just it Lissy," spat Anne. "It's always about you isn't it and how shitty you feel? Did it ever occur to you that I may be feeling shitty myself? Did you ever stop to think what my life's like? It's not exactly the bed of roses you're used to you know. Some of us have had to fend for ourselves."

"Gosh Anne…I…"

"*And*, Miss High and Mighty…" Anne went on, "… how do think I felt with you going on about your mother all the time? Bitching on about how unfair it is and all the time you have two parents that think the sun shines out of your ass when my mum wouldn't give a fiddler's fuck if I fell off the face of the earth."

"I…I told you. It's not the same." Lissy was shocked at the outburst and was feeling extremely uncomfortable. The guilt that up until now belonged firmly in another lifetime was stabbing and taunting at her now saying – *I told you it's all your fault. You're a terrible person.*

Anne wasn't finished and to Lissy's great dismay she went on hatefully – "And now you're gonna be a mother yourself. Well, let's see how long that poor child lasts before it's running a mile from you. Probably better of if it dies at birth."

"Anne, how could you?" Lissy's voice broke and the tears that had been threatening to come for the past two minutes cascaded down her cheeks. She found that she was shaking she was so upset, but it wasn't with anger. Why wasn't she angry? She had every right to be after Anne's performance but she wasn't. She was guilty and defensive and scared but she wasn't angry. The memory of her past life mother dying in the blitz came crashing into her thoughts and she felt overwhelmingly responsible. What the hell was happening to her? She wanted to run and hide. She wished John was there and Mum and Dad. They wouldn't tell her it was her fault. They wouldn't make her feel like this – like everything that ever went wrong in the world was down to her and they certainly would never dream of accusing her of not protecting her baby and letting something terrible happen to it. She ran to the bathroom in tears. What was happening to her? Why was she feeling so dreadfully unhappy when she ought to be over the moon with joy at all the wonderful things she had in her life? She sat down on the toilet and buried her face in her hands and wept until the guilt and fear left her and she could think straight again – until she was Lissy Brenning again. Then the anger came – it was all Rose McDevit's fault. The guilt was hers. "How dare she abandon me and then leave me feeling guilty for just being alive?" She said out loud. She jumped suddenly, the bathroom door had opened.

"Lissy? Are you okay? Oh Lissy, I'm so sorry. I don't know where all that came from. I didn't mean it, I'm sorry." Anne seemed genuinely worried about her.

"You meant it," Lissy replied getting up off the toilet and putting on a show of pride. Then she thought twice. It didn't feel right. How many times had she behaved like that when faced with adversity? She did it every time. Anne had been right. She *was* a spoiled bitch who expected everyone to bow down to her. She never stopped to think how others felt except when she was trying to make an impression. She was a selfish spoiled bitch and that was the truth of it. "No, I'm sorry. You're right Anne. I've been awful this last while."

"Well you've had a lot on your plate."

"Maybe, but I've been a bitch and I'm sorry. It'll be different from now on I promise. You're right – I have so much to be thankful for and I am thankful you know, I really am."

"I'm sure you are," Anne told her. "It's me – I get jealous I suppose and you all seem to get on so well with Linn. I've always been jealous of her you know."

"I know. Linn told me. She doesn't have a clue why, you know, and neither do I for that matter."

"Well, she's so nice isn't she? Everyone loves her."

"Everyone would love you too if you just stopped being so defensive all the time. We've had some great nights out haven't we? You're a lot of fun when you want to be."

"Yeah, what are we like eh? Tell you what – let's call a truce and start again. What do you say?"

"I say yes please," said Lissy and gave her a hug. "Now can we sit down and have something to eat? I really am bushed."

Anne laughed. "I never asked you what happened in Ireland. You just seemed to give up on all that. Have you?" she asked genuinely interested.

"Yeah, in a way. I did find out who she was actually."

Anne's eyes opened wide – "Oh!"

"Her name's Rose McDevit. She's not well though and I don't think she wants to get in touch with me anyway. Best left alone."

"You don't sound convinced," said Anne, "want to talk about it?"

"No, not really. Besides, if I was able to find out who *she* was then she should be able to find *me*." Lissy remembered the fortune teller's response when she asked if she would find her mother. She had said - *no, I'm afraid not but she will find you*. Lissy couldn't think how that would be possible with no adoption records and a family who wanted the secret buried firmly in the past.

"Well, at least you know now where you came from," Anne told her kindly, "and now that you're a mother yourself you can give your child that holy love you believe in so strongly." She patted Lissy on the abdomen and thought she was being consoling by saying – "This one will never come to any harm. Not with you as a mother."

The words hit Lissy like the hurtful blows Anne had dealt previously. This one will never come to any harm with her. Why did that make her feel like she didn't deserve to be a mother at all? What was the origin of this awful guilt she was feeling? And why did she feel that Rose McDevit was the only person who could tell her the answers?

Chapter Twenty Three

The Group

Rose loved her life. She loved who she was and as the pieces of the jigsaw came together one by one she was beginning to see a more beautiful picture than she had ever thought was possible. The key was she was being real and, more importantly, she now realised that enjoying the ride was an essential aspect of that.

Carrick Glen, November 2005

Another car pulled up in the yard. "Shit Rose, how many people are comin' to this thing?" Jack asked his wife.

"Whatever – 'bout twenty or so," was the reply.

"Hope we have room for parkin'. If any more come we're gonna have to park in the garden."

Rose was hosting a drum circle. She had invited Rich Barker, a well known drum circle facilitator from County

Clare to come for a day. She had met him and his assistant David Brown in Wicklow last year when she attended a drum circle there. It had been a wonderful day in which they all drummed and sang and performed a Native American Sun Dance. Rose had enjoyed it so much she had promised herself she would bring Rich and David up to Mayo so that her friends could experience it for themselves.

"Well, that's eighteen so far counting Rich and David," said Rose, "but Gertge has still to come and she's bringing Lisa with her."

"Who's Lisa?" asked Jack.

"She's from Holland as well. She's been working with Gertge for about a year now. A lovely woman, about sixty or so and more life in her than most twenty year olds. I really like her. She's funny you know – would get on well with you."

"There's Gertge now," said Jack as Gertge's car pulled into the yard. Jack went off to direct her to a parking space.

By the time everyone was seated in a circle, drums ready, they were twenty two in all. It was a fine autumn Saturday and the windows were flung wide open to let the fresh breeze sweep throughout the room as the drum rhythm got faster and louder entrancing the drummers into a trance-like state with its heightened drone. Rose was as high as a kite. She was still high that evening when everyone had gone home.

"What planet are ya on today?" Jack asked in jest. He loved to see Rose enjoying herself.

"God knows," she laughed, "'cos I don't and May and Black Elk don't apparently. They're nowhere to be found."

"Are ya okay?"

"Grand. I need to come down though for I'm not protected. I'll be shattered later." If Rose thought she would come down that night she was wrong for something else happened that left her reeling with anticipation. She had a phone call from Wales. It was Marjorie Armstrong.

"I'm just finished writing my book dear," Marjorie said, "and I was hoping to have a little meeting with friends - a gathering for psychic development. Just a few chosen people dear, not a lot. It would be nice if you came. Would that be possible?"

"Yea, I think so. That would be great. You're writing a book then?"

"Oh yes – just finished. Are you not well today dear? You're shaking. I can feel it"

Rose realised how tired she was. She was indeed shaking. "I'm exhausted. I've had a big day today. Lots of people here for a drumming circle."

"You need to be more careful dear with your energy. You can be stripped very easily. That is something I can teach you when you come – it's called psychic protection. Tell you what, I have a friend here with me at the moment. She's a healer, dear. Would you like her to work with you now?"

"That'd be great," accepted Rose with relief.

"Ok then, let's do that and we shall call back in twenty minutes or so."

"Great, thanks."

Twenty minutes later the phone rang again. It was the healer - "Hello Rose. I'm Georgina. My word, you're like a little light bulb aren't you?"

"Hello Georgina. Aye, that's what everyone says about me. It's just I can't seem to protect myself," explained Rose.

"Well you *are* protected," said Georgina, "You're very well protected actually. I spoke to your guide – Black Elk?"

"That's right." Rose was blown over by Georgina's accuracy.

"You're much too light now for anything dark to harm you. You just need to learn not to give your energy away. You have amazing guides, honey. My word, such power! What were you like when you were a child?"

"The same, only I hadn't a clue what I was doing. My guides just kinda took over."

"You have amazing power but I see a huge fear. Sadness and fear. Oh, I am sorry – I can see your pain. But, that will all go. We must see each other. We must work with shifting that old energy into the light. We won't talk now – you need to rest. Speak to Marjorie and we can arrange to get you over here, yes?"

"Fantastic, thanks Georgina." Rose said feeling somewhat better already.

"Well it's fine isn't it? We *will* work together and that's what we do isn't it? And it will be an honour to meet you," said Georgina enthusiastically. "There are two others who will attend this meeting and I feel you have a connection with *him*. His name is James. It's probably more about him than you but I think you will know what that is."

Rose thought for a moment and then remembered that Francie had once told her that there was a man coming into her life who would work with her at a point of transformation. She told Georgina about this. "I remember I said – 'yes, his name is James and no other person in the world would be able to work with me in the way he will'. Do you think that's him?" she asked.

"I don't know – I don't think so but you will know," Georgina reassured her.

Georgina Knight was a seer and a healer. She had been working with Marjorie Armstrong, editing her book and preparing it for the final stage. All her life she had helped people with whatever their passion was: she had healed people, taken care of people and generally opened her home and her heart to any needy person who asked for her help. Lately she had been focusing her time and effort into people whom she believed had something special to give to the world. Marjorie's book was good. A lot of people would benefit from hearing her story and Georgina felt if she could do anything in her power to bring that to fruition, then so be it. But what about her? What did she want from life? She would have liked a husband and children – a family, but that wasn't to be. If the truth be told, Georgina was quite content with how things were. She was making a difference, bringing light into the dark shadows of people's lives. She knew she could do so much more, though. She had been feeling restless lately and she knew she had much more to give. She had had a dream. It was of a sanctuary – a place where people would go and spend time relaxing and healing… Georgina could feel it within her heart; she could see how it would look and what treatments would be available. The only thing standing in the way was the lack of location. Georgina was constantly looking for the right location but she hadn't yet found it. Some day she would – when the time was right; and until then she trusted the universe to provide her with the pointers she needed to keep her firmly on her path. Georgina knew that she had a purpose and now she knew that the woman she had spoken to this evening – Rose Farley, was one more step on the way to fulfilling that purpose.

John Lennon Airport, Liverpool January 14th 2006

"I will know you," Georgina had told her on the phone. Rose picked up her bag and made her way to the arrivals lounge. As soon as she stepped foot inside there was Georgina grinning from head to toe carrying a little smiley face on a stick. Rose was tired but a wave of energy swept through her and she felt overjoyed to finally meet her new friend. Without a word the two women embraced each other with a hug. It was like coming home. Rose instantly knew without a trace of a doubt that Georgina Knight was a familiar soul – someone whom she had been close to many times on her soul's journey – a soul sister – one of her group of seven.

"My husband, Jack is one of my soul group," she told Georgina on the car journey to Wales, "I think it is very likely that you are as well."

"Well yes, we've worked together many times I feel. I'm getting a feeling of France. We were sisters in France."

"That's a lifetime I have been working on for quite a while now," replied Rose astounded at the powerful energy she felt between herself and this woman. She felt she had to elaborate and told Georgina what she remembered – "Jack and I are married and we're standin' at the river bank with our two children. There's a fracas goin' on in the city – Paris, and he goes to fetch someone and gets killed."

"You and I both were killed that night," Georgina said, "burned as witches. We were in a sort of sisterhood – Cathars I think."

Rose felt a familiar shiver up her spine that told her she had spoken or heard the truth. She thought of a nightmare she had a lot when she was a kid. "When I was a child I had this dream a lot," she told Georgina, "In fact, I've had it lately again. In the dream I'm being ambushed by a mob and they carry me to a huge bonfire. The next thing I know is I'm on the top of this fire tied to a stake and I'm not afraid. I say no in my mind and I reach out my arms. A blinding white light comes from my hands and feet and my heart and then everyone suddenly is unaware of what they were doing and they go away and I am safe."

"I think you are ready to stand in your great light," Georgina told her. "This is it for you. This is the final incarnation when you will fulfil your soul's purpose."

Rose got the shivers again. "Then that's true for Jack and you and the other four members of the group as well because we are all in it together. One purpose. Am I right?"

"I hope so," Georgina had tears in her eyes. "I just feel so tired of this world you know. It's like I don't belong here and it's so painful to be here. Sometimes… and I know you will understand this Rose … sometimes I feel like all of the world's pain and suffering is passing through me and it feels unbearable. If I had more support maybe, but I don't know – maybe this is how it will always be for me."

Rose cried for her soul sister. She did know how she felt but she also knew that it was different for her. "Georgina," she said softly, "I do know how you feel but it's different for me. I'm lucky I suppose in that I'm protected from the world's cruelty although God knows I had my share of it. But now, well it's like there's a barrier against that and I'm in my own little cocoon where I'm me and Black Elk can do his thing and everyone wins. You on the other hand are here to channel that darkness through you, transforming it back to the light and then letting it flow into the earth. That is what you are about and it's shit at times, I know, but it's your purpose 'cos *you* can do it – not me – you."

"Well you're right. I know that and I can do it, yes."

Georgina took several deep breaths. "It would be nice though if I had some support."

"You've got me. That's why we're together now. I know that 'cos Black Elk is tellin' me all this stuff. It's not comin' from me you know – it's him."

"It is, yes, but it's also you."

"Ah well, I know what ya mean." Rose understood that although Black Elk was telling her what to say – it was really her because he was a part of her – probably the best best part of her.

"Who was Jack going to fetch?" asked Georgina suddenly.

"What?"

"In France. Who was Jack going to fetch?"

"I dunno. It wasn't you?"

"No, but whoever it was, he could stop you from doing what you were going to do. Jack wanted him to stop you. What were you going to do?"

"I dunno."

"You will."

They arrived at Marjorie's place in Wales at eleven am. Marjorie was on the front doorstep to meet them. "Hello, hello and welcome!" she yelled before they had even got out of the car. Rose studied her closely – she didn't recognize her. Spirit had obviously used her as a means to connect with Georgina. She was lovely though – getting on in years and not in the best of health. Apparently she had died three times on an operating table as a young woman. She told them how she had been sent back to work as a medium.

"You died dear, you know," she said to Rose again, "you have a lot of work to do." She introduced them to the rest of the small gathering. "This is James and his wife Maria. James is trance as well." Rose shook his hand and she knew – it wasn't the James she was waiting for. Marjorie introduced Maria - "Now Maria, this is interesting – she is a psychic artist."

"What exactly is that?" Rose asked the dark eyed young woman.

"I take a pencil and paper and I just start to draw" Maria told her warmly. "I don't think about what or who I'm drawing – it just appears. For example I drew a likeness of you recently. Of course, I didn't know it was you or I would have brought it with me." The dark eyes flashed as she spoke and Rose thought that she had never met anyone before with this amount of passion for what she did. Naturally, she wondered why Maria had drawn a likeness of her.

"Why did you draw me, do you think?" she asked.

Maria smiled broadly and looked at her husband. James put his arm around her and addressed Rose. "She drew it for me," he said to Rose's surprise. "I had a premonition." He paused and seemed to be deciding what he should say. "In the premonition I was watching this woman who was in a deep trance. I asked her a question I have had for a very long time and she answered it for me. The amazing thing was she answered in a man's voice." He noted Rose's reaction and realised his thoughts were correct – this was the woman from his premonition.

Rose decided to say nothing about Black Elk at this stage – she wasn't sure she should talk about it at all. She glanced at Georgina who said nothing. As the day went on Rose noticed that Georgina seemed to take a back seat altogether when it came to discussing matters of psychic development. She managed to get her on her own that evening before they finished up. "I noticed you were very quiet Georgina. May I ask why? I would have thought you would have much more interesting things to say than anyone else."

Georgina's answer wasn't at all surprising. In fact, it was what Rose had herself been thinking more and more as the day went on. Georgina said – "Sometimes with these gatherings Rose, there are too many people vying for the position of top dog. I can't be bothered with such games. I prefer to stay centred, coming from a place of love rather than from the perspective of my ego."

Rose thought she knew what Georgina had meant. "I think I know what you mean" she said, "Sometimes my good friend Jonathan Kane would say to me – Rose, you have humility. Don't lose that."

"It doesn't do to be getting involved with power struggles," added Georgina. "Remember, it's not you who does the work – it's the power of the divine working through you. We're all capable of great things as long as we know that basic truth."

Rose thought about something Black Elk said about Jonathan. She told Georgina - "Jonathan is a really humble person and he's got amazing healing ability. Black Elk calls him *the monk*."

"Well you have it right too I think," Georgina told her. "In fact, you don't own your power enough I'd say. Plus, you have integrity, I'll give you that."

"Definitely, but that has always been the most important thing in the world for me – truth. I've strived towards it my whole life – truth in all things. Nothing else matters."

"What did you think of today?" Georgina asked.

Rose had had a great day. It was good to be in the company of people who didn't think she was crazy or making it all up. Marjorie had taught her quite a bit about protecting her energy and had even invited her to accompany her to Carolina in The States to meet with some Native American teachers there. She had invited them all actually but like Rose no-one seemed to feel optimistic that they would be able to go. Rose certainly was not fit enough yet after the accident to endure such travelling and finance would be a big problem. Still it was exciting to be asked and if spirit wanted her to go then they would find a way for her to do so. James had been great. He really was a good medium. He had read for Rose and to her immense delight who should come through for her … only Uncle Gerry!

"I'm getting a man here," James had said. "He feels very wheezy in his chest. Two plastic hips? Yes – two."

Rose was overjoyed. "My uncle Gerry," she smiled.

Gerry had been wonderful. He talked about many things to prove that it was he who was there. Rose cried when he referred to the apples.

"Why would he be giving me apples?" James had asked. "He says – *a wee…lock...o' apples…?*" James struggled with the accent.

Rose laughed. "That's what he used to say – *here's a wee lock o' apples for ya – they'll do ya good.*"

"He's serious now. He says tears of sadness – very unfair – but now tears of joy. A great future ahead. He did his part and he's proud of you." Rose was crying. She hadn't realised she had loved Gerry as much as that and just how much he had loved her. She could feel him around her – she could even smell the pipe smoke. James went on – "He is talking about his hips. He is saying that he did it and you will do it too. You will be able to get about much better in the future – the choice is yours." Rose cried a lot more and everyone was respectfully quiet. They could tell that this Gerry had meant a lot to her. Marjorie put her hand on Rose's and told her softly –

"Black Elk spoke through Gerry."

July 2006

Rose had been dreaming. She sat up in bed and glanced at Jack. He was sound asleep. *Good*, Rose thought, *I'd best write this one down*. The dream had been one of those dreams that seemed real. She knew through experience that they were a bit like premonitions. They were her spirit's way of telling her conscious mind something significant. She turned on the bedside lamp and reached for her dream diary. *'21st July 2006'* she wrote – *'I dreamed I was in a foreign country and I was looking for a man. I knew when I found this man that he would recognize me instantly and that one day he would work with me. I don't know the name of the man I am looking for but in the dream his name was Mr Holland.'* She turned off the lamp again and settled back down to go to sleep but she found she couldn't sleep. Her thoughts were full of who this man might be. Was he one of her group of seven? Rose found that the more she thought about him the more she felt wide awake. At one stage she was so alert she began to connect with the many spirits that were constantly around her just waiting for an opportunity to get through. Most of the time Rose ignored these spirits – she had been practicing the techniques Marjorie had taught her to protect herself but she still hadn't managed to shut herself off completely from constant communication. However, tonight as she lay there in the dark, wide awake and receiving, the spirit of an elderly woman came through very clear. Her face flashed before Rose's closed eyes and Rose jumped to attention once she heard one word – *'Grace'*.

"Who are you?" Rose asked.

"*Grace's grandmother*," was the reply. Rose said nothing and waited. Suddenly there flashed another picture. It was of a little girl about five years old, dark auburn hair and bright blue eyes. She was the image of Rose.

"Is that her?" Rose asked the grandmother, who indicated that it was. "Is she okay?"

"She's fine – not damaged – a little spoiled and looking for you." Rose smiled. Her Grace was okay – she wasn't abused. The grandmother left as quickly as she came but before she disappeared completely Rose caught something else. She wasn't sure but she thought she heard – *'Dorset'*.

Next morning she was up earlier than usual. The dream and the communication with Grace's grandmother was fresh in her mind and she sang happily as she got herself ready for the day ahead. Gertge and Lisa were picking her up at eight am. They were going to Galway for a singing workshop. Rose had been looking forward to it for quite a while. On the way down to Galway in the car she told Gertge and Lisa about the previous night's events.

"Will you try to find her in Dorset?" asked Gertge.

"No, not yet anyway. I don't feel it's the right time and besides, how would I find her without a surname? Something else that bothers me too is that the grandmother was Irish. Maybe she's not in England at all. No, I'll wait and follow my gut feeling. If I'm to find her then I will when the time is right."

"You are so right," remarked Gertge and Lisa agreed. Rose had never really had the opportunity to talk with Lisa at length before so today she made a point of getting to know her friend a little bit better.

"I go back to Holland soon," Lisa informed her, "in

August. Before I go though I would like to come to your home and visit you if that is okay?"

"Aye, that would be grand," Rose could think of nothing nicer.

"I would be happy for you to read the cards for me. Is that something you can do for me?"

"Not a problem as long as you know it's only a bit of fun really. I don't like to predict the future you see. The future is very fickle. Two things can happen if I tell you something. You could either bring it about by focusing on it or you could change it altogether. Do you see how fickle it is?"

"Well, time is not something I think too much about. I feel that the past and the future don't exist really. Now is all there is."

Rose took the opportunity to speak her truth – "That is so true Lisa. You know, when I'm moving about from one dimension to the next and my guides are with me of course – it's like there is no such thing as time. What I mean is, it doesn't go in a straight line like one would think it does. What is real is that time is kinda circular – not even that but it's like it's just a dot and everything exists within that dot – every person, every lifetime, all dimensions, everything there is." Rose was getting carried away with her excitement. She felt such a feeling of freedom and power when she was speaking out all those things she had kept inside all her life. All those things she thought that when added up meant that she was mad – born bad. But all those things were the truth as far as she was concerned now and she longed to speak it – she was born to speak it.

She went on - "I believe that is how time travel is possible. The dot is like the world wide web and one can experience any time or dimension one wants just by surfing the net."

Lisa looked at her with amusement. It wasn't very often she met someone as real and as raw as Rose. She only hoped that her obvious vulnerability wouldn't fall into the wrong hands. She made a mental note to keep in touch with Rose after she had gone home. *At least she has Gertge*, she thought thankfully – Gertge was a warrior. She wouldn't let Rose get too dragged away. "Rose" she said later that day, "I am thinking – you are so special but you need to be protected. I think that is very important for you. Do you have anyone you can talk to for support? I know it is difficult being you in this world."

Rose noted two things at once that filled her with encouragement and a sense of achievement. She noticed that more and more people were being kind to her, wanting to encourage her and she noticed that she was starting to react to that with a sense of value for herself. Both these things were quickly becoming commonplace with her and she liked it. She was being herself and not pretending any more. She was being real and attracting more and more people into her life that verified and encouraged who she was. Life was so much different than before the accident – before the awakening. She hung her head and cried; tears of resentment and sadness for her lost years mixed with relief and joy for what she had accomplished. She felt blessed – truly blessed. Lisa waited. She knew why Rose was crying. She needed time and space to heal – to release all the residual pain she had carried around for so long. When Rose was done she took Lisa's hand. It felt as if she had taken the hand of a long lost love – someone who had been a crucial support for her many times before. The two women silently looked into each other's faces and they felt a big love flowing between them – heart to heart.

"Thank you," Rose breathed deeply.

Lisa was sure that there was only one thing she should say – "That is why I am here." And Rose knew – Lisa was the fourth member of her group of seven.

"Ok, let's see what's goin' on here then," Rose said lightly, pouring over the layout of cards on the table. She and Lisa each had a cup of hot tea in their hands and they were ready for some fun. The reading was a good one, which was what Rose always said when she provided some truth for folk. The lady, May, was close by, ready to be of assistance. As it turned out Rose was to be forever grateful for May's guidance that day. As soon as she set eyes on the cards she saw him and May confirmed it – it was the man from her dream. "Lisa, do ya remember that dream I told ya about? This is him – the man in the dream," said Rose with excitement.

"Has he a connection with me?" asked Lisa.

"Definitely. He's a healer May is tellin' me. He lives in Holland. You know him very well – you are close."

"It is Hans. He is a healer yes. He treated me for an illness years ago. You dreamed of Hans?"

"It's him. Of course! Holland! I called him Mr Holland in the dream but his *name* isn't Holland – he *comes* from Holland. I must see him. May is tellin' me that I must go to him."

"Well that is no problem," said Lisa. "I go in August and you go too. I will telephone him and let him know you are coming."

Later that afternoon Lisa telephoned Hans and spoke with him. It was a brief call and was all in Dutch – Rose never understood a word. "So there we are," Lisa said in English when she put down the receiver.

"Well? Can he see me?" asked Rose breathlessly.

"It is arranged. He needs to know when you wish to come and he will have two days free for you. He is quite excited. Hans is very tuned in to truth – he knows it is important."

"Grand. Oh, this is exciting. I have had loads of healin' before y'know but I think it is more about meeting him than anythin' else." Rose already knew that Hans was an important piece of the jigsaw.

"Well, he works very different from any healer I know," Lisa told her. "It is quite special what he does."

The arrangements were made to suit everyone and four

weeks later Rose was on her way to Amsterdam by air. Lisa went that morning by ship with her car and belongings. Rose always hated sailing. Any time she got on a ship she would feel unhappy and uncomfortable with a great big gap in her solar plexus. Flying it had to be. Hans met her at the airport and he felt to her just as she thought he would. She had spoken to him on the phone last week.

"I work with the zero point of time," he had told her. "Do you know what that is?"

"I've never heard the term before but I do know what you mean," she had replied. He meant the dot that she had realised was all there was.

"I take you back to the zero point of time – to the original blueprint and that is where transformation occurs" Hans went on to say.

Rose was impressed. Another person she could be real with – fantastic! She told him a little about her self and about Black Elk. She told him about the voice-over during her sleep – "It's just practicing I suppose."

"No, it is so that you will not be frightened when the time comes. I have never witnessed this phenomena before but I know it happens" replied Hans. "We were together in France I think" he added.

The realization hit Rose suddenly. She didn't know why she hadn't realised it before. Hans was the person Jack had been going to fetch when he got shot. Black Elk began telling her now the way it was, and she related it to Hans - "Yes, I was killed and so was my husband. He had been running to fetch you. There was something only you could have stopped me from doing. I don't know what that was. Anyway, you didn't come because my husband was killed before he got to you. It was in Paris in thirteen hundred and six. Many women were burned that night as witches."

"We worked with herbs and crystals then," added Hans enthusiastically, "I do now too."

"I work with crystals as well," Rose told him. "I do shamanic healing and I use crystals as well. I'm very interested in them – in all stones and in trees too."

After that initial conversation over the phone, Rose had a vision about Hans. She had been meditating and Black Elk and another spirit helper, Sparrow Hawk, had lifted her up and taken her to the temple to commune with the Master Hilarion. She had learned many things that time and had seen much of her truth. It was as she was on her way back to the earthly dimension that she had the vision. She saw Hans as a scientist, standing in a laboratory. The lab was filled with shelf after shelf of large bottles of liquids and oils. She was there although she couldn't see her self – she was experiencing it from the perspective of the first person. Hans turned to her in the vision and said – "The world is not ready for this."

Now as she sat beside him in his car speeding towards the south of the country where he lived she could feel his reluctance again to bring his work out into the world. When he turned to her, taking off his glasses and said – "You know

Rose – the world is not ready for this," she could have cried out loud.

You have been saying that for so long, she wanted to scream, *trust – trust in the universe – trust in me – I won't let you down this time.* Where did those thoughts come from? She didn't know but she was filled with a guilt from long ago – that same guilt she had felt when she had the birth chart done with Glenda from London. Was it possible that Hans had been one of the people she betrayed then? If indeed he was then that meant she was working with the same soul group since then, thousands of years ago. *Get the finger out and get this purpose done already,* she laughed to herself.

The day had been full of surprises and when she walked into Hans' place and saw what was there she was bowled over at the accuracy of her vision. In Hans' place was a laboratory lined with shelf after shelf of large bottles of liquids and oils. Rose laughed out loud and told Hans of her vision to which he reacted with some interest but Rose noticed – a lack of enthusiasm. The pang of guilt hit her again and threatened to ruin her enjoyment. She brushed it aside.

"Shall we have a coffee?" Hans suggested.

"May I have tea please?" she replied, wondering when Lisa would arrive. They drank their beverages and ate bread and cheese. Rose's mood lightened and she began to enjoy Hans' company immensely. He certainly was knowledgeable. She listened to him talk of things she had often wondered about and was so relaxed she almost fell asleep on the sofa.

"Are you tired?" Hans asked after they had finished their snack. "I would like to show you my stones."

Rose said she *was* tired but she would love to see the stones and she could sleep that night anyway. Hans led her up the stairs where he had devoted an entire room to storing his crystals. The walls were shelved as in the lab. On the shelves were at least two hundred transparent boxes, each containing one crystal. The crystals were large and as Rose took several out of their boxes and held them in her hands she could feel many different energies from them.

"Wow," she said quickly replacing one very large crystal in its box, "I don't like that. It makes me feel panicky."

"That is very special," Hans told her, "it channels our dark power." Rose was enthralled. Her guides often told her she was afraid of her own power. Lu and Jonathan had said the same thing. "You must pick it up before you leave tomorrow," Hans said. "I think you will feel very different to now."

Rose smiled. She was feeling very content. She was in the right place at the right time and here was another member of her group of seven. The jigsaw was looking good – the picture was becoming clear. *Soon I will be who I am in my wholeness*, she thought to her self beaming with happiness.

And the prophecy will be complete, added Black Elk in her heart.

Downstairs they heard someone call to them. It was Lisa. Hans called down to her in Dutch and soon she appeared at the top of the stairs. There was much delight and hugs as the old friends greeted each other. Poor Lisa was exhausted. It had been a long journey. After Lisa was well looked after and everyone was eager to begin, Rose was taken into another room that contained a healing table and a selection of little phials of the oils from the large bottles downstairs. During the first healing session several of the phials were strapped to her. The whole thing was very emotional for her and she must have cried bucket loads in one hour. The next day she had two more sessions during which she was more able to take an active interest in what was happening. By the time they had finished she was feeling brighter, more alert and totally content. Black Elk and Hilarion had participated in the healing sessions throughout and provided everyone with their wisdom and amazing presence. Rose left Holland with a deeper knowledge of her self but before she left she wanted to hold that crystal again. This time, to her immense pleasure, she felt nothing but peace when she held it. *Thanks guys*, she said silently to her guides.

At home Rose spent the next few weeks resting mostly. Besides taking care of her children and generally seeing to the family's needs she did nothing but sleep. *The long sleep, Jonathan calls the way in which people are unaware of themselves – well this is my long sleep,* she smiled to herself. She had noticed the difference in her legs almost as soon as she arrived back from Holland. Now the arthritis was gone completely and her joints were no longer paining. "All I have to do now is get the muscles built up," she said to Jack who was delighted and amazed at the way in which the transformation had taken place. He suggested she went to a physiotherapist. There was one not far from where they lived apparently and Jack had heard that he was very good.

"Several people have recommended him to me," he told Rose. "I don't know why I hadn't thought of him before."

"It wasn't the right time," said Rose.

Roger Dowlings, the physiotherapist lived just one mile from Rose as it turned out. She made an appointment and arrived at his house one morning four weeks after her trip to Holland. "Hi, I'm Rose Farley," she said to him, "from just down the road. It's nice to meet ya."

"Nice to meet you Rose," the haughty man replied. The appointment went well and Rose was optimistic that she could get her legs back to a good working order in no time. She had already thrown away the walking stick. In fact what had happened was, it had broken in the airport on the way home from Holland. Rose liked Roger but there was something about him that perplexed her. Although he was very pleasant and agreeable there was a pride in him that she felt was touching on arrogance. That morning after the first appointment, Rose was in her healing room. She had found as the time went on that she needed to devote an entire room in her home to healing work. In this room she kept a healing table, a glass cabinet full of crystals and gems, and an altar on which she kept various sacred objects. On the walls were hung several beautiful pieces of art which were both healing and inspirational to look at. Vicky had painted her a huge piece depicting her as a Native American woman standing naked before Wakan Tanka at the dawn of the day. Rose called it *The Dawn* and it was very special. She never tired of gazing at it, reminding herself of who she was and the prophecy which was to be fulfilled on earth. This morning she sat on the floor below *The Dawn* and communed with her guides and spirit helpers.

"Do you know who Roger is?" Black Elk asked her. Rose noticed that at the mention of his name she had stiffened and had become resentful. *"Relax and I will take you on a journey so that you can understand."* Rose closed her eyes and took several deep breaths. In moments she was spinning out to a time seven hundred years ago.

It was thirteen hundred and six and she was once again standing on the riverside walk by the River Seine in Paris. She and her children said goodbye to Jack and waited for him to return with Hans but of course, he didn't return. Rose was aware this time that she was about to do something very dangerous. She believed that she could ingest a poisonous substance and live because she would be able to shift her consciousness to a level where the vibrations of her bodily cells would be so light that they would completely disperse and she would vanish. She believed that when she lowered her vibrations again she would be transformed in pure spirit and thus healed. Jack had been terrified when he realised what she was about to do and had insisted on fetching Hans. When Rose eventually became aware that Jack wasn't coming back she began to go to the city to look for him. At the end of the riverside walk was a doctor in a doctor's buggy. It was Roger and he had been lying in wait for her. He persuaded her to come with him in the buggy to find Jack but instead he betrayed her and gave her over to her executioners. What became of the children she never knew.

Rose brought her awareness back to the room. "Could I have done it?" was the first thing she asked Black Elk. The answer came back very quickly –

"It was not the time. Hold the 'Red Stone' close to your heart and when it is time the stone will sing and the prophecy will be fulfilled."

"The 'Red Stone'?"

"The 'Red Stone Of Power' given to you in Lemuria. You hold it within your heart. Soon the prophecy will be released and the stone shall sing."

At that moment Rose felt an ancient power stir within her heart and she knew without an inkling of doubt the meaning of Black Elk's words. "Thank you," she said. Then, there rose within her the same old guilt from thousands of years ago and she asked – "I know I have betrayed Hans and the group, Black Elk, yet I know that it was from a time long before Paris. Why is Hans so angry with me after all this time? Why doesn't he trust me?" As soon as she had asked the question she knew the answer. "It is because he thought I revealed his secret to Roger, isn't it? Roger and he were brothers in the royal house of Paris weren't they? His family exiled him when they discovered his secret life as an alchemist. Hans thought I betrayed him but it wasn't me."

"That is so," confirmed Black Elk. Rose felt distraught. How would she convince Hans of the truth? "*White Buffalo, you must remain grounded in this lifetime,*" Black Elk told her. She understood and brought her awareness firmly back to the here and now.

For days following that journey Rose thought of how she had gone so terribly wrong and what a mess she had made of everything. Such negativity was damaging to her and she began to attract discontent and anger into her marriage and other relationships. Her guides had to step in and intervene but it was several weeks later before Rose finally listened to what May was trying to tell her.

"Rose, my dear," May had said to her, "don't you see what happens? When we are aligned with a certain level of awareness as you have been, then two things naturally occur. Firstly, we go through a period of integration during which we re-integrate the information into our conscious mind. Secondly, we then test ourselves by attracting the old energy attached to that particular information. You see how upon re-integrating the memory of the happening in Paris, you attracted anger, discontent and distrust into your self? Now Rose, you must choose to let go off that old energy and free your self from that negativity." Rose understood and adjusted her thinking to a more positive and joyful outlook. Within days she noticed the change in her relationships, particularly with Jack and when the following month she received a phone call from a loving and trusting

Hans she knew that all that energy was now coming back to her transformed into peace and harmony.

Hans had been lost to her but she had found him again in a dream. He was the sixth member of her soul group but who was the seventh and final member? She had been contracted to find her spiritual family and this was to be reflected in her earthly family. Could it be possible that the one person she hoped to find in this lifetime was the seventh member? Was her daughter, Grace the final piece of the jigsaw?

Chapter Twenty Four

The Temple

What exists in spirit shall exist on earth – and what shall be on earth, it already is in spirit – it will be but a reflection – a shadow of what is real.

Holland, December 2006

Hans had been talking to Rose on the telephone. He said goodbye and flung himself down on the sofa. What should he do? He was torn in two – his heart was telling him to go to Ireland. There was work to do there with Rose, but his mind was saying no, he had work to do here as well. Besides, so many people relied on him to help them. What would they do? – Where would they go to for help if he left and went to Ireland for – oh, how long would he be gone? He had to think about that too. His guides had told him who she was. That they had worked in the same way with each other for thousands of years. He understood that she was one of a group of seven souls who were incarnating together again and again in order to fulfil a common purpose. He knew intuitively that the purpose involved him doing what he did so that Rose could channel a higher wisdom. His guides had showed him a vision last night. He had been talking about it to Rose just now on the telephone – "We were on a stage," he related to her, "and behind us was a huge white cross. I think it was significant to what we were doing there. I talked for a bit and then we got to work. Several people from the audience asked questions and you answered them. Rose, it was not your voice that spoke – it was your guide...*erm*..."

"Black Elk," offered Rose.

"Yes, Black Elk. He spoke many wise words but when I came out of the vision I could not recall them."

As Hans spoke Rose was experiencing the familiar warmth of truth sweeping throughout her and after some time she said – "Hans, I was being prepared for this work for a long time and the white cross – it is a symbol of my path. Black Elk taught me about the two roads that cross over in the centre just like a cross. When I was a child he would talk to me about the two roads and teach me many things from his Native American beliefs." She hesitated as she became aware that Black Elk was telling her to do something. "He wants me to do something now," she told Hans, "Can you connect with the time in France?"

Hans was silent for a moment as he concentrated, and

then he said that he was there.

"Good, how do you feel about me at this moment?" Rose wasn't sure what she was doing but she trusted her guidance.

"I feel angry and frustrated with you," replied Hans.

"I was going to do something very silly,"explained Rose, "that is why you were angry. I was going to ingest poison and then heal myself immediately by raising my vibrations to a higher level in which the cells would completely renew themselves. I wasn't aware at that time that I wasn't ready."

Hans had been feeling something very strange. He could relate to what Rose had just said but he felt as if he wanted to rant and rave and tie her down so that she couldn't do any more damage than she already had."I think you were always headstrong and impulsive," he said suddenly, "that is why I feel that it would be a mistake to trust you. I fear that you will take our work and bring it into the wrong hands."

Rose felt the guilt once more and she swallowed hard, tears stinging her eyes. Hans' words had hurt her and the worst thing was that he was right. She knew that she had betrayed them once before, long before France, and that it had been a massive betrayal – much bigger than doing something silly like getting her self killed through her own misjudgement. She could remember that now. That was the real source of her feelings of guilt…"You refer to the Order of Delphi, don't ya?" she asked, now seeing back through time.

"Yes!" said Hans, with excitement. "I knew when I saw you that there was some connection with the Order and when we were working on the healing I was given the information. Now, it feels like I have never forgotten you."

"I know I betrayed the Order," said Rose, "and I was wrong – very wrong. I feel a terrible guilt over it but I am wiser now." All was becoming clearer to her now – the Order had been infiltrated by dark priests and she was led astray; it was the downfall of the Order. "One of the infiltrators tried to pull me back many times," she told Hans, "and he even tried in this lifetime, but I was wise – I knew I shouldn't follow him. His name is Francie Connor. He is a good man but his unconscious shadow self still attempted to lure me away from my path."

"Well done!" said Hans, "I have no doubt you will stay true to your path. And Lisa is happy that we have met. She thinks we will do great work."

"And Georgina is aware as well," said Rose, "Jack and Roger, though, would probably prefer not to talk about these things."

"Well… they are doing their part whether they know it or not," said Hans.

"Of course," agreed Rose, "Jack looks after me very well and keeps me grounded which is an awesome task I have to say." Rose laughed at herself and Hans agreed that he was exactly the same. "Jack is doing that and Roger – well, I believe his part was always to do with earthly healing. He may have rejected our work with alchemy all along but I feel now that physical healing is every bit as important as spiritual healing, don't ya think?"

"I do. A balance of spiritual and vibrational healing as well as traditional medicine is best."

"And I had the spiritual healing for my legs with you and with Jonathan and now I come to the reflection of that on the earth, which is the physiotherapy," pursued Rose.

"What do we do now? – that is the question," asked Hans, wondering should he go to Ireland to be with Rose. Maybe Lisa would go back to work there and he would go with her.

"*It is not necessary to connect on the earth just yet,*" Black Elk told Rose, "*you must go to the Temple and connect with him there. There you will relate on a high level.*"

"Black Elk is telling me that we should connect on a higher level, in the Temple. Are you aware what that is?" Rose asked Hans.

She heard him take a deep breath before he revealed to her that his guides had also said they must do this. "To the Temple of Truth, above Crete," he confirmed.

"Aye," said Rose, "To the Flame of Truth. Black Elk is telling me that the Master Hilarion will be waiting for us at the temple and that we will learn there how we are to work together." Hans felt happy to travel to the Temple but he wondered if he knew how to do that. As if she had read his mind Rose said next – "You can go during meditation – just intend that you do and you will spin out through your solar centre, or if you are uncomfortable with that go during your sleep. Simply ask your guides or angels or whatever to guide your spirit as you sleep to the Temple of Truth to commune with the Master."

"And you think I could do that – spin out through my solar centre and travel through dimensions?" Hans knew it was something Rose had been doing since she was a child but he wasn't altogether sure he could do it.

"Well you can Hans. You do it for other people all the time although they're not aware of it. But I believe everyone can if they raise their consciousness enough. Of course, you would need to be really well advanced in psychic development but it is possible for anyone to do and you are more than well enough advanced. You simply have to believe you can."

"I agree," said Hans, wholeheartedly. "I think that more and more people are learning to do this thing that you do so naturally. It is not that easy for most people of course."

"Do ya know what I always think about?" she replied, "The Master Jesus said that in order to enter the kingdom of heaven you must first become like little children. Do ya know what I think that means? It means that unless you can have the faith that little children have you cannot enter the kingdom of heaven – you cannot raise your consciousness to a level where you are in the light. Therefore, in order to travel to the Temple of Truth in the etheric realms you must have the faith of a child. Believe and it will be so."

Hans contemplated what Rose had just said – she was right of course. Anything is possible if you believe it strongly enough – faith can move mountains and all that. Suddenly he felt a wave of certainty sweep through him and he knew that he could trust her now. She had grown in wisdom. "Rose you are quite special," he told her, "and you have gained much wisdom. I think you have many wise words to say that many people would benefit from hearing."

"I believe that is down to Black Elk," said Rose. "He was taught by the powers of the universe in his great vision and he passed that wisdom on to me. It's not me that needs to speak – it's Black Elk. That is why he will come through me and speak. But first, I have to write. I have to write my story. I have known this for so long…but I still procrastinate. Perhaps the time isn't right yet?"

"It is not the way you see it. You will write it very differently from how you think now," Hans offered. Rose had agreed – she felt the truth of those words.

Now as Hans relaxed on his sofa he wondered again should he go to Ireland. Perhaps he needed to work with her on this book? Or maybe they should engage in higher healing, but then that was something they would do at the Temple. No, perhaps he would go to Ireland at some time – when the time was right – when the stage work was to begin, whatever that was. But first it was sufficient to meet at the Temple and if Rose was to write this book then it would be a while yet before she was ready to be in the public eye. "I only hope she can cope with that, he said to himself as he closed his eyes for a nap, that is one thing I can do with confidence but I'm not so sure about her. She will need plenty of help and support because she is vulnerable. Yes, she is still very vulnerable indeed."

<u>*Carrick Glen, December 2006*</u>

Rose had been very happy to speak with Hans on the telephone, although it did drag up that dreadful guilt she was still carrying around. It felt to her like a ball and chain, weighing her down and preventing her from flying. Hans hadn't pulled any punches – she was guilty of betrayal and that was the truth of it. Two years ago when she first re-integrated the memory, Black Elk had told her that she alone was holding on to the responsibility of it – she was forgiven – but if *she* could forgive herself she would set herself free. Still, she continued to feel guilty. However, now that she had spoken her shame to Hans, who knew of her error, she felt that maybe now she could lay it down.

The following morning when the kids had left for school and Jack for work Rose sat in her healing room and connected with all her guides – "Guys," she said, "there is something I wish to do. I wish to let go of the guilt I feel about the Order. I intend to do that now and I ask you all to gather around and lift me up – give me the power to become a shaman." She closed her eyes and listened to her heart beating. Soon, she began to see beautiful colours and she knew she was centred in spirit and was ready to begin.

Black Elk was at her right hand side. She began to feel an energy that was increasingly becoming close to her heart. It was Sparrow Hawk. She spiralled out to him and he lifted her up to a high place. Black Elk, Rose and Sparrow Hawk stood at the bottom of the steps of the Temple of Truth. "This is as far as I go," Sparrow Hawk told Rose and he turned into a Sparrow Hawk and flew away.

Rose asked Black Elk – "Why does Sparrow Hawk lift my consciousness when you and I can do that together?"

"That is the way you would have it," replied Black Elk. He looked towards the Temple. At the top of the steps was a beautiful entity. She wore long flowing clothes and held a sceptre in her hand. In a thought Rose and Black Elk were before her.

"Pallas Athena," said Rose.

The beauty bowed her head and said – "Eliza." Rose felt the power of the name fill her heart and giving her strength and wisdom. She felt her self come completely alive – so alive that her body was tingling all over. When she looked at her body she saw that she was a zillion particles of light vibrating at high speed. She felt the question hurtle towards Pallas Athena and the answer came back in the same instant –

"Yes, you are Eliza. It means one who climbs the heights of heaven reflecting the mind of God." Pallas Athena opened the huge doors to the Temple and Eliza and Black Elk entered. Inside was filled with an emerald green light. Many people stood in circles around a giant emerald flame.

"The Flame of Truth," said Rose as Eliza.

Pallas Athena led them to the left into a circular room. In the centre of the room was a glass case containing a huge red ruby stone. Beside the case stood Hilarion. He held out his arms to Eliza and Black Elk and they moved towards him and were taken into a warm embrace.

"I am proud of you my chelas," he said - meaning 'my students'. He put his hand on Eliza's crown and said to her – "you wish to know yourself. That is good, and first you must witness the error for it is in understanding that you gain wisdom." He touched her forehead.

Immediately she saw that she was a priestess in the Order of Delphi – a priesthood that worked to serve mankind on the fifth ray of Truth. The Order was under the direction of Pallas Athena. Eliza had worked to help mankind know the difference between truth and error but dark priests had infiltrated the Order and Eliza was lured away – had fallen from grace. The Order was abolished and the service was taken away from mankind. As she experienced again the betrayal and shame she understood why she had fallen and she vowed that she was forgiven and released from the error. When Hilarion removed his hand from her she opened her eyes and said to him – "I forgive my self for the error. I am a humble servant of Truth."

Hilarion smiled and led her and Black Elk around to face the glass case. He stood side by side with Pallas Athena and they held out their hands. The ruby stone in the case rose up and Eliza vanished as it came right into her heart. She saw as Black Elk also vanished – the ruby stone also in his heart. As the stone shone from the centre of each of them its dazzling light became all that was and Eliza was aware that she *was* that light – as was Black Elk. The light began to come together into a circle and when Eliza reappeared she and Black Elk were as one.

Hilarion spoke to them – *"You see that you are one soul with twin flames. The Red Stone of Power is now in its place. When the Stones sings the prophecy will be fulfilled."* With that Black Elk stood beside Eliza once more and they were ready to leave the Temple.

When Rose opened her eyes her face was wet with tears and she was exhausted. Picking herself up off the floor she went to her bedroom and lay down on the bed. She fell asleep and didn't wake until Olly and Jerry were back from school and were knocking on the front door to get in. For the rest of the day Rose walked as if in a dream and for several days following she found it difficult to ground herself. In a way she was more alive than ever before. Wherever she went colours seemed more vivid and sounds seemed more keen. She saw beauty in all things – she heard beauty in all things and she felt more beautiful – as beautiful as the most dazzling sunset and as beautiful as the lowest flower. She went for walks and communed with the many wonderful spirits of nature. "Look at you!" she exclaimed to the primrose in the hedgerow, "aren't you beautiful?"

She walked into the forest and sat on a tree stump among the giant standing ones. Amidst a young sapling she saw the light flicker and change as a little being came into view. He was a merry little fellow with a body somewhat similar to a goat. He giggled when she greeted him and ran off stopping every now and then; he wanted her to follow him. He led her up a trail that climbed steeply and although her legs hurt she pushed onwards determined to see where the little nature being was taking her. As she paused to rest she heard giggling coming from the thickets on both sides of the trail and when she looked there she saw many of the little beings all hiding and giggling at her presence. She felt truly blessed and in wonder of them and she didn't wish to frighten them away so she pretended she didn't see them and went on after the one who had been brave enough to show himself. Up and up they went until at last the little fellow stopped and disappeared. Rose hurried to where he stood. The first thing she saw was some broken glass. She was annoyed – *some inconsiderate visitor has smashed this with no thought to the little forest animals who could get badly hurt*, she thought. She made a mental note to get Jack to drive her up here in the car so that she could lift the glass with a shovel. Just then she thought she saw the light flicker among the trees. Stepping among the trees she picked her way on the soft mossy ground strewn with dead pine needles. The waft of pine and bark filled her nostrils and she thought of the little wood at Granny Doyle's old cottage. She sat down and rested her back against the trunk of one of the huge standing beings and thought about how she used to play among the trees in Granny's wood. *Hide and Seek*, she said to herself with a smile as she remembered how she would hide from Wind and how Wind would always find her. "Funny, Black Elk," she said out loud, "it was nearly always when I was there that you and May lifted me up for one of my lessons. I guess I was more relaxed and at one with the centre."

"*White Buffalo, look before you. See who appears. She will help you,*" Black Elk whispered to her. Rose looked and tried to focus with her inner sight. Some distance away she saw a white glow and as it neared her she saw that it was a woman. The woman had long brown hair that reached to her naked feet. On her crown she wore a garland of daisies and on her body was a long flowing gown of greens and browns. When she walked the light flickered on her gown and Rose could see that it was made of all manner of forest life. By the time she stood before Rose the woman was immense in size. Rose looked up into her face and waited for her to speak –

"*I greet you Eliza,*" said the woman. "*We have waited for you to come back to us for a long time. We ask for your assistance. You see the many beings that are here in this place – they are ailing and we wish for you to re-align with us so that we may live.*" Rose understood in an instant – She was to reconnect with the joyful earth beings of her childhood. By doing so she would essentially be healing the consciousness of her childhood – her inner child. She thanked the beautiful deva and promised to focus on healing their relationship.

"Mitakuye Oyasin," Black Elk whispered, *"and the nation shall live."*

"There is no separation," Rose understood.

The deva beckoned to her –*"Come and sit with your relatives,"* she said indicating the base of a large cedar.

Rose sat again and at once began to see what the deva wished for her to see. She saw the spirit of a man – she knew it was her twin brother. He came to her and embraced her and said *"I was never meant for this world. I was to awaken you to the twin flame that is Black Elk. I am proud of you sister for you are true."* With that he left and Rose cried for him. She cried for the loss of a brother whom she never knew, for the loss of a mother to affirm her worth and for the loss of a daughter to teach her the power of her feminine self. When she was at peace within she left the earthly Temple and thanked the nature beings for their healing.

As she walked down the trail the voice of her brother spoke to her once more – *"Sister, the power of the will of God the Father you have witnessed in the outer realms of Father Heaven. Now, you have witnessed the power of the love of God the Mother here in the inner realms of Mother Earth. Balance in all things."*

Loss was no stranger to Rose. She had lost much in her life but she had also gained much. As Christmas loomed ahead she thought a lot of her childhood and what Christmas had meant to her then. Her father had drunk more and there were more parties and celebrations which for her, always meant one thing – more suffering. Suffering was in the Catholic way, she supposed, the equivalent of Black Elk's fearful road. At Easter time she would have always attended service on Good Friday – the day in which you remembered the crucifixion and death of Jesus. She would go to the altar and light a candle and stare up into the face of Jesus on the large crucifix in St. Agnes' in Hexton, Belfast. As she looked the eyes of the Christ would look into her heart and she would feel His healing power. Writhing in agony and tears she would look away. Even during the reading of the passion she would experience one of her Christ episodes, as she called them. When it came to the part of His death on the cross and the priest would read out – *My God my God, why have You forsaken me?* Rose would feel so much pain and loss in her heart. Now, what seemed a lifetime later, she knew that she had been witnessing her own pain and loss. When she felt as if it were her nailed to the cross and she felt that immense love and forgiveness mixed with the heartfelt plea for respite, she knew she was experiencing her own Christ Consciousness within – that place in her heart that she always knew held something good – that salvation that she prayed would shine into her life – the little spark of the Divine – she knew now that it was the flame of her origin – of her own creation – her and Black Elk. On Christmas Eve she took two strips of wood and joined them in a cross. Then she painted the cross white and placed it in her new rose garden. *I want to place the white cross all around the world,* she intuited. Black Elk had taught her many times of the two roads that crossed over each other – the fearful road and the good red road. She had walked the fearful road all her life most of which she suffered greatly but it was always when she remembered to come into the centre that she found her respite. It had been a long way but now, as she walked, Wakan Tanka would light the way for her – the Christ Energy within her lifting her up so that she could fly with wings of light. She found a piece of paper and a pencil – she could feel the words coming through. Black Elk and she had the poem written word for word within minutes. This is what they wrote –

A long way we have travelled a road
That twisted and turned
And blistered and burned us
Until we could no longer endure
The starkness of its hard black surface.
But to turn about face
And race our opponents
To the finish line of white tape
To break through the glue
That held our feet to the ground
And to soar with wings outspread
We have found
Our respite.

The fearful black road. The powers of the universe had shown Black Elk how he could use the power gained from knowledge of that road to destroy his darkness and how he could use the power gained from the good red road to bring that darkness to rebirth. Rose understood that they meant his shadow self – in its destruction and rebirth into pure consciousness – its crucifixion and resurrection – Black Elk will have walked the two roads coming always to the centre where he was complete – perfect in his true self – where the flowering tree would blossom and the nation would live. It was the centre of all things – the centre of the cross – the meeting of the four directional powers of the universe and the meeting of heaven and earth – balance in all things.

Rose found her self crying again. They were tears of respite – of joy. Uncle Gerry had said her tears of sadness would be tears of joy. How right he was. The very nature of who she was could be defined in those words. She had once heard that the word 'shaman' means wounded healer – one who turns pain into joy – destruction into rebirth. Just then Uncle Gerry showed up. He was smoking his pipe.

"*You see who you are Rosie!*" he said. "*Do you see who I am?*" Rose wondered for a moment what he could have meant but then in a flash she understood. Gerry was telling her that he was connected to Black Elk. "*We share soul energy,*" he said, "*I have been assigned to care for you since you were born.*"

"I can accept that for Black Elk told me of how I share soul energy with his son Ben," replied Rose "but it's a bit confusing, isn't it?"

"*You will come to understand and this is something that you will teach for you have much knowledge of these things"* Uncle Gerry explained to her.

"If what you say is real and I'm not imagining it just 'cos I would like it to be so, then come to me with some proof. Have someone talk to me about a pipe."

"*Do you see this girl*?" asked Uncle Gerry as a picture of one of Rose's friends, Sinead flashed before her.

"Aye."

"It will be her."

The following morning as Rose and Jack dropped the boys at yet another birthday party she saw Sinead with another friend – Gary. They were both smoking cigarettes. The first words Sinead spoke to her were – "I shouldn't be smoking these. My Granny died of throat cancer from smoking a pipe."

Gerry had spoken the truth. Black Elk was not only guiding her and looking after her spiritual needs but he had also been working through Gerry on the earth looking after her psychological needs. Gerry had always been the only adult in Rose's childhood to affirm her worth often telling her in various ways that she was valuable and special. He had kept her from losing her grip on the physical reality by bringing Black Elk's amazing presence close to her being to heal her. At a time when she was so shut off from her true self, Gerry was there with the connection she needed to prevent her from losing her shattered consciousness completely. Rose realised now how blessed she was. She had come into this world with all the tools she needed to survive. She thought about the time she was suicidal. It had been a long dark time but she had survived because there was never going to be any other way for her. She remembered how at that time she had believed that there was no other way for her but hell. Now, she didn't even believe in hell or the devil. She believed that you created your own heaven and hell and that a balance between the two is where you find peace.

"Oh Black Elk," she cried, "I am ready. Let the stone sing. I hear it calling to me."

January 2007

Rose believed she was ready and she was but she had yet to complete the jigsaw. She had been to the Temple many times since she last spoke with Hans and although she could never recall their meetings there she knew that progress was being made and a higher healing was taking place throughout her being. Hilarion spoke to her often of her progress and how she was to know herself in her wholeness.

"Do you see Eliza, how each member of your soul group is a part of your wholeness?" He went on to explain – *"You have manifested your shamanic identity and each member of the group is a manifestation of one of the seven aspects of you. Similarly, for each of them you represent part of their wholeness."*

Rose thought about what Hilarion had said – it was

so true. She went through each member individually and thought about their power and what that was. Hans, she could see manifested the masculine Will of the Divine whilst Lisa was obviously a manifestation of the Divine Feminine Love. Georgina was the wise spiritual healer and Roger was the earthly physical healer – balance in all things. She, of course was the channel – the child – the perfect centre, rooted to the earth by Jack's earthly presence. That left only one other – the wounds of the shaman – the manifestation of the journey on the fearful road.

That is it! she exclaimed to herself in a moment of clarity, *Grace is the seventh member – she is the wound. She has manifested through the earthly body and so is the earthly wound – a perfect manifestation of the fearful road. In a way, I suppose she is the crucifixion for her birth was the culmination of my difficult path. And the resurrection of course, is the renewal – the healing – a perfect manifestation of the good red road. So what is the purpose for all this? Of course, it is what I have always said I desired – to know my self – to know the truth. And the only place I can find it is in the centre where the two roads meet. A balance between heaven and hell – between pain and joy.*

Hilarion was pleased with his chela. *"Come to the Temple,"* he told her, *"I will show you your woundedness and you will be healed."*

On the second day of the year two thousand and seven Rose and Black Elk journeyed to the Temple of Truth and were shown much of their soul's journey. Pallas Athena met them on the steps and opened the way for them to enter the Divine Temple. Inside, Rose stood as Eliza, facing the East. Black Elk was within her being – they were one soul. The Emerald Flame of Truth burned brightly in the centre of the Temple and Hilarion was the Flame.

Eliza heard the words – *"I am Hilarion – I am the Flame of God."* Eliza understood. The Flame was the centre of the Master – the perfect centre – and it was the centre of her and of Black Elk.

She repeated the mantra in a loud voice – "I am Eliza – I am the Flame of God."

Hilarion was before her then and he spoke: *"Look to the Flame."*

She looked to the huge emerald Flame and began to see in it the journey she had walked on earth. She saw a temple of stone and a chamber in that temple where there were two stone slabs. On one slab lay a woman who was her and on the other slab lay a man who was Black Elk. They had a great love for each other. There came before them an earth goddess and she was of a dazzling red light. The light came down over the two lovers and was a red stone in their hearts. As they watched the goddess shape-shifted into beings of all kinds. Eliza felt a tug on her heart when she saw the man who was Black Elk flicker out of sight. He was gone and Eliza understood that they had been separated. It was the beginning of the journey.

The picture changed and she was in Lemuria. From the sky came a huge golden light that was the Will of the

Divine. Eliza heard the words now as she had heard them then – *"You must hold the Red Stone of Power in your heart until it is ready to sing. It will call to you."*

The picture changed many times and she saw that she was a shaman many times. She saw once more how she had betrayed the Order of Delphi. She saw Black Elk living on earth and having his great vision. And then she saw how she had erred in France. The picture came to rest on a time not long ago. She was an explorer and she was among the great pyramids in Egypt searching for the truth. The picture changed again and Eliza saw that her soul reincarnated as a Mexican child. She saw that the child was paralyzed with fear and that she died aged four. Suddenly the picture vanished and she was looking into the Emerald Flame. Throughout all of these lifetimes she could feel the longing for her twin flame, that male part of her that was incarnate as Black Elk.

"I have searched for my twin flame for so long" she said, "and now we have been reunited. He is Black Elk, and his spirit name is Eagle Wing Stretches and here I am, Rose, and my spirit name is White Buffalo Woman" she concluded. "Together we worked to conquer the fear, and we've done it, haven't we? The stone is calling to me."

Hilarion smiled and said *"Together you are one – you are Eliza."*

He took her hand and they rose up until they were above the Flame. They spiralled around and around until they had come down into the centre of the Flame where they vanished. In a thought they were before the Flame once more and they were transformed. Eliza looked to her body which was vibrating again with a zillion particles of light. When she looked to Hilarion, He was a higher being – the Master's Master.

"I am Na – ther – n – a," he said. *"Look to the East for there you shall be exalted."* Eliza looked and she saw that he meant the land of Egypt. However, she did not understand how she was to connect with that.

"It will be revealed," Natherna said to her.

Balance in all things – was Rose's truth. In Black Elk's lifetime the powers of the universe taught him that whatever is in spirit is real – the manifestation of that on earth is but a reflection of what already is. Rose understood this for Black Elk had taught her that truth many times. Now, he reminded her of the natural order of things. *"White Buffalo,"* he told her, *"you have transformed in the Temple and now you shall be transformed on earth."*

When the telephone rang one afternoon and it was Gertge inviting her to meet with an American couple who were visiting her, Rose accepted immediately. She could feel the warmth spreading throughout her being.

"They are James and Jenna from Santa Fe, New Mexico," said Gertge, "He is an amazing psychic. I feel it is important that you two talk."

Rose knew – it was James – the one who was to work

with her at the point of transformation. "It *is* very important that we meet," she replied. The meeting was set for that Friday morning at Carrick Glen.

"You need to write" James told her. They were sitting opposite each other at the kitchen table and he was looking deep through her eyes into her soul.

"I intend to write, but I was waiting for the story to be complete. Maybe the time is right. I should begin."

"Yes, although it is not as you think it is but it will be revealed to you. I feel an Egyptian energy from you. You are quite likely not aware of it."

Rose shook her head to say that she wasn't - "Unless Natherna is Egyptian?" she added.

"He's a very high intelligence who first incarnated in Ancient Egypt" said James. "In fact, he's a higher part of your own soul."

Rose smiled – she knew Hilarion was a higher part of her and Natherna was a higher part still. "Y'know James, this is all big stuff an' I'm not sure if I can do this. I still feel a bit fearful of it all an' I know there's important work in the near future. Sometimes I wonder if I will fail and fall flat on my face." Rose spoke those words and she could hear herself speaking those words but it was as if someone else was speaking them – not her. It had been a long time since she was that afraid of failure.

James saw it in her eyes – "Rose, this is your woundedness speaking. It will always encourage you to be negative and fearful for that is how it survives. You have worked through that I can tell, and you have brought it to the point of transformation. You have even been reborn in spirit – now you must be reborn on earth."

"Black Elk said almost those exact words. But I don't know where I am going wrong. The woundedness should be gone although it does feel like it is no longer real – like it is a memory."

"Or a picture?" suggested James. I see it when I look at you. Everyone you meet sees it. It's like you offer them a picture of your wounds but it is so superficial – it no longer exists as your shadow. I think you need to put it to rest in some way. You will know how to do that. Then you will be able to move on into your wholeness." Rose got up and walked about the room for a while. Her woundedness - Grace was the representation of her woundedness. How could she put Grace to rest – did she want to?

"I know," she told James, "the child I had through the abuse – Grace – I have to put her to rest. How do I do that?"

"Well you will have to say goodbye in some way I suppose, and not remain attached to the hope that you will find her some day."

"I know I will find her," replied Rose, "she's in Dorset." She had said it and she believed it – her daughter was in Dorset. And then it came to her – she knew exactly what to do.

The next day was Saturday. Rose had agreed to make a

visit to Gertge's home at Willow Community to work with James on a healing session. Black Elk and her guides had shown her the origin of his spinal problems and she felt it was important that they clear that old energy not only for James' well being but for her as well. The healing session was more amazing than any she had participated in so far. At one stage James' guides had her move to one side. They lifted her up in spirit and changed her energy completely, shifting her up and aligning her with James' consciousness before proceeding. When she looked into his face then he showed her who he was and what connection they had. His face changed into that of a Mexican man and Rose knew him to be her grandfather – from the life when she had died as a four year old Mexican girl. He had been partly responsible for her premature death. Her love for him had led to her death. As James he sought to reconnect with her on the earth and balance out that energy.

Rose also thought of Carlos and the little boy he was then. *Wonderful Carlos*, she thought, *may you also come to know who you really are*. By the time James and she had finished working both of them were transformed.

"We are in a new energy," James stated, "I shall never be the same again." Rose grinned, she too was in an entirely new energy.

On the way home she and Jack drove out to Cloughbeg. They went to Granny Doyle's cottage and entered the little wood there. Having greeted her old childhood friends she took the little white cross she had brought with her – the one she had made for her rose garden and she placed it on the ground amongst the trees. On the cross she had scraped out one word – GRACE. She took out another item she had carried with her. It was a doll she had kept since she was small. She had called the doll Jenny but now she was to represent Grace. "My thinking is quite simply this" she had told Jack in the car on the way there, "When I was pregnant with Grace I thought she was the devil didn't I?" Jack cringed. "Sorry darlin' but I want ya to understand why I must do this. Anyway, Collette tried to make me believe that she was a doll. So, I'm thinking – the devil represented all the dark crap in my life and I need a symbol of that to bury. A doll is the perfect answer. Plus, it was my doll so in a way I am putting my childhood to rest." Jack had agreed that it seemed a perfectly good explanation to what looked like a crazy act.

"Y'know what's interestin'," she went on, "I had two dolls in my life. One I called Lucy and the other Jenny and I had one daughter whom I called Grace. Black Elk had only one daughter called Lucy and he had sisters called Jenny and Grace."

Now, she placed the doll on the ground alongside the cross and began to dig a hole into which she then placed the doll – Grace. She covered her over with earth and planted the cross at her head. Moving back a bit she surveyed her work and she cried. Her guides gathered around in a circle and she was grateful for their love. She spoke a word of gratitude for all the blessings in her life and for the many childhood friends she was now with again. She spoke a word of gratitude for the blessing that was Grace. Grace was the wound, the manifestation of the fearful black road – the darkness of her childhood. Through putting her to rest, Rose was resurrecting her childhood into joy.

"If it wasn't for you my darling," she said, "I would not have made the journey back to wholeness. You were a gift of hope, a light in the darkness and I shall always love you with all that I am, wherever you may be. I set you free my darling – I give you back to where you came from – to your Mother Earth. Be at peace." Blinded with tears of joy Rose got up and blew a final kiss to Grace and then she turned leaving the wood and walking forwards into a great future.

The jigsaw was complete. Rose could see who she was and she was beautiful in her wholeness. The Red Stone of Power called to her beckoning her forth into the final dance. All around her the powers of the universe were in joy and harmony and all things in heaven and earth were in balance.

Chapter Twenty Five

A Mexican Tale

Mexico City 15th June 2008

Lissy and John finished their early lunch and went to their hotel room to freshen up for today's excursion. They were going to an ancient city called Teotihuacan only an hour's drive from the hotel. Lissy was feeling on top form. She had stopped being sick in the mornings and had regained a constant flow of energy. "You will be okay darling? You don't want to overdo it," John said for the third time that morning. "I mean, we've done a lot so far. No harm in taking a few days rest." But Lissy had never felt so good. Since coming to Mexico it was as if some part of her had come alive and she wanted to go on enjoying it for as long as she could.

"Darling, we'll never be here again. I want to do it all. If we're just gonna laze beside the pool we should have gone to Benidorm. So, please stop asking me if I'm okay. I'm fine, honestly. I've never felt better."

"Well as long as you're sure," John fussed, "You will say if you feel queer or sick or whatever. I know pregnant women can swoon at the blink of an eye."

"Darling," she laughed, "no-one says swoon any more and for fuck's sake, stop worrying. I'm pregnant not terminally ill."

John didn't laugh. He couldn't help but worry about her. "Are you sure it's not too hot darling. We could always leave it and see if the weather cools a bit."

"And risk missing it altogether? No way, fussy drawers. What are you like, eh? It's like taking my mother on holiday with me. Now you're really pissing me off. I mean it – I'm fine and we're going and that's that."

John gave up and checked his wristwatch – it was one pm. "Get a move on then," he said in a flat tone, "it's one now and the bus leaves in half an hour." Obviously, the heat affected him in the same way as when he was hungry.

Men, thought Lissy disgusted, *no staying power.* "When the going gets tough the tough hide away in their hotel room," she teased. This time it was John's turn to pummel her with pillows. "Okay, okay, I deserved that," she squealed.

"Who gave you permission to tell the jokes? That's my job." John couldn't be in bad form for long with Lissy. For weeks now she had been wonderfully huff free.

She looked at him seriously and said – "This is the new

me honey – get used to it."

The bus left at one thirty on the dot. There were very few passengers on board and John was grateful for the extra space. The heat was stifling even with the air conditioning going full welly. "Phew!" he said fanning himself with the excursion brochure, "this is the hottest day so far."

"It'll be even hotter by the time we get to Teotihuacan," Lissy told him, "I just hope there's a bit of shade somewhere."

John was pleased now that he had sussed it out beforehand – apparently, although the bus would arrive there during siesta – the hottest part of the day, the actual tour didn't start until three thirty."There will be. There's a reception area that everyone gathers in first. It has all the essential amenities. Then a bus takes you out to the sight at three thirty. I have it all checked out for you honey." He beamed with self-satisfaction.

Lissy smiled and took his hand."Oh, thanks darling. You look after me very well," she said sweetly. John beamed even brighter and he puffed out his bodyguard's chest with pride. "Let's see that brochure again," Lissy said.

John opened the brochure and read aloud from it. "'Teotihuacan – The City of the Gods - is situated about forty kilometres north of Mexico City. It is a metropolis of pyramids, terraces, sacred roads and temples. The two main interests there are the Pyramid of the Moon and the Pyramid of the Sun on top of which would have been a sacred temple, although all that remains of the temples are parts of walls. The Avenue of the Dead runs alongside the Pyramid of the Sun and leads to a vast plaza known as the Ciudadela which houses the Temple of Quetzalcoatl.'"

"*The Pyramid of the Sun*, that's what Jim talked about. He learned all about it on the Discovery channel apparently," said Lissy.

"So we have the Discovery channel to thank then," John laughed, "If it hadn't been for it I would be lying by the pool right now with a big shady umbrella over me and a pint of ale in my hands. Oh what bliss!"

Lissy thumped him – "Think of it as getting a bit of culture. If you want to marry me then you ought to smarten up in the artistic world. Take *A Mother's Love* for example – now there's a bit of culture and no mistake." She laughed – it wasn't exactly *The Mona Lisa*.

"Seriously honey, you will be a famous artist some day," John told her brushing a curl from her eye, "That painting you did of Mary Doyle's cottage was sheer genius. You can actually feel the sadness just looking at it."

"That's because you've been there silly. Other people will just see an old cottage and nothing else."

"Where will you put it? You can't leave it in the cellar with all the rest can you – it's special?"

"No I don't intend to. I think when it's framed I'll hang it in the hall with the other one. It'll be a constant reminder that my mother is actually a real person with a real life, even if it is a sad one. And you never know – maybe one day I will give it to her."

"You mean you might contact her after all?" asked John in surprise.

"Maybe, just to see if she's okay. Besides, what if something happened to her and I never got to know her. It kinda would be a shame wouldn't it?"

"Lissy Brenning, as long as I live I'll never figure you out." John was gob smacked. He wondered should he tell her now about what Jim had found out. He reckoned he should. "Honey, what would you do if you knew right now exactly where Rose McDevit is and that she's perfectly sane?"

Lissy stared at him thinking very quickly. It was obvious he knew something. It was written all over his face. "What? What do you know?"

"Jim did some searching after we left Ireland and he found her. Honestly, she's absolutely fine – nothing wrong with her." Her face went pale and in her eyes he could see that she was afraid. *Shit! Did I do the wrong thing?* he thought. But then suddenly she smiled and was asking all sorts of questions –

"Where is she? And she's not mad – not in the slightest? Did he tell her about me? Tell me everything John. When did he tell *you* this?" John relaxed a lot and was relieved at her excitement.

"The night he arrived for the party. You went to bed remember? He told me then."

"Why didn't you tell me? What's all the secrecy about?"

"You didn't want to know, honey. You said it was a closed chapter and that was that. What was I supposed to do? I didn't want you getting all upset again." He prepared himself mentally for one of her storms but it didn't come. She seemed quite agreeable and a whole lot excited. She said nothing, evidently waiting for him to carry on. "And she lives very close to Cloughbeg actually – in a place called Carrick Glen. Do you remember we were thinking of going to that forest?"

"Gosh, yes, I do."

"That's where she lives. Jim was talking to her brother-in-law and her name is now Rose Farley. Remember that little Irish bar we sat in? You thought it was cute?"

"Aha."

"Her husband's name is Jack Farley. That's his family's place."

"No way!" she exclaimed. John nodded –

"Yes way. *And* she has children. Oliver and Jerimiah are ten and eleven and she has a stepdaughter called Emma." Lissy grinned with pleasure. It was more than she ever hoped for. Her mother was normal and she had children.

"Shit, I've got two little brothers and a step-sister as well. Does she know about me? Oh please tell me she knows about me?"

"Well, she's bound to know about you but I wouldn't think she knows who you are?" replied John, "How would she know?" he asked shaking his head.

"She knows – she has to 'cos she will find me, remember?"

"Yea, but honey you can't go by what a fortune teller says. You gotta be real."

"I am real. I know it. Don't ask me how – I just do. She knows where I am. Maybe she doesn't yet know *who* I am but she knows where."

The City of the Gods was amazing. It wasn't exactly John's thing but Lissy was enthralled with the tour guide's tales of ancient civilizations and human sacrifices. She wandered about after the guide for the best part of an hour in the blazing heat and although she was feeling somewhat sluggish on the outside – on the inside she had come alive. Everything about the place screamed at her that she belonged here. At one stage she left the group entirely, wanting to do her own thing – go her on way. John was getting increasingly worried about her. "Honey, I think you should rest. You don't seem yourself."

"I'm not myself," she replied, "something is happening deep within me. I bet if I asked Bobby he'd agree that I have a deep soul connection with this place." John said nothing. He had learned recently just to let her do her thing and not ask too many questions. She was quite plainly going in a direction he knew very little about and if he was to hold onto her then he should listen carefully and be ready to catch her should she fall. "You know what I feel like doing?" she said getting up and pointing towards the temple of the Sun, "let's go up that pyramid and sit in the temple at the top."

"Honey, we should wait for the tour guide. It might be dangerous."

"Poppycock, we'll be fine. Come on darling." With that she sped off. He caught her up.

"Okay then, but the first sign of tiredness and we come back down, understand?"

"Understand."

The steps of the pyramid were quite big and it took a lot of energy to get up. From the bottom they seemed to never end. They were only a little way up when she began to feel the guilty feeling again. She sat down – the step was hot and burned her bare legs. She didn't move them away. *It feels like the pyramid itself is pulling it out of me*, she thought astounded at the strength of the feeling. She thought of her mother in the past life she had remembered – when she was a little girl in wartime Britain. *Why do I feel responsible for my mother deserting me?* she asked herself.

"Are you okay honey?" John asked concerned at her silence.

"Fine, I'm just thinking, that's all. Give me a moment please." The guilt was growing stronger. She could almost touch the reason for it. *If I could only know where it's coming from. What is it about?* The stone step seemed to get hotter and her legs were becoming sore but she didn't have the strength to pull away. The overwhelming feeling of responsibility had gripped her senses with its searching fingers and she felt as if she would die right there on that step. Part of her would have welcomed death – released from the terrible burden of guilt. She gulped down some lukewarm water and wiped her forehead and the nape of her neck with a wet hand. As the world began to spin away from her she heard John calling out –

"Lissy!"

She felt his hands grabbing her as she fell. In the very last moment before she gave her self over to the power of the guilt, her thoughts were for her unborn child. *I won't lose you. Not this time*, she thought and then the world went dark. In the darkness she was experiencing a time long ago. It was a past lifetime…

…She was dressed in black, appropriate for the mourning period. "The mourning period" she moaned resentfully to her husband. "As if when the time is done I will suddenly stop being destroyed and act like it never was – like *she* never was. As if it wasn't my fault…like I deserve to be happy." He looked at her with blank eyes – his Maria was gone – he was dead inside. "I shall never be happy again," she told him, "until I have her back with me."

"That can never be," he replied abruptly. Even he knew it was her fault. She didn't deserve to have her back. She reached out to him to comfort him – to console him in his grief but he pulled away. Turning his back to her, he walked away. She had waited for him to come back but he never came.

Years passed and she grew old and tired weighed down heavily with grief and guilt and the terrible abandonment thrust upon her by her husband. Juan had been her greatest love, always sharing every possible moment together and when Maria was born she cemented their union with the greatest joy. Now Maria was gone and only four years old and he would never forgive her for it. Years later, as she lay on her death bed, friends and family gathered around her but no-one had ever filled that gap in her life where Juan had been and Maria had embellished so with so much beauty. Before she passed from her anguish, she saw once again the vision of her child's perfect little body crushed and paralyzed. She should never have taken her there. They were excavating at the ancient city of Teotihuacan. Maira had wanted to see her grandpapa who was working there. She had been very close to her grandpapa and would get dreadfully upset when she couldn't be with him. Her husband had forbidden her to take the child there because of the danger but she had disobeyed him and taken her anyway. Her father had warned her as well – "stay away daughter" he had ordered her, "this is no place for the child." They had been leaving when a great heap of large rocks fell trapping Maria beneath them and snapping her spinal cord. Her little body would never have survived the damage her mother had incurred upon it.

"I should never have taken you there my love," she said to the vision of Maria as she lay dying. "I shall soon be with you but I promise I will never rest until I pay my debt to you." As she took her last breath she was consumed with guilt and terribly alone. Those who were there with her heard her cry out – "My darling Maria, I swear that one day

I will bring life back to you so that you will be the beautiful woman you were always destined to be."

"Lissy? Can you hear me honey? Lissy?" she heard John's voice coming from somewhere. It was so distant she could barely make out if it were him or her Mexican husband, Juan. As her head began to thump with pain and she felt the heat of the sun on her body, she became confused as to where she was. John pulled her up into a sitting position and offered her a bottle of water. Several people were climbing the steps towards them.

"What happened?" a dark haired young Mexican man asked, "I heard you cry for help. Is she okay?"

"I hope so," replied John, "she just kinda blacked out completely. I was shouting to her and all but she wouldn't come round." The young man climbed the final step in front of her and sat down beside her.

"I am a nurse. May I?" he asked. John nodded distraught. "Hello Senora, can you tell me your name?" Lissy couldn't speak. She was still reeling from the loss of her past husband and child.

"It's Lissy," said John, "she's pregnant. Will she be okay?"

"It's probably just the heat," the young man replied, "let's get her down and under shelter. I'm sure she'll be okay." He checked Lissy's pulse and looked at her eyes. She seemed fine. "Lissy, can you hear me? My name is Juan. I am a nurse." Lissy nodded. John sighed with relief.

"Honey, you're gonna be okay now. Here take some more water." Juan spoke to the group of people who had followed him up – "Stand back please and let us through." Two of them offered to help carry Lissy to the ground.

As they lifted her up she groaned "Juan, don't leave me." Juan looked at John who was just as surprised as he was.

"I won't leave you," he said, "let's get you cooled down and you'll be fine."

Someone had placed a chair at the bottom of the steps and they sat her down on it. Juan checked her pulse again and reassured John that she was okay. "Because she is pregnant, it would be good that she see a doctor. They will arrange it at your hotel okay?"

"Yes, thanks mate. Thank you very much." John shook the young man's hand and then knelt down in front of Lissy. "Honey, you'll be fine." Lissy still looked very distant. "Honey, can you talk to me please, you're scaring the hell outta me." He took her chin in his hand and lifted her face to look at him. She looked pale and scared.

"I killed her, oh John, I killed her – my own child." She grabbed him around the neck and held onto him tightly.

John, half relieved that she was talking and half frightened by what she had said, wrapped his arms around her and cried. He snuggled his face into her neck and moaned "Darling, don't say that – the baby is fine. You just blacked out for a bit. You're both fine."

"But you don't understand," she wailed, "she's my mother and I killed her and Juan will never forgive me."

"What are you talking about? Lissy, look at me. Are you okay?" He shook her slightly in an attempt to wake her up. She looked around her and seemed to come back from wherever she was. Looking at John again she recognized him as who he was – her fiancé in this lifetime. Juan and Maria were past and they had already begun to fade from her memory.

"John…I…I don't know what happened."

John closed his eyes and cried some more. *If there is a God*, he thought, *then thank you for bringing her back to me.* "You passed out honey. It was all too much for you what with the heat and all. I shouldn't have let you come. I knew it was a stupid thing to do."

"No, no darling, I'm fine now. I am and I think it was a good thing that I came here." John was confused. How could this possibly have been a good thing? He was prevented from asking her what she meant when Juan came back over to them.

"Hello Lissy," he smiled glad to see her more alert, "How are you feeling?"

"I'm fine thank you. It was kind of you to help me… *erm*…"

"Juan."

The look on Lissy's face had both men once again perplexed at her reaction.

"You are staying in Mexico?" Juan asked. She nodded yes. "I leave soon to go to Mexico. I think perhaps it would be good if you allow me to drive you to your hotel."

"Well we have the bus, Juan, but I certainly would feel much better if we travelled with you. Just in case you know?" said John. That way if Lissy was feeling ill then they would be in a better position to help her. He held out his hand to Juan and shook once more – "I'm John. Appreciate it mate. Thanks a lot."

On the way back to the hotel Lissy couldn't help but study Juan's face and mannerisms. He was so familiar to her and he had the same name as her past husband. Juan was aware of her interest in him and was beginning to feel quite uncomfortable. Still, he had wanted to help them out. There was something about Lissy that made him feel protective over her. Not only that but he felt as if he owed it to her to help her. *Loco*, he said to himself and shifted his attention to John. "What is the name of your hotel?" he called to him in the back seat.

John took the brochure from his pocket. It had a stamp on it with the name and address of the hotel. "Here mate. This is it, and the address. Do you know it?"

"Ah yes, it is easy to go there now."

Twenty minutes later Juan parked the car and went with them into the hotel foyer. He spoke to the receptionist in Spanish telling him what had happened and insisting that a doctor be called at once. That night after the doctor had left Lissy told John of what she had remembered. She was sitting up in the bed since the doctor had told her she must rest.

"Don't you see," she said excitedly, "Maria is my mother, Rose M'Devit in a past life and I was her mother. I was responsible for her death and I've never let go off the guilt I felt because of it." Her eyes flashed as she spoke and John was never so pleased to see that passion he loved about her. She really and truly had experienced something strange and crazy he supposed, but he couldn't bring him self to believe that she was remembering a time when she was someone else altogether.

"You should be sleeping," he said, "not getting all worked up over a dream."

"It wasn't a dream," she practically yelled at him, "why won't you believe me. We went there because it was there that I took Maria when she was four and the rocks fell on her and then she died. I had to be there to remember it. It's why I have been feeling so guilty and why I have always been abandoned. First I was abandoned by my husband, *Juan*, and then I was abandoned by my mother during the war and now I have been abandoned by my birth mother in this lifetime. It all makes sense. Juan abandoned me because of what I did and I have punished my self ever since by being abandoned." She took a breather and looked pensive as she was trying to figure parts of it out. John lay down on the bed beside her and let her go on. "Of course, she is Rose, my mother in this lifetime and I am her daughter. The roles are reversed. It's almost as if this is the time when things are put to rights – balanced out."

"What do you mean?" John was more interested than

he would have liked to admit.

"I swore before I died that I would bring life back to her. I need to do something for her now. Something that would make a big difference to her life – change it for the better. She did have a shitty life. There's no denying that but instead of me being born making things worse for her, maybe I was born to make things better. But what could I possibly do to make her life better?"

"Dunno, maybe she wants to have you in her life. Maybe just by being there you will be making her happy."

"I'd like to believe that."

What Lissy didn't know was that she had already saved Rose and brought joy into her life. By being born as she was, she helped Rose to go right into her fear. It was the only way she could bring the crucifixion to it and be transformed into her true self. By being born Lissy had fulfilled the oath she made as Maria's mother. She had brought life back to Rose so that she could be the beautiful woman she was destined to be.

After five minute's silence when John had thought that she had fallen asleep, Lissy said "Juan is Juan."

"What?" John asked confused.

"Juan is my husband back in that other lifetime in Mexico. He's still called Juan and still lives in Mexico." She gasped as she realised the way it was – "He still lives there because he couldn't let go. He had abandoned me then because he couldn't cope with the reality of what I had done. He blamed me and it separated us but he never stopped loving me. So, he hung about until I came there again and when I did, there he was waiting to hold out his arms to me and forgive me." She turned to face John who stared at her, his mouth hanging open in disbelief. "Of course he doesn't know it, but that is why he was there - to help me, why he gave us a ride back here. He was making it up to me *and...*" she was on a roll now and the answers were flooding in, "...he was making sure I didn't lose another child. He had said that I could never have her back with me but he softened – by helping me today he told me that it's okay for me to have a daughter again. Oh John, isn't it amazing, the way it's all connected? The self never dies. It just keeps changing bodies."

"You seem to have it all worked out honey" he replied softly.

"But you do see it, don't you?"

"I don't know. You make it sound so straightforward and I must admit I'm beginning to feel very queer like I know what you're saying is real, but it's just so mad. You'll have to give me time."

Lissy beamed – John was beginning to realise the truth as well. "Oh my God!" she exclaimed, "John is English for Juan. Isn't that peculiar? I wonder what that means?"

"It means you can't stay away from Johns," he jested, "*Now sleep!*"

She nestled down into the bed grinning with delight at the latest revelation. "What a journey it has been. These past six months or so I have gone from not knowing who

I was at all to not only knowing who I am in this lifetime but also in previous lifetimes. It has been so healing and now look! I'm about to get married and become a mother as well."

"I agree. It's been an amazing journey."

"The journey to wholeness – to happiness. You know what I think darling?"

"What do you think?"

"When I get home I'll contact Rose and invite her to the wedding. Let her know she's gonna be a grandmother."

"I think that's a very good idea. Now sleep."

Chapter Twenty Six

The Wounds of the Shaman

When we know who we are, why we are here, we open ourselves up to the wisdom and knowledge of the ancestors. We become a clear channel for that wisdom and it is that which is our greatest gift – our saving grace that nurtures us on the fearful black road.

London England, 16th June 2008

Bunty Gordon opened the door slightly and peeped into the huge conference room. It was packed to bursting as usual. The tour was going well. In fact it couldn't have been more successful. She smiled, pleased with herself. She had intuited that this one would be big. Ever since Marjorie had spoken about Rose and said that she would be a great medium one day she knew she needed to snap her up.

"The spirits say that she is the light of a new era for

religion," Marjorie had told her, "She will lead many people into a new faith and it will be a huge flame of hope for mankind."

Bunty could see now how that might be – Rose was in contact with her spirit guide Black Elk who had taught the Native American people about Christianity. Now, he was speaking through Rose, or Eliza White Buffalo as she was known, and he taught a belief that incorporated his Christian teachings and his Indian way too, but was largely about a great vision he had received when he was nine years old. The Two Roads was quickly becoming a way of life for a lot of people. Bunty didn't know about a new era for religion but it certainly was something that more and more people were interested in.

She went to the room where Rose, Hans and Georgina were preparing themselves for stage. "How's it going? Ready?" she asked.

Georgina put her finger to her lips to hush her and nodded at Rose who was sitting with her eyes closed. She ushered Bunty out to the hallway and closed the door behind them. "She's been like that for ages…having one of her moments…best to leave her to it." Bunty looked a little confused. "She's clearing emotion" explained Georgina. "Gets like that, especially since we've been discussing Grace."

"Well, when will she be ready?"

"She'll be ready, don't worry. All in divine time. If she doesn't clear this it'll make it more difficult for Black Elk and May to do their thing."

Bunty wasn't feeling so relaxed. "Ever since we got back from Ireland she's been like this. She's not upset by Joe's death is she?"

"Goodness no, Rose can cope with bigger things than that. I think she's just indulging in some wishful thinking. She went out to the little grave where she buried Grace you know…that day you were visiting with your mate Breda. Apparently someone had been there. It was obvious that someone had tidied the grave and planted some crocuses there under the white cross."

"I see," said Bunty, "tell her I'm ready anyway. We can't leave it much longer."

Georgina went back inside. Rose winked at her and said – "Still flappin' about is she?"

Georgina's smile said it all. Poor Bunty. She had been in the entertainment business for the best part of twenty years. One would think that she'd be used to it by now. "She was asking about Ireland. Wanted to know if you were affected by the funeral."

Rose shook her head and smiled – "Not at all. He was a good man but death is just part of life – the best part some would say."

Both Georgina and Hans pondered what Rose had just said. Lately, she had been so in tune with Black Elk it was hard to know if what she said was her words or his. Georgina changed the subject. "Have you cleared?"

"Some, I can't help but wonder who it was that tended to the shrine. I want to stop thinkin' about it but it's as if spirit says otherwise."

"Do you want our help?" asked Georgina. Rose nodded, so joining hands with Hans and Rose, Georgina tuned in and began. "That's strange" she said, "all I get is Dorset."

"Just what I thought," replied Rose, "Dorset. It's either Grace's grandmother that won't let me forget her or I still have an attachment to the hope that I'll find her." She had specifically asked to do an audience in Dorset. Grace's grandmother had not let her forget that Grace might be there. The audience was scheduled for twelve days' time – the twenty seventh. "That's not the only thing" Rose added. "There's something about Mexico still coming up since yesterday. I have to look at that too."

"Yes, I have it" replied Georgina tuning in some more. "An oath has been fulfilled. It has freed you up even more. You were tied to Mexico by an oath your mother had sworn and she has just released you from that."

"Definitely, it happened yesterday. I felt it as soon as I woke up and I had bin dreamin' about Mexico. Adios Mexico then." She shrugged. She had struggled with that energy all her life. Especially as a child, she used to feel as if she couldn't lift her head off the pillow or move at all in fact. It wasn't surprising that she had hurt her body so badly in this lifetime and was paralyzed for a short time. However, she had resolved some issues with Carlos and had worked with James to balance things out and now she was free of all cords binding her to that lifetime. The issue now at hand was Dorset.

"What about Dorset then? Is it the grandmother or your inner wishes?" asked Georgina.

"Dunno. Either way I wish to clear my self of it or I'll never get going tonight."

"What does Black Elk say?" asked Hans.

"It's done. Alley bloody looya. Shall we go? Do you feel okay to go?"

Hans and Georgina agreed – they were ready. Going out the door Georgina needed to pass on one more thing - "She'll be there...in Dorset."

By the time the audience was over Rose was shattered. She was so tired she only sat for the scheduled thirty minutes book signing. Usually, she signed on, bringing it up to an hour and sometimes longer in places that had an unusually big crowd. "People want to speak to me personally," she had explained to Bunty, "they don't just want a signed book when they can have it signed personally to them. Plus sometimes they just want something clarified and then I pass them on to Georgina or Hans, but when it's something only Black Elk can answer I hate to turn them down."

"You must learn to say no, Rose," Bunty had replied. "The time for questions is on the stage and not after."

"I know, I know. Georgina's sick of tellin' me the same thing but sure she's just as bad as me, so she is."

"Hans and Georgina can look after themselves but you need to rest after channelling for an hour and then answering questions for another hour. The signing must be kept to thirty minutes strict."

Rose understood Bunty's concern but still she signed away until the last book purchaser had left the room. Tonight though she was so tired she could have fallen asleep over the books. She had been working earlier today on her second book – well, hers and Black Elk's really, since he was the main author. She simply typed the words. She signalled to Bunty that she was ready to finish and said her apologies to the disappointed queue as she passed them on her way back to the private room. Once there she collapsed into a comfy chair and fell asleep within seconds. It had been such a journey getting here. Ever since that day in Cloughbeg eighteen months ago, when she had said goodbye to woundedness and embraced her wholeness, she had been working long hours – firstly writing her book and then studying past life regression therapy before beginning her work with Hans and Georgina. Her book – *The Wounds of the Shaman* was a best seller. She had wasted no time in getting it written. It had been easy since it had written itself basically. That was one of the things she would say about it on stage during the introduction –

"It already was written and existed in spirit. All that remained was to download the reflection in the physical realm," she would declare and then hand it over for Hans to explain. Yes, it had been such a wonderful journey. She had thought that she would never top her journey to hell and back and then that amazing journey to her heavenly centre, but these past eighteen months had blurred past in great joy.

It all began when she flew to Liverpool to visit Georgina in February 2007. On the plane Black Elk told her that she was to begin the book and when she and Georgina were eating breakfast the next morning, he had come directly through Georgina and told her the format it was to have. Within fifteen minutes Rose had the full story in her mind. She began as soon as she got back home and six months later had it completed.

Lisa had told her at the beginning – "Rose, when you have the book written you will be in a very different energy." Rose knew exactly what she had meant. As the time went on and the chapters flowed into their fullness, Rose understood much more of who Eliza and Black Elk were and why it was important to bring her story and His wisdom out into the public. Black Elk had had his great vision over a century ago and he had taught the Christian way to his people in his later years. Eventually, with the high perspective of the eagle he understood the comparisons between the teaching and symbolism in his great vision with the teachings and symbolism of the church. Through his twin flame in the earthly realm, Eliza White Buffalo he was ready to bring that understanding to the great nation – to all his relatives – *Mitakuye oasin.*

"*The flowering tree will prosper*," he told Eliza, "*and the nation shall live.*"

Rose woke and wondered where she was for a moment before remembering – she was in London and it was the second week of the tour. Two more days and then she would go home to Mayo to Jack and the boys. She always missed them when she was away but it was always so sweet to come back to them. A week at home and then she was off to Dorset for an audience in a town called Lanesworth. She smiled to herself – *she will be there.* May had been the one to tell Rose that she ought to start talking on stage about Granny's wood and the little white cross that bore the name Grace.

"She knows who she is," May had added. Although Rose understood what it was like to be confused about one's parentage, she knew that it was not crucial for her to be in Grace's physical presence and for Grace to be in hers but she wanted to connect with her on that level and thank her for giving her the hope and strength to be who she was. Had she not embraced her woundedness she would not have known the Eliza within and she would not have written *The Wounds of the Shaman*. Then Black Elk's prophecy would never be fulfilled – not in this lifetime. As she contemplated how it would transpire the door opened and Georgina and Hans came into the room.

"Are you okay Rose?" Hans asked her. She was exhausted and emotional but yes, she was okay. She nodded but he could see that she needed rest. "No more thinking," he ordered, "put it away until we go to Dorset and the spirit world will bring her to you."

"Yes," agreed Georgina, "and then it will happen as it has been laid down." Rose nodded again. All in divine wisdom. Still her heart leapt with hope for Dorset.

Lanesworth, Dorset, 26th June 2008

Lissy closed the book. Normally it would have taken her weeks to read a book but she couldn't put *The Wounds of the Shaman* down. It was a good thing she still had a few days holiday left or she would not have been able to cope at work. Eliza White Buffalo's story of a child named Lucy had shook her world entirely. So much so that she had to stop reading every so often and allow herself to cry, sorely. She cried for the child in the story but in reality she was crying for herself – for all that she had lost in her own story. Each day brought new emotions and memories of her own childhood – things she had forgotten – like when she was twelve years old and the girls at school were laughing at the way her mum picked her up each day. She had so begged her mum to let her walk home with her friends but the answer was always no. She had bragged to them that she was adopted and that she had two mothers and that one day her birth mother would come and she would be so cool and let her do anything she wanted because she was special. Lissy hadn't understood then why the girls had laughed so much but as she grew older she saw that her mum had filled her head with notions of grandeur and that was what the girls found hilarious.

"They're only jealous. Take no heed of them," her mum

had told her but Lissy was gutted. All she ever wanted was to fit in.

She had many painful memories before she had finished reading the first part of the book but when she came to how Lucy became pregnant and how she had talked to the priest in her grandmother's parish and how the baby was sent to a priest in England for adoption, she thought she would die of crying so much. The comparisons between her mother's story and this one were phenomenal. The writer wrote of how Lucy was subjected to terrible abuse including occult like ritualism and she described Lucy's grandmother's cottage which was in Kerry in Ireland. The similarities between it and Mary Doyle's cottage could not be ignored. It seemed to Lissy that the two were one and the same cottage.

She had shown it to John who read with growing astonishment and then said "Blimey honey, this could be Rose McDevit's story."

"But Lucy was from Kerry not Cloughbeg."

"Yes but she spent her early years in Northern Ireland , didn't she? And then she came to live in the South when she was what age?"

"Thirteen."

"Exactly. When Rose was thirteen she came from the North to the South. Was Lucy pregnant when she came to Kerry?"

"Yes."

"There you are."

Lissy wasn't so sure. It seemed sort of unreal. The idea

that this actually was Rose and not some other poor bugger whose story was very similar was too crazy to be true and this kind of thing was common in those days – she had researched it on the net. Apparently most of these stories were of a similar nature. But the dates added up and as she read further into the book it became increasingly clear that there was a real possibility that it was Rose's personal story…Lucy had been interned in a psychiatric hospital and had gotten herself well. And then she went on to marry a local man and have two sons and a step-daughter. She and John had thought that that had been the real clincher.

"The children are the same ages as Oliver, Jerimiah and Emma," she gasped holding her hand to her throat to stop her self from crying out. She just did not know how to react to it all.

"It's her Lissy. It has to be," John repeated until he had convinced himself as well as her. "Fuck, we have to phone Jim – let him know."

"No…no darling, please. I don't want anyone to know just yet. I can't help thinking it's all a dream – a big mistake and tomorrow we'll look really silly if we tell Jim and we're wrong."

"How the hell could it be anyone else?" But Lissy was adamant. "Let's finish the book and see what else there is," John decided.

If they had been shocked at the description of Lucy's family then they were in for an even bigger shock. Lissy read about how Lucy wished to put her woundedness to rest by burying a symbol of her daughter, Grace. She gasped out loud when she read how Lucy had taken a little white cross and placed it in her grandmother's wood and how she had buried a doll there. She had even scraped into the wooden cross the name Grace. "Oh my God! John, come here – quick."

John came running downstairs and was at her side in seconds. "Tell me. Is it her? It's her isn't it?" he asked breathlessly.

"It's her – it's my mother," she replied through streams of tears. She handed the book to him and he read. When he had done he plopped himself down on the sofa looking completely mesmerized. Lissy was crying uncontrollably. She had been on such an emotional journey not only these past six months but especially these past few days with this book. She did not know how to feel any more – all she could do was cry.

"Who would have thought it?" John scratched his head and looked around the room as if he would find the answer there. He held out his arms – "Come here darling." Lissy threw her self into his arms and cried until all traces of her inner tremor were gone. After ten minutes John said – "That woman, Eliza White Buffalo, that's Rose."

Lissy sat up straight and nodded. Her face was soaked. She wiped her nose with her sleeve and sniffed. "We're all going tomorrow. Me and Anne and Linn and Mark."

"So you'll see her. It'll be her."

Lissy nodded and sniffed again – "Yes…Oh John, what'll

I do? What'll I say? What if she doesn't like me? Oh God! What if she doesn't want me? What if I'll be messing things up for her?"

"Blimey honey, you'll be fine. She wants to know. It's obvious. What's that part in the book? *I will always love you with all that I am, wherever you may be."*

Lissy gave him a smile and she laughed as she said – "Crikey, it's really her isn't it? Tomorrow I'm gonna meet my mother." John began to laugh as well and he couldn't stop. Whatever it was it was very funny indeed. "What?" asked Lissy laughing nervously.

"Well…ha ha ha…she's not in a loony bin…ha ha…but you've got to admit…ha ha ha ha!"

"What?"

John was splitting his sides laughing. He fell back onto the sofa holding his belly. "She's a…hee hee hee…a right weirdo….ha ha ha hee hee hee."

Lissy laughed at him. She had to agree – Rose McDevit had turned out to be even more of a weirdo than she was. "Blimey, now that I think about it," she said, "she really is something. Oh...my…God, this is incredible. My mother – best selling author and psychic."

"General all round weirdo," laughed John who was rewarded with a thump on the arm. He sat up straight and fixed himself, taking huge breaths in order to stop laughing. "Ahem," he coughed, "what does the rest of the book say?"

"Oh shit," Lissy squealed, "I haven't finished it. Shove off you and give me peace to read my book."

John shook his head giggling some more as he went to the stairs – "Now you sound like Russell," he laughed and had to duck as a cushion came hurtling towards him.

Carrick Glen Ireland, 19th June 2008

It was a beautiful summer morning. The long stretch of hot dry weather had been broken during the night with prolonged showers and this morning the glen was drenched in freshness. Rose went for a walk drinking in the wonderful aroma of the wet hedgerows. It was still early – only six thirty and although the sunrise had been almost two hours ago a wonderful aura of mysticism lingered in the air. As she walked a young breeze met her, gently blowing the cobwebs of the big city from her being and renewing her with joyful youthfulness. She sang at first, as she walked – a song that sprang from deep within. It had no words but its meaning was clear…

…Come Breath of Life – breathe into every cell of my being and lift me up as I dance the good dance.

The breeze blew on and she could feel it come within as she reached a higher and higher consciousness. Above her a sparrow hawk soared and circled and below the many nature beings whispered to each other of her presence. She stopped walking and stood still for a moment eager for all the delights of nature. Breathing in deeply through her nose, the heady perfume of hawthorn flower wafted towards her, surrounding her with its beauty. The breeze hummed in her ears a psalm of love and the warmth of Mother Earth's quenched soil married with the heat from Wakan Tanka's powerful rays filled her nostrils. She was nestled in the arms of her sacred parents – nothing could disturb this precious moment. Somewhere close by a woodpecker could be heard tap tap tapping on the bark of a tree and in the distant field came the song of the cuckoo. They played a rhythm joining in with the gentle drumming of her heart and when the breeze picked up into a warm wind she embraced the childhood friend who had played hide and seek with her and they both began to dance. They moved and swayed to the rhythm of the bird song and as her heart beat faster and the wind blew harder they laughed together amidst the joy of life. As Rose began to spiral outwards she welcomed the process trusting Wind and knowing that Black Elk was always with her. Her feet seemed to leave the ground and they soared together as one.

High above the forest they flew – over the giant standing beings that were swaying in timely motion and far across the mountains out to sea. As they moved gracefully above the ocean they picked up the white billowy clouds and sailed along on them whilst all the time Rose held tightly to the hand of Black Elk.

"Where are we going?" she asked him.

Black Elk answered – "When I was on the earth plane the Great White Buffalo would come and carry me to my loved ones so that I could know that they were good and safe. Now I carry you just as you have done for me."

And then he pointed towards the distance and said – "Look to the clan of Cassidy. When she looked she saw in the distance a clan of beautiful people and she knew them to be good and honourable. They came closer and she saw that one woman was very old – as old as Mother Earth and she saw that she was beautiful. Rose and Black Elk stood before her hand in hand and Rose knew that she was Grace's grandmother.

"Follow me," said the grandmother and she changed into a white buffalo calf and ran off towards the North. In a thought Rose was on the top of the world. The grandmother stood before her and said – "Look to the East."

Rose looked and what she saw there pleased her greatly and she understood for it is from the East that we gain understanding. There in the East was a building. Rose read the name – *The King's Arms*, and she knew that it was the venue for the audience in Dorset. Walking into the building was a young woman with beautiful long auburn hair. She turned as if she was looking for someone and Rose's gaze met with hers. As they saw each other Rose knew her to be Grace and she knew Rose to be her mother.

The scene ended and turning to the grandmother Rose said "Thank you for showing her to me."

The grandmother began to change and she changed into many women. She no longer was Grace's grandmother. She was all things feminine.

"You see Eliza," she said to Rose.

Rose saw…the grandmother was White Buffalo Calf Pipe Woman, the Great Mother, the epitome of all that is feminine, who brought the gift of wisdom and peace to the Indian people, long long ago. She became the white buffalo calf and ran to the North.

As she vanished from sight Rose heard the words again – *Look to the clan of Cassidy.* In a thought she was on the billowy clouds once more and Black Elk spoke to her –

"White Buffalo, this is but a tiny piece of the freedom available to you. From this moment you will come to know that all doors are open to you. Your playfulness is your signature tune and the joy that you create is the source of life for all things. It shall take you to new heights where you and I shall dance forever among the great ancestors."

"The great vision…" she said, "…I see it – not as you have shown it to me when I was a child but as it is now - The Two Roads. It has changed."

"Not changed, rather turned to be viewed from a higher knowledge" said Black Elk.

Rose contemplated this and then asked "All those things you say when we are on stage – Is that it? Is that the end? The prophecy is complete so is that all there is – no more?"

"It is the beginning and the end. What form it takes in the middle is your choice. I have shown to you the wisdom of the ancestors. It is with that wisdom that you will choose how it will be shown on earth." Rose understood – time does not exist. The beginning and the end exist as one in the dot that is all there is. The middle is the earthly journey

– the manifestation of the dot. It was her choice now how she was to carry on with Black Elk's teaching of his great vision.

She pondered this for a moment as he waited for her to manifest the wisdom in her heart. She lifted her face to him and he saw that she was growing more aware. The stone shone radiantly from her being and the history of creation was written in her eyes. It had always been her choice. She had danced the good dance on earth as he had also done and she had made the choices that led her to wholeness as he had done. Now, through her middle world journey she had brought the prophecy to completion – as it is in heaven, so it now is on earth.

She spoke quietly and peacefully "The choice was always mine," she said and he bowed his head to her.

"I am so proud of you my little calf."

He took her on his lap and she saw that she was nine years old once more. Nothing had changed and yet all had been transformed into the beauty and wisdom of a pure and innocent child. She lay her head on his chest and enjoyed the feeling of her transformed childhood.

In his heart she could hear the earth goddess of Lemuria calling to her – "*It is done.*"

The exceptional little girl who is Eliza White Buffalo, hugged her twin flame and long lost love to her – they would never be apart again.

As the wind began to turn and they began to spiral inwards, the world began to change and when Rose opened her eyes where she stood on the trail to the forest, she knew that she had always been in her wholeness. The long sleep was over and the dream was no more. She brought her being right into the earthly realm and looked about her. Wind had said her farewells and a stillness had filled the glen once again. There wasn't a sound to be heard as she walked slowly on into the forest where she could feel the warm welcome of her old friends – the standing ones. She sat on a tuffet of moss offered to her by an old old spruce and she closed her eyes to sleep. She slept still and safe for ten energizing minutes. There wasn't one other human there to disturb her. When she woke she spoke a word of gratitude for the shelter and then made her way back to the house where her earthly family were just waking and starting their day.

The Heart of the Child - Rose McDevit's heart had been transformed – washed clean by the sacred waters of the Good Red Road. We all come to the world with a perfect heart that can never be destroyed. For the heart is divine and infinite and as long as one remembers to come into that centre where the two roads meet, they will always find their wholeness there.

Chapter Twenty Seven

Grace

We all like to have a sense of purpose in life and we all ask the same questions – Why am I here? What is it all about? Many have, like Rose, discovered that when they come to that place of stillness where the two roads meet they find a simplicity there that contains all the answers they need. Life itself is simple, and when we let go off the reins and become like little children holding onto the hands of our sacred parents, we know that our childlike questions are heard and that they will be answered – when we are ready.

Lanesworth Dorset, 27th June 2008

Rose woke early. It was four fifteen am. The hotel room was flooded with the quiet half-light that only came in the few minutes before sunrise. She got up and went to the huge window that reached from ceiling to floor. She had deliberately left the drapes open last night so that she would be woken for this time. Sitting on the floor she rested her arms on the sill and took in the beautiful view across the bay. There was a clear sky this morning and on the watery horizon the first mystical light of the sun rose and spread over the still water highlighting it with little silver sparkles. Rose waited with bated breath. This would be the first sunrise of the rest of her life – when she would finally look her daughter in the eye with honesty. Last night she had thought about the moment it would happen, keeping herself awake until long after midnight. She wondered would she know her when she saw her? Would she know who she was like May had said and come looking for her, or would she be totally unaware of the identity of Eliza White Buffalo? So many questions raced about in her mind, which was heavy and groggy from lack of sleep. "Be quiet!" she told it.

The sun was just beginning to peep over the water. It would happen quickly this morning, she knew. She opened the window wide to let in the fresh new air and all the noises of nature that jabbered with excitement in response to the early morning herald. Soon the morning was alive and busy with waking life. She thought of a poem she had once written on a beautiful spring morning – *'lift me up and sing to me with words long since denied'* she had requested. Her heart swelled with gratitude now as she surveyed the early morning theatre. Nature was lifting her up – singing to her of *'newness and sweetness and wonders of yonder'*. Today was to be a day of newness. The sweet invigorating taste of a hopeful relationship with Grace would be the frosting on the cake of her life.

She sighed blissfully. How wonderful everything was now. What a journey it had been getting here and it was worth it. She would do it ten times over again if it meant always getting to this moment. But not just for her, for Grace and especially for Black Elk. She meditated for a few moments on what the journey had meant for him - the expression of *his* self, *his* truth, in the completion of the prophecy. In his elder years on earth he had prayed to Grandfather Spirit. He would sit by the fire and the sweet aroma of the wood smoke would fill his awareness lifting his prayer to the creator –

"Oh Great Spirit, You have made me just as You have made all my relatives on our Mother Earth and beyond Her You have made as well. All there is You have made. I come to You now as a child comes to his father and I ask that the prophecy will be complete so that the flowering tree will prosper and the nation will live. I ask not for myself but for all my relatives so that they may have health and help."

Rose got up off the floor and flopped back into bed. She would need lots more sleep if she was going to channel tonight. Plus she, Jack and Georgina had planned to take in the sights of the Jurassic Coastline today. Hans was going back to the airport to meet Lisa who would be flying in from Amsterdam at lunchtime. Lisa had never met Georgina before and Rose was looking forward to having so many of the group together. Hans had met Roger last month at Carrick Glen and the two men had got on like a house on fire, discussing the benefits of alternative health therapies. Rose had been interested to note that at first there did appear to be some caution exercised between them, especially on Hans' part, but as they talked they relaxed and before long they were as long-lost brothers, each one complementing the other nicely. Yes, it would be very nice to have so many of the group together. Rose and Jack had left the boys in Emma's capable care and Jack had come to Dorset also to support his wife with finding Grace and if Grace would be willing to integrate her self into the group also then everyone would be here bar Roger.

"Oh Grace," Rose sighed as she snuggled up under the duvet, "please be here…please." She had been guided by the Master, Natherna, in the next step of the reconciliation and as she drifted back to sleep with thoughts of Grace, she dreamed…

…She was in Mexico and she was in a coma. Around her bed stood her parents and grandparents. "Maria" her mother was crying, "I am so sorry my child."

She rose up out of her body and left the room to seek her playmate, Eduardo. She walked to his yard but he wasn't there and everywhere she searched for him she didn't find him. With a heavy heart she returned to her room where she saw that everything had changed. People she didn't know stood around the bed on which lay an old woman.

As she neared the bed the woman called out to her. It was her mother.

"My darling Maria," her mother called out, "I swear that one day I will bring life back to you so that you may be the beautiful woman you were always destined to be." With that she rose up from the bed and embraced her.

Rose woke suddenly. *That was Grace*, she thought. "That was Grace," she said out loud so that she could hear the words spoken to her. "My mother in Mexico was Grace. That was the oath sworn by her and now it is fulfilled."

She shook her head in amazement at how everything had been so connected and had played itself out like a perfect play on the perfect stage. For that is what it really was – a story - the dream of the long sleep. Now, the final act was to come and the story had revealed itself and the main player had discovered at last her true identity on and off the stage. There was nothing standing in the way now for Rose and Grace. They could finally come together again with freedom and honesty.

"Maria!" Lissy woke suddenly. It was four thirty am and the sun had just risen. She had cried out in her sleep. John lay next to her still sleeping. She lay still, quietly crying tears of contentment. Her mother had come to her. She had found her in her sleep and had come to say that the time was right. They would be together today. Lissy took a deep breath and visualized the dream she'd just had...

...She was in a desert, walking aimlessly around until she came to an oasis. In the oasis were many strange people all offering to help her find her way. They led her to a room lit up by the brightest light and standing in the centre of the room was a child. She could barely make out the features of the child since her face was of a blinding white light. On all the walls appeared words saying – the time is **now**, freedom is **now**, the way is **now**. Lissy had understood the words and knew that she would never get lost again. The room began to fade and as she began to move backwards she saw the child's face. It was Maria.

She got out of bed and went downstairs to the kitchen for a drink. Having poured her self a large glass of orange juice she wrapped a throw around her shoulders and carried her drink out through the back door to the garden. The ocean could be seen just beyond the fields at the bottom of the garden.

"I owe you an apology," she told it, "you told me I would find myself when I found my mother, and you were right but I didn't know the full story then and I thought you had tricked me. I'm sorry I didn't listen when I should have done."

The ocean had spoken the truth that morning she stood with John on the cliff side. It had entranced her and whispered to her heart promises of love and fulfilment but her impetuosity had held her back from seeing the truth in certain matters and she had reacted with anger and dismissal. Now she knew that no matter where she would be in life all she had to do was to stand back and in a place of calm and detachment she would find the answers to her questions.

Jack woke to the gentle sound of waves lapping onto the shore. Where was he? Oh yes, he was in Dorset with Rose. He turned and pulled her closer to him. She murmured happily in her sleep and he smiled. It had been a long time coming, this day. He had hoped and prayed that she would find Grace and now everyone was certain that the day had finally come. What a journey it had been! He had stood by and watched her fall apart over and over, ripping herself to shreds and almost destroying any happiness they had together. It hadn't been easy for him. When he met her he knew it wasn't for the first time. He had loved her since the beginning of time itself and he would love her till the end of time and throughout it all, he had suffered greatly. He had watched her rise and fall many times and each time she would get right back on her feet and reach for the highest stars. He was always there to catch her, grounding her energy and pulling in the ties that kept her secure. She was convinced that they had spent lifetime after lifetime not only with each other but with the other five members of the *soul group* as she called it. He didn't know much about soul groups or past lifetimes but he knew that he was beginning to feel the truth of her words and if there was one thing he knew to be absolutely solid, it was her integrity. If she knew it to be true then so it was.

He shivered a little - from being cold? He wasn't sure, but he got up and closed the window in their hotel room. She must have opened it during the night. She slept on peacefully, her face displaying an inner contentment. He remembered when her sleeping face displayed a different inner world. It had been a terrible world and it had been his job to protect her body while Black Elk protected her soul. What was his job now that she was well? He sat on the floor by the window and watched her sleeping. *She still needs me*, he told himself, *to protect her from others more than herself. She's so vulnerable and as long as I have breath in my body no-one will ever hurt her again.*

He hung his head as the thought of what they had done to her came back to him. He didn't like to think about that any more, especially since she was so sure it was over and would never affect her again. But he was still angry, still churning with inner pain whenever he thought of it. If it had been his Emma he would have stopped at nothing to ensure they were brought to justice. Rose on the other hand, displayed such immense forgiveness and was perfectly content that all was in order within the world. In one way, he understood where she was coming from, for when he was at the river fishing and being alone with the sounds of the birds he felt a completion like everything was in its place.

"Take the stillness of the river and feel it wherever you go," she had told him on several occasions. "When ya sit quietly bring your attention into your heart and remember what it feels like to be at the river. When ya have that memory feel it with all that ya have until it is so strong it is as if you're there. Then you *will* be there." She had smiled, so sure of her words.

He tried it now as he sat there on the hotel room floor. He closed his eyes and brought his attention to his heart. When he began to picture the river and all that would be there he focused until the memory was so strong he began to hear the water rushing by and the birdsongs. Soon he began to see a picture and he was there…

…Casting the fly over the surface of the water he watched intensely as the salmon rose and snapped. He struck, hooking the fish, his heart thumping wildly. He could hear it beating louder and louder within him. As he lifted the fish out of the water and placed it on the river bank he was jubilant with achievement. He threw himself down on his back onto the grass as the early morning sun rose up into the sky. As it rose, it shed its light over the river preventing him from seeing into its depths. The fishing was over for the day. But as he lay there on the grass he could still see the depths of the river in his heart and the passion he had felt getting there had become an inner peace filled with salmon and birdsong and the gentle flow of the water.

Jack opened his eyes. He realised that he had been crying and that he felt at peace. *So this is what you've bin harpin' on about?* he silently asked the sleeping Rose. He realised quite a while ago that he ought to follow her into her world or risk letting her drift so far from him on the current her life was taking her on, that he would lose her forever. As he still felt the peace in his heart now in a hotel room of all places and not the river bank, he knew that he had started that journey to wherever she was and that he wanted to go there. He had a glimpse of it now and there was no turning. *Full steam ahead,* he grinned as he lay back down beside her. She opened her eyes and smiled at him before she took him in her arms.

"Good morning Jack Farley," she murmured, "what were ya thinkin' about just now?"

"How do ya know I was thinkin' about anythin'?"

"Ya were thinkin' nice things. I know ya were. I had a vision. You took me by the hand and said – I'm ready to let myself be happy."

Georgina woke to the sound of music playing. It was one of those beautiful classical symphonies but it was one she had never heard before and it had sounded as if it were her own voice – coming from deep within her. She sat up in bed. The music stopped but she still felt its presence in her heart. She sighed deeply. She was so at peace with herself. It had been a long journey but she had come to a place where she knew she could finally say that she was fulfilling her purpose for being here on earth.

"Sometimes it's as if it's just too painful for me to be here," she had told Rose on the day they first met. "It's as if I don't belong here."

She and Rose had met often, supporting each other and lifting each other up so that they could work together on a high level. Many words of wisdom were spoken between them and they had grown with each other into wholeness. She had taught Rose to have confidence in herself – to listen to her guides and her inner wisdom and follow that with all her heart. She had taught her how to manage her emotions and Rose had taught her how to take the rough deals that life throws at you and turn it all into honesty and truth.

"We mirror to each other our deepest questions," Rose had said, "and the answers are sometimes there to be seen but sometimes we have to look much harder to find them."

Georgina had always felt that she needed some way to express her innermost identity to the world. Rose had seen it way back. She had sent Georgina a book about a man who had gone into the light and had come back to establish a group of centres around the country. In these centres people could avail of all sorts of treatments from float tanks to group healings and from support with the dying process to support for pregnant mothers.

"Black Elk says that you will do this work but that you will take it to the next level," Rose had told her. "He has shown me a vision of a circular building which you will establish. In this centre you will provide an environment where people can find ways of becoming one with their true selves."

Now Georgina had her healing sanctuary well established. It was a circular building located over a ley line within the earth. The energy the line emitted was of the Great Mother– what Georgina called the Magdalene Energy. She hugged herself warmly as she thought of how she had always been drawn to that energy. Now the sanctuary was in its rightful place in her heart and on the earth and she was able to go back and forth from there to working with Rose and Hans. The work that she did with them complemented the work that she did in the sanctuary. She could take her truth out to the world as she did on stage and when she needed to retreat she would work from the sanctuary where she could enjoy the nurturing closeness of the Magdalene Energy.

"Thank you Magdalena," she whispered into the stillness of the morning and once more she could hear the distant angelic notes of harmony play within her soul.

Hans woke just before dawn. He and Rose had agreed that they would each leave the drapes open in their hotel rooms so that the early morning energy would wake them in time to greet the day. Rose had requested that he work with her at that moment to project her spirit towards Grace. The Master Natherna had told her that it was the way forward not only for her but for Grace and the entire group. It had been He who insisted that Jack join them on this occasion.

"*You shall need his energy when the time comes,*" Natherna had told her. "*Roger shall remain in Ireland and ground the group to the earthly dimension.*"

"I will do as He asks," Hans had told Rose.

He got up and went to the window. He hadn't slept much at all last night. A lot was resting on this day. The sun was almost up and he waited. As soon as the sun had risen he was to give her a moment of reflection and then he was to begin his work. It was almost half past four when he began. When the work was done he sat quietly staring out through the window. *What a beautiful country this is!* he thought wistfully. He had never wanted to leave Europe before he met Rose and Georgina. He had worked quietly all his life helping the sick and needy. He and his wife had humbly raised their family in a simple life, never asking for more than they needed to survive and they had been happy. All the time he was building something special. He had a deep knowledge of herbs and crystals and worked closely with the spirit world in his alchemical practices. His wife had never understood him though and when she moved on years later, he continued to live in simplicity devoting his time and energy to his passion which was his soul's purpose. Rose had told him that he had said to her many times that the world was not ready for his work. Was that still the case now? It appeared not. Perhaps, he had been wrong – afraid that he would be rejected.

But now – wow, he thought, his heart leaping at the sight of a seagull soaring up into the sky and folding its wings to dive, *now I feel like that bird soaring high above the world but for one purpose only – to do what I was born to do.* The seagull had no fear and neither had he. He had worked towards this time all his life – many lifetimes in fact, and he had always kept it quiet, sometimes totally secret, but now it was time and he felt safe and confident in taking it out into the world. He smiled at the visual thought of him self on stage spreading his arms wide and shouting – *here I am, this is me, this is my life!* The world could do whatever it wanted – react to him in whichever way it would but it could never waver him now. He was confident in who he was.

Closing his eyes he recollected the Master's words last night. The Master had talked to him after he had agreed to help Rose. He had told him that Grace's reconciliation with the group was imminent and that he would fulfil a longing in his heart that he had denied for so long. What would today bring? Who was this Grace and what was her connection to him? He nodded off to sleep and soon was dreaming…

…He was in Paris. It was the year thirteen hundred and six. His brother had come this morning. How he had found out where he was he had no idea, but he had come and he was angry.

"That…witch" the brother had spat at him, "she has put a spell on you and now when her wickedness has been challenged she tells me that she had learned it all from you, my brother. Come away with me now and I will protect you."

He knew his family would never forgive him if he didn't leave his work and go back to being an aristocrat but how could he turn his back on who he was – what he believed in? He had lived this secret life for so long and she had assisted him for the past ten years. Could it be possible that she had betrayed him? – given him over to the authorities?

He would go on questioning her loyalty for the rest of his life. But he could not turn his back on her children. He found them in the rubble. The little girl was crouched over her dead brother, blood pouring from a gunshot wound in his head. He had taken her that day as his daughter. They fled France with the help of his brother and spent years fleeing from country to country finally ending up in Holland. She had been everything to him. He taught her all that he had taught her mother and more. He had always loved to paint. He made the pigments himself from the fruits of the earth. She had proved to be a promising student and by the time she was grown she was painting beautiful images that the masters themselves would have been proud of. She had seemed happy but sometimes he would see a far away look in her eyes and he knew she was longing for her mother. It had broken his heart that he couldn't mend hers.

At seven thirty Hans opened his eyes. He had dreamed of Grace – she had been a little girl tragically torn from her family. He had tried for so long to heal her – to mend her heart, but she remained alone and abandoned. He hung his head and cried as his heart ached with a need to help her and as he wiped his tears away he remembered the Master's words and he was filled with hope –

you shall fulfil a longing in your heart that you have denied for so long.

Soon, he would see her again and the Master's prophecy would be complete

<u>*Holland, 27th June 2008*</u>

Lisa woke to the sound of the alarm clock ringing. It was six thirty. Today she was to fly to England to meet with Hans and Rose. Jack would be there too and she was to meet one other, an English lady called Georgina Knight. It had been a long time since she had seen Rose. She was very fond of her. The last time they had seen each other was two years ago when she had come to Holland to meet Hans. Now, Lisa was looking forward to seeing them both again and witnessing their work. Apparently, London had been alive with talk of *The Wounds of the Shaman* and now the whole of the British Isles was talking about it. Soon, it would be launched into Europe. Lisa could feel its success.

"Hans, listen to me," she had told him one evening when he was still unsure whether to go to Ireland or not, "this is not just about Rose and *The Wounds of the Shaman*. This is about the entire group and the teaching that we hold as one. You must leave behind this quiet secret way of living and go onwards with confidence because I can see that this work will make it to the USA. Rose needs you, and Georgina. She cannot do it alone. It is about the group as a whole and you three are crucial to the teaching. Please Hans, say you understand because a lot depends on you."

So much had happened since that conversation and Lisa was content that she had done her part. Now, the seventh member was to be reconciled with the others.

Poor Rose, Lisa thought as she drank her early morning coffee in the garden, *she has come through so much for this day and now that it is here she will need much love to help her to cope with whatever happens. Maybe the girl has no love for her at all. She may simply wish to see who Rose is and walk away. That is unlikely, I think but it is a possibility. Then there is the likelihood that she expects too much from Rose and she will upset her greatly. Rose has much to give, I know but she is so vulnerable. Oh Divine Mother, look after my Rose for me and when I go to her I shall do all in my power to protect her delicate heart.*

Lisa wrapped her shawl about her shoulders and shivered a little in the cool early morning air. She looked around her little garden. In the short year she had been here, she had transformed the unkept garden into a little paradise. It was her talent – that one special thing that every person has to give to the world – this was hers. It was the ability to bring divine love into all things transforming them into their full beauty. So many people did that in so many ways and were unaware of it. Lisa knew her purpose was to mirror that quality to them so that they might see them selves in her. Rose, she knew portrayed the innocence and beauty of a child which was plain to see in *The Wounds of the Shaman*. From what she had been told about Georgina it was clear that she also was a talented writer and artist.

A butterfly flew off the bloom it had been sitting on and came to rest on Lisa's bare foot. It tickled a little and she laughed quietly so as not to disturb it. "Your beauty is so obvious," she whispered to it, "what beautiful colours you have. You have been painted with all the colours of heaven."

The butterfly responded to her admiration by fluttering up to her knee and when she held a finger to its little legs it did not resist her touch but climbed upon her finger and allowed her to lift it up for a closer look. "So graceful," she whispered and with that the butterfly fluttered away to go in search of the next beautiful bloom.

Lisa leaned back peacefully in the garden chair. "So graceful with all the colours of heaven," she repeated. The awareness came to her in a moment of clear sight. She saw a beautiful young woman with her long auburn hair held up in a butterfly clasp. She was painting a picture with the most heavenly colours Lisa had ever seen. When the image faded she smiled sure now that Rose would be fine. The young artist was Grace and Lisa had had a glimpse of her spirit and she was divinely beautiful, spreading the colours of heaven wherever she went.

"So that is your way Grace," she said, "I shall look forward to seeing your work."

Ireland, 27th June 2008

Roger woke at five am. His head was groggy and heavy. He had woken several times during the night. He had been dreaming about being in France a long time ago.

"That man, Hans from Holland," he told his wife, "You know the man Rose Farley had said I should meet?" His wife nodded sleepily. "He had gone on about he and I being brothers in a past life in France."

His wife sat up and looked at him as if he'd gone mad. "What did you say?" she asked him.

"That I couldn't say I believed it or not." He shook his head and looked as if he were about to continue but instead got up hastily and began to dress for the day.

"Roger dear, it's your day off. Come back to bed and sleep. You've been working too hard this past while." He ignored her and put on his shoes. "Why are putting those shoes on? You promised you'd mow the lawn today?"

He left the bedroom and went downstairs to the kitchen where he prepared himself a strong coffee. *Has he put ideas into my head?* he asked himself, *talking about witch hunts and aristocracy?* Every time he had closed his eyes last night the same dream kept coming back again and again…

...He was in France and the year was thirteen hundred and six. His mother had been distraught and had feared that his brother had been involved with witchcraft in some way. She had got it into her head that a spell had been cast upon his brother and that he would bring terrible shame upon their noble name if it got out that he was consorting with witches. He had been sent to seek him out and capture the witch responsible. He had done so as well and had urged his brother to come home with him so that he could protect him. However, the plan had backfired and his brother had hidden among more of the witch's kind. He had discovered where he was but by that time he had been troubled greatly with terrible dreams. In these dreams his brother had gathered around him five others who had sworn to protect him and his work. They would stand in a circle and when he came and broke that circle he would see a long line of women and children screaming and writhing in agony – their bodies ablaze with flames – his own children and wife among them. In some of the dreams he would take the offered hand of his brother and join the circle making it seven. Then they would rise up into the air and on the ground he saw the women and children once more but this time they were happy and well. He knew they were merely dreams but by the time he discovered where his brother was and who was hiding him, his conscience troubled him greatly and he believed that should he be responsible for his brother's demise then he would be damming many women and children to a terrible fate. He said nothing of his knowledge and instead secreted his brother and a young girl out of the country. He painfully regretted the lives he had put to death and vowed that he would keep that circle of six people safe as long as he lived.

Roger took his coffee and sat in the conservatory. He couldn't help but wonder if his dream had been real. Had Hans spoken the truth? He and Rose had talked about a circle of seven people responsible for bringing certain truths into the world. They hadn't said anything about saving people from a terrible fate though. He sat drinking his coffee and pondering what it all could possible mean. An hour went by and he fell asleep with the cold coffee cup in his hands. He slept peacefully for another hour and woke refreshed and ready to start the day. *Catch yourself on Roger,* he told himself and happily changed into his walking boots. "I'll mow the lawn tomorrow dear," he called to his wife who was still sleeping upstairs, "I have an urge to spend some time in the forest this morning and later I wouldn't mind going out to that stone circle place outside Drumgar. I've never been there but I think I might check it out. I'll eat in Drumgar dear. I want to catch up with my thoughts."

Off he went to Carrick Glen Forest Park. He passed Rose's house and wondered should he call but remembered that she and Hans were away this weekend. He spent a lovely morning wandering about and filling his senses with the smells and sights of the forest. After a huge lunch in Cloughbeg he drove out to the stone circles and lay on the grass there enjoying the alone time. Every so often images from the dream flashed into his mind and before long he began to understand that there was more to him that just who he was today. He thought about the group of six in his dream and smiled to himself as he imagined taking their hands and making it seven. By the time he collapsed into bed that night, he felt as if he were a new man.

"Remind me to contact that man Hans," he told his bewildered wife, "I think he and I have much to talk about."

Lanesworth Dorset, 27th June 2008

Lissy and John decided to walk into Lanesworth. It was a gorgeous evening and the show didn't start until seven pm, lots of time to walk in and enjoy the cooler evening air.

"It'll help you calm down honey," John had said.

They met Linn, Anne and Mark as soon as they set foot inside the foyer. Linn took Lissy's hand and squeezed –"Ready?" Lissy shook her head, not able to speak. "You'll be fine," Linn stressed.

Lissy glanced at Anne who gave her a big smile. "We're all here for you," she said. The time was six thirty. "Hey guys, what do you say we go in and get good seats? Not much time for a drink." Everyone agreed and went to the conference room doors with their tickets. An older woman with bleached blonde hair was standing there chatting to the ticket collector. Lissy recognized her and nudged John.

"Bunty Gordon. I knew I'd heard that name before. Remember at the funeral tea in Ireland? Mrs Doyle's friend."

"Oh yeah." He pulled Lissy suddenly to the side.

"What?"

"She said her client was appearing here in June. Lissy... she was talking about Rose."

Lissy's face opened wide in astonishment. "Shit John. Just how close did we come to Rose over there?"

"Pretty close," he shrugged with a huge grin and threw an arm around her shoulders. "Looks like the forces of the universe have been working overtime to get you two together."

Lissy looked serious –"You may joke but I think that's exactly what happened."

At seven on the dot Bunty Gordon strutted onto the stage and announced the programme for the evening. She brought two others onto the stage before Rose. A Dutchman called Hans Pieters and a Liverpool woman called Georgina Knight. They talked a bit about the book and then Georgina announced – "And so it is my honour to introduce to you Eliza White Buffalo."

Lissy looked at John and everyone looked at Lissy. Linn reached for her hand and squeezed it tight. Lissy thought her heart would be heard beating on the stage as she watched Rose come on and smile among cheers of admiration for her book. She shook as she watched her sit down on a chair placed centre stage. Tears stung her eyes and rolled off her cheeks.

John pulled her closely to him and kissed her head –"*Shhhh…*" he whispered lovingly, "…don't cry. Take deep breaths – you'll be fine."

She smiled weakly, her jaw trembling. She didn't once take her gaze from Rose. She was just as she had imagined. Shorter maybe but then she was sitting down so it was hard to tell. Her hair was so like her own, the same waviness but a little darker in colour maybe and not so much red. She wore the ruby necklace she wore in the picture on the book but her hair was down instead of braided. A plain red band stretched around her head.

Much nicer, thought Lissy. Rose wore a white dress with long sleeves and a flowing skirt that reached to her ankles. On her feet were plain moccasin type sandals. Lissy thought that the overall effect gave one the impression of a young innocent girl and she found her self questioning what she believed to be true. *Could this really be my mother? She looks younger than I do.* Her heart thumped nervously. The woman was still smiling – the claps of appreciation still resounding around the room. Lissy wanted to get out – run. She grasped John's hand tightly and swung around to speak to him but just as she were about to utter the first word a voice spoke. It came directly into her mind –

"Grace!" She halted, staring at John, her mouth hanging open. *"All is well."* Her heartbeat slowed and she swallowed hard relaxing back into the chair.

"Are you okay honey?" John's voice seemed strange to her. She looked at him again and when he smiled warmly she melted into his arms.

"I'm fine darling" she sighed relaxing even more…"it's fine."

Rose began to speak – "Thank you, everyone, thank you so much. It is lovely to have such a warm welcome. I'm very happy to be here this evening. Actually, this is a very big day for me not only because we are all here together and we shall do some great work as a group here this evening, but also because there is someone here in this room now who I have been hoping to meet for a long long time. So, if you will excuse me the indulgence, I would just like to say one thing and then we shall commence with the work. I would like to say to her that you are greatly loved and have been greatly missed and it will be a huge honour for me to finally meet you."

There was lots of murmuring among the audience as people speculated on who Eliza White Buffalo had been addressing. Lissy beamed with pleasure and began to feel heaps better as she exchanged glances with her friends.

"Oh my God John, she knows I'm here," she whispered. They put their heads down close to one another.

"She will find you, remember?"

She nodded grinning. "And, she's psychic. So she will have known I would be here."

"Shh, she's gonna speak again."

Rose began to talk about her book and how she had

been guided to write it. She spoke of pain and grief and how everyone has their own 'stuff'. She talked of the shaman inside us all, the hero that comes along when we finally have had enough and we give the controls over to a higher power within us -

"It is only by accepting our crucifixion and letting go of the controls that we die to our lower selves and are resurrected into our power – our true identity as powerful spiritual beings walking the earthly path."

The audience was still – every person in the room was captivated. Rose had said that every single person here this evening was meant to be here. No-one was here by mistake or circumstance – they were all here to learn from others and to give to others of their wisdom and knowledge. She had said - "I will say something tonight or maybe it will be Georgina here or Hans. It may be Black Elk or it may be the person sitting next to you but whoever it is, that person or several persons may say some one thing that you need to hear, and when you truly hear that message and understand it you will know that you are in the perfect place at the perfect time."

Lissy listened to Rose's voice with growing awareness that she was without a shadow of a doubt, her mother and that she was everything she had always thought her to be – good and holy – divine and unconditionally loving. She was realising that these past few weeks the horrible stuff connected to her mother had begun to wane away because that was not what she was – it was what was done to her.

She wasn't going to meet all that horrible stuff - she was going to meet her mother.

She whispered to Anne sitting to her left, "Remember what I used to say about her? Before I went to Ireland?"

Anne nodded enthusiastically. "Yeah," she replied. Anne was deeply enthralled with Rose's words. "You were so right babes. You can feel the love just falling off the stage." She paused to clap as Rose stood up to announce a short interval. "You'll have to introduce her to me."

"Don't worry. I will. Now that I've found her I won't be letting her go any time soon."

"Do you think she could heal me?" Anne added.

"Haven't you listened to her?" Lissy replied. "She said we are all are own healer. We all have the tools to heal ourselves."

"I know, but do you really think I could do it? Just an ordinary woman like me? I don't have the power she does."

"Oh you're not powerless, believe me – you can do it. Take it from someone who has already started the process. How do you think I got to this moment?"

Anne looked at her workmate with a fresh perspective. She certainly did seem very different since she came back from Mexico. "Will you teach me?"

"We'll teach each other Anne," Lissy said lovingly.

The rest of the evening went very quickly. Rose had gone into some kind of trance and was channelling her guide

– Black Elk. There were all sorts of gasps and noises from the audience as he began to speak and Rose's voice came out all male and eerie. Lissy wasn't sure she liked that aspect of her mother but decided that because it was apparently this Indian man that was speaking and not her then it wasn't actually her that she felt uncomfortable with. The Indian man was asked lots of questions by the audience. Many people broke down and cried at the answers he gave. Others were jubilant and cheered him. Most were silently in awe of the whole experience. Lissy desperately wanted to ask if she was psychic but was too nervous at addressing the stage.

One man in the row in front of her put up his hand. "Yes!" called Georgina Knight, pointing down at him, "the gentleman in the blue shirt." A girl passed a microphone down the row of seats to him.

"You say the prophecy is complete" he asked addressing Black Elk, "that the flowering tree is healthy and the nation is happy. I can see how you and Eliza White Buffalo are at peace but I don't understand how the rest of the world is still in a state of unrest."

The answer came quickly – "When we come to the centre where all things are, we see that there is only light. When we choose to look to the light and not to the shadow that it casts, we see what really is - that the nation is whole and there is no separation. You are me and I am you. Look away from the shadow my brother and know that all is well."

At the end of the session, Rose left the stage and went to

her room. Jack was there preparing her a strong cup of tea with sugar. "Oh Jack, thanks darlin', just what I need right now." Jack was pleased - "There's nothing like a good cup of strong sweet tea to ground myself after channelling," she always said at home. She had twenty minutes before she was to return to the conference room for signing.

"Do ya think she's here?" Jack asked meaning Grace.

"She's here." May and Black Elk hadn't stopped grinning all day. Grace was there alright.

"Should ya say somethin'?"

"Already have. She'll come to me. I doubt very much if she'll go home without coming to me, and if she does then she'll come tomorrow."

"Ya sound very sure about that."

Rose simply smiled. All was perfect in the world. At nine twenty five she went back to the conference room with Jack and took a seat behind a desk in the back of the room. A queue of people stood waiting for her to sign their individual copies of *The Wounds of the Shaman*. Rose was amazed to find that she was not at all nervous. Every so often, she would look a young woman in the face only to know that it wasn't *her* but she wasn't disappointed, not even when the queue was coming to an end and she could see that there were only a few gentlemen left.

At ten past ten the conference room was almost empty. Rose was in deep conversation with the man who had asked Black Elk the question about the prophecy. He was quite a humorous guy and had her in fits of giggles with his mirth. She was still laughing as she walked into the bar to join the others.

"Excuse me," came a small nervous voice from behind her, "Are you Rose McDevit?"

She turned to see the lovely young woman with the auburn hair.

"I'm Lissy Brenning…I'm..."

The woman's face was ashen with nerves and she trembled as Rose held out both hands to her and said "Grace."

It was the end and the beginning.

Breinigsville, PA USA
14 June 2010
239883BV00001B/24/P